I0651341

William Dalton

Will Adams

The First Englishman in Japan

William Dalton

Will Adams
The First Englishman in Japan

ISBN/EAN: 9783337184278

Printed in Europe, USA, Canada, Australia, Japan

Cover: Foto ©Raphael Reischuk / pixelio.de

More available books at **www.hansebooks.com**

WILL ADAMS,

THE FIRST ENGLISHMAN IN JAPAN.

A ROMANTIC BIOGRAPHY.

BY

WILLIAM DALTON.

LONDON:

CASSELL, PETTER AND GALPIN,

AND 596, BROADWAY, NEW YORK.

[The right of translation is reserved]

TO

THE RIGHT HONORABLE

THE EARL OF ELGIN AND KINCARDINE,

K.T., G.C.B., &c. &c. &c.

THIS STORY

OF THE FIRST ENGLISHMAN WHO SET FOOT IN JAPAN,

AND WAS THE MEANS OF ESTABLISHING

COMMERCIAL AND FRIENDLY RELATIONS

BETWEEN THE SUPREME RULER OF THAT EMPIRE AND

HIS OWN SOVEREIGN THE KING OF ENGLAND,

IS

MOST RESPECTFULLY DEDICATED,

BY THE AUTHOR,

Who is unwilling to let pass so appropriate an opportunity of offering his "mite" of admiration for those great qualities and indefatigable exertions, by means of which his Lordship secured for his countrymen a Treaty with Japan, the full and singularly-important advantages of which time will develop, but which may not be entirely understood, except by those who have made a study, not only of the history and characteristics of the people, but of the great mineral wealth and resources of the land they inhabit.

PREFACE.

WILL ADAMS may not inappropriately be called a representative Englishman, for though neither General nor Admiral at sea, nay, but little more than a simple shipman, he was one of the "fathers" of our navy. Not for that reason, however, was he chosen as the hero of the following narrative, but because he was the *first* Englishman who ever set foot in Japan, in which land he lived, for some time a prisoner, then as the friend and confidant of the Emperor (Ziogoon), negotiated a treaty for his country, married a native lady, had children, and lastly, after a twenty years' sojourn, made a will (which was afterwards brought to England), and died. Of the history of this fine old English shipman, and founder of the Dutch and English commerce with Japan, we have but fragments in the shape of letters written by him and some of his contemporaries; but from these we gather the facts that he was born at Gillingham in Kent; was apprenticed to a shipmaster, one Nicholas Diggines, of Limehouse, near London; and that he married, served as master and pilot in the navy of Queen Bess, again in the service of the worshipful Company of Barbary merchants, and lastly in the Dutch fleet which sailed from the Texel in 1598 ; and that, after a disastrous voyage, accident threw him, with several shipmates, upon the land of Japan, about April 1600, in which empire he remained till his death in May 1620 ; and this, and much more that has enabled me to give the fortunes of my hero, we have upon authorities which may be found collected and collated in the admirable work of Mr. Thomas Rundall, printed for the Hakluyt Society, and entitled "Memorials of the Empire of Japan in the Sixteenth and Seventeenth Centuries."

The gaps between the fragments of authentic knowledge of Will's history I have endeavoured to fill in with pictures of the people and the time; a time, be it remarked, which forms a singularly interesting epoch in the history of the children of the sun goddess ; for just before Will arrived, Japan had buried her Cæsar, Tiego-Sama, who, satiated with minor conqûests, had resolved upon subduing the then mighty Chinese empire. Upon Will's *arrival*, a usurper filled the imperial seat, who might be likened to our Henry the Seventh, for, finding the numerous kinglets weakened by long intestine wars, he crushed their power and curtailed their number. From' this sovereign, Will, who had ever an eye to the interests of his beloved England, obtained for James the First a free-trade treaty. Again, during the period of Will's sojourn in the land, happened the many intrigues of the Spaniards and Portuguese to exclude all other Europeans from commerce with the natives, and began also those plottings of the Romish priests with the heir of the late Ziogoon, which caused the fearful persecutions of the

Christians shadowed forth in the narrative, and which terminated in the Japanese St. Bartholomew, the terrible massacre of the Christians at Simabara, and the extirpation of Christianity from the empire.

Of Melichor von Santvoort, all that is recorded is, that he was one of the Dutchmen who landed in Japan with Will Adams, and that he was *still* at Nangasaki six years after his shipmate's death. That little, however, the Author found sufficient for his purpose, which was the penning of Will's character and adventures by one who *must* have well known and *probably* loved him ; and having thus introduced the Dutchman, by weaving his fortunes among those of the historic names of the period, he sought not only to give additional interest to the narrative, but, at the same time, to illustrate the character and manners of the people and the times.

Of the other personages of the story,—the Jesuit, Pessoa, the Lady Mary, and her brother, the King and Queen of Tango, Sir Martin of the Gilded Spurs, the Author has only to remark, that although he has freely used the licence permitted to the writers of such narratives, they all once lived in the flesh ; and that, if an apology be at all necessary respecting them, it must be alone to *their* shades, for the feebleness of the hand which has attempted to pourtray their characters, and picture to another age their varied fortunes.

There may be *one* among my readers who holds the popular but erroneous notion that Japan, having been so long " a sealed nation," so little is known of its people that he can place no reliance upon the descriptions in this narrative. To him it may be answered, that till after the death of Will Adams, Japan was free and open to all comers and goers.

By the way, referring to "this early intercourse between the empire of Japan and the states of the West," Mr. Rundall writes—

"The government of Japan is exhibited in a most favourable light. It was distinguished at that period by high-bred courtesy, combined with refined liberality in principle, and generous hospitality in practice. Without any reservation in regard to circumstances, rank, calling, or nation, the hand of good fellowship was then cordially extended to the stranger. In the instance of a Governor of the Philippines, although shipwrecked and destitute, the claims of rank were admitted. He was received with the honours due to a prince; while he sojourned in the land, similar honours were paid him; and, to facilitate his departure, he was furnished with all the means generosity could dictate. The lowly-born William Adams, when cast in wretchedness on the shores of Japan, was not, indeed, received as a prince; yet this man, commencing life in the capacity of 'apprentice to Master Nicolas Diggines, of Limehouse,' eventually attained rank and acquired possessions in the empire equal to those of a prince. With no claims to consideration but talent and good conduct, he became the esteemed councillor of the sagacious and powerful monarch by whom the land that had afforded him shelter was ruled. In the course of his career, this man of humble origin appears as the negociator between the sovereign of his native country and the foreign sovereign by whom he was patronised; and in that capacity securing for his countrymen important advantages and privileges. Merchants, for a century, found a free and open market for their wares. They realised enormous profits, if cent. per cent. may be so deemed; and, if reliance may be placed on the imperfect materials that exist for forming an estimate, they were enabled to enrich their native lands with stores of the precious metals to an incalculable amount of value. Missionaries, from their advent, were allowed to commence a career of proselytism, and they pursued it with zeal and success."

Now among the visitors to Japan were many who, having been for a number of years domiciled in the land, with liberty to traverse the empire from shore to shore, either themselves wrote, or supplied the materials for lengthy and elaborate histories, graphic sketches, and painstaking details, that have since so well stood the test for truth, that, apart from some personal observations, the main work of modern writers has been to confirm and reiterate. Indeed, to give a list of the writers of every shade of religious and political opinions—Jesuits, Dominicans, Franciscans, Protestants, sailors, merchants, and simple travellers, would be to catalogue a library of no small dimension; but from this library the Author has drawn his facts, and those facts, side by side with the accounts of the most recent travellers, tend to prove, that whatever may be the *future* of Japan, the manners and customs of the people of 1600 and 1860 differ but in a shade, and that, for good or for bad, the old Adam, aye, and the Cain too, still lies but a little below the surface of their nature.

In concluding the labour of many months, the Author would only add, that, as he has attempted rather to *amuse* than *presumed* to instruct, if the perusal of his work serves but to pleasantly while away a few hours the object of his ambition will have been attained.

WILLIAM DALTON.

CONTENTS.

Illustrations.

———o———

WILL ADAMS,

THE FIRST ENGLISHMAN IN JAPAN.

CHAPTER I.

SANGUINE PROSPECTS, BUT SAD PARTINGS.

ALTHOUGH at this writing I am a man deep in years, still, praise be to God for ever and ever, my faculties are as clear as upon that memorable day when I joined the fleet of the noble General Jacques Mahay, which at the instance of Master Verhagen, the rich merchant of Amsterdam, and by permission of the good Prince Maurice, put to sea to make the voyage to the Indies ; and inasmuch as, being of fair scholarship, it was my custom to make notes of events nearly as they happened during my long sojourn in the East, the reader may rest assured that the incidents and adventures set down in the following narrative are true, albeit some of them may smack of romance ; but regarding this last word, I must chronicle it as my belief that the incidents in the lives of many of the soberest men, if collected and brought together upon paper, would, in the reading, relish more of romance than many of the wildest coinings of the most ingenious brains.

But to begin. I am, then, that Melichor von Santvoort, late of the Dutch factory at Nangasaki, and the same who accompanied the ill-fated Verhagen fleet in the year of grace 1597, now at this present writing fifty years

1

ago ; by which you will please to consider, that as, at the
time of the setting out of the fleet, I had not completed
more than twenty summers, you will find my age to be
seventy years.

Although descended from a good old Flemish stock,
many of the members of which had been sufficiently noble
to hold notable offices at the courts of the Dukes of Bur-
gundy—indeed, my father had been one of the chamber-
lains of the Duchess-Regent, the sister of Philip of Spain,
tyrant of the Netherlands, who, praise be to God, was
ultimately discomfited by that noble prince, William the
Silent, whose assassination by the miserable fanatic, Bal-
thazar Gerard, deluged the land with the tears of a loving
people—of my nobility I had but small cause to be proud,
for at his death, my father left me little else but a stout
frame and an intolerable hatred of the cruel, avaricious
Spaniard, a hatred for which I had good cause. Both
my parents had fallen victims in the bloody shambles of
the red-handed Alva, while I, their only child, escaped,
owing to the good offices of Master Verhagen, at that
time a prosperous burgher, and one who, having more
regard for his worldly than his spiritual interests, so
held the candle to the devil, or, in plainer words, so con-
formed to the doctrines of Rome, bent his neck and
opened his purse-strings to the ruthless Duke, that he
was permitted to hold his own, while thousands of his
more obstinate fellow-countrymen fell beneath the rack,
fire, or swords of the Spaniards. But, be that as it may,
Master Verhagen, who in early life had received many
benefits from my father's family, had sufficient gratitude
to protect the orphan in his hour of trouble, so for my
safety he took me with him upon one of his trade journeys to London, in which great city he left me with one
Master Saris, under whose care I was to learn the huma-
nities, and, for the better advancement of my future
career, pick up some knowledge of barter and the ways
of traffic ; and in London, praise be to Providence, I did
learn the English language, and many other matters of
great use to me in after life ; and by the time I reached
my twentieth year, I had also learned to regard one

member of the good merchant's household after a fashion
which he did not deem advantageous, either to myself or
the person in question, who, indeed, was no other than
his comely daughter, Maud.

By reason of the discovery of certain passages between
Maud and myself, he wrote complainingly to Master Verhagen, begging that he would advise him whether he held
me in such love as to provide me with a fortune, or such
means of making wealth that befitted the husband of the
only daughter of so wealthy a merchant as himself; but
of this question I knew nothing, till one day Master
Saris placed in my hand a sealed packet that had just
been brought to him by a ship-master who had recently
arrived from Holland. The packet contained a letter
from Master Verhagen, drawn up in friendly terms, but
still upbraiding me for practising upon the affections or
the daughter of one who had treated me so kindly, and,
moreover, commanding me to return to Amsterdam.

Now at this writing I know not whether I felt most
angry or pained at the contents of the letter. Anger, I
suppose, must have been uppermost, for Master Saris,
taking me by the hand, said—

"Melichor, thou hast not the right to be angry for
this thing, which, although thy first trouble, is for thine
own good. Thou hast high blood, high pride, yet but a
low purse; qualities which, neither together nor sepa-
rately, fit thee to be the son-in-law of one who owes all
he possesses to the work of his own hands."

Now to this speech I should have made answer in
words that would have troubled me till this writing, had
not the good man added almost affectionately, "Still,
Melichor, thy scant purse would not have stood thine
enemy in my eyes, for that might be mended; but I have
observed that amidst all thy good qualities—and I admit
many—thou hast a pride and restlessness that would
unfit thee for the plodding life of a trafficker in cloths
and other goods: but," and as he spoke he shook me
warmly by the hand, "let us not part in anger, for to-
morrow thou returnest to Master Verhagen's house."

"Nay," I replied, warmly, "that will I never do; for

it is he,—he too, who received benefits from my father, who hath made this mischief."

"Tut, Melichor, thou must, for the good merchant stands to thee in the light of a parent; and if thou art so unruly as to disobey him, even if hereafter thou obtainest the wealth of the Indies, thou shalt not have Maud to wife."

"Then," said I, a gleam of hope flashing across my heart, "may I ever dare?"

"By my faith thou mayest, and there is my hand upon it," replied he, adding, "but remember, Melichor, providing only that thou returnest to Master Verhagen, and so fittest thyself for trade and traffic, that in a few years thou mayest think the fluid in thine ink-horn of more real nobility than that in thy veins."

"Master Saris, I will obey thy behest," was my reply; but my heart sickening at the consciousness of my poverty, I added, "But, alas! what may I do without gold among traffickers in goods? No, the sword is my inheritance, and by that alone can I hope to gain either wealth or Maud; so will I at once to Master Verhagen, and having claimed some monies of mine own, then seek the brave Stadtholder Maurice, and, reminding his highness of my father's services and fate, claim a place in his ranks."

But a frown darkened the countenance of Master Saris, and, clutching my arm, he said firmly—

"Young man, it is as I have said, thy stomach is too high for a home-stayer and trader, yet shall no swashbuckler of the sword wed my daughter. But," he added, "there is yet another course. Thou art restless, bold, and fearless, qualities which, although they will neither serve thy object here nor in Amsterdam, yet might advantage thee in the Indies, where the rascal Spaniard is reaping such golden fruit that the good merchants of London and Amsterdam are well-nigh mad with jealousy. Nay, even now while we speak, a fleet of good ships is lying in the Texel, in which Master Verhagen has ventured so much of his substance, that it is even called after the worthy burgher's name."

"Aye, Master Saris, I have of late had much speech with certain ship-masters concerning this fleet, and its destination, which, although it promises much of mischance, yet holds out such hopes of repairing fallen fortunes, that I will crave Master Verhagen's permission to accompany it," I replied ; adding with enthusiasm, " aye, if it be but as a ship-boy."

" Now, Melichor, boy, thou art in the right mind, and of the same, too, as Master Verhagen ; for see what he writes." So saying, he placed in my hands a letter he had received from my guardian, in which I now found that it was the intention of the latter to send me to sea as purser, or keeper of the merchandize, in one of his ships ; and, disloyal as it may seem to the god Cupid, for the moment I felt more over-joyed than if Master Saris had there and then bestowed upon me the hand o Maud, but then my readers must remember that the recent voyages and adventures of the navigators, Drake, Frobisher, Candish, and Hawkins, with the sound drubbings they had given the Spaniards and Portugals, and the wealth they had conquered from them by their own bravery, had set the brains of all the youth of England and the United Provinces of Holland on fire. Indeed, the blood of that man must have been thinner than water who could have contented himself at his ease, either in palace or warehouse, while the best of the land, either as officers or common ship-men, were scouring the great ocean with the hope of benefiting their fellow-men by the discovery of new, and the opening to traffic old countries, and that, too, with many opportunities of drubbing the Spaniards. Now anent this madness for voyages to the East, you must know that for more than a hundred years after the discovery of the Cape of Good Hope by Vasco de Gama, the profitable traffic of the Indian seas was monopolised by the Portugals, to the great hurt and jealousy of all other nations, who, being too weak at sea to dispute this ocean sovereignty, were compelled to purchase Indian merchandize at the city of Lisbon, by reason of which that city soon became the richest and most populous of European capitals.

When, however, the Spaniards discovered another passage to the Indies, by way of the Straits of Magellan, they, after the same fashion, claimed the especial sovereignty of that new sea-road, and by every means of knavery and defiance endeavoured to prevent the ships of other nations from floating in those seas ; and so strong and of such great force were they, that, for a time, the English endeavoured to make a road of their own by way of a north-eastern, a north-western, and even a northern passage to India, directly over the pole. As for the Dutch, while subjects of the Spaniard they were content to purchase Indian merchandize at Lisbon, to sell again in the markets of northern Europe. But upon the termination of the great and blessed revolt of the Netherlands, and their erection into the United Provinces, my countrymen determined to punish their late tyrants in their sorest place, the South Seas, and so gain a share of the Indian traffic ; and this determination fell out as I will relate.

When, in the year 1580, the Spanish and Portugal dominions became united under the Spanish crown, the latter sovereign not only commanded that the Dutch should be excluded from all trade with Lisbon, but that their ships then in port should be confiscated, and their masters imprisoned. Now it fell out that this tyrannical act brought down its own punishment, for Cornelius Houtman, being one of those ship-masters who were thrown into prison, got into such conversations with some Portugal sailors, that he obtained from them all their knowledge of the Indian seas and countries ; and so full was he of this information, and upon his return to Amsterdam such tales did he tell, and so well did he work upon people's minds, that a number of merchants agreed to associate together to fit out a fleet of eight vessels, four being to avoid the Spaniards and Portugals, and thus make the experiment of a north-eastern passage, while the other four were so armed and manned that they might, if necessary, contest the passage to India, and the Portuguese road of the Cape of Good Hope. The first fleet, under the command of Hugh Linschooten, made the discovery of Nova Zembla, which, although a loss to the merchants in the sense of lucre, was attended with important results, as it evidenced the boundaries of man's knowledge of the globe. As for Houtman's fleet, it produced an immediate effect, for that general reached the west coast of Java, and, notwithstanding signal opposition from the Portugals who were established in Bantam, and with whom he had to fight many bloody battles, he managed to open up a trade with the natives ; and the success of this expedition, although not great as a trading matter, so whetted the appetites of the merchants for further trade direct with the Indies, that in the year of our Lord 1598, they fitted out four separate fleets, in one of which it was the pleasure of my guardian, who was half owner of the vessels and goods, to ship me in the capacity of purser.

How the ships of the Verhagen fleet were ordered and commanded, Master Saris read aloud to me from my guardian's letter. The first ship was the 'Admiral,' and was to carry the general, Sir Jacques Mahay ; the 'Charity,' which was the vice-admiral, and carried the lieutenant-general, Simon des Cordes ; the 'Faith,' Captain Sebald de Wert ; the 'Fidelity,' Captain Binningham ; and the 'Good News,' Captain Borkholt ; all names, as you will see, of good omen, and piously given. Moreover, for the better safety of the expedition, the worshipful merchants had engaged as pilot-major one who had not only seen much service, he having served the greater part of his life in the ships of the queen of England—indeed, he had been in Master Martin Frobisher's ship at the time the drubbing had been given to the Armada, so boastfully by the Spaniards called the Invincible. Then in the same fleet with this brave pilot was another pilot, his friend, called Timothy Shotten, who had made the voyage round the world with Master Candish, and there was the brother of the pilot-major, and one Spring, another English mariner, great in his knowledge of navigation, besides several other Englishmen of bravery and experience, but of lesser note among shipmen and navigators, all of whom, being English, served the Netherlander merchants, because those of their own country, not then being given to commerce upon so large a scale, had not employment for such adventurous spirits as had been round the globe with Drake, Frobisher, or private adventurers like unto Master Candish, who could equip a fleet out of his own estate, and that, too, after such a fashion, that it might defy the ships of the Portugals and Spaniards, the enemies of almost all other Christian people.

The remainder of the day upon which I received this news I was mightily joyful, thinking over my new prospects; but the next morning the presence of Mistress Saris made me sad at the thoughts of leaving England, and for her I would have resigned all my bright hopes; but then it was for *her* those hopes had been built, for *her* it was that I was about to encounter unheard of dangers; at least, I thought, or tried to think, that it was love, and not ambition or gold for its own sake, that had so engaged me. But it is even now an unpleasant theme, and therefore will I at once dismiss it. Be it known, therefore, that after a sad parting with Mistress Maud, an exchange of vows and plain gold rings, I took my departure the following day for Chatham, at which place lay the ship which was to take me to the Texel. The same night I slept at an inn, near the great dock then building for her Majesty's ships. The next morning, followed by a porter who carried my small amount of luggage, I proceeded down to the river, and hailed a boat.

" To the Dutchman, my master?" said an old Armada veteran, pointing to a small lugger-built vessel lying out in the middle of the Medway, and with the flag of the United Provinces flying from her mast.

" Aye, aye, as speedily as may be," said I; but as I stepped into the stern-sheets, there came some half dozen men, who, from their maimed and wounded state, I could see belonged to the " Chest," an institution which, by way of parenthesis, I may say had been established some twenty years before by the sailors of her Majesty's ships, each of whom contributed from his pay a portion for the relief of their fellow-countrymen who had been wounded in the great drubbing of the Spanish Armada.

Two of the lesser disabled of the veterans were carrying a heavy sea trunk, and as they almost hobbled along, lustily repeated the popular song describing the defeat of the Don, the refrain of which was taken up by the four others, who, however, no sooner saw me, than stopping at once, they cried out to me to unship myself for a better man.

"Belay there, mate, this springald is bound to the same craft as our old shipmate," said the owner of the boat.

"Howsomd'ever that may be, he does not ship himself before his betters," was the reply; and I believe they would instantly have dragged me ashore, but at that moment their attention was arrested by the coming of some other persons, cheered along as they came by some fifty or sixty veterans. Taking advantage of this opportunity, I laid backwards in the boat, indeed, behind the sail.

As they approached the boat, the veteran escort formed to the right and to the left, leaving a channel which disclosed to me a man whose dress bespoke him to be a sea officer, although of what rank I could not tell. He was of tall stature—taller than any around; his limbs were stalwart and sinewy, his face deeply bronzed, and lined as if with wear, tear, and care; his forehead was broad and prominent, the lips were thin and close, the nose large, and nostril extensive, as is the case with most men of great and generous motives; the eyes were large, lustrous, full, deep blue, and his hair was of light brown, long, and flowing over his shoulder; his moustache was thin, but lengthy, and his beard short and pointed. Indeed, from the fall of his footstep, the firmness in which his features were cast, and the inflated nostril, whoever he might be, he struck me as one in whose mind execution waited upon conception, as the report and bullet upon the flash. The veterans had moved aside to permit him a farewell word with his wife and two boys, all of whom, like himself, had the light hair and blue eyes of the Saxon.

They were a brave family: whatever tears might have been shed in private, neither mother nor children wore

aught but smiles; nay, their eyes sent forth glances of
pride, as if at the past and future of their dear relation,
of his dangers and triumphs, of joy, as they saw the estimation in which he was held by the brave men, once
his companions in arms and danger, around them.

The family group stood alone for some minutes in
whispered conversation, the veterans looking on with dry
eyes.   They had conversed earnestly for some minutes;
the father embraced the two boys; then, as if the leave-

taking had passed, the veterans gave a volley of cheers.
This aroused the officer: he would postpone the last,
the sacred farewell, the one dear hand that should touch
his last, the full melting eyes, whose glances should min-
gle with his, and fall into his innermost heart, there to
remain indelible in far distant lands, and so he unclasped
his wife's hand.   It was time if he would preserve his
manliness, for both pairs of blue eyes were full: one
tear drop had fallen.   He ran towards the veterans; lustily they cheered, and warmly they shook him by the

hand, and now, with choking voices, bade him God speed, and if he ever fell in with the Dons, to remember good Queen Bess, and Drake and Frobisher, and the drubbing they had received in sight of the white cliffs they had sought to darken with their black countenances. Then the feeling of glory was uppermost : the boys flung their tiny hands in the air, and the bold Saxon woman, worthy sister of the great Queen her sovereign, whose glory had made the women of England like those of old Sparta, waved her fair hand also ; but notwithstanding the knitted brow and the compressed lip, the dear arm was no sooner around her neck, and the warm lips upon her cheek, than the tears bedewed her face.

"Now God take thee in his keeping, Bess, for thou art but a woman, though a brave one."

"God help me, dear Will ; I am but a wife, no more ;" and she now sobbed aloud, for her pride was gone ;—no, not gone, for it was her woman's pride that the wife's love, in its weakness and its strength, should be uppermost in her brave heart.

"Tut, dear Bess, this voyage—my last, I promise ye —may make thee flaunt it among the best dames in the land ; for call ye not to mind the glories of Drake and Frobisher ? and they were my generals." So saying, he impressed one long kiss upon her forehead, leaped into the boat, and waved his hand, amid the cheers of the veterans, and cries of "Success to the brave Will, and may it be thy lot to meet many a whiskered Don !" But while the boat moved toward the ship, the fearless seaman held his head upon his hands, strained his eyes towards the shore, and sobbed aloud like a child, as indeed he was at heart.

Not till the boat grated against the sides of the ship did my companion turn his gaze from the shore, nay, nor till the " How fares it with thee, Master Adams ?" of the master aroused him from his sorrowful reverie. Then, however, he hastily sprang up the sides, and, as his feet once more felt the deck, and his hand grasped that of the Dutch captain, his countenance brightened, and the bitter pangs of parting with his family became softened by the

professional pride of the pilot, which I soon divined him
to be; for having answered the captain's greeting, he
proceeded at once to busy himself with the men, who
were letting the ship down the river, and that, too,
chiefly, I believe, that in the bustle he might lose all
present thoughts of those from whom he was about to
be severed so long—aye, God only knew how long!
This, then, I thought, as, mounting the sides after him,
I heard the greeting of the captain, is *the* William Adams
to whom the Amsterdam merchants have entrusted the
pilot-majorship of the fleet, *this*, then, is the man who
has traversed the globe with the greatest navigators of
the age, and with whom I am to sail; and so great was
my joy, that I longed to make it known to him I was to
be his shipmate on the long voyage. At *that* time, however,
my wish was not to be gratified, for so busily was he engaged in his duties during the day, that I could get no
speech with him, and when night came, by which time
we were off the North Foreland, I felt so ill with sea-
sickness, that I took to my berth, and there remained in
my great misery, longing rather for instant death, than
desiring to make discoveries, or gain riches in the Indies.
This want, however, of my sea-legs brought with it its
consolation, viz. that speech with Master Adams I so
much desired; during my illness, at which, although
very severe, the captain of the vessel and the mates
laughed and jeered, he, who had traversed well nigh as
many seas as those boasters had countries, stood by me,
at least when the duties of the ship permitted, and tended
me with the loving-kindness of a parent, so I soon found
an opportunity of telling him that we were destined to
sail together. I was somewhat chagrined, however, to
find the small opinion he had of my powers of withstanding danger and fatigue; for once, and that was the day
we entered the Texel, after I had spoken with undis-
guised exultation at the prospects of the voyage, he replied, "Verily, Master Melichor, it is not a pleasure-
voyage in a gilded cock-boat that we are going, but one of
so much peril that it will try the powers of stronger
built, if not braver-hearted navigators' than thyself; yet

if it be the will of the worshipful Master Verhagen that
thou shouldst encounter these perils, it is not for me his
servant, or thou his ward, to cry nay, but to obey cheerfully, and trust to the mercy of God, whose name be
praised for ever and ever."

Thus it was I made the acquaintance of William
Adams; but now, that the reader may not be kept in suspense, and too long a time from those adventures, which
must be chiefly interesting to him, as they happened in
the far off land of Japan, I will pass over such matters as
my meeting and farewell with Master Verhagen, and proceed at once to relate the main incidents of our most disastrous expedition.   For those who may be curious as to
the details of many mishaps which happened to that fleet,
its officers and crew, they will find them related in sundry
letters writ by Master Adams, and likewise in the account
given by Master Sebald de Wert, one of the only two
captains whom God permitted to re-visit his native land.

CHAPTER II.

THE GREAT FLEET AND ITS FORTUNES.

NEVER was a gigantic bladder of human hopes set afloat
under happier auspices; nay, nature herself aided to puff
it to its greatest extension, and so delude the vanity of
Dutchmen.   The shores were lined with holiday-dressed
spectators, the waters were covered with freshly-painted
and decorated barges and other craft, bearing the princes,
merchants, magistrates—in a sentence, the stateliest,
wealthiest, and most beautiful in Holland.   From mainmast tops to their keels, the gallant vessels were crowded
with men whose courage was undoubted, even if their experience was small, and whose hearts were filled with delight, no less at the prospect before them, than at the
sight of the fluttering flag of the United Provinces, then
new, but which soon promised to be as victorious in the

great South Seas and islands of the Indies, as had been
that of the Spaniard and Portugal, with which it was
destined it should so soon and often come into bloody contact. Loud was the roaring from the ordnance on shore,
and return salutes from the great brass pieces on board
the vessels which held the merchant adventurers then
initiating the birth of the since so great and wealthy
Dutch East-India Company; for sad as was the miscar-
riage of that particular expedition, it was yet the first
germ of that mighty Society which now rules the seas, albeit our worthy neighbours and friends of the English
nation, emboldened, or rendered envious of our successes,
have since formed, I hear, a somewhat similar Company,
and establishment in the Indies. Then, as the anchors
were lifted from their briny beds, as much by the bound-
ing hearts as by the hands of the sailors, amidst the thun-
dering of the cannon, the sun shone, as it only shines in
June, and then but rarely, as it did, at least, to my thinking, (who from that day for more than twenty long years
thenceforth saw it shine in widely distant latitudes,) on
that twenty-third day of June, in the year of our Lord
fifteen hundred and ninety-eight, when the celebrated
Verhagen fleet sailed from the Texel.

Great as had been the liberality of expenditure in the
doings on shore, it was equalled by the profuseness on
board the vessels: indeed, had there been a judicious
economy pursued at the commencement of the voyage, it
would have prevented much suffering and real starvation
ultimately; and that was the opinion of Master Adams:
for one day, while becalmed off the coast of England, the
officers had met to enjoy a last glorification previous to
entering upon the serious business of the voyage in the
cabin of Jacob Quackernack, the master of the vessel in
which I sailed, and which ship was the admiral. There
were present a young man, one Detson Hudcoopee, who
was not only of kin to the lieutenant-general Simon des
Cordes, but in great favour with Sir Jacques Mahay, our
general, Master Adams, pilot-major of the fleet; Thomas
his brother, the master, the mates, and myself the purser.
Well, being off the coast of England, the master Quack-

ernack, out of courtesy to the Englishmen present, chal-
lenged the health of their queen, which being drunk, he
proceeded to glorify our merchants for their liberality,
saying—

"What think you, Master Adams, of the cheer provided
by our worshipful merchants for those who sail under
their flag?"

"Truly it is a question that may not be answered in
this presence without churlishness," was the reply.

"Nay, to my thinking 'tis the more churlish to deny
answering such a question, Master Adams, since the worshipful Company have entrusted thee with the care of
their fleet," said Hudcoopee.

"Then, by the favour of this good company, will I by
way of answer honestly tell thee, that at the commencement of a voyage it is the way of us English to have some
godliness, more discipline, and less good cheer, for fear
there may chance to be short allowance and little bodily
strength or good humour upon our homeward passage,"
said Will.

"Tut, man! thou art doubtless a bold shipman and a
skilled pilot, but methinks thou wouldst make but a sorry
steward, at least in the men's minds, for good wine makes
the spirits flow, and 'tis the humour of the men that
makes the ships to go," said Quackernack.

"Under thy favour, Master Quackernack, I take it, it
is not the wine, for the sooner that becomes scarce the
better for discipline, but the water and the live meat, that
my brother begrudges," interposed Tom Adams, and Will
bent his head approvingly.

"Beshrew me, man, but thou art forgetful of the islands
in our course, where goats, beeves, and other animals are
to be found," said the master.

"Thou hast been misinformed, Master Quackernack, by
my faith thou hast, or my experience goes for nought,"
replied Will sturdily.

"Aye, but even should it be so," replied the master
quickly, and with some alarm adding, "what wouldst
thou counsel?"

"That these recommendations of the gracious Elizabeth

to the crews of the fleets of the worthy knights Drake and Frobisher, should be enforced," replied Will, pulling from his pocket a printed paper.

"By my honour thou art a careful pilot, and worthy of thy business to be so prepared. Let us hear the contents of that paper, Master Adams," said Hudcoopee, and Will complied with the request. The recommendations were to the following effect, that

"Commanders of ships should pay the strictest attention, First, that Divine worship be performed twice a day. Secondly, that all blasphemous expressions, profane swearing, lewd conversation, dicing, and every other description of gaming, so often the cause of quarrels which lead to murders, the especial object of God's indignation, be forbidden. Thirdly, that every kind of filthiness be removed from within board, cleanliness being a notable preservative of health, and want of cleanliness the cause of breeding sickness. Fourthly, in their intercourse with strangers, particularly with uncivilized people, the crews are directed to avoid every kind of violence, to conduct themselves with civility and kindness, which tends to promote the honour of the country. Fifthly, that the men, after having been long confined to sea-fare, may not injure themselves, either by eating immoderately, or by partaking of improper food. Lastly, That care be taken not to allow waste of the fresh meat, and that the comfortable things wherewith every ship is furnished be not spent in rioting and banquetting, so that the sick may hereafter perish for want of things needful.

"By my hope of meeting a Spanish galleon, no bad articles either, providing they could be carried out," said Quackernack, who had been attentively listening, with his head upon his hands and his elbows upon the cabin table.

"Thou art in the right so to say, Master Quackernack, and, by God's grace, will I endeavour to persuade the general to the same way of thinking," replied Will.

"Beg of him also to ship a priest at the first port we make, or we cannot carry out the English article number one," said Hudcoopee, with a sneer.

"By the Stadtholder, it would be no such bad notion either. Let us learn where we may, that's my mind," said Quackernack.

"Faith, it would bring a smile into the face of the bloody Spaniard himself, to hear of us Dutchmen getting our sea-schooling of the English," replied Hudcoopee sneeringly ; but as it was ever the habit of Will to avoid disputes, and moreover that he knew Hudcoopee possessed the ear of Sir Jacques Mahay, he replied by draining off a horn of wine to the success of both Dutch and English, and confusion to the Spaniard, which, restoring the good humour, ended the matter.

The next day, however, Will did endeavour to persuade the general to more economy and discipline, but Hudcoopee, being dead against all his suggestions, matters continued as they were till about the twentieth of August, when we were running near the Cape de Verds, by which time our provisions had become so scarce, that the whole of the crews were placed upon half rations, a regulation that was necessary, but which speedily produced both scurvy and discontent ; and to such an extent did the latter prevail in our ship, that for fear of open mutiny, the officers kept themselves upon the alert, and doubly armed both by night and day.

At the sight, however, of the De Verds, the hearts of all but Will Adams and his brother rejoiced, and the general ordered the signal to be made to summon the captains and pilots to a council on board the admiral. Well, when the council was sitting, and Thomas Adams and I were leaning against one of the great guns, anxiously awaiting the result, and conversing upon the chances that provisions and water were or were not to be had for the landing, word was passed through the ship for Gilbert de Canning and Absolon van Owater (both old shipmen) to attend the council, when, as they passed, Thomas Adams muttered—

"By my life but those knaves should be strung up to the yard-arm."

"Wherefore ? What mean you by these words ? they are two of the quietest men in the fleet," said I.

"Aye, doubtless, but by that reason they are rogues, I tell ye, Master Melichor : that fellow Canning has soft-talked Master Hudcoopee into a belief that yon islands abound with goats and other eatable animals."

"Then by my honour, if it be true he should be re-warded well, for we are in sore want of food," said I.

"Tut, tut, man alive, it is a lie : of my own knowledge it is a lie, and told, that the general may send him with a party ashore."

"Even so : there can be no great harm in the fellows' wanting to stretch their legs after being so long cooped up aboard," said I.

"Nay, listen," replied he : adding, in a whisper, "It is that they may desert the ship, for so I overheard them plan during last mid-watch."

"Mutiny by heavens ! and the general should know this," said I, startled at the intelligence.

"Aye, aye, Melichor, even now he may have know-ledge of the knaves' intention ; that is, if my brother Will has deemed it wise to tell him ; but I misdoubt not that he has, for when I reported to him what I had over-heard, he said, ' Keep thy discovery to thyself, brother ; for if the council act upon the lie of Canning, it will be time sufficient to arrest them ; but if not—and it shall be my endeavour to prevent them—the rascals will be better at their work than in irons, as assuredly they must be placed, should the general come by this know-ledge.' "

We were not long kept in suspense as to the result, for the council breaking up, we saw the two men, Can-ning and Owater, brought forth between a file of soldiers. "Ah ! the rascals have so nearly had their way that Will das been compelled to checkmate them with their own plan," said Thomas.

"Thanks, then, to thy quick wit, we shall not remain upon this pestilential coast," said I.

"Nay, thou art too quick at conclusions, Master Meli-chor," said Will, coming behind us ; adding, "for although the cunning of these fellows is circumvented, Master Hudcoopee and the master have such faith in the existence of food and water upon yon island, that they have persuaded the general to come to anchor, and land the sick upon St. Jago, where they are to remain while our foraging party is to be sent into the interior ; moreover, their worships the captains have taken in such high dudgeon the opposition of master Shotten and myself, that they have ruled that for the future no pilot shall take his seat at the council table."

Thus, by the perverseness of some, and the jealousy of others, we were detained at St. Jago for twenty-four days ; at the end of which time, namely, the 15th of September, we left the island, not only without adding to our stock of provisions, but with one-half of the men down with the scurvy, of which fell disease, soon after, when we had passed the line to two or three degrees south latitude, died our general, the gallant Jacques Mahay.

The new General, Simon des Cordes, whose ship now, instead of ours, was made the admiral, ordered the fleet to bear for Cape Gonsalves, upon the coast of Guinea, where we again landed the sick for the bettering of their health, but where, alas! the greater part died. We again set sail, and kept on our course till we fell in with the Isle of Annabon, at which place we were in such misery and desperation, that we determined to obtain provisions, or leave our bones upon the land ; therefore we attacked the town, and thereby obtained some relief, yet in so small a degree, that when we sailed therefrom, the rations per diem for each man were only a quarter of a pound of bread, with a like small proportion of wine and water, which scant allowance brought so much feebleness and ravenous hunger that our poor men fell to eating even the calf-skins with which the ropes were covered. All this, however, was but the beginning ; for although we entered the first narrow of the Straits of Magellan upon the 6th of April, we did not leave that sea for five months ; and notwithstanding that, during that time, we found great stores of penguins, one hundred of our men died, and that by reason of so much toil, that was rendered more irksome and miser-

2—2

able, inasmuch as nought they could do would further
our voyage. Truly, nothing in this world could be more
miserable than those months passed amid incessant snow,
hail, hunger, losses of anchor and masts, sickness, death,
want of stores, and the great cold, which, by increasing
our appetites, made scantier our small supply of provisions.

At last, upon the twentieth of August, we entered the
great South Sea, but, seven days afterwards, there
happened such a great storm, that our ships separated
from each other, nor did we again fall in with the
admiral ship and our general until the 9th of October.
Then we set sail for the coast of Chili, which, upon our
setting out, had been appointed for our general meeting,
and which coast we were right glad to reach, for we had
great hopes of bartering some of our merchandise with
the natives for provisions ; but some knave Spaniards
being amongst the savages, they not only prevented this,
but, after their like, treacherously endeavoured to entrap
the chief among us on shore. Then, having fruitlessly
waited twenty days for the coming up of the rest of our
fleet, we again set sail, and ran by Valdivia to the Island
of Mocha, at which place happened a great misfortune,
as I will relate.

Now during our great distress no man had stood up
so manfully, ever working, never repining, like Will
Adams, and of a verity it seemed as if his good spirits
brought their own reward ; for although almost all of us
had, at one time or other, been laid upon our backs by
sickness, he continued sound and whole. So far had
Will remained unscathed by misfortune : his turn, however, came soon after our arrival at Mocha.

The appearance of our ship was the signal for the
gathering of the naked but well-armed savages along
shore, and that, too, evidently for the purpose of preventing our landing. Starve, however, we would not, so
land we must : therefore, as Will Adams and his brother
were the only officers on board with health and strength
enough, they, accompanied by thirty men, took to the
boats, and, after a desperate fight, in which the greater

number were wounded with arrows, effected a landing, and drove the savages some distance inland. Then, believing the time had come for a parley, the two brothers held above their heads knives and pieces of cloth, making, to the best of their endeavours, signs that they wished to exchange such articles for food, fruits, and water. Whereupon several, who seemed to be chiefs among the savages, advanced some distance in front of their people, gesticulating and chattering in a language which Will making out to be Spanish, he called out to his men to know if there were any among them who knew the knave Spaniards' tongue.

"Canning knows the lingo," was the reply.

That Canning should be the only man on board who could converse with the natives was unfortunate, for it was scarcely prudent to trust him ashore ; yet such was our strait, that Will had no choice but to send his brother to fetch from the ship this fellow, who was released from his irons.

Canning, being then sent forward as ambassador, and finding the savages acquainted with sufficient Spanish words, held a long conference with the chiefs, who, he told Will, would willingly barter with us on the morrow, but that night he and his party must return to the ship ; —a scurvy concession, it must be owned ; still it was all he could get, and so Will bade Canning tell the chiefs the party would come ashore again in the morning ; but no sooner had Canning delivered the message, than he was seized from behind by two of the savages.

"Treachery ! To the rescue !" cried Will, and on the instant all those who were not too badly wounded sprang forward with their muskets in their hands ; fire, however, they could not, for the cunning wretches held Canning in their front.

Then Canning cried out to his shipmates not to advance, or the savages would murder him. Then, with the two parties within a few yards of each other, Canning called out to Will that the chiefs intended him no harm, but that as a shipful of white men had some time before landed, plundered and killed many of their people, they

had seized him as a hostage that our crew should not do
likewise ; moreover, they intended to keep him with
them till the next day, when, providing no greater
number of persons landed than was sufficient to barter
and carry away the provisions, they would let him
depart unharmed ; and again Will was obliged to comply,
and so, in no very great spirits, the party returned on
board.

The next morning a council was held in the captain's
cabin, consisting of Master Adams, the chief officer,
Quackernack, Thomas Adams, and myself, when it was
resolved that the shore-going party should be headed by
the captain himself, who took with him Thomas Adams,
and about thirty men, nearly all, indeed, who had any
strength. Will Adams and Master Quackernack were
left in command of the ship, while I accompanied the
party. When we were almost in shore the savages ges-
ticulated for us to land, but for a time the captain refused. At length, however, finding they would not
advance to the boats, he commanded the men to land,
and, dividing them into two parties, one under the command of Thomas Adams, and the other under his own,
he led the way with his party, but as he advanced the
savages receded ; seeing which, Thomas Adams ordered
his men to advance in support, but, strangely as I thought
at the time, shook me by the hand, saying, " God help
us, Master Melichor, I fear me some villainy is at work ;
but should I get knocked off the hooks, tell my brother
he will be indebted for my loss to Gilbert Canning."

Alas ! the meaning of those words, or rather presenti-
ment, soon became apparent ; for as the first party, led
by the captain, entered the village, arrows flew from
every nook and cranny of its double row of huts, with
such deadly aim, that at least one-half of the men fell,
our gallant captain first. Maddened at this treachery,
the party under Tom Adams, which he had formed back
to back, sent a storm of bullets. The reply to this exhibited the trap into which they had fallen ; for now it
was no arrows, but a heavy rain of lead. The Spaniards, the hated, treacherous Spaniards, were upon the

island, and in league with the natives, whom they had
persuaded to decoy our people into the village.

Enraged at their fatal rascality, I should have leaped
from the boat and joined in the fight, had I not been
rudely forced back into my seat by the men who had
been left with me in the boat, and who wisely pulled
out from the shore, keeping their hands upon their oars,
to be in readiness to receive any fugitive; but alas! instead of fugitives, the savages, with bows and spears,
came yelling towards us. To escape them, we pulled
lustily, and fortunately reached the ship without a wound,
but in deep sorrow for the fate of our companions.

Even sorrow, however, was too great a luxury to be
indulged in by wretches in such miserable plight; for
now, after this great loss, we had scarce men, or at least
manly strength enough on board to lift anchors; and
embittered with the increased suffering which this sad
event promised the men, they received the news in
moody silence, and, I am afraid, selfish sorrow. As for
Will, that others might not be still more discouraged,
the bitter, though uncomplaining agony he felt for the
loss of his much-loved brother was never shown, otherwise than in the words, "Praise be to God, he is spared
much misery."

That night and the next day we hugged the shore,
with the hope of picking up some fugitives; but hunger,
weakness, and thirst kept us from staying longer; and
so we passed over to the island of Santa Maria, where,
to our relief, we found the 'Hope,' that is, the admiral;
but oh, how quickly was our joy at the meeting turned
to grief, when, upon going aboard, we found that the
sufferings of the crew had been as great as our own.
Then we heard that they also had suffered from the
Spaniards' villainy; for it appeared that some days previous to *our* arrival at Mocha, the general, and twenty-
seven of his men, having landed upon that island, had
been treacherously slain.

Then, in this sore trouble, Master Hudcoopee, who
had become sobered down, being chosen general, and
Master Quackernack, captain of our ship (the 'Charity'),

we took counsel together what should be done to get
food, for we were all well nigh starving.   Alas ! nothing
could we do but take upon us the character of pirates,
and so land, attack and plunder the town ; yet even for
this we were not in sufficient force.

God, however, in his mercy, at length took compassion
upon us ; for while we were pondering what to do—as
to sail we could not without food, while to land with so
small a force, would have been certain destruction—a
boat put out from the town with two men in her ; but
when they came aboard, the crew, finding they were
Spaniards, so remembered their slaughtered companions,
that they would have been hung up to the yard-arm, but
for Will Adams, who, smothering his own indignation at
the treachery which he believed to be hidden under the
fair words by which they sought to persuade us to land
and accept their hospitality, advised that they should be
kept prisoners until they had written to their fellows in
the town to send us beeves, sheep, and water, moreover,
threatening them with death if this were not done ; and
so greatly were the cowards alarmed at the aspects of
the few desperate men among whom they found themselves, that before night they had saved their lives by
helping us to sustain ours with food.

Having thus obtained relief for ourselves, we began to
think of others, and so held council together as to what
we should do to make our voyage profitable to our merchants ; but as our merchandize consisted chiefly of
woollen cloths, which it was not reasonable would be
found saleable in hot places like the Moluccas or the
Indies, where the people for the most part wear little
clothing, we were sore hard in our minds what was to
be done ; but even then, fortunately, Providence had
placed on board one Derrick Gerritson, who had been in
Japan with the Portugals, and he told us that woollen
cloths were in great estimation in those islands, and so
to direct our course to Japan we all agreed.

CHAPTER III.

AFTER MUCH AND LONG SUFFERINGS, WE ARRIVE IN JAPAN.

THUS providentially relieved from our sore distress, and having resolved upon our course, we left the coast of Chili, in thirty-six degrees south latitude, in the month of November, when, again passing the line, and after divers months, during which we had a fair wind, we fell in with certain islands in sixteen degrees north, the natives of which were men-eaters. Now at these islands the great justice of God in punishing crime was clearly shewn, for seven of our men, making up their minds to quit the ship, took a large pinnace, and made their way ashore, but no sooner did they land than they were killed, and afterwards devoured by the savages : and thus, although they had wickedly left their suffering shipmates, they met with their reward.

Then again, as if to add to our wretchedness, in the last week of February we lost sight of our general's vessel, and never saw her more ; an accident that was doubly unfortunate, as our ship, the 'Charity,' had by that time scarcely men enough left to work her, and but a wretchedly small store of provisions. Nevertheless, we still went on our course for Japan ; but in March, when we reached the island called Una Colonna, so many more of our men had died, and so many of the others were sick nigh unto death, that, with the exception of John Owater, whose duty it was to keep on the look out for land, Master Adams and the present writer were the only two persons on board who were whole. As for Master Quackernack (the captain) he was stretched in his cabin in hourly expectation of a summons to the other world ; while the nine or ten men who, by strength rather of mind than body, remained upon deck, were in such weakness that they could only move about upon their hands and knees.

In such straits, but which day by day were getting
worse, we continued for many weeks, (it being by God's
providence alone that all the time we could hold the ship
under hand,) till on the night of the 10th of April 1600,
when it did appear to us all that we had arrived at the
crack of doom, for there happened a heavy storm: the
lightning played about the heavens, and the thunder came
in such shocks as were beyond my past experience, but
by far worse were the groanings of the captain, who kept
praying to God to deliver him from his misery by death,
and the mutinous moanings of the men, who, maddened
by their long sufferings, now gave way to hopeless despair.   Indeed, one who, for charity's sake, I must deem
to have lost his wits, after much moaning, wailing, and
gnashing of teeth, crawled down the hatchway, when
Providence setting a spark of suspicion in the mind of
Master Adams, he left the helm at which we were both
standing, and followed him.   He had not disappeared
down the hatchway many minutes, when, with the poor
fellow in his brawny arms, he threw him upon the deck,
saying to the men around—

"Look well to this madman, my men : he would have
fired the powder magazine."

But the men, moving neither hands nor feet, stood de-
mentedly, as if they regretted that the attempt had
failed.

For a minute there was a dead silence.   At length,
however, one bolder than the rest confessed that the act
of the one had been the act of all by agreement, but that
having drawn lots among themselves who should be the
one to fire the magazine, the duty had fallen upon the
miserable wretch whose attempt Will had frustrated ;
when, as quick in action as thought, Will drew a pistol
from his belt, saying—

"Cowards ! infidels ! would you doubt the justice of
God ? Back, I say, to your posts and your duties as best
you may."   And then, as the cowed men obeyed, Will
added, "My men, your miseries have been great, but
your rewards are to come.   Would you, then, at the last
hour, lose all hope of that heaven to which, even now in

this dire misery, you are as near, as if treading the land of your birth ?"

At this the men, growing ashamed of their despair, gave cheers for Master Adams, and to the best of their strength did their duty, and so, by God's help and Will's strength of mind, kept the ship's head straight, and thus we weathered the gale, and, better, soon after day-break the next morning heard from Owater, the look-out man, the welcome words, "Land ahead !"

"Land ahead !" the words fell upon our hearts as refreshingly as the first drop of water upon the tongue of a man dying of thirst, or, and I mean it not irreverently, as the call up to heaven to a soul scorching in purgatory.

Again the words were now taken up and repeated by the hoarse faint voices of the whole of our poor fellows. God help them, they had not even then done with suffering.

" The coast of Bungo, it is," cried Owater.

" Make you out our whereabouts, Owater ?" said I.

" Aye, Master Santvoort, it is the coast of Bungo," was the reply.

" Then, by God's mercy, we have at last reached Japan," exclaimed Will.

But shortly afterwards there came on a dense fog, such a one indeed that is to be found in no other latitude. Moreover, it fell over and around us so thickly, that the men again lost their spirits, and then sickly voices moaned and groaned as if it had been an infliction, but Will chid them as if they had been guilty of blasphemy.

For three hours the fog continued, but then it was burst asunder by the resplendent sun, which was a fortunate chance, happening as it did at that moment, for we saw that we were standing right on to the land, and in dangerous proximity to the rocks.

"Let go the anchor," cried Will. "Hoist a signal, Melichor, for a pilot." But so miserably weak were the men, that it was with difficulty the order could be obeyed. Indeed, had it been to weigh anchor, it would have been impossible.

" Shall we discharge the great gun, and so signal to them our distress, Master Adams ?" said I.

" And thus bring a whole fleet of these Japanners upon
us ?   Nay, Master Melichor, better bide our time, bide
our time," he replied.

Then the noise of casting anchors, the bustle upon
deck, called up a little life into our captain's body, and
assisted by Owater and Derrick Gerritson, who was but
in a trifling degree stronger than himself, he crawled
upon deck, and stood upon the forecastle, propped up
his back against some bread bags and rope, when, shaking Will by the hand, he said, " Under Providence we
owe our lives to thee, Master Adams."

" To God alone, who has preserved the strength of a few,
are we all indebted, Master Quackernack, and by your
leave I would have it that a prayer be offered up for
bringing us so far through our dangers."   So replying, he
fell upon his knees, and then earnestly, and in so solemn
and firm a tone of voice, did that bold seaman offer up a
prayer of thanksgiving for God's goodness unto us all,
that even those whose impatience and want of knowledge
had caused them to blaspheme in their utter miseries,
incontinently joined in repeating the words after his slow
and distinct utterance ; and then, when the thanksgiving
was finished, did Master Quackernack again seize Will
by the hand, saying, " It is even as thou saidst at starting, Master Adams, prayer should have been repeated
twice a day from the outset of our perilous voyage, yet
I doubt me that any minister could have wrought upon
the hearts of these fellows as thou hast."

" Tut, tut, Master Quackernack ; every man has a
minister in his own heart which should teach him his
duty to God," was the reply.

But that which affected me most in this scene was, that
the most ruffianly, mutinous, and blasphemous man of our
crew stumbled forward, and saluting Will as if he had
been the general of a fleet, said, " Hang me, or pardon
me, as thou wilt, Master Adams ; but when a shipmate
of Drake's like thyself, who can keep his feelings all taut
while he is starving and expecting to go to the bottom,
can pray till he cries like a woman, I for one will believe
that he must have some powerful minister inside ;" and

as, with a tear trickling down his cheek, he timidly held
out his hand, which Will shook forgivingly and heartily,
there was not a dry eye in the ship.

As the fog cleared off we saw several vessels making
towards us : they were fishing-boats about five tons each,
with bamboo sails, ropes of straw, and sculled by eight
men, four upon each side ; the oars rested upon pins in
the side of the boat, to which they were secured about
the middle, so that they poised themselves. The rowers,
instead of sitting to their work like our men, stood
upright and pulled with marvellous rapidity.

As these boats neared us, the captain gave the order
to prepare to give fight ; an order which made us laugh
in spite of ourselves, for there were only three able persons on board. In a very short time our deck was
crowded with short sturdy men, with bare feet, and hair
shaven backwards from the forehead to the nape of the
neck, the little left about the neck and on the temples
being well greased and turned up in a cue, which was tied
with string made of white paper; as for their clothes,
perhaps the least said the better, at least for decency's
sake, for although a few wore a loose blue or brown cotton
gown, the greater part were more than half nude.

When they had reached the deck, and saw but three
men standing upright, while the rest were either lying or
reclining helplessly upon the boards, and so knew that
resistance was not intended, the masters of two of the
boats, approaching near Will and the captain, put off
their straw shoes (for they were the only men among the
new comers who were not barefooted); then each clap-
ping his right hand within his left, put them down
towards their knees, and in that stooping position waved
their bodies to and fro, that is sideways, and cried—

" Augh ! Augh !"

" By the Lord, I would give a bale of cloth to know
what these fellows mean," said the captain.

" It isn't mischief," replied Will, making an English
bow.

" They are making us welcome," said I, imitating
Will's bow, at which the Japanners laughed and mut-

tered words that we could not understand. We must have made a very strange and foolish appearance, for there we stood, making dumb motions to each other, until Derrick Gerritson, who I have told you had been in Japan before, said—

"Welcome to us they mean! Well, I'll see that in the turn of a handspike," so first, to draw their attention to him, he coughed and cried "Augh! Augh!" then, having pointed to the sick men, including our invalided captain, he said, as he rubbed his stomach and put his fingers in his mouth—

"Saki, saki; Sokano, sokano." The masters evidently understood him, for instantly one of them, turning to a sailor, gave him some order, which caused him to return to his boat and row towards the shore.

"By the great Harry I have done it," said Derrick.

"What?" asked several voices simultaneously.

"Why, the only thing that'll do us any good. I have asked them for saki, that is a queer kind of Schiedam; and sokano, which means something to eat."

At this reply the sick men gave a cheer, but the Japanners, supposing it to be our mode of salutation, imitated it immediately to the best of their endeavour, and then laughed heartily, as if delighted at the success of their attempt.

In less than an hour the sailor returned to the ship, bringing with him several large flasks of spirits, and a large box of fruits, figs, nuts, rice, cakes, dried fish, and tea-dust. The famished men would then and there foolishly have eaten and drunk to their great hurt but for Will, who, with my assistance, stood before the good things, and doled them out in small quantities,—the spirit first, for acute hunger had long since destroyed their natural appetites. Of this spirit, diluted with warm water, we all partook, and it was strange its different effects: it revived the strength of the weak, and to the sick it gave repose, for they all went to sleep. As for the captain, getting one of the flasks in his hand, and having no control, he drank the whole of the contents, when suddenly, from the lowest state of weakness, he

became possessed with the strength and violence of a
raving madman. Then the Japanners came to our assistance, for with marvellous dexterity they passed cords
around his arms and legs, and helped us to carry him to
his hammock.

After this, we worked hard at dumb motions, to let
them know our distress, and that we wanted to take our
sick ashore. This, however, they gave us to understand
could not be, permitted, until they had received orders
from the authorities on land.

Admirably as we had managed so far with our new
friends, towards evening an incident occurred, which
nearly caused our destruction, and this fell out as follows : Polite and good-natured as these Japanners appeared, they possessed a curiosity as insatiable as it was
unpleasant, and the ship was such a wonder to them,
that they searched every part of her, closely examining,
not only all her points, but every article upon which they
could lay their hands : some carried writing materials
and a small note-book, in which they appeared to be
compiling an inventory. One of these worthies seemed
to have a genius for drawing, and so, approaching John
Owater, who had managed to take sufficient saki to make
him both quarrelsome and vain, tried his skill upon him,
and delighted with his own success, exhibited it to John ;
but the sailor, instead of being gratified, was so indignant at the likeness, that he attempted to tear the paper.
The artist endeavoured to save his work, and a scuffle
ensued, when John, in the height of his indignation, but
I believe by accident, gave his antagonist a blow, that
sent him down the hatchway upon the heads and shoulders of several of his inquiring countrymen, who, with
indignant countenances, and sharp knives in their hands,
immediately ascended to avenge the insult.

Will Adams, witnessing the fray, at once placed himself between the enraged Japanner and the drunken
sailor, but seizing the latter by the arm, with so great a
show of indignation, that the Japanners, who are well
trained to obedience to superiors, with very many bows
and bendings, signified their willingness to leave the

punishment of the culprit in the hands of his superior officer.

"Drunken knave, thou hast endangered the safety of us all by thy villainous temper," said Will.

"The heathen made a picture of me that would disgrace the figure-head of a Dutch beer-barge," was the sullen answer.

"What matters it, thou fool?" said Will.

"What matters, Master Adams? why it——"

"Tut, tut, thou mutinous dog," interrupted Will, passionately. "Get thee a bucket of water and sluice the beast apart from the man;" and the fellow, being sufficiently in his senses to fear being again put in irons, slunk away.

Early the next day the waters swarmed with boats and galleys of various kinds, from the simple fishing-boats to the gorgeous barges of the nobles and the princes; and as we stood watching the approach of this fleet towards our ship, Will exclaimed—

"By the great Harry, Melichor, we are making a sensation among the heathen!"

"By my faith, if they attempt to board us we shall soon get to the end of our troubles," I replied; adding, "but see you after what fashion these boats and barges are being formed into double lines?"

"Aye, that roadway is doubtless for their chiefs, who are about visiting us," said Will, and soon after, three richly-gilded galleys made towards us; one crowded with ladies; another which, from the silence and respect as it passed through the lines of boats, we guessed to hold the king himself; and the last, with the great nobles in attendance. Then, when they scrambled aboard from all sides, in a singularly disorderly fashion, Will Adams took upon himself the duty of receiving their majesties. I say their majesties, for there were two of them, and as neither party could understand the language of the other, a very strange reception it was.

The two kings, whom we afterwards discovered to be father and son, and who reigned jointly, after the fashion of the Roman emperors, were alike dressed in brown

silken gowns, girt close to their bodies, fine shirts, large
trousers, and sandals, which were fastened to their feet
by means of a button between their toes; their heads
were closely shaven, their hair long behind, and tied up
in a knot, and without any kind of hat. Each wore
two swords, one being about half, and the other a quarter of a yard in length. As for their general attire, it
was nearly the same as that of the nobles who attended
them.

Although father and son, these two princes bore small
resemblance to each other. The father, a man about
fifty-five years of age, was short, even for a Japanner,
but stout, with even features, and although obliquely-
placed eyes, little black orbs that seemed brimming over
with good nature, and a nose—I must say it—that told
at once that good cheer was no novelty in Japan. As
for the young king, as became, perhaps, the greater fresh-
ness of his dignity, his stature was tall, his figure slim,
and his countenance stern—nay, almost ferocious. Thus,

3

while I at once fell to liking the father, for the son I felt
a repugnance, and that, too, notwithstanding that he affected great politeness.

Of the ladies—of whom I should first have spoken—
there were two score, the greater number being of the
household of the young king ; and although, to the taste
of a European, but few of them were beautiful, inasmuch
as they were very low in stature, and wanted blush in
their faces, and, moreover, had their lips painted crimson,—not to mention those who, being married or betrothed, had had their teeth dyed a deep black, yet they
had very good complexions and comely features. The
dress of these ladies consisted of silken gowns, and each
wore so many one over the other, that she made up a
size ten times larger than Nature had given her. They
wore no stockings, but instead, a sort of buskin, bound
with a ribbon about the instep ; their girdles were like
those worn by the men, only much broader, while their
hair—which was very fine, plentiful and black—was decorated with flowers and ribbons, and held in shape by
large bodkins of gold and silver ; and this description
may pass for all the court ladies but one ; the exception
I shall deal with hereafter. The queen, notwithstanding
her blackened teeth, was of noble presence, being taller,
fairer, and of higher carriage than her women, having,
moreover, a countenance full of amiableness and intel-
lect. As for the lady above excepted—well, then, it was
a shame that she should have been born out of Europe,
for she was young, shapely as the fawn, with the eyes of
the gazelle, and yet a complexion fairer than the women
of Holland ; and though not, perhaps, quite equal in
beauty to the daughters of England, she possessed a
comeliness of person, and a swan-like symmetry of neck,
that bespoke the inner pride, or rather dignity of soul,
which kept that beautiful frame in motion. This lady
kept close to the side of the queen, and like her mistress,
seemed to be watched with lynx-eyed caution by the young
king, who, as the reader will hereafter discover, was
of a jealous nature.

Now the politeness of these great personages was sur-

prising to us, for no sooner did they see Master Adams,
who advanced to their front, than they put off their sandals, and made obeisances similar to those performed the
day before by the fishermen sailors, and which we returned by bowing as lowly as possible, crying, "Augh,
augh;" but when they found us dumb and looking
foolish, by reason that we knew not what to say, the
kings looked at each other, and laughed, the old king
most heartily. Then the latter, bethinking himself of
the best way of promoting good feeling between us,
spoke some words to a noble by his side, who, going to
the ship's side, signalled to the fleet, and shortly afterwards our awkward position was somewhat relieved by
the arrival of a craft, filled with nobles, each bringing a
servant, who carried a present of venison, fowl, fruits,
fish, and saki, all of which required no interpreter to
understand. When the viands were properly adjusted
upon the deck, the kings sat down upon some rich mats
their nobles had brought for their use, and motioned us
to partake, sending, at the same time, small lacquered
boxes of viands to the men, at the receipt of which the
sailors cheered, and the kings laughed. Then the old
king, receiving from a lad a large lacquered cup, containing about a quart of spirits, placed it first upon the
top of his head with both hands, and then, with a merry
eye, drank the whole off at a draught.

"The old toper means us to do likewise," said Will;
adding, "they are drinking our healths; let us return the
compliment." So, taking smaller cups, we followed the
royal example, and the king laughed heartily; then, bethinking himself, he spoke to us in a tongue which, although we could not understand, we took to be the
language of the Portugals, and so we sent for John
Owater, who made out that his majesty intended sending
for us ashore the next day; whereupon we endeavoured
to express our thanks by pointing to the land, and bending our heads, and again the king laughed.

Now as soon as his majesty found that one of our
party knew a little of the Portugals' tongue, he made
many attempts to ask questions; but as Owater's know-

ledge was but small, and that of the king's still less, their organs of speech became, as it were, disagreeably entangled ; all of which being put down by Owater to the stupidity of royalty, he became so much irritated that he forgot himself so far as to express his contempt in good round Dutch oaths ; but fortunately for us, his majesty's ignorance of the latter tongue led him to take so comical a view of their mutual predicament, that he well nigh choked himself with laughter.

After this passage, the kings, their nobles, and the ladies, proceeded to examine the ship, and not a pole, or a spar, or scarcely a rope did they pass without notice, or desiring one of the lords, the old king's secretary, to make a note thereof in the memorandum-book which he carried in his hand. They even insisted upon examining the captain's cabin ; and although we endeavoured by many signs to make them understand that it was occupied by a sick man, they still persevered. I opened the door, and the old king endeavoured to enter ; but the opening being very narrow, and his majesty very broad, he stuck half way, and that so tightly, that we had some fears for his health ; his cheeks were flushed, his eyes distended. His son, however, with the aid of a noble, having first asked his permission, taking hold of his arms, by a long pull and a strong pull brought him back into position, when the royal old gentleman, perceiving the anxiety depicted upon the countenances of his people, laughed himself almost into a fit ; but although deprived by nature of the gratification of his own curiosity, the good-natured prince commanded his lords to go forward. The junior king was the first to enter, and he was followed by a young lord, who, seeing before him a picture of Venus and Cupid, to the astonishment of all, fell upon his knees, and began to mutter in Latin.

"The heathen !" said Will, in disgust.

"Nay, Master Adams ; it is my belief he is a Christian, pupil of the Portugal fathers."

"Christian ! what ! and fall upon his knees before that baggage Venus ?" replied Will.

"They mistake it for the picture of the Virgin and child," said I.

" Tut, tut ! our good Bess would make short work of these papists, and such scurvy teachers of Christianity, Melichor, that their scholars don't know the difference between that heathen woman and her imp, and the Madonna and child."

The young king, however, was apparently no Christian, for, in an angry tone, he muttered a few sharp words to the kneeling youth, who at once, with great humility and down-cast eyes, arose to his feet. As, however, the king turned his back, the lad's whole countenance changed, a glance of unmistakeable, although suppressed hatred shot from his eyes, and the fingers of his right hand nervously twisted about the handle of his sword; but that right hand wanted its forefinger. I do not know that such an event was any thing very remarkable among so barbarous a people ; yet it warmed my curiosity, nay, troubled me. Who was he ? what his history ? why that glance of intense hatred ? and—and—why that maimed hand ?

The inquisitiveness of all these high personages having been appeased, they left the ship, courteously, however, leaving with us an officer of two-sworded dignity, to protect us from the impertinence of people of low condition, who not only visited us to gratify their curiosity, but to purloin any articles upon which they could place their hands.

CHAPTER IV.

WILL ADAMS'S EARLY HISTORY.

ALTHOUGH Master Quackernack had recovered from the first violent effects of the spirit, yet his health and body were so shattered, that Will retained command of the miserable remnant of our once fine crew ; and so, the day after the royal visit, calling the few who could stand upright, he prayed them, for the honour of their country, to furbish themselves up as sprightly as might be.   This address was received with the heartiest cheer their weak lungs could send forth ; and scarcely had they obeyed, and made something approaching a decent appearance, when three of the king's barges came alongside.   One of them was padded with soft carpets and mats, for the comfort of the sick ; another, similarly arranged, for the express and separate comfort of the captain ; while the last was for those who were whole.   Moreover, that the sick men should be safely landed without further harm to their health, two of the king's body physicians were sent to take charge of them.   So when we set out, one of the latter seated himself in the captain's barge, and the other in that which held the sick men.   When we reached the beach we found it covered with thousands of people of all ranks, who had come down to get sight of the foreigners ; but to prevent any discomfort that might have occurred from the crowd, the good-natured old king had sent down a number of odd-looking sedan-chairs, called 'cangos,' besides two 'norimons,' that is, others of a superior class, for the conveyance of the officers.

Thus were we taken to Fuchay, the capital of the little kingdom over which the two kings held rule.   The house appropriated to our use was of great extent, but only two storeys high, and built of wood and plaster, the outside being whitewashed to look exactly like stone.   The horizontal beams were supported by posts, placed at some distance from each other, the spaces between being filled with interwoven bamboo canes, the interstices of which were again filled up with clay, sand, and lime.

The interior of this building formed, in reality, but two rooms, one above and another below ; the latter, or basement, was divided into three compartments, the first for the sick men, the second for the captain, and the last for Master Adams and the present writer.   The divisions were formed by wooden frames, pasted over with thick painted paper, and so that they would easily slide in wooden channels or grooves, above and below, and by reason of the thinness of these partitions, it was necessary for a tenant of either to speak in a whisper, if he would not be heard by his neighbour. The windows, of which there were many, consisted of light moveable frames, divided by slender rods into squares, pasted over on the outside with fine white paper, through which the in- mates could see without being seen. The roof of the house, which was covered with copper-plates, and shone in the sun like burnished gold, projected some distance beyond, so that at the same time it formed a covering for a long gallery which ran before the windows, and from the extreme edge of this roof, slanting inwardly, hung blinds made of rushes, which were to protect the paper windows from the heavy rains.

Of the interior of the apartment we occupied, I shall say but little; that little, however, will help to complete the description of a Japanner's dwelling. The fire-place, to which there was no chimney, stood in the middle of the room, and was nothing more than a large copper-pan, with projecting edges, and over which was suspended a kettle, full of water, heated by a charcoal fire. The ceiling and walls, which were covered with a gold and silver flowered paper, were soiled with smoke. The floor was covered with mats, made of rush (the *Juncus effusus*) interwoven with rice straw, at least three inches in thick- ness, and two yards in length by one wide ; and this size is worthy of note, for, by law, it is established that every mat in Japan must be made exactly of the same size, and thus it is that a mat is a standard measure throughout the empire. Of furniture, I can say nothing, as there were neither cupboard, bureau, sofa, bed, table, chair, clock, nor looking-glass.

When the porters placed our chairs in front of this house, I felt a glow of satisfaction that the time had again arrived to practise the use of my legs ashore. It must be remembered that we had been nearly two years aboard ship. As, however, I put my legs out of this little vehicle, you may imagine my surprise at finding them suddenly hoisted over the shoulders of one man, while another behind supported my body, and so carried me forward into the room I have heretofore described, and this, too, I afterwards found, by order of the king, who had commanded our conductors thus to carry us, to prevent our feet from getting wet, and so doing an injury to our health.

"The fellows must have strong limbs and big hearts that will catch me in that rat-trap again," said Will surlily, looking at the norimon, shaking his body into its natural shape, and rubbing down his legs, as soon as we had both been carried into the room after the above fashion.

"Nay, nay, Master Adams, it is churlish to complain, for it was kindly meant," said I.

"May Beelzebub take such kindness, Melichor," replied he; but the sight of a man with a large lacquered tray, furnished with some pieces of a fish esteemed the rarest delicacy in Japan, swimming in brown sauce, some other fried fish on skewers, lemon peel with sugar, and several slices of mange, that is, a kind of round cake as big as a hen's egg, but made of flour and sugar, and steeped in a brown sauce, highly flavoured with ginger, restored him to his humour, and he said—

"May be this is too good to be lasting. Let us, however," he added, as he seated himself upon a matted carpet near the viands, "be thankful for anything that is wholesome, and pray that we mayn't have fallen in with a parcel of land pirates, who are blinding our eyes while they are plundering the ship of its merchandise, to the cost of our worshipful masters the merchants."

"Nay, nay, Master Adams, these fellows, though heathens, are not fools to bait the trap when the rat's caught without," I added, as I tasted a piece of fish, which was not at all to my liking: "it is poison they mean."

"Aye, aye, I have heard these Indian people have a trick that way," said Will, taking my jest in earnest, and holding up another piece upon one of the little sticks which served for knife or fork, before him suspiciously; but one of the attendants, as if comprehending the sign, took the piece of fish from the skewer, and immediately swallowed it.

"Bah! I am but a lubber to have taken thee for a Roman or a Spaniard," said Will; adding, as he bowed and smiled, "and if you only understand English signs better than the English language, you'll see I mean to ask your pardon." And the man did understand, for he bowed down to the carpet, and then, as he arose, laughed heartily.

"By Beelzebub, the land shark's laughing at us," said Will petulantly.

"Then let us laugh, too, Master Adams, for from peasant to king, in this part of heathendom, laughing seems to be the law of the land."

"Thou art right, Melichor, lad, for from the laughter that lights up the eyes and hides the teeth no great harm can come," replied Will; adding, however, as another attendant came into the room, and placed by our side, upon a large brass tray, a small fire-pan with coals, a spitting-pot, a small box filled with tobacco, and three large pipes with small brass bowls, "By the head of Sir Walter, these heathens have even the Virginian weed itself;" and as he filled a pipe he contemplated the whole smoking apparatus with silent astonishment, but, after some dozen solitary puffs, he said—

"By the great Harry, Melichor, to find Sir Walter Raleigh's plant here but ten years after the worshipful knight first brought it into our own Christian land would puzzle the learned head of Master Dee the astrologer."

"Tut, tut, Master Adams; it wots not by what means it came here, so that thou hast it to enjoy; for my own part, I like not the weed, for to me it seems but to be making a chimney of one's throat," said I.

"For the first thou art right, Melichor, as it is but a tempting of Providence to catch and bottle up the wind that has helped us into a good haven; but as for thy dislike of so solacing a plant, thou art an ass," he replied with a laugh; which, however, soon subsiding, he began in silence to draw at the pipe, till the smoke came forth like that from the chimney of an Amsterdam still.

Thus for the first few hours were we well tended; but at night, notwithstanding our objections by signs, we were forcibly introduced into a large tub of hot water, and rubbed down as if we had been horses; but after that we were left to the enjoyment of our beds, which consisted of soft mattrasses, stuffed with cotton, spread upon the mats, and some twenty cotton gowns which served for sheets, blankets, and pillows, made of six thin lacquered boards : the hollow part serving for the safe and cleanly keeping of comb and brush.

Three days and nights we passed after this fashion, alone, and nothing would have better pleased us, if we could but have prevailed upon our attendants to permit us to exercise our legs about the town, and Master Adams had not been in great anxiety about the safety of our goods.

Upon the fourth day the old king came, bringing presents of fish and saki, stopped with us several hours, laughed and drank heartily; and although to all our endeavours to make him comprehend our wish to visit our captain and shipmates he only laughed, and replied, ' Tsusi,' which, I afterwards discovered, meant 'interpreter,' he had no sooner left us than two of the attendants led us to the room where our captain was lodged. The poor fellow lay stretched upon some mats, with his back upwards; two men were holding his head, and two others his feet, while an elderly two-sworded gentleman, with abundant hair upon his head, which denoted him to be a physician, was kneeling by the captain's side, busily engaged in tending a number of small cones, which were smoking away like so many volcanoes.

Now the instant Will saw his commander's plight, he ran forward with a look of horror and indignation, crying, "To the rescue, Melichor! the land-sharks are putting the skipper to some infernal torture, to make him disclose the hiding-place of the coin on board ;" and in another minute the astonished Japanners were sent flying to the four corners of the room, and the physician

lay upon his back by the side of his medicine-chest,
struggling to regain his feet, and the volcanoes were
swept from the back of the patient, whom Will had
turned round, when, holding his hands, he said—

"Cheer up, Master Quackernack, the enemy has hauled
down his flag."

The surprise, however, of the whole party at this onset
was only equalled by Will's horrified astonishment when
the captain, in angry but weak tones, and writhing as he
spoke, replied—

"Belay there, Master Pilot; the good heathen is a
chirurgeon, and by thy rashness thou hast undone the
operation by which I was being relieved of these pains."

"God's mercy?" exclaimed Will, aghast, "I have run
my keel upon a reef in good earnest." Helping the
fallen leech to his legs, he added, "But the caravel never
floated that was not likely to get adrift, and even Master
Frobisher has made a wrong reckoning before now: so,
comrade, I ask your pardon;" and he held out his hand
to the chirurgeon, who, however, comprehending nothing
but war by the action, seized hold of it with both hands,
called out to his men, and in a moment we were seized
from behind, ropes tied round our arms, and thus led
back to our room.

"God's mercy, but I am an ass to have gone so far
out of my reckoning as to mistake a chirurgeon for an
executioner."

"It is a sad mishap," said I moodily, "a sad mishap,
Master Adams, and I pray God that he may speedily
send us an interpreter; for it is my belief that He alone
can persuade these heathens thou didst not intend
murder."

Fortunately, however (as I heard afterwards), the
notion of the Japanner was that we had both suddenly
become *possessed with the fox* (*i.e.* mad), and therefore they
kept us bound till the old king had been informed of
the affair; when again, fortunately for us, his majesty
came to see us, and having, by many questions put to
the attendants, guessed at the real cause of Will's raid
upon the chirurgeon, he ordered us to be unbound, par-

took of a bowl of hot saki, and, after a hearty laugh, quitted the room, shaking his venerable head, and muttering the word ' *Tsusi.*'

This apparent torture, which we had seen Master Quackernack undergoing, I now know to be the favourite medical remedy called *moxa-burning.* This moxa is the finer part of the young leaves of the wormwood (*artemisia,*) and is procured by rubbing and beating the leaves till the green parts separate, and nothing remains but the wool, which is sorted into two kinds. When applied, it is made up in little cones, which, being placed upon the part selected for the operation, are set on fire at the top ; they burn very slowly, leaving a scar or blister on the skin, which, some time after, breaks and discharges. The operation is not very painful, except when repeated in the same place, and is, moreover, esteemed throughout the empire to be a catholicon.

For a long time our position was as if we had been living in a country inhabited by dumb creatures, for we could only make our wants known by signs and motions, and those oftentimes so ridiculous, that the Japanners, as well as ourselves, laughed outright. To relieve, however, the irksomeness of our confinement, Master Adams would relate stories of adventures through which he had passed during his career. One of these, which is not only agreeable in itself, but necessary for the understanding of this narrative, I will now relate. It was on the morning of the fifth day of our confinement, that he said—

" Mayhap you know the town of Gillingham ?"

" Nay," said I, " I have but little further knowledge than that it adjoins Chatham, and is nigh by the new docks now building for the queen's ships."

" Well, then, in antiquity, I must first tell you, that it is second to no town in England, for although now it is but a huge workshop for manufacturers, it was on the site of that town a great battle was fought between King Edmund Ironside and Canute ; there the 600 Norman gentlemen who came over in the train of the two princes, Alfred and Edward, were all barbarously put to

death by the great Earl Godwin ; there also, for many
centuries, stood the shrine of the saint the Papists call
our Lady of Gillingham, to which pilgrimages were made
from all parts of England ; there was born, also, the
famous scribe, William of Gillingham, who writ a history of England in the days of the second Richard ; and
there, although now in ruins, stands the ancient palace
of the Archbishops of Canterbury, and for these reasons,
as well that I was born there, am I proud of the place ;
and hark ye, Melichor, I would not give a rope's end,
save, indeed, it might be athwart his back, for the man
who is not proud of his birth-place."

Then, when he had re-filled his pipe, after pondering
for some minutes, he said—

" Melichor, the picture of the past is now before my
mind. It is the year of grace, 1577. There is the large,
old, ruined house, aye, and the great oaken room ; logs
heavier than usual are heaped upon the fire, to which the
group are drawn nigh unto scorching their feet, for it is a
cold, biting November night. But the family : well, here
they are. First, a tall, square-built seaman, the redness
of whose face seems borrowed from the burning coals,
upon which his large, laughing blue eyes are fixed ; he is
seated upon an oaken chair, his arm around the waist of
his wife, who is sitting upon his knee, attentively listening to the story he is telling ; scarcely, however, so attentively as the two boys, who are kneeling by his side,
or the tall, fair-haired, blue-eyed girl, who also is kneeling, with her elbow upon a stool, and her lustrous eyes
glistening in the face of the happy seaman. That seaman
was very happy, for he had but just returned from a
voyage which made the name of Frobisher famous for
all time. Twelve months before, the good ships the
' Gabriel' and the 'Michael,' under the command of
Master Martin, had started from Greenwich under the
happiest auspices, and with the good wishes of the nation, which had hopes that the gallant vessels would
make the long-desired north-west passage to Cathay.
As the ships passed Greenwich the lords came running
out from the palace, the Queen waved her hand from the

windows, and, moreover, sent a noble gentleman on
board to make known her pride of her adventurous subjects, and also to command the general to come and take
his leave of her; while the mariners, apparelled in sky-
coloured cloth, manned the yards and decks, and dis-
charged their ordnance according to the order of war,
insomuch that the hills sounded therewith, the valleys
and the waters giving an echo, while the beholders on
each shore shouted after such fashion, that the sky rang
again with the noise.

" Well did the listening family remember all this; the
voyage had been prosperous, and again the welkin was
ringing with joy at the return of the two ships. And
now the mariner is relating how that they had discovered
a land inhabited by strange infidels, whose like had
never before been seen, and whom, as they crouched down
in their small boats, the crew had mistaken for porpoises.
At the account of these strange beings, and the news
that one had been caught and brought home for the delec-
tation of the Queen, the girl claps her hands together
and laughs. Then, at the wonderful bravery of Master
Martin Frobisher, who, by his own sole hands, rescued
the crew from a watery death; and at the great fights
with savages, the boys swell out with pride and emulation,
till they seem to have grown an inch in height, and burn
with hope for the day when they may themselves accompany their bold father. But with what a thrilling terror
the mother listens to the tale of five men having been
captured and eaten by the savages; for, but for God's
providence, might not the speaker have been one of
those unfortunates? So, he telling and the others listening, the evening wears on without either noticing how
low has burned the fuel in the fire-place. Then the
speaker proudly contrasts those brave English adventurers, for the greater part men of gentle blood and fortune, who, in the frailest of vessels, have traversed seas
perpetually agitated by storms and encumbered with ice,
with the pure and honourable desire alone to benefit the
human race by the discovery of new lands, with those
dark Spaniards and treacherous Portugals, who, being-

but men of desperate fortunes, had sought the Indies selfishly, and only from a love of gold, by reason of which, not only had they, by their murders and robberies, forfeited their souls, but for ever made the sight of white men hateful to the Indians.

"And this," said Will, taking the pipe from his mouth, and looking earnestly in my face, as if he wished to impress a moral, "I would have you to note, Master Melichor, was true when that brave mariner spoke, for up to that period, Englishmen had made these voyages out of mere love of honourable adventure."

At this speech, however, I could not help smiling, for I well knew the instinct all men have, that gold is to be found in foreign countries : but noticing this, Will said—

"By God's grace, Master Melichor, it was from a desire to discover new lands, and another passage to the Indies, that those voyages, of which the good man spoke, had been made, for at that time the existence of the metal was not even dreamed of in the seas that had been traversed, and better had it been if they had never suspected it, for one lump of gold soon after caused the ruin of Martin Frobisher, and his patrons, the merchants and others ; but of that anon," and he continued—

"Now, so interested was the group in the narrative, that the fire would have gone quite out, had not my father—for need I tell you that I was one of those boys —shrugged his shoulders, and gently putting his wife aside, said—'By my faith, wife, but we shall be frozen if thou dost not replenish the fire.'

" 'That will I do, my father,' interposed the girl, at once running towards the fuel cupboard.

" 'No,' said my brother and I, running after her. The girl, however, won the race : nay, before we had reached the cupboard, she had snatched up a black lump and thrown it upon the expiring fuel.

" 'Mercy on me, thou little mischief, it is the trophy thy uncle brought from the lands of ice and men porpoises, that thou hast mistaken for sea-coal,' exclaimed my mother, as she jumped from her chair to the rescue. She had taken it from the fire, but the heat causing her to let it fall upon the stone hearth, it split into two pieces.

" ' God's mercy ! what have we here ?' she cried, as she picked up the black stones and threw them upon the table.

" ' 'Fore heaven, wife, thou art as much scared at the breaking of a trumpery stone as if it had changed into the evil one himself,' said my father, laughing.

" But for a minute my mother kept her eyes fixed upon the stone, then clutching both pieces, she said nervously, with a flush of excitement upon her face—

" ' Didst thou indeed, my husband, find this stone upon one of those icy lands thou tell'st me of ?'

" ' Aye, aye, lass ; and where there is enough left, if need be, to supply England with sea-coal for the next fifty years.

" ' This is not coal ; it is—' but my mother stopped for a moment, as if the deep thoughts passing through her mind had tied her tongue-strings.

" God's mercy ! then what is it ?" cried my father, who was no less astonished at his wife's strange behaviour than we children.

" ' The hand of Providence is in this,' replied my mother, adding slowly and seriously, ' for it is gold ore, pure virgin gold.'

" ' Thou art mad, wife,' replied my father ; but taking the pieces in his hands, and perceiving the glittering of the yellow metal streaked amidst its black surroundings, his eyes flasked strangely for one who had so well rallied the Portugals and Spaniards for their love of the metal, and his voice trembled with joy as he said—

" ' 'Fore God, wife, but thou art i' the right.'

" Now this discovery was not much in itself, for the quantity of gold was small ; but my mother being a practical woman, explained to us, before we sought our beds, that in the earth from which that stone had been taken there still remained vast quantities, by reason of which, and my father having made the discovery, he would be richly rewarded, if not desired to join an expedition for the expressly finding of gold ; for there could be no doubt

that now not only private gentlemen, but the merchants
of London, the Court, and the Queen herself, would
openly countenance and aid such an enterprise ; moreover concluding by piously remarking that God had
doubtless opened up this knowledge, that in the search
for gold many new discoveries would be made, of benefit
to the human race. Thus did this small finding of gold
disturb all present and future tranquillity. For my own
part, so excited was I, that I at once boldly declared that
I, too, would become a mariner, a discoverer of strange
people, and a finder of gold ; at which the little girl,
throwing her arms around my neck, exclaimed—

" ' Oh, that is brave, Will, for thou wilt become a great
man, like Master Frobisher, and I will be thy wife, and
go with thee to these strange lands :' and with such
thoughts we went that night to rest.

" Now matters fell out much as my mother had pre-
dicted, for the stone being proved by the London gold-
finers to contain the precious metal, a great gold fever
raged throughout the land, sums of money were collected
from stay-at-homes, and three ships were fitted out,
having Master Frobisher for general, one belonging to
her Grace the Queen, who threw over his neck a golden
chain, and thus, manned with gentlemen of blood, soldiers,
and mariners, the ships sailed from Greenwich ; but this
time Master Frobisher was commanded to search for
gold, and to defer further discovery until another time ;
and with that expedition commenced my troubles, for
therein my father was drowned, by falling overboard,
and my mother died of grief that she had persuaded him
to join the ships. The events, however, of that November
night fixed my career ; and I, who had no mind to be
any thing but a mariner, was bound apprentice to Master
Nicholas Diggins, of Limehouse, near London. My
brother Thomas, whose death, please God, I may live to
revenge, was apprenticed to a Master Best ; and so, in
learning the duties of a mariner, and in making many
small voyages, !were the next twelve years of my life
passed ;" and Master Adams stopped to refill his pipe.

4

"But of the little girl," said I, for it seemed to me that he avoided speaking of her.

"Aye, aye, it is of her that I have now to speak ; but stay Master Melichor, the memory unmans me ;" and he turned his head aside. Indeed, he must have been moved powerfully within, for great tears stood in his eyes. Soon, however, recovering himself, he continued——

CHAPTER V.

THE GREAT ARMADA, AND HOW WILL OBTAINED HIS WIFE.

"THAT pretty, brave, glorious girl, with the fair wavy hair and blue eyes, was my cousin, and the only daughter of a rich London merchant, one Master Saris."

"The only daughter of Master Saris," I repeated with surprise.

"Art moonstruck at a name, Melichor ! Aye, aye, but I see from what quarter the wind blows," said he laughing ; "for," he added, "thy brains are upon the pretty Mistress Maud, whose worthy father made me informed of some passages between you : but fear not for thy sweetheart, my lad, for the Mistress Saris of whom I speak, although first cousin to Mistress Maud, is, by reason of this, the daughter of a much older brother, some twenty years over and about in age. But, to continue my tale, Mabel, for that was her name, was wont, during my mother's lifetime, to pay long visits to our house at Gillingham, for the benefiting of her health, and so, by way of return, Master Saris would have it, that, at all holidays during my apprenticeship, I should pass my time at his house in London ; and thus, to cut a long rope short, some passages happened between us, which, being discovered by Master Saris, caused him to address me in such rude and violent speech, that I should have laid him at my feet, but he *was* her father, and for *her* sake I promised not to see her again till I could shew enough of the accursed metal, the desire for which had now turned the heads of great and small, to satisfy his avarice, Mabel, upon her part, declaring that she would be the wife of none other ; but as gold is not to be had for the mere longing, we did not again meet for seven years. This long absence was, however, somewhat consoled by the crossing of many letters between us, which was managed by one or two of my shipmates, who made the journey to and from London on the business of my master, whose ships brought merchandize from Holland to Master Saris's storehouses nigh by Deptford.

" Now, at the beginning of that ever-memorable year 1588, a report, which had long been current, growing stronger, that Philip of Spain was preparing a great armament for the conquest of England, good Queen Bess bethought herself, that, if such were the case, it would be but courteous to give the Spaniards a noble reception, and having made her mind known,—and while English hearts beat upon English ground it will never be otherwise,—the means were but a short time coming ; for while one half of the people got ready for sea, the other half prepared to line the coast ; but as her grace required good sea-officers, I, by means of my experience, was engaged as master and pilot on board one of Drake's ships, a fleet anent which I will now say but little, for its glory stands chronicled in the breasts of Englishmen as an example to future generations ; but in addition to the Queen's own fighting ships, the fleet was speedily swollen to the number of one hundred vessels by the efforts of the merchants' marine and the gentlemen of estate, who volunteered not only their private means and pleasure ships, but their *personal* services. Well, upon the 8th of July, the worshipful Sir Francis having received sure information that the Spaniards had put to sea, but that some of their ships had speedily become so disabled by a storm, that they had been compelled to put back into port, determined to drub them in view of their own people. When, however, we came within sight of their coast, the wind turned so suddenly about to the south, that the general, bethinking himself that the enemy might pass him unobserved, returned to England, but, upon his arrival at Plymouth, greatly to his indignation, he found such news had been received at court that the Spaniards could not put to sea that year, so the Queen had ordered four of her biggest ships to be brought about, and laid up at Chatham ; whereupon Sir Francis Drake, fearing the worst, made such representations, and begged so hard, that, even at his own cost, the ships might be retained, that the order was countermanded, and fortunate it was, for one Captain Fleming arrived soon afterwards, bringing the news that the Spanish fleet was then in the British seas, and that, too, off the Lizard.

" How that mighty armament came, shaped like a half-moon, how we met, chased, fought, destroyed, and took the Spaniards prisoners, it is not my business to tell, at least more than is sufficient for my story. This, however, is a token which may serve as a reminder to future generations of foreigners what they have to expect from all similar attempts." So saying, he showed me a silver medal, upon which was stamped a fleet flying with full sails, and a motto, " Venit, vidit, fugit."

" Upon the 23rd, the day of the great fight, the Spaniards, taking advantage of a favourable wind, tacked about upon the London volunteer ships after such a manner that the latter had become hemmed in, and were in great danger. Our squadron being ordered to the rescue, commenced a fight that lasted with great fury the whole day. Before dark, however, they were beaten back, riddled with the fire of our great guns and culverins ; and sore it went to every man's heart that we could not follow them up, by reason that each of the Spanish ships were filled with soldiers, while in our squadron there was not one ; but it is of the smallest of the London volunteer ships that I have to tell you. Now, although this little vessel had borne the heaviest fire during the whole day, her crew had manfully prevented the enemy from boarding her. Night however drew upon us, the Spaniards skulked off, and she signalled that she was disabled nigh to sinking, when our captain sent me with a boat-party to her assistance. Well, I boarded her, and, to my astonishment, found standing upon the half-deck, ready to receive me, no other than John, the son of the youngest of the Saris brothers; when, forgetting his straits, and thinking only of the glory their little ship had earned, I caught him by the hands, saying, 'Well hast thou done thy duty, cousin mine: this nutshell is the wonderment of the whole fleet. But,' I added, 'art ashamed of thy good name, man, for of a truth report hath it that one Master Lock commands this ship?'

"'Then this time, Cousin Adams, report is no liar; for Master Lock, peace be to his soul, and glory to his name, *did* command this ship, till the rascally Spaniard shot him off the deck into the sea.'

"'Then thou art his successor, cousin?'

"'Nay, his successor, and, as for that, his forgoer as well, inasmuch as he who is the owner of the ship is in yon cabin, and even now, awaiting speech with thee;' replied John, leading me to the cabin.

"'But,' said, I seeing him make way for me to enter the cabin first, 'hadst thou not better report my coming on board?'

"'Nay, he expects thee,' was the reply; whereby I at once entered the cabin, when—when, Master Melichor, I felt as if hit by a cannon-ball; for before me, in the midst of broken pikes, shot, powder, spars, against a great cannon, and withal corsleted and helmeted, stood —whom do you believe, Melichor?" said Will, stopping for my answer.

" By heaven, it is impossible for me to guess; without, indeed, mayhap it might have been the general of the Spaniards in irons."

" Thou mightest guess till the crack of doom, and then be adrift. Well, I will tell you—the little, fair-haired Mabel Saris."

" God's mercy! is it possible?" I exclaimed.

" Aye; and the moment her eyes rested upon me, her helmet was upon the floor, her glorious tresses hanging dishevelled, her head upon her shoulder.

" 'Well, dear Will,' she cried, 'our early dreams have

become true; we stand together in the same ship; we have
shared the same danger: but,' she added quickly, ' the
vessel is sinking.   Would we were far from this.'

"For my own part, I felt as if stunned by a spent
ball.   I could not speak.   No, by my faith, no more than
clasp her in my arms, and cry ' Mabel.'

"She was the first to recover her presence of mind, and
she said, 'Thou art surprised; but this, dear Will, is
neither time nor place for explanation.   Hie thee to thy
commander, beg of him to send a chirurgeon on board;
but beg of him to let thee come also, for our own pilot-
master has fallen, and we have none on board.'

" ' Nay, nay, not even for thy dear love will I quit my
ship till every Spaniard be driven from the sea,' said I.

" ' True, thou art right so far; but hie thee, Will, hie
thee on the instant, that aid may reach my poor maimed
men : but have a mind, Will, that thou report to thy commander that Master Lock's gallant conduct should be
brought to the hearing of our Queen, whose own gracious
example has placed men's hearts in the bosom of her
women, and made them soldiers and sailors.'   And as I
stayed to gaze upon her glowing face, she stamped her
pretty foot.   'Hie thee, Will; not a moment is to be
lost; for I also choose duty before love.'

" ' Nay, Mabel, thou art offended,' said I, at the moment forgetting all about the duty I had flaunted in her
face; and by God's grace, I believe a word from her at
that moment would have made me change into anything
but a knave Spaniard.   Seeing, however, that I lingered,
the little termagant answered only by going to the door,
and calling to her cousin—

" ' John Saris, see you that Master Adams leaves the
ship, for by God's mercy I will let him know that I command at this present time.'   And so determined was she,
that had I refused, I believe of a certainty she would have
sent me back to my ship in irons."

" Truly a brave girl, Master Adams," I replied.

" Brave, aye, as a lion, yet gentle as a lamb; though
of the first I take it not more than the rest of her countrywomen; for at the period of danger, Master Melichor,

neither English maid nor mother was to be found who
would not have done likewise ; and God, I believe, had
specially planted such feelings in them for their own protection; for had the bloody-minded Spaniards kept to
their boastings, and put the crown of England upon the
head of the spurious son of Philip, neither maid, wife,
widow, nor child would have been spared, as even boasted
the prisoner Pedro to the lords of the council. But I'll
just overhaul that conversation, Master Melichor.

"This knave prisoner, Don Pedro de Valdy he was
named, was taken by Sir Francis Drake before the lords
of the council, by whom being asked, 'What was the in-
tent of their coming?' he answered, 'To conquer your
nation, and root it out.' 'What, then, did you intend to
do with the Roman Catholics?' 'To send them, good
men, directly to heaven, as well as you that are heretics
to hell,' answered the knave. 'But,' said the lords, who,
to my thinking, should there and then have strung him
high as Haman, 'for what purpose brought you the gold
and wire whips, whereof you had such numbers in your
ships?'

" 'With them,' said he, 'we intended to whip to death
the heretics who had assisted our royal master's rebel
subjects, the Hollanders, and done such dishonour to our
Catholic king and people.'

" 'And what would you have done with their young
children?' asked the lords.

" 'They,' replied the villain, 'which were above seven
years of age should have gone the same way with their
fathers: the rest should have lived, only we would have
branded them in the forehead with the letter L. for Lu-
theran, and kept them in perpetual bondage.'

"And this declaration being taken down and repeated
by Dr. Sharp in his sermons to the soldiers, from whom
it became known throughout the fleet and kingdom, kin-
dled a flame of hatred in the hearts of Britons, that in-
creases in fierceness the deeper it sinks by time. But to
conclude my story—

"When I made my report to the captain, he sent two
chirurgeons on board to attend the wounded, and myself

to pilot the ship to London. So, when I had delivered
my commission to my petticoated commander, the woman's heart beat its way through the corslet of steel, and
she promised that we should become partners for good or
for evil ; and so we did upon the ninth of September, the
day after the general thanksgiving for the defeat of the
Spaniards, when the Queen. God bless her, rode in state
in a chariot, beneath a gilded canopy, drawn by white
horses, through streets hung with blue cloth, and lined
with the train-bands, to the Cathedral of St. Paul, from
the lower battlements of which hung, as they will again
should such another thievish invasion be attempted, eleven
of the Spaniards' standards. But I have not told you
how it came about that the fair-haired girl became a helmeted and corsleted leader of ship-men. Well, then, it
was just this : but I will tell it you in her own words—
    " ' Know you, dear Will,' said she, 'that the promise
made by the little girl on a certain November night was
ever uppermost in the mind of the young woman ; so that
when, about twelve months since, my poor father insisted
upon my becoming the wife of a city councillor of great
wealth, I determined, immediately, to attire myself in the
clothes of a ship-boy, and join the crowd then gathering
to man the ships ; but, alas ! my poor father had no sooner
equipped his volunteer vessel than he died. My grief was
great, but it became lost in the indignation,· which, in
common with the rest of my countrywomen, I felt at the
report of the coming to England of the Spaniards, with
the talk of whose bloody cruelties, in the Indies and the
low countries, the kingdom was ringing; and so, taking
Master Lock, and our cousin John Saris into my confidence, I e'en braced up my woman's heart and brain in
steel, and went aboard my own ship, for such it had become by my father's death.'
    " ' But the hurricane of shot, the flash of steel, the hel-
lish fire-ships, were no fit sight for thee, Mabel,' said I.
    " ' Look I the worse, Will ?' she asked archly.
    " ' Nay, Mabel, but a stray shot, or the Spaniard.'
    " ' What, would you that the men-creatures should
alone make up the rays of glory of a woman's reign ? But

now, Will, no more anent this. What I *have* done, I
have done, aye, and will do again upon a like necessity.
As for the Spaniard, I was prepared: I should never
have been taken,' and she held before me a small dagger.

" 'Tut, Mabel, such things are not for thee,' said I.

" 'Nay, but very fitting for the Spaniard,' she replied,
laughing.

" 'Yet, dear Mabel, I cannot rid myself of the thought
of what a stray shot might have cost me.'

" 'The trouble only, dear Will, of looking for another
wife.'

" 'Not so, Mab; for, by God's mercy, the woman does
not exist who could have replaced you in my heart.'

" 'Tut, tut, Will, so say you all; but nevertheless will
I try you, and there's my hand upon it,' she replied.

"And, as I have said, we were married. The rest is
soon told. Mabel's father, the rich Master Saris, died a
poor man, leaving scarcely the value of the ship he had
fitted out. I then entered the service of the worshipful
company of Barbary merchants, with the hope of acquiring in those miserable countries sufficient wealth to
leave the sea, of which I had become heartily tired. In
that service I remained, that is, at home and making the
voyages, nearly twelve years, when, hearing of the Indish
traffic of the Dutch, and the gold and rich merchandize
that was being brought home by them, I applied to my
wife's uncle, Master Saris, for some sort of letter of re-
commendation to Master Verhagen, and, by consequence
of the employ being what I desired, and my experience
being that of which he stood in need, I was appointed
pilot-major of the luckless fleet in which we both left
Holland; and now you have the whole of my story."

CHAPTER VI.

THE SPANIARD AND THE JESUIT.

Upon the fifth day of our incarceration, for such it was, we received a practical lesson in the chief virtue of the country, namely, cleanliness. Hitherto one tub of water per diem had been regularly placed in the room for our use; that morning, however, about the usual hour for the appearance of the tub, we received, in lieu, a visit from the chief of our attendants, accompanied by two of his men. At his entrance we arose, and he, in acknowledgment of the courtesy, made a bow by custom established, that is, bent his body till the two ends of his scarf touched the ground, then rising, and pointing to the door, he said—

" Froo, froo, cisfroo."

" Froo, froo, cisfroo — yes—cisfroo ; but who is he ?" repeated Will, greatly puzzled to know to what great personage we were now to be introduced. But the chief only laughed ; indeed it was his only refuge.

" God's mercy ! but I'd like to work out the meaning of that grin upon the face of the heathen," said Will angrily.

" Froo, froo," repeated the chief, again pointing to the door.

" Froo, froo. Yes ; froo, froo, it is ; but as this froo, froo is neither an Englishman nor a Dutchman, I am adrift as to your meaning," said Will ; but, losing all patience, he added to me, " Mayhap, Melichor, you can make out the fellow's signals." When, observing that while the chief kept pointing to the door he moved backwards in the same direction, I said—

" He means that he wishes to take us out for a walk."

" By the great Harry ! it may be so ; and that the heathens have come at last to a right notion of the real use of our legs," said Will joyfully ; adding, however, surlily, to the men, as they hemmed us in upon all sides, " A

little more sea-room, shipmates;" at which, notwithstanding the roughness with which Will elbowed them,
they all laughed, and we all proceeded at a slow pace into
the garden, which, although not more than thirty feet
square, was yet laid out in shrubberies, flower-beds, small
woods, smaller mountains, rocks, and rivulets, and inter-
sected with paths of wondrously clean gravel, and polished
sea-shells and stones.

"Hilloa, Melichor, are we to bring ourselves to an
anchor in this hen-coop," said Will, as, passing through
a little miniature forest, we approached a low, narrow
building of cypress wood, from every chink and cranny
of which were issuing volumes of steam.

"Froo, froo, cisfroo," said the chief, perceiving Will
staring at the building.

"Froo, froo, cisfroo," repeated Will, now out of all
patience. "A murrain on the heathen, what meaneth
he ?"

But before I could reply, we were both politely hustled

through the doorway into a room filled with tubs, some of which were half full of boiling water.

"It is to put us to death by scalding they mean ; let us knock them over, and run for it," said Will, looking around savagely. And I believe I should have agreed with his suggestion, but that the chief, as if guessing our fears, ordered the men to leave a greater distance between us ; and then, by way of making us comprehend his meaning, untied his girdle, so that the whole of his clothes fell to the ground, and the next instant himself immersed his body in one of the tubs.

"Why, what dolts we have been, Melichor, not to find out that 'Froo, froo, cisfroo,' means a tumble into hot water."

Then, when the chief saw we understood him, he jumped out of the tub in great delight ; but finding from our signs that we objected to the use of such an ener- vating eastern luxury, he muttered a few words to the men, when, not a little to our surprise, and in less time than we believed it would have taken to have unrobed, we were stripped and forced into the tubs ; and vexa- tious as was the compulsion, we afterwards found that the baths had been commanded by the king for the bene- fit of our health.

Thus did we obtain experience of the Japanners' great virtue, cleanliness, which, albeit it may be next to godli- ness, is, in Japan, oftener next door to immodesty and unchasteness ; and to this remark I am led, inasmuch as the commoner kind of people, who cannot afford to have a froo—that is a hot or sweating house, or a cisfroo, as they call a warm bath in their own grounds—have tubs near their doors, in which men, women, and children, bathe at the same time, and in sight of each other ; a custom which some simple people believe arises out of innocence, but it is my belief that it is mere wantonness, for it requires too much credulity for me to think inno- cence a staple virtue in a land in which the painted Jeze- bels, who swarm to double the extent of those to be found in any other country, serve a regular apprenticeship of sin, and are competent, at its ending, to be received as the friends and equals of the well-conducted of their own sex, whereby there is neither emulation to virtue, nor punishment for vice.

" How feel you, Master Adams, after your dip in the water," said I to my now grim-looking companion, as we were being marched back to our apartment.

" As good humoured as a half-scalded pig in a brine-tub," he replied, shaking himself.

" Yet it was but a well intended courtesy, Master Adams ;" but turning upon me almost savagely, he replied—

" Now look ye, Master Melichor ; to force a bolus into the mouth of a horse may be well intended, but the animal will kick nevertheless ; and by God's grace, if I ever catch one of these rascals on plank of mine, I'll have him dipped in the cook's slush-tub, till he comes out with fat enough upon his hide to supply him with candles for the rest of his life, and mayhap that'll teach him to froo, froo, and parboil one of Queen Bess's master pilots."

How long Will's ill-humour would have lasted I know not, if, upon reaching our apartment, we had not found refreshment, tobacco, and saki, ready for our use. The sight of these things restored his humour, so filling a bumper of saki, he made an awkward attempt to pledge the chief by holding it above his head. The Japanner not backward to understand him, answered the challenge by first filling, and then draining the vessel at a draught, a feat which seemed so astonishing to Will, that, taking the Japanner's hands in his own, and giving them a hearty shaking, he exclaimed—

" By my faith ! shipmate, but a man who can take such a hearty draught, must have a fair wind, and with a fair wind who ever heard of aught but fair sailing ?"

But so hearty was Will's grasp, that although the chief smiled, the smile was spasmodic and sickly, and a small tear started in his eye, as if his mental satisfaction had been a little damped by physical pain.

Being thus restored to good humour, Will signalled to the other attendants to sit round the fire with us. Such a proceeding, however, being against their notions of discipline, the chief ordered them to retire, after which he himself squatted down upon his heels, and having carefully hidden his feet beneath his gown, quaffed another cup of saki, and laughingly muttered, " Froo, froo," by which he probably meant to ask how we had approved our bath. But be that as it might, Will, putting his own interpretation, started up at the words, laid down his darling pipe, and with a very determined look, commenced—

" Look you, shipmate——" but suddenly bethinking himself that the chief could not comprehend him, he shook his head in disgust, saying, " Bah, I am an ass : it would be as easy to whisper though a hurricane to the man at the main-top ;" after which he smoked his pipe in surly silence, till interrupted by the trampling hoofs beneath our window, and hearing the sounds, I ran into the balcony followed by the chief, who, seeing the cause of the noise, cried, " Tsusi ! tsusi !"

" Tsusi, tsusi," repeated Will, " what's in the wind now ? no more Froo, froo, I hope."

" It is the king," said I, " and with him——"

" Tsusi, tsusi," repeated the Japanner.

" By Beelzebub there is Tsusi again ; what does the fellow mean, Melichor ?"

" Interpreters, by Neptune," said I, jumping at that conclusion from seeing two Europeans by the side of his majesty.

" Interpreters ! then we shall make head through this fog at last," said Will joyfully ; and the next minute our attendants were upon their knees before the old king, his son, the young noble with the maimed hand, and the two Europeans.

Of the latter, one was tall, lean, and sleek, with short upper lip, large nostrils, and a pair of grey eyes, as piercing and inscrutable in expression as those of a cat ; moreover, about the whole man there seemed a velvety softness, a *suaviter in modo*, that entirely threw you off your search for the *fortiter in re*, and which was not at all diminished by the simple clerical garb which bespoke him to be a member of the Society of Jesus.

The other carried his character in his very gait : he was a short man, of robust frame, large features, dark skin, deeply bronzed, but whose fiercely curled moustache, plumed hat, half armour, and swaggering gait, told you at a glance that he was one of those Spanish adventurers, part seaman, part soldier, part trader, but *all* robber, whose deeds of unjust avarice and cruelty then filled the world with terror or disgust.

Now, as the Jesuit and soldier entered the room, they were in earnest converse with the king ; but at a word from his majesty, they stopped to gaze at us ; the Jesuit with a smooth smile that would have roused the hopes of a condemned criminal ; the soldier with the eye of a connoisseur in men, at least of men fit to serve beneath his flag.

" God's mercy, Melichor, but we might as well be in the hands of the devil, as in the power of these hounds of Portugals and Spaniards," said Will.

Then an ironical smile played across the Jesuit's features, as he muttered some words in his native tongue, and at which the latter seemed greatly excited, and curled his moustache and frowned darkly upon us. Oh, oh, thought I, the priest understands English, and has translated Master Adams's speech to the soldier. The Jesuit, however, simulating ignorance of English, addressed us in the Dutch tongue, asking us what countrymen we were, and what had brought us to Japan. Whereupon, as Master Adams did not speak Dutch very fluently, I answered for him, repeating the story of our voyage, excepting only those passages wherein the Spaniards or Portugals had been concerned; and concluded by begging that the good father would faithfully translate to the king the history of our misfortunes, and beg of him to give us, in exchange for woollen cloths and other merchandize we had brought with us, sufficient of food and other matters for our homeward voyage, with some balance of gold, or other commodities produced in his country, for the benefit of our merchants. To all of which the father gave a quiet hearing, and replied—

"The story of thy misfortunes will I relate to the king: as for the request to trade with the Japanners, that must you urge to His Excellency here, Don Andras Pessoa."

"Not I, by Neptune; I ask no other favour of Spaniard or Portugal but the fair play due between enemies," said Will angrily.

"Who art thou? what thy rank, my friend?" said the soldier clutching the hilt of his sword.

To which Will replied quickly, and, as I thought, madly, "A follower of Drake and Frobisher, names a SPANIARD should know, Will Adams by name, pilot-major by rank, and, to boot, one who manfully helped to whip the tyrant Philip's ships out of England's seas."

And truly I thought these would have been his last words; for in an instant Pessoa's sword was flashing before our eyes. At a word, however, from the king, the weapon was stricken from his hands; and with a look of intense hatred towards Will, the haughty Spaniard muttered some words of apology to the king.

Then the Jesuit and Pessoa held some short converse together in Spanish; after which the priest addressed the old king, and our hearts rejoiced, for we thought he was repeating the history of our misfortunes. Great, however, was our surprise, when, at the close of the Jesuit's speech, the king, instead of laughing as usual, frowned terribly, and having given some order, at once left the room, accompanied by the whole of the party.

"Ugh! there is an evil wind blowing up from some quarter," muttered Will when we were alone.

"Thy haste and imprudence has ruined us, Master Adams: even now it is my belief that the Jesuit and the Spaniard have made up some tale villainously to our hurt," said I.

"Tut, tut! it wots not. Had I licked the feet of the Spanish knave and the Jesuit both, it would have been the same; for is it not the business of the priest to cheat, as it is of your swashbuckler to lie and plunder?" replied Will; adding: "Look you, Melichor, from the moment the eyes of those hounds set upon us we were doomed: but it wots not, it wots not; I am prepared: as I have lived, so will I die, with a high heart and open eyes."

"Nay, nay, Master Adams," I replied, for I was not so well prepared to die; "the good-natured old king will never put to death twenty mariners, whose sufferings have impressed their misfortunes even upon their faces, at the will of two such miserable knaves."

"They have the game in their own hands, Melichor,'' said Will despondingly; adding, as some dozen of the king's soldiers arrived, armed from head to foot, "See you the tragedy is even now commencing?"

And truly the beginning was tragic enough; for, forcing us upon our knees, the rascal Japanners trussed us up after such a fashion that tears started from our eyes. They bound us with their cords, but so precisely alike as if they had been practising an art. The cords had the same number of knots and loops, both being placed at equal distances; they placed nooses round our necks and breasts ; our elbows nearly touched each other, and our hands were tightly secured together, leaving a long cord to be held by a soldier, who, upon the slightest attempt to escape, could, by a single jerk, make the elbows come in contact, and so cause excruciating agony ; and which was so adjusted that the one jerk would at the same time tighten the loop about the neck almost to strangulation.

" Are the cowardly lubbers afraid of two unarmed—" But before Will could utter more, his rope was pulled across a beam of the room, and naught but a gurgling sound came from his throat, so that I thought his last hour had come. But it appeared the men were only amusing themselves, for the next instant they loosened the rope again, and Will cried out—

" Devils ! would that I had you yard-arm and yard-arm but for five minutes."

" This villainous work is the doing of the Portugal captain," said I.

" Or the Jesuit, or the GOOD-NATURED old king, it matters not a rope's-end," replied Will ; adding : " Ugh ! these cords are searching to the bone : but cheer up Melichor, for come what may, and doubtless it will be a short shrift and a quick end, the devil shall see how a Drake's man and a pilot of Bess's can die."

Now, although the ropes were somewhat loosened about our neck, they were thrown across a beam, the ends being held by the men, and in that position they kept us for at least an hour, when some other soldiers brought two broad planks, to the ends of which were attached rope loops : these being slung across poles, we were stretched upon the planks, and thus carried forth from the house, guarded upon all sides with as much care as if our limbs had been at liberty, and thus we were taken through the town to a large farm-like building, in which there was a number of small cages, made of thick wooden palings, with small holes for the entrance of the prisoners, who, to my horror, I saw were our shipmates, at least those who were sufficiently well to bear such confinement.

Passing through this apartment, they carried us into a thickly-matted room, in the walls of which were driven hooks; to which, when they had fastened our body ropes, they inclined the planks, so that we immediately slid down upon the mats, and felt very grateful for the little ease they afforded us, notwithstanding we were in great pain from the bleeding wounds caused by the tightness of our temporary shackles.

Without a murmur, and with simulated indifference, we bore the agony, and thus I believe we should have died, had not our pale, swollen faces, and the blood that trickled from our wounds, alarmed our guards, who, I suppose, had been bribed by the Spaniards to exceed their king's orders, at least in the matter of unnecessary cruelty; for, perceiving our danger, they loosened the cords, and poured some warm saki down our throats, which, bringing some of the blood back to our faces, they then gave us eatables.

CHAPTER VII.

THE SPANIARD'S OFFER, AND ITS REJECTION.

THUS bound like wild beasts, we were for days kept, not without food, but without water to perform our ablutions, until, with our long shaggy locks, and hirsute and unclean faces, we resembled the monsters it afterwards appeared we were then believed to be. Moreover, we had but little doubt that we were being reserved for some terrible punishment, for such care did they take that we should not commit suicide, that even the mouth-pieces of the pipes which we were permitted to smoke had large balls affixed, so that we could not swallow them. Another proof that we were regarded by the natives as monsters was the number of men, women, and children who came to gaze at us through the window; a sight, by the way, I afterwards found our keeper turned to good account, by charging two copper coins each person for the show: moreover, ladies, even of the highest rank, when they came to gaze at us, notwithstanding that they were surrounded with attendants, and we were bound hands and feet, stared at us from a respectful distance, startling timidly at our slightest movement.

For six days did we continue in hourly expectation of being put to death, but upon the morning of the seventh, shortly after we had been fed, for fed we were, the food being put into our mouths to obviate the necessity of knives or spoons, with which our gaolers believed we might destroy ourselves, we received a visit from the Jesuit father, and thus did Will welcome him—

"Out on thee, Sir Priest! Didst not promise to encompass our release from this cursed country?"

"Not so, my son; for such a promise would have been vain on the part of a minister of religion."

"Minister of religion ! Minister of the devil ; for none other could have wrought so much wanton rascality as the torture of a whole crew of shipwrecked mariners, and those, too, fellow-Christians, whom an adverse fate has thrown into this heathen land," said Will.

"Thy words, my son, are as irreverent as is thy misbegotten heresy, and thy traitorous rebellion against our Catholic and Sovereign Lord Philip."

"Let go your anchor there, priest," said Will. "That I am a heretic I thank my father who made me so; but as for being traitor to bloody Philip, it is a lie, for I am a born subject of good Bess of England, who whipped the knave Spaniard from her seas."

"Nay, my son, it matters little that I have confounded thy country with that of this thy companion; neither will it tend to advantage thee the one way or the other, for the punishment of thy heinous crimes is sure and certain."

"Crimes ! thou false-hearted priest," I cried : "what is this crime which doubtless thou and thy knave companion have charged against us? for else we should not have been suddenly chained up like dogs or thieves."

"It is not for me, my sons, to inquire into these charges ; *my* mission is one of Christian charity : it is, heretics though you be, to see that ye are not sent from this world without confession and repentance of your manifold sins against God and your fellow-men," replied the Jesuit.

" Now hearken, priest : like all other men I have my sins to answer for, but they are none to which I am amenable to living man : therefore, if I am to be murdered, so let it be, and be quickly. I will die as I have lived, praising God and blessing my Queen. So, having thy answer, if, coward like, thou wilt not tell us the crimes of which we are accused, get thee hence, or mayhap, in my rage, I may even now burst these bonds and do thee some harm."

" Neither thy irreverence nor thy vain boasting can advantage thee, my son ; yet, notwithstanding both, will I, out of Christian charity, tell thee these charges, nay, perhaps even open up to thee a prospect of escape from the crucifixion, to which thou and all of thy companions have been doomed."

" Tut, tut ! The crime, the crime ; tell us that, priest."

" Piracy and murder," replied the Jesuit seriously.

" A lie of the Spaniard, and told to encompass our undoing," said I. As for Will, he seemed stricken dumb with astonishment. Looking, however, stedfastly at the priest, he said—

" Father, wilt pass thy word as a Christian priest honestly to give to the king, or kings, my answer ?"

" As heaven and martyrdom is my hope will I, my son," replied the father, with, as I thought, more earnestness than could have been shown by one who meant us false.

" Then say that I am ready to prove its falsehood upon the body of my accuser ; and if that be not permitted, all I ask is time sufficient to learn enough of their language to prove that treachery has brought us to this pass."

" This will avail thee but little, my son, if thou canst not disprove that the fleet in which you sailed attacked and plundered a galleon of his most catholic majesty, as well, also, as his town of Annabon."

" Ah ! how know you all this, my father ?" said Will,

with surprise ; adding, " but even so, my father, it was lawful warfare, for which one Christian nation would not put to death the subjects of another."

" My son, the Indies and their seas are the patrimony of the catholic king, and the gift of the holy father : to make war therein is piracy ; to slay his catholic majesty's subjects is murder."

" Aye, father, it is an old yarn that such is the doctrine of the rapacious Spaniard and Portugal, and the time will come when it will be drubbed out of him ; but, even so, Philip has no power in a neutral country, whose king and people own not his rule," replied Will.

" Where, oh, my son, in the East, is the land in which the catholic king has not, or hopes not to have, amity ? but with this land of Japan he has especial ties of friend-ship, and the Japanners place their friends so near their hearts, that they hold it a crime not to punish trans-gressors against them as if against themselves."

" Hold ! let go your anchor, father, for I am of too plain speech to chop logic with schoolmen. I can only pray you get us time, and send us a teacher of this heathen tongue."

" But, my son, I spoke of another course, another chance, by which you may save your lives," said the priest.

" Hold, father ! you have wasted too much breath upon these rogues already," said Pessoa, entering the room.

" Rogue in thy teeth, coward," exclaimed Will.

" Coward !" returned the captain, placing his hand upon his sword. But then, with a dismal smile, he added, " Tut, tut, I am not here to cross words with such as thou : but listen, fellows, and you, master pilot, especially."

" Would I might answer thee with my sword, or, better for thy small purpose, a rope's-end," muttered Will.

It did not, however, suit Pessoa to notice the affront, so he continued, " I have heard all that has passed between thee and the good father."

"I could have sworn it, for thou couldst as well be guilty of eavesdropping as thieving," said Will.

"But," Pessoa continued, "thou hast not denied the attack upon the catholic king's settlements, and the plunder of his subjects."

"The fortune of war," said Will.

"Aye, fellow, the fortune of war; the same fortune that has now placed you in my power."

"Thy power, miserable rogue!" exclaimed Will.

"Aye, fellow, a power that can send thee to the cross, for such is the punishment of pirates in this country."

"Pirate! again thou liest in thy teeth," said Will.

"Tut, tut! listen, comrade," replied the captain, with an ill-disguised attempt at good-humour; adding, "what I have to say is for thy benefit. As I have said, I heard thy request to the father to procure a teacher of the language, that you might answer this charge. Now, if you persist in this obstinacy, your death is certain; for although such is the justice of these heathens, that were there any doubt as to thy crimes against their friend, the catholic king, they would grant thy request, and time might then make them change thy punishment to perpetual imprisonment, they have already proofs, not only of crimes committed against their ally, but of others intended against their own country."

"Hold there, knave! What jargon is this about crimes intended?" said Will.

"Thou art a bold fellow," said Pessoa, ironically, "and if thou hadst had but cunning, success might have attended thy scheme; but as it is, mark you——"

"As it is," replied the tantalized pilot. "If you are not even a more cowardly hound than you look, you'll cut these infernal cords, and measure swords with me."

"Aye, aye, comrade, even that in good time, if thou wilt be reasonable; but as I was about to tell you, one of your shipmates has been before you, and wisely made his own bargain."

"Thou liest, thou rogue: no shipmate of mine."

"Stay; thou art hasty, comrade, and forgettest one Absolon von Owater."

"The rascal! Aye, well, what said he?"

"But little, comrade ; yet enough to crucify thee, if I make it known," replied the captain, sneeringly ; adding, "Well, it appears that this poor man, Owater, was the owner of the ship and merchandize."

"The devil!" exclaimed Will, too much astonished to say more.

"Aye, comrade, it was a trick worthy of the devil ; yet I like the boldness of thy plans : for were not you as pilot, your comrade here as purser, and the rest of the crew hired at Amsterdam by Owater, to take the ship to the Moluccas ; but upon the voyage you seized and put him in irons, the marks of which remain even now upon his legs and arms."

"The rascal was put in irons for mutiny," said I.

"Aye, aye, that of course," replied the captain ironically ; continuing, "then, changing your course, you came to the coast of Bungo, with the hope of selling the merchandize ; and, moreover, of plundering any town upon the coast which you might find sufficiently defenceless. Now, my brave fellow, this being made known to the king, what mercy think you he will shew you?"

"Hold, man, thou art a fool as well as a coward ; but it is impossible that thou canst believe .his tale ; it is moonstruck nonsense," said Will.

"I am not at confession that I should tell thee what I *believe ;* it is sufficient for me to convince you that the *king* will *believe* if *I affirm*, and the poor man, who speaks enough of the tongue, as well as one of his shipmates, also declares it to be true."

"Bah, bah! thou art at most but a clumsy rogue : for think you that any other of the crew, or the captain, will be found to support these lies?" replied Will, laughing.

"Stay, comrade ; thou art nearer the cross than thou art aware."

"Out upon thee for a lubber, get thee gone," said Will, with a violent tug at the cords.

"Now, comrade, I have the ear and friendship of the king and his lords, by reason of the trade I have estab-

lished between Bungo and Macao and the Philippines.
He will, therefore listen to my statement; and his hate
once excited by the account of your piratical intentions
upon his own coasts, especially now he knows you to be
pirates, the cross may be changed for a slower, but more
terrible death."

"Tut, tut! thou art a mountebank ass; for are there
not eighteen or nineteen of this rascal Owater's shipmates
to give thee the lie?" replied Will exultingly.

"Is it not thou who art the ass, to forget that these fellows know no more of the natives' tongue than the natives
know of theirs?" replied Pessoa; adding, with a meaning smile, "while *I* speak both."

"God's mercy! I am indeed a dolt to have forgotten
this," exclaimed Will. Then, looking at the Jesuit, he
said, "But thou, O father, a Christian and a priest, canst
not stand by and see this wrong done."

"Listen to the noble Andras Pessoa, and there may be
no wrong done, my son," was the only reply.

"Then we are lost in a net-work of villainy, from which
none can save us but thou, O my God!" exclaimed Will
piously.

"Not so, comrade," replied Pessoa, chuckling that
Will's stern spirit was bending. "Thou art a bold seaman and a good pilot; I have need of such on board my
carac: moreover, thou hast influence over the crew of thy
ship; I require seamen."

"How now, thou lubber; what wouldst thou?" said
Will fiercely; but the captain, interrupting him, said—

"Be not hasty, but listen. Accept service, thou and
thy men, as far as thou art able to persuade them; and
if they do not listen to thee, other means shall be found
to compel them: and I will promise thee, not only the
living of a general, but the means of acquiring wealth beyond thy wildest imagination."

During this speech Will's eyes swelled from their
sockets, the muscles of his whole body grew distended;
but when he had concluded, with choking voice he
said—

"Hast done?"

"Think well of my proposal, man: crucifixion, or liberty and wealth," said the captain.

Will, however, having managed to work one of his arms free, gradually shuffled to the length of the cord which held him; and on getting near the captain, struck him a heavy blow, which laid him low, saying—

"Then that be my answer, knave."

The captain had recovered his legs, his drawn sword was in his hand, but the astonished Japanners darted between them, and secured Will's arm to his side, and drew his ropes near the wall. Having done this, they smiled with contempt at what they thought to be the cowardice of Pessoa, who, sheathing his sword, said—

"Even thy attempt, albeit it was cowardly, I can pardon; and, moreover, again ask of thee to think well of my proposition; I will give thee till my return voyage from Macao, for which place I weigh anchor to-morrow, and during the interval I will beg thy respite from the king." So saying, accompanied by the priest, he left the room.

Chequered as had hitherto been my life, I soon found that in my composition there was none of the material out of which heroes and martyrs are wrought; and this was never shewn more plainly than during the six days following the visit of Pessoa; for with limbs bound tighter than ever, a lesser quantity and coarser quality of food, our guards increased, and in hourly expectation of being led forth to crucifixion, my sufferings, both mental and physical, were very great. By contrast, Master Adams put me to the blush, for he bore all with resignation, or, at least, defiantly. Nay, his mind dwelt not upon his sufferings, but upon the Spaniard's rascally offer, anent which, by the way, I differed from Will, in believing it had only been Pessoa's intention to get us into his power, that he might ship us all as slaves to New Spain, or the Philippines; for it was the policy of the Portugals and Spaniards to crush in the bud the remotest chance of the English or Dutch opening up commerce with Japan.

"Nay, *nay*, Master Melichor," said Will to this; "the knave could never dream of shipping nigh twenty sea-

dogs as slaves. By the Great Harry! I doubt if the
black-hearted Philip has a colony that would hold them.
Nay, nay, lad, every great rascal believes all other men
made of the same metal as himself, and so the knave
tried us. As for the yarns about the treachery of some
of the crew, I don't value it at a rope's-end."

"But how obtained he such close knowledge of our
voyage, even to the attack upon his countrymen?"

"Aye, aye, that gets one in a fog, Melichor." As,
however, he spoke, the Jesuit made his appearance, accompanied by an officer of the old king's guard. "Bah!
the knave priest again," said Will contemptuously.

"But, nevertheless, thy *friend*, my son," replied the
father; and, as he spoke, the officer drew his sword across
the ropes which bound us.

"God's mercy, but this is a friendly act, albeit I misdoubt me that it is to answer some purpose of thine own,"
said Will, shaking his stiffened limbs now that they were
released, but adding, " Yet, priest, if thou thinkest either
that my conscience will take service with thy idolatrous
worship, or my body and mind with the rogue Pessoa,
thou hadst better treble than unloose these cords ; for I
fear me I shall do thee some mischief at the outset of the
proposal."

" My son, thou art wanting in charity ; for know, that
it is to my intercession thou art unbound."

" Thy intercession ! Tut ; to what end : for art thou
not in partnery with the rascal Spaniard ? I tell thee,
priest, fortune has given thee speech with these heathens,
and therefore thou hast the advantage ; and, having it, I
know full well, wilt use it to suit the purpose of thy Pope
and king."

" It is mine to bear revilings, therefore exhaust thy
venom, my son," replied the father meekly.

" Nay, nay, an' thou wilt fight neither with sword nor
tongue, it were poltroonery to attack thee thus ; therefore henceforth, father, am I silent," replied Will ; adding wistfully, " yet for this release from these infernal
cords would I——"

" What wouldst thou, my son ?" said the priest.

" E'en let thee know how we shake hands in England, did I not think that even now thou art sailing beneath false colours."

For an instant something like a frown appeared upon the priest's brow ; it remained, however, but for an instant, and with a strange earnestness for one who was our enemy, he replied—

" That I mean you well, my son, know that not only do I bring thee release from thy cords, but respite from the death to which thou wert most assuredly doomed through the hatred of Don Pessoa."

" The gift is scarce worth the having, father, if it is accompanied with perpetual confinement in this hole," said Will.

" Didst thou not pray for time and a teacher of the language, that thou mightest answer for thyself the charges brought against thee by one who is all powerful, at least in this small kingdom, by reason of his traffic with the king ?" said the father. "And this boon have I obtained by intercession with the Daysu Sama, or regent, himself, to whom I am interpreter, and who has sent his commands to King Foyne, that you all be kept in confinement till he has the opportunity of questioning you himself : till when, my sons—for the regent is at present engaged in a civil war with many refractory princes of the empire—I will visit you daily, and endeavour to teach you what I may of this idolatrous tongue."

Then Will, as if suddenly convinced of the good faith of the priest, and with strange celerity for one who had so obstinately doubted, took the right hand of the Jesuit between his own, saying—

" Father, from my soul I believe and thank thee ; the more so, that I may yet have the chance of crossing swords with this rascally sea-rat, Pessoa."

" Of the captain beware, my son, for he hath mysterious knowledge of your doings at sea ; and, moreover, the power to turn it to his own account against thee," replied the father.

" The rascal," exclaimed Will ; adding, " but one question father—The captain of my ship—the crew ?"

"Are closely confined, yet cared for, like thyself."
"Aye, aye, that is well. But this Pessoa's words; his
story about the ownership of the vessel, and the mutiny
of Owater?" said Will.

"My son, I believe it is even so; but more I may not
say." And not another word could we get from the
priest upon the subject, greatly to Will's annoyance.

The father kept his promise; and for nine months following, during which we were confined in the same apartment, not a day passed without bringing him to us; and
during that period, he not only taught us much of the
language, which, by reason of our not having other means
wherewith to vary the monotony of our existence, we
assiduously studied, but also imparted to us much information, which, as it imports the readers of this narrative
to know, I have endeavoured to collect together in the
form of a regular narrative.

CHAPTER VIII.

THE STORY OF CHRISTIANITY IN JAPAN.

AT the period of the new moon, in December of the year
1547, a great tempest ravaged the whole coast of Can-
goxima, bringing destruction upon the shipping of all
nations; indeed, one who was present says, "that out
of nearly two thousand vessels (an incredible number) but
ten or twelve weathered the hurricane. And in one of
the fortunate few sailed the renowned traveller, Fernam
Mendez Pinto, a man whose so-called "marvellous lies"
the light of passing time is gradually transmuting into
more marvellous truths.

The storm having subsided, Pinto and his companions
disposed of their merchandize, the profit being the
greater, inasmuch as so many of their competitors had
been swallowed by the sea; and joyful at their own luck,
though sad at the loss of so many lives, they prepared to

set sail for home. Three several times, however, did
they start, and, from some accident or other, as many did
they put back again. The last accident was the running
away from the ship of two of Pinto's slaves. "But the
escape of these men," say the Jesuit fathers, "was directed by Divine Providence for the furtherance of a
great end." And, verily, to say the least, it was remarkable : for when Pinto, accompanied by two companions,
rowed towards the shore in search of the slaves, and the
boat just felt the ground, three horsemen, who had been
at full gallop, leaped from their horses, which, like their
riders, were spent and almost breathless, and, running
towards Pinto, the chief of the party, in bad Portuguese,
but in tones which plainly told that he was pleading for
his dear life, said—

"Noble sir, the haste and danger we are in admits of
no delay : being in great fear of some enemies who are
in pursuit of me, I beg of you, for the love of God, that
without suggesting doubt or weighing inconveniences,
you will take me at once on board your ship."

Taken aback by this strange occurrence, and fearing to
do that which might embroil his countrymen with the
rulers of the country, Master Pinto was for a time greatly
embarrassed ; but having a fellow-feeling, by reason he
had been in similar plights himself, and remembering
that he had seen the gentleman before on shore, and,
moreover, being spurred to a decision by seeing at a short
distance a number of horsemen at full gallop towards the
sea, he, without further parley, helped the fugitives into
his boat, and immediately, with his two companions,
made towards his ship. When, however, they had pulled
a bow-shot's distance from the land they saw the horsemen flinging their arms about in great rage, and heard
them cry, "Give up that traitor or we will kill you."

"For the love of your God, noble Christians, rest not
upon your oars until you reach the ship," implored the
alarmed fugitive ; and, as they manfully pulled away
again, the horsemen on shore cried out—

"If thou dost carry off that Japanner, know that the
heads of a thousand fellows like thee shall pay the forfeit."

" But," here remarked Father Rodriguez, " the Holy
Virgin, who had directed the accident which sent the boat
ashore in the very nick of time, deafened Pinto's ears to
their commands, and turned to her purpose the heart of
the captain of the ship, for the chief of these men was
one Angiro, whom she had selected as the instrument by
which the faith of Christ was to visit the hearts of the
Japanners.

Now, when the noble Angiro and his servants got on
board, great was his gratitude, and many his thanks to
Don Alvarez, the captain, who, being a devout man, felt
his heart thrill with delight and astonishment when the
noble Japanner fell upon his knees and muttered a prayer
before the picture of the virgin and child, which hung in
his cabin ; but, observing the captain's surprise, Angiro
said—   .

" The capitan sama (lord captain) is filled with wonderment that a child of the sun goddess should seek the God
of the Portugals ; but let him listen ;" and so Angiro
said—

" A chadamodo by rank, and of more than sufficient
wealth, my soul had long thirsted for more substantial
food than that provided for me by the priests of Xacca,
Quanwan, or Buddha ; and although I knew not my pre-
cise wants, a something, a longing, a feeling had sprung
up within me, the mere gratification of which caused me
to fall into a settled melancholy. To cure this, I sought
pleasures, physicians, and, lastly, residence and prayer in
a monastery of Sintoo priests. But it was in vain that I
sought relief, till chance made me acquainted with the
noble sea-captain, Alvarez Vas, who, however, upon my
making known to him my complaint, opened up to my
ears that a God had been born, and had died upon the
cross, for the sins and benefit of all. Many were the
inquiries I made ; many were the conversations we had
together ; and then he discoursed to me of a wondrous
man, the fame of whose great goodness and sanctity is now
filling the world, but more especially the Indies, where
the Portugals and Spaniards held rule, and whom he exhorted me to search out and consult. Thus, from that

moment the desire to seek the holy man—Francis Xavier he named him—became the passion of my soul ; but, alas ! the difficulties and dangers to be encountered were so great, that my melancholy became more and more settled ; nay, it so showed itself to all, that I became the object of pity to many, banter to others, but this day, a nobleman jeering me upon my state of mind, we quarrelled : I drew my sword, and, in the moment of my rage, he fell. Having done this deed, I fled homewards, and was about calling my family around me to offer the only reparation I could to the dead man's friends—that is, perform the hara-kiri (rip open the stomach) ; but remembering the teaching of the noble Alvarez Vas, that he who slew himself destroyed his own soul, yet knowing also that to evade the hara-kiri was to bring disgrace upon my family for ever, I became distracted, and fled to the sea-shore, accompanied by my faithful servants."

"Truly herein is displayed the hand of Providence, for we are even now upon our course for Malacca, where the holy Francis is at this time engaged in his labours among the heathen," said the captain. Whereupon Angiro testified his delight in the most lively manner.

The noble Japanner, however, was doomed to disappointment, for, upon the arrival of the ship at Malacca, he found that Xavier had left, and for some reason, known only to himself, the vicar of the Bishop of Goa, who resided at that place, refused to baptize him. Thus disappointed, he determined to return home, but not finding a ship bound direct for Japan, he embarked for a port in China, from whence he started in another vessel to his own land ; but a great typhoon coming on, the ship put back into the Chinese port ; and then again was the finger of Providence displayed, for in the harbour he found his old friend Alvarez Vas, in command of a ship on her way back to Malacca. This captain begged of Angiro to accompany him, and, upon arriving at Malacca, the first person they met upon landing was the Captain Alvarez again, who immediately brought him to the presence of the fathers Francis Xavier and Cosmo de Torres, both of whom were so delighted with the zeal and earnest-

ness of Angiro, that they received him and his two servants into the bosom of the church, Angiro being baptized
by the name of Paul of the holy faith, and the servants,
one by the name of John, and the other Anthony; and
these three were the first Japanners converted to Christianity.

The life, the soul of the accomplished and high-born
co-founder of the Jesuits, Xavier, was devoted to the pro-
pagation of his faith among the people of Asia; and that,
too, with a zeal that neither danger, poverty, nor the most
intense suffering could damp; therefore it was with an
extacy bordering upon delirium he heard from Angiro that
many thousands of his countrymen, of equal intelligence
with himself, were as a flock gasping for the water of
life, and he at once resolved to seek the land of Japan.

This resolve was attempted to be changed by the
friends who loved him: they pointed out the immense
length of the voyage; the dangers from the pirates who
infested the seas; the unsurveyed coast of Japan, which
never more than two out of three ships reached in safety;
the whirlpools, the tremendous typhoons; at all of which
the good man smiled, saying—

"It were a shame that I should be afraid to venture,
for the sake of the faith, where sailors and merchants go
for the mere love of lucre: no missionaries should have
less courage. It is the will of God that fills me, and go
I will."

Xavier kept his word, and, accompanied by two brethren of his order, Angiro and his two servants, he landed
in Japan, and then commenced a propagandism which
met with such success, notwithstanding the continual
wars that were being carried on between the independent
sovereign princes, the jeers of thousands, petty persecutions, scoffs of others, and the violent animosity of the
priests of both the Sintoo and Buddhist faiths, that in
less than thirty-two years they had made one hundred
and fifty thousand converts, appointed a bishop, and
established numerous churches, seminaries, colleges, and
hospitals. Nay, so fervent were the Japan kings who
had become Christians, that, in 1582, they sent an em-

6

bassy to the Pope. The party consisted of three princes, sons of kings, and two of the highest nobles. The embassy, under the charge of Father Rodriguez, reached Lisbon in August 1584, at which place they were received with great pomp ; from whence they went to Madrid, where Philip himself received them in the midst of his family. Then, making a triumphant progress through Italy, they arrived at Rome in time to be at the enthronization of Gregory XIII., the manner of whose reception may be imagined from the fact, that the moment the foot of the charger of Mancio Ito, who headed the party, touched the bridge of St. Angelo, the guns of the castle fired a salute. They were answered by those from the Vatican ; and long ere the echoes had died away a strain of delicious music filled the air, and it was amid a flood of harmony that they drew bridle at last before the gates of the Vatican. And moreover, as if the Pope knew not how to make enough of his "dear Japanners," as he called them, not only were they fêted and splendidly entertained in all manner of ways, but he conferred upon them the knighthood of the golden spur, on the eve of the Ascension, in the presence of all the foreign ambassadors and native nobility of Rome, himself presenting sword and girdle, while the ambassadors of France and Spain buckled on the spurs ; after which ceremonies, the Pope, throwing golden chains around their necks, embraced them all in turn.

Now, although these and many more ceremonies were performed, apparently for the advantage of the people of Japan, they were really to further the private ends of the Pope, the Portugals, and the Spaniards ; and this I state, not because I am a Protestant, and a good hater of Portugals, Spaniards, and all popish ceremonials, but because facts justify the declaration ; for certain it is, the priests did that which rendered the two years' journey of these princes but of little good to the Europeans, and monstrous harm to the Japanners.

For two years after the return of the ambassadors to Japan, the tide of success flowed steadily onward ; during those two years, namely, 1591-92, twelve thousand na-

tives were added to the army of Christians ; nay, even
the reigning Ziogoon, Tiego-Sama, had so favoured the
new religion, that it was expected he and his whole court
would have been baptized. But success had flowed too
quickly ; it caused the priests to become insolent, and so
aroused the hatred of the native bonzes, who found their
revenues shifting into other hands, that they left no stone
unturned to injure the Christian missionaries. But, to
sum up a long and much-vexed question, although this
hatred of the bonzes had been long smouldering, and an
uneasy sensation had been growing among those of the
nobility who had no liking for the new religion, the first
sparks of persecution became almost simultaneously
ignited in three different places.

The merchant captains, upon their touching at Goa,
Malacca, and the Philippines, exhibited such certain
proofs of the wealth of Japan, and told such wonderful
stories of the progress of the Jesuit father in the hearts
of the people, that numerous Dominican and St. Franciscan friars burned with such religious emulation, that
they insisted upon being taken to Japan, where, upon
their arrival, in despite the laws of the Emperor, who
had become either tired, or fearful of receiving so many
foreign priests, and the advice and earnest entreaties of
the Jesuits to remain *perdu*, they formed processions, and
preached in the public streets of the great city of Macao,
built new churches, and, in a word, set at defiance the
laws and customs of the Japanners. The Franciscans
quarrelled with the Dominicans, and both became at open
enmity with the Jesuit fathers, to the great shame of
their holy calling, and the astonishment and disgust of
native converts, who, remembering the poverty, humility,
and good works of the followers of Xavier, saw that their
spiritual teachers aimed more at making money than saving souls.

Again, the wealth of the missionaries had so swollen
out their pride, that they refused the prescribed marks
of honour to noblemen and princes of the highest rank.
The truth must be told : being in the midst of luxury
and heathens, their vanity led them to act as if they had

6—2

been so many little popes, endeavouring to outvie each other in dignity. Too proud to walk on foot, they must be carried about in gilded chairs, and put themselves upon an equality with the mightiest in the land.

Now the Emperor Tiego-Sama had long been the friend of the Christian priests, although, since his majesty had destroyed by fire and sword some thousands of his native bonzes in the towns and monasteries at Frenoxima, and had willed that, at his death, he should have a statue erected to his honour, by which he was to be worshipped as the god of war, it must be questioned whether he ever really intended to support Christianity, except as a make-weight against the bonzes, whom he hated; however, their *protector* he might still have continued, but that, according to the custom of the country, wishing to raise a native Christian lady to the honour of his harem, and meeting with refusal, he became so enraged with the religion which taught such contumacy, that he issued an edict forbidding any more priests to be brought into his empire.

The edict, however, as I have shewn, was disregarded by the Dominicans and Franciscans, who still continued to smuggle themselves into the empire: but Tiego's rage cooling, partly it is believed, through the influence of good Father Rodriguez, who was his interpreter and friend, little notice was taken of their doings, and, indeed, their permanent establishment might have been effected, but for the two acts of insolence, one upon the part of a priest, the other upon that of a sailor.

The first was the arrogance of a Christian bishop, who, chancing with his retinue to meet the procession of a great prince, refused not only the customary homage of all in the empire to so high a personage, namely stopping his chair and alighting while the grandee passed, but caused his attendants to rudely hasten and take precedence of the roadway. This act of insolence, being reported to Tiego, much enraged the monarch; but again the good offices of Father Rodriguez warded off evil consequences.

Unfortunately, however, shortly afterwards, a Japan

lord, hearing a Spanish pilot boasting of the world-wide dominions his king had conquered, the nobleman asked him how it was that a sovereign, whose native territories were so small, as they appeared to be upon the map, managed to conquer so many and such far distant countries. " Nothing can be easier," replied the boaster: " for when my king desires to take possession of a country, he begins by sending missionaries ; and when the holy fathers have converted large numbers of the natives, his majesty sends after them soldiers, by whose means, aided by the holy fathers and the native converts, he subdues the whole nation."

This speech was the one live coal wanted to light up the flames of persecution ; for although, for a time, the emperor's great regard for the Jesuits still kept him from ordering any overt act, soon after, some additional insolence upon the part of the Franciscan and Dominican friars, in which Tiego believed he saw being played the first part of the programme of conquest laid down by the pilot, caused him to place guards at the house-doors of all the Christian priests, and issue an edict for a census to be taken of the native Christians.

Now, although the cruel purpose of this census was publicly known, such was the frenzy for martyrdom to which the priests had worked up the minds of their converts, that thousands came forth willingly and anxiously to enrol their names for the coming shambles : and now the first persecution broke forth. The friars were condemned to lose their ears and noses, and then to be crucified. And, as a warning to others, twelve of those Christians who had most frequented the church were included in the same sentence ; as were also a Jesuit father, two Jesuit novices, and some young children, who chanced to be in one of the houses when it was surrounded.

But no cruelty seemed capable of damping the burning ardour of the fathers ; for after the amputation, and when a portion of the bleeding ears was carried to the superior of the Jesuits, with tears of joy he offered them up to God, exclaiming—

"Behold, O Divine Saviour, these first-fruits of our labours in Japan! Grant that this blood, poured forth upon the earth, may make it fruitful with faithful souls, who shall glorify Thy name in this unknown and distant quarter of the globe!"

But the details of that tragedy are too terribly interesting to be told in other words than those of an eyewitness; therefore I give the following from letters, written years after by one of the fathers who was present:—

"The martyrs were conducted in carts about the city, their sentence being carried upon long poles before them. Far, however, from the insults and derisions, which usually accompanied similar processions, the crowd had nothing but respectful sympathy to offer to the present victims; many were moved to tears, as the cart containing the children passed along, and they were seen standing together with their hands tied behind them, and their little faces bathed in blood, while with their innocent voices they still sang hymns in honour of their God."

Marvellous indeed must have been the fortitude and earnestness of that band of martyrs, if (and I see little reason to doubt) there be truth in the letter, to which I have heretofore alluded, and which continues—

"Father Baptist, the superior of the Franciscans, continued to preach as they went along, as also did Paul Milki, the Jesuit, who even converted two of his guards in the course of their journey to Nangasaki, the town destined for their execution, and to which place they were sent so badly mounted and so poorly clad, that, but for the charity both of heathens and Christians, they must have died on the road from the inclemency of the weather. None of the Jesuits were permitted to accompany them; even the bishop was obliged to send his blessing by proxy. Father Rodriguez, by the connivance of one of the officers, managed to obtain an interview with the prisoners just before they entered Nangasaki, and then a reconciliation of the two orders took place; for the superior of the Franciscans asked pardon of the Jesuit on his knees for the injury which he now felt that his brethren had brought upon the mission.   Father Rodriguez, not to be outdone in humility, also asked pardon of the Franciscans in the same lowly posture, if haply he or his brethren had done aught contrary to Christian charity.   The condemned Jesuit thanked the Franciscans *so* fervently for the share which they had had in the happy consummation of his labours, that the heathen guards were filled with wonder, exclaiming—

" ' What manner of men are these, who go to destruction as others to a banquet or ball ?   Who ever saw so much sufferings and so much joy—a hymn of triumph, and a felon's death ?' "

" They might well ask the question," says the same writer ; adding, " and greatly must their astonishment have increased, when, upon drawing near Nangasaki, and the crosses destined for their execution became visible, the martyrs burst into fresh exclamations of joy and devotion.   One of the little boys, named Lewis, upon seeing three crosses smaller than the rest, eagerly and joyfully inquired which was to be his, and embraced it as soon as he reached the spot.   Little Lewis was but twelve years of age, and might easily have escaped when first taken at the convent, but preferred dying with the fathers to living without them.   Neither was this," says the Jesuit writer, " a mere momentary impulse of enthusiasm ; for every one of these poor children had remained firm from the first to the last, and in vain did the parents of one of them beseech h.m to have pity upon their grey hairs, and purchase safet at the price of his religion ; in vain did the great officials offer life, and even favour and promotion, if they would abandon their religion.   No ; they were determined, young as they were, to die with the fathers."

The Japanese mode of crucifixion is as follows :—The victim is fastened to the cross (not nailed) by the hands and arms, and by an iron ring passing round the neck, so as to keep the head in an erect position ; and a sharp lance then driven into the heart extinguishes life in a moment.   Such was the death which the martyrs were now to endure ; and, lying each upon his own cross, they

waited for the moment when they were to be lifted up on
high.   Troops had been arranged round the foot of the
hill, in order to prevent any but the nearest relations of
the martyr from approaching the spot; but t ie vast
plains, extending from that point to the city, were
thronged by a dense mass of people come to witness the
execution.

At first, a solemn silence reigned throughout that
mighty multitude: every voice was hushed, every heart
and eye was fixed upon the fatal spot; but when at a
given signal the crosses were raised, and the martyrs were
seen hanging, each from his own cross, with an executioner at his side ready to strike the fatal blow, the feelings of nature could no longer be repressed; and from
the plains below there arose a mournful cry, that reached
even the ears of the dying saints.   They responded not
to the lamentation: on the contrary, Father Baptist began
the ' Benedictus;' and, at the sound of his voice, the
others took up the strain, and continued it to the end,

with a devotion which quite electrified the spectators.
The children then asked Father Baptist to sing with
them the 'Laudate pueri;' but, absorbed in profound
contemplation, he heard them not; and they sang it
therefore themselves, never ceasing until their innocent
voices were hushed in death. They were all struck
nearly at the same moment, and all met their fate with
the same courage and constancy as from the beginning.

The place of execution was not that for ordinary malefactors, but a hill bordering on the sea, since called the
Mount of Martyrs. The earth, wet with the martyrs'
blood, was sedulously gathered up by the bystanders;
" and," say the Jesuits, " in spite of the care with which
the bodies were guarded, those of the Jesuits were conveyed across to Macao, where they are still preserved as
relics."

" This tragedy (the opening of a series which was to
follow, after an interval of some sixteen years, and marks
the cruelty, ferocity, yet firmness, of the native character),
took place in the year of our Lord 1597, and was immediately followed by a great transportation of Christians
as soldiers into the Corea, with which country Tiego was
then at war; and a new edict for the banishment of the
Jesuits. Their churches were everywhere destroyed,
their colleges broken up, and thus inevitably would
Christianity have been expunged from Japan, but for the
death of Tiego, who, notwithstanding his ferocious policy
towards the Christian priests—a policy induced chiefly
by their own conduct—was the greatest sovereign who
had ever sat upon the throne of Japan."

CHAPTER IX.

THE CÆSAR OF JAPAN.

Now as it is at all times pleasant to read the history of celebrated men, and inasmuch as it is desirable the reader should know somewhat of the distracted state of the empire at the time Master Adams and myself were thrown into the land of the Japanners, I will, with as much brevity as may be, lay before him a view of that emperor's life and character.

Tiego Sama, then, may, in some sense, be regarded as the Cæsar of Japan ; for albeit he was ugly and disagreeable to look upon, of small stature, enormously fat, with six fingers upon one of his hands, eyes so forward that they seemed to be starting from their sockets, beardless chin, and features altogether so moulded, that he was like unto an ape, which, indeed, he was nick-named, was yet of wondrous strength, great activity, spirit, and daring, and, moreover, of large mind.

When a boy his occupation was that of a carrier of water and a cutter of wood. Great talents, however, seldom go long unobserved, and so the mean boy was taken into the service of one of the princes attached to the court of the reigning emperor, Nobunaga, who, being a great judge of character, speedily transferred him into his own army, where his talents so marvellously developed themselves, that he soon arose to a separate command ; and as at that time every one of the many petty kings' hands was against the other, and all against the emperor, the new general met, engaged, and defeated them one by one, till he had crushed the rebellion ; services which his imperial master requited by creating him second person in the empire. While the emperor lived, Tiego remained stedfastly loyal ; but when his royal master was murdered, so powerful was he by reason of his great popularity, both with the troops and the people, that he seized upon the throne, and obtained of the mikado, or spiritual emperor, the illustrious title of Tiego Sama, which means, "The most high and sovereign Lord."

Once enthroned, Tiego's great talents as a *ruler* began to shew themselves, for he crushed the power of the turbulent kinglets and princes ; conquered the land of Corea ; but what was greater to his credit, raised the character of the people by revising the laws, and, by his wisdom and justice, so enlarged the influence of Japan, that its emperor was known, and his alliance courted, both by the king of Spain and the emperor of China : the latter, indeed, he intended to conquer had he lived.

Now, although Father Brixiano, in his letter, will not have it that Tiego was cruel, and gives as a proof of the cause of his great successes, his clemency to the conquered princes, none of whom he ever put to death after having once promised them their lives, I must think that the man who, because he had conceived a jealousy of his nephew, whom he had himself made a colleague in the empire, deprived him of his authority, caused him to cut himself open, and publicly beheaded the thirty-one wives, their children, and all the known friends of the prince, to say nothing of his proceedings against the Christians, must have possessed much of the nature of the tiger. That, however, if remorseless and hypocritical, he was also of great policy and wisdom, may be seen by the account of his rise and rule, which he gave to the ambassador of the Spaniards.

"Know," says Tiego, "that Japan containeth above sixty states, which had from long time been sorely afflicted with internal broils and civil wars, by reason that wicked men, traitors to their country, did conspire to deny obedience to their sovereign lord. Even in my youth did this matter grieve my spirit ; and from early days I took counsel with myself how this people might best be made subject to order, and how peace might be restored to the kingdom. That so mighty a work might be brought about, I especially essayed to practise these three virtues which follow : therefore I strove to render myself affable to all men, thereby to gain their good-will ; I spared no pains to judge all things with prudence, and

to comport myself with discretion : nothing did I omit
to do that might make men esteem me for valour of heart
and fortitude of mind. Now, by these means have I
gained the end I sought. All the kingdom is become as
one, and is subject to my sole rule. I govern with mild-
ness, that yields only to my energy as a conqueror. Most
especially do I view with favour the tillers of the ground :
they it is by whom my kingdom is filled with abundance.
Severe as I may be deemed, my severity is visited alone on
those who stray into the ways of wickedness. Thus hath
it come to pass, that, at the present time, peace univer-
sally reigns in the empire, and in this tranquillity con-
sisteth the strength of the realm. Like to a rock, which
may not be shaken by any power of the adversary, is the
condition of this vast monarchy under my rule."

The good father, Rodriguez, from whom I learned so
much of the history of Japan, had been the favoured Jesuit at the court of Tiego. He was the interpreter, and
had, by all manner of means, sought his conversion.
" But," said the father, who was with the Emperor at
the time of his death, " as he lived, so did he die. I
tried in vain to arouse him to the contemplation of
eternity ; even in the agonies of death the ruling passion
of his life was strong within him, and his soul was en-
grossed by his anxiety to secure the succession to his son
—a boy of eleven years of age—and to procure for himself the honour of being placed among the gods of Japan.
The latter wish was the easiest of accomplishment ; for,
soon after his death, a temple was erected, and a statue
which, during his lifetime, he had had modelled after his
own likeness, was set up for public worship."

The death of Tiego terminated the new Corean war, in
which he had engaged, chiefly for the purpose of exiling
his Christian princes and their followers. The latter thus
being returned to their own dominions, Christianity once
more flourished, churches were rebuilt, and colleges re-
established ; but, alas for the people ! the great Tiego
was dead, and his heir a minor ; and out of that minority
sprang forth evils which deluged the empire in blood.

The better to secure the succession of his son, Fide

Yori, Tiego, upon his death-bed, established a council of
regency, composed of forty-nine of the petty kings, placing
at their head Gejas, King of Bandora, a district so large,
that, besides the five great provinces called the Quanto,
in which were situated the great cities of Seruga and
Jeddo, it embraces also three other kingdoms, all of which
had been bestowed upon him by the Emperor Tiego, who,
the better to secure his fidelity, had caused his son and
heir Fide Yori, to be married to his powerful subject's
grand-daughter.

As, however, with many other princes who have been
similarly placed, Gejas, notwithstanding his connection
with the young emperor, found the possession of power
too sweet to look forward to its resignation with pleasure :
he soon resolved to seize upon the throne itself, and to
secure this consummation he set intrigues afloat among
his co-regents.   Among these were many who regarded
the memory of Tiego with affection, and who, moreover,
were but little desirous of exalting Gejas.   These, quickly
discerning the chief regent's ambitious projects, formed
themselves into a party for the protection of the young
Emperor.   The council of regents, however, being pretty
nearly divided, an appeal to arms followed, a civil war
broke out, and the party opposed to Gejas was led by a
certain illustrious Christian, named Augustine, King of
Fingo, and grand admiral of the empire.

At the time of the arrival of Master Adams and myself
in Japan, the war was raging in the Quanto, or hereditary
dominions of Gejas, in all its fury, the victory being sometimes upon one side, sometimes upon the other, the misery
and turbulence being similar to the wars of the Roses in
England, when great feudal princes were opposed to each
other ; and thus it was that the chief regent could not
gratify his desire of examining us *vivá voce* ; therefore,
perhaps at the trial of my readers' patience, have I endeavoured to place before them a slight view of the state
of Japan, and Christianity therein, during the last five
years of the sixteenth, and the first year of the seventeenth century.

CHAPTER X.

EIGHT tedious months were we kept in this place, the monotony of the confinement being varied only by hard strivings to learn the language, and listening to the relations of the Father Rodriguez touching the doings of the independent kinglets and princes, for and against the boy Emperor, Fide Yori, who was then residing, under the guardianship of his wife's grandfather, in the fortified palace of Osacca, in a mock-regal position not unlike that of the two sons of the fourth Edward, while England was under the protectorship of their uncle, Richard of Gloucester : at the end of that period, however, Father Rodriguez, who had regularly kept us informed of the progress of the civil war, brought news that the chief regent, who now called himself Ogosho-Sama, had beaten his enemies back from his own private domains, the Quanto, into the other states ; and, consequently, now having time upon his hands, he had commanded that we should be taken to Osacca, then his head-quarters, that he might discover for himself whether we were the terrible thieves our enemies, the Spaniards and Portugals who had speech with him, affirmed us to be ; and the day after the arrival of this command we were shipped on board one of this Ogosho's own galleys, which was manned by sixty men, fifty of whom were rowers ; and oh how grateful did we feel for that voyage ! The change from the prison-room to the keen, biting atmosphere, the bright seas, the rugged, picturesque rocks, the countless islands, invigorated our frames, enlivened our hearts, and delighted our eyes, notwithstanding the occasional dense fogs, the frequent shocks—really young earthquakes—that so vividly proclaimed to us the truth of the report, that out of three ships, never more than two reached the coast in safety.[1]

Then the majority of the numerous islands, alongside and between which we passed, were teeming with human life, and often occupied by great towns, at which, when we stopped, as often times we did, we were, although prisoners, treated very courteously. The most remarkable sight we met with was the number of women, who seemed to be more like fishes than human beings, for, getting their living by fishing, they reside upon the water in great boats. As for the manner of their fishing, it is sufficiently curious, for not only do they use nets and lines, but, should a particular fish escape their net, they make no more ado than plunge into the depth of the sea, after the fashion of ducks and swans, and it is said that they never fail to secure the fish : neither are they afraid of the whales, porpoises, or other great fish with which those seas abound, for they carry with them a long shark knife, or spear, ready for defence or attack, as the case may be ; and this particular race of women may always be known by their eyes, which, from continual diving, grow of blood-red colour.

As for the fish, they are, excepting the whales and porpoises, and such like, as curious as the women themselves. One of these is the furube, which can blow itself out into the shape of a ball. There are three varieties of this fish ; two of most delicious flavour, but, if not properly cleansed, very dangerous to eat, because of their poison, and yet the people will not forego the fish, for all that so many people die from eating it : soldiers, however, are forbidden to buy and eat it ; and if any one dies of it his son is denied succeeding to the father's post. The other sort is mortally poisonous in *every* instance, and is eaten by all who, having resolved to kill themselves, wish to die after an agreeable manner.

Another fish is the satisfoko, and is to be found in no other country : it is of great length, from two to six fathoms, with two long tusks standing out upwards from the mouth : it is used chiefly to ornament the tops of houses. The Japanners tell strange stories of this fish, which, they say, is a great enemy to the whale, and of so cunning a nature that it can kill the monster by creeping into its mouth, and devouring the tongue ; and this the satisfoko can do, because, as it creeps in, it puts its head and teeth in such a way that they are no hindrance.

Another fish is the sea-dog, which is about the length of a boy of ten years of age, without scales or fins, with a big head, mouth, and breast, and a large thin belly, like a bag, which would hold a great quantity of water, and thin sharp teeth, like those of the shark, with two feet, not unlike the hands of a child, by which means he creeps at the bottom of the sea.

These sights and natural curiosities served to amuse us till the twentieth day, when we arrived at Osacca, at which we were greatly rejoiced, for we thought that then our long confinement would find its end, either in liberty or death ; but proportionate was our disappointment, when an official, putting off from the shore, ordered us to proceed on to Seruga, for which place Ogosho had left some days before. So we continued our voyage till we came to the garrisoned town of Fusimi, where we were taken ashore, and lodged in the castle, which was a great building of freestone, and entirely surrounded by a ditch.

This place had been strongly fortified, and garrisoned with three thousand men, by the late Ziogoon, or Emperor, Tiego, for the purpose of holding in awe the two great cities of Meaco and Osacca ; and, that the soldiers might not, by long residence, become localized, and so forget their allegiance, it was the custom to change them every three years.

Now as it so happened that the change of troops took place the day after our arrival, we were transferred by our conductors to the charge of the out-going soldiers, who, under the command of their general, the King of Tango, were returning to Seruga ; and so well were we mounted upon horseback, that the journey would have been very agreeable, but that Master Adams and I were kept so far apart from each other, that we could not hold converse.

In the morning, as we rode forth, we met, and stood aside, drawn up on either side of the road, to permit the ingress of the new comers, who, in their full battle array, made a marvellously goodly show. That they were of haughty bearing was not to be wondered at, for the soldier class is held of the greatest rank in Japan, the commonest among them being entitled to wear two swords, and assume the title of Sama, his rank, moreover, being hereditary.

The incoming garrison consisted of three thousand men, mostly in the prime of health and strength, and their discipline was to be commended, although their habiliments and arms seemed to me to be somewhat cumbersome. Being imperial troops, instead of cotton—which is worn by the soldiers of the petty kings—their clothes were made of silk : they wore short, but very wide breeches, and jackets embroidered with gold, over the back, breast, and arms of which were suspended chain armour, and even the thighs, from the waist to the knees, were armed. Upon their heads they wore large hats of lacquered copper, and vizors over their faces.

The order of march was well disciplined, for they came five abreast, every fifty having an officer at their head : all wore the two swords, but they were divided into companies of five hundred, three hundred, and some of only half the last number. First came those armed with calivers ; then pikes ; then those alone with swords and bucklers ; then bows and arrows ; and, lastly, a company armed with waggadashes, that is, a weapon resembling a Welsh hook ; but they had neither flags, drums, nor, indeed, any other musical instruments of war. The first company of those who were armed alone with swords and bucklers had their scabbards of burnished silver ; while another company, who were next the general, had their scabbards of gold. In the midst of every company were three horses, very richly caparisoned, with gilded saddles, some covered with costly furs, some with velvet, and some with broad-cloth ; but every horse had three slaves to attend him, who led him with silken halters, which was necessary, for the eyes of the beasts were covered with leather. Every officer rode upon horseback, with his bed and other necessaries neatly packed, and poised upon either side. Over this package, upon a covering of red felt, the officer sat cross-legged, and in this order they took possession of the castle.

It was after a similar fashion that the outgoing garrison marched towards Seruga, except that we had with us the governor-general, the King of Tango, who, at a long distance in the rear, followed in great state, with many hundreds of attendants, horses, hounds, and hawks, with which he amused himself hunting at those places, either in the woods, plains, or mountains, which happened between the numerous towns, cities, and villages; and very solemn, dignified, and quiet was the order of the march, not a word being spoken that was not necessary, at which the reader will wonder, when I recount the incidents we met with during our six days' journey.

The road upon which we travelled is called the Tookaido, and is a sample of all the great roads in the empire—that is, of gravel and sand, so clean that you might eat therefrom, and wide enough for the princes and their trains, frequently marching as many as twenty thousand, to pass each other, without confusion or delay. At this passing, a stranger to the customs of the land cannot refrain from a feeling of disgust at the indecent dress of the pike-bearers and chair-carriers, who wear their clothes tucked up about their waists, and nothing but a small girdle of cloth about their loins: so that, with their naked legs, for the greater part tatooed, they resemble savages, nor to forbear laughing at the folly of these men, who, as well as the pages, umbrella-, hat-, and chest-bearers, and all the liveried footmen, make grimaces at each other, and jump about, between a mimic march and a comic dance; for at each step they draw up one foot as high as their backs, stretch out their arms on the opposite side as far as they can, seemingly to imitate swimming through the air, the pikes, hats, umbrellas, chests, boxes, or whatever else they may be carrying, all the time dancing about with them.

These great roads are marvellously pleasant, being planted on each side with beautiful fir-trees, with fountains at intervals, and well drained by means of ditches, through which the water flows in plentiful streams, serving to irrigate the neighbouring fields. At the distance of every league are two small mounds, one upon each side of the road, covered with grass, in which is planted a fine pine-tree, trimmed and fashioned so as to form a harbour; but which are at the same time intended as mile-marks, that the hackney-men may know the distance to charge their customers. Then there are numerous temples or monasteries, erected in the pleasantest places, castles of the nobility, built somewhat after the fashion of those old feudal houses in England; and very numerous are the monstrous idols, or images of gods, to be found stuck up on the roads at hilly points. In the great cities, and even in villages, I observed the regard which the great people have for teaching the poorer class the laws; for in each town, in the most public square, was stuck up a fudanotsui, that is, a small place encompassed with gratings, for the *supreme will*, as they term it; that is, a tablet for the placing in a conspicuous view all imperial orders and proclamations, and signed by the prince, lord, or governor of the province, who, by the way, upon the same tablet issues his own private orders and proclamations. The worst sight at the entrance of many towns is the place of execution, whereat may be seen heads of malefactors, upon poles, and decaying bodies upon crosses.

But by far worse than white ants, musquitos, terrible fogs, devastating fires, terrible earthquakes, begging priests, and little cur dogs which (by all but those who have become Christians, being held sacred) may snap at your legs with impunity, are the multitude of painted Jezebels: they swarm everywhere—in the grandest houses, in the greatest cities, at times upon the roads, under the disguise of mendicant nuns, at others upon the door-steps, and at the windows of the tea-houses, which are as infamous as they are numerous; yea, at the doors of houses, upon the parapets, at every turn, at every step, they flaunt themselves before the eyes of the traveller. Yes; this people, who affect to carry honour to the highest point, not only tolerate, but warmly encourage and foster this lowest degradation of humanity.

Yet are these poor creatures the most accomplished and best educated of the women, and, by consequence, frequently make good marriages ; after which they are ever held in high esteem. And now respecting the mis-statements of those writers, chiefly Jesuits, who have reported of the Japanners that they are every way amiable, I will affirm that intoxication by means of saki is a vice so common, from king to norimon-bearer, that it is held to be no blemish to the character of either; indeed, the stronger the drink, and the more copious the draught, the more manly and brave is the toper esteemed.

Then at length we reached Seruga by the great Tookaido, a road so well made, so clean, and bordered for a great part with such beautiful gardens, and enchanting scenes of hill, dale, wood, and water, all of which natural beauties being heightened and improved by the art of man, prove his power of subverting, or rather moulding nature to his necessities and refined tastes : but how much more beautiful would it be but for the tea-houses and saki-shops, which so thickly blot the picture, that, to Christian eyes, the beauties seem but a mass of corruption ; for corruption beginneth at the heart of things. Yet a wonder—a miracle of man's power over inert matter, a wilderness of rugged rocks mid-ocean, uncertain of existence for an hour—for it is a part of a chain of volcanoes, enveloped in fogs, and lashed by seas that sink one ship out of three—yet conquered by man, or comparatively so by man, who, alas ! in erecting it into a Paradise, has so chipped out from his own heart the impress of God's image, that it seems at last to be peopled by a race, which, notwithstanding their ape-like politeness, in moral dignity are no better than South Sea savages.

Arriving within an hour's journey of the city, our whole party were drawn up in double columns, there to await the arrival of the King of Tango, who, being a great distance in the rear, did not reach the main body till near night ; but then when he passed through the lines with his face partly averted from where I was stationed, it occurred to me that I had seen him before ;

and while I was making an effort to remember when and
where we could have met, my eyes lighted upon a splendid norimon, that is, a kind of chair or portable room,
of oblong shape, made of twisted bamboo, japanned,
painted, and gilded ; and which, from the size of the
poles, the number and livery of the bearers, I knew
belonged to some lady of his majesty's family ; but the
features of its occupant, of which I just caught a glimpse
through the partly-drawn silken curtains, those glistening black eyes, and that fair skin,—surely they were
familiar to me, at least I seemed to have the same dim
remembrance of them as of the king ; but his majesty
and the lady passed on, leaving me lost in conjecture, in
the midst of which we were resigned to the charge of
three soldiers, who, throwing cords around our arms, led
us into a kind of barn, where, notwithstanding I put
several questions to them—for we now understood sufficient of the language to hold some converse—they
remained as mute as if they had been dumb. Delighted,
however, at finding ourselves together again, I took no
notice of the churlish brutes. As for Master Adams,
shaking me warmly by the hands, he said—

" How fare ye, Melichor, and how like ye this being led
about, like dancing bears at a fair ?"

" Well, Master Adams, thanks be to Providence ! But
in the present case, methinks it be the men who are being led by the bears ; for these heathen fellows be both
as dumb and as surly."

" Their dumbness matters not, for I fear me the brutes
could say but little that would benefit us to hear ; but,
God-a-mercy, man ! I believe me they are going to fasten
us up like beasts," said he, pointing to some hooks in
the wall ; and then turning to our guards, he said, as
best he could, in their own tongue—" Tell me, my masters, are we to be hauled up to these hooks?" But the
men only shook their heads and laughed ; at which Will
became so enraged, that he lifted his leg, as if to kick
them ; but fearing the consequences, I cried, " Have a care,
have a care, Master Adams." To which, desisting, he
replied—

" Thou art right, thou art right : it would be pleasant, but not prudent, to chastise these fellows." However, the appearance of a man with a large tray of refreshments entirely restored his good humour : but casting his eyes over it, and seeing no tobacco or pipe, he said— " The good-looking and polite gentleman has forgotten the solacing plant."

"That is true ; but the noble Sama must pardon his servant, for the great Ogosho has forbidden the use of the plant, under penalty of imprisonment for the first offence, and death for the second." And as the man spoke he bowed himself out of the room ; whereat Master Adams spoke not, but soothed his disappointment by a low prolonged growl. And here I may remark that Ogosho's disgust at tobacco-smoking was quite equal to that which James of England exhibited not long afterwards.

Now, first having loosened our cords that we might partake of the good things before us, and then having tightened them again, and passed the ends through the before-mentioned hooks in the wall, so that we should be secure for the night, our three guards squatted upon the floor to amuse themselves by asking each other riddles, the punishment for incorrect answers being the tossing off a cup of hot saki, but to my thinking, it was their opinion that the loser had the best of the game ; for certainly the incorrect replies were so many, and the forfeits so often paid, that before long they were all sleeping beneath the tightest of night-caps, accompanying each other with the loudest, if not the most harmonious of music.

CHAPTER XI.

WE GO TO COURT, AND OUR ENEMIES ARE CIRCUMVENTED.

VERILY, the news must have spread rapidly through the city that two ferocious pirates had been taken ; for the next morning, as we were carried in cangos to the palace, the crowd of men, women, and children was so great, that the ottonas, *i.e.* heads of streets, and the watchmen, could scarcely keep us from being crushed beneath the weight of their curiosity : neither did they appear particularly well-disposed towards us ; for while some of the lower rabblement shouted at us, " Core, cocore, ware," which meant, " You Coreans, with false hearts,"— a kind of stock cry, which had come into fashion half a century before, in consequence of the wars with Corea, and the great hatred entertained towards the Coreans— others who had been taught by our jealous enemies, the Portugals and Spaniards, repeated certain doggrel verses, which set forth that we were blood-suckers and sea-monsters, who had no homes but our ships, and no means of living but by plundering the vessels of the Portugals and Spaniards.

Thus, after about one-hour's jolting up hilly streets, we reached the royal residence, which was built after the fashion of the great palace at Jeddo, then occupied by the heir of Ogosho Sama : it resembled a huge town, at least five Japan miles in circumference, and was made up of three different castles, each being strongly fortified, and enclosed within a separate ditch.

In the fort and outermost castle resided the princes of the empire, with their families, in great stately palaces, built in streets, with spacious courts before them, and shut up by strong heavy gates. In the second, the most important personages of the court had their lodgings ; but the third was the real palace of Ogosho. It was seated higher than the others on the top of a hill, enclosed with free-

stone walls and bastions, which were supported by great
ramparts of earth, upon which stood the houses of the
imperial guards ; but all the structures which went to
compose the entire castle were of uncommon strength,
being erected of freestones of great size, but laid upon
each other without being fastened either with mortar or
bars of iron, so that in the event of earthquakes the
stones should yield to the shocks without damaging the
wall itself.

The most ornamental portion of the inner palace was
a great white tower of many stories, adorned with bended
roofs, covered with golden dragons, built for the pleasure
of the sovereign, from whence he could view miles of
rising ground, laid out in magnificent lawns, gardens,
orchards filled with trees and fruits, and works of native
manufacture of the rarest kind, and terminating in a pleasant wood, planted with rare plane-trees.

Crossing the great ditch, and entering the palace
through a pair of enormous gates, which were guarded by
a company of soldiers in black silk, we came to a large
guard-room, hung about with cloth, and arms of all kinds
—pikes, targets, bows, arrows, and swords. Having
passed through this first enclosure, and by the houses
and palace of the princes and lords, we came to the second
castle, which was fortified after the same fashion as the
first ; only the gates and inner grounds were much more
stately and magnificent. At this spot we were commanded to alight from the cango, and then led across a
stone bridge into the great and principal guard-room,
where, to our surprise, we found the Jesuit Father Rodriguez, who, approaching us, said in a low voice—

" Welcome, my sons. The great Ogosho has at length
listened to my pleadings, and sent for you."

" Would that I could sufficiently thank thee for bringing us even to this end, whatever it may be," said Will.

" Hush ! follow me, and keep thine eyes and ears open;
but, as you value your lives, utter not one word, whatever thou mayst see or hear."

" As quiet as a caravel in a calm ; as dumb as a dead
shark," said Will.

"But thou mayst hear harsh words spoken, villainies charged against thee that will raise thine ire."

"For such am I prepared, aye, and also how to answer them," replied Will.

"Nay, my son, listen, but for thy life speak not till I tell thee."

"Father, I misdoubt me thou art playing us false. I *will* have speech with the emperor."

"Shame, Master Adams, the good father means us well," said I in a whisper, but angrily, and catching hold of Will's arm.

"If I have not thy word to this, I will even now leave thee to thyself and thine enemies, who are powerful," said the priest.

"Then be it as thou wilt," replied Will surlily: and the father, who seemed to know and be known to the officers and attendants of the palace, led us across a large square to the royal apartments, the outer chamber or hall of which was thronged with courtiers, guards, and servants. Making way through the crowd, he led us up a staircase into a spacious room, the walls of which were decorated with cranes and tortoises, where he bade us await him. After an absence of about half an hour, he returned, and whispering to us to take off our shoes, he again conducted us, through a doorway to the right, into a very small box-like cabinet, darkened by a silken curtain; then, cautioning us not to move, or speak above a whisper, he glided from the room. But, drawing aside the before-mentioned curtain, imagine our surprise at finding that a lattice-work of bamboo splints, covered with fine transparent silk, with openings of not more than a span broad, alone divided us from the hall of audience, into which we could see and hear all that passed, without ourselves being visible. These latticed boxes are now used by the degenerate descendants of Ogosho, not only for the *midia*, or empress, and her court ladies, but from behind which the emperor himself now gives audience.

The hall of audience, of which we had a complete view, was the scene of much barbaric grandeur, for the usurper

Ogosho had just returned, flushed with victories, and the consciousness that he had at length secured the supreme power. It was a vast apartment, opening upon a large balcony, before which spread a garden of great beauty, and divided by richly painted and gilded screens into five divisions, each division being raised one step above the other. The first served as an ante-chamber, or hall of waiting, for the gentlemen in attendance ; the two next served a similar purpose for the kinglets, great lords, and officers of the empire, who were all arranged in order of their precedence ; the fourth was tenanted only by two persons, a priest, who held the first dignity in the household of the *mikado*, of whom Ogosho *nominally* held his power. The first floor of these divisions, or apartments, was magnificently decorated and carpeted, but exceeded by the last and highest, in which, upon his heels, sat Ogosho, in a kind of square box, raised about two steps from the floor, richly ornamented, and, moreover, railed about by a gold lattice-work, six feet high, in which were small doors for the egress and ingress of the princes or others who might be called from the crowd. There, upon an ottoman of blue satin, worked with stars and half-moons of silver, sat Ogosho-Sama, the supreme ruler of the empire. His age was about fifty-two ; he was of middle stature, of full form, and, greatly to my surprise, of a countenance that one could not look upon without liking, for although it bespoke great firmness, there was a playfulness about the lip, and a brightness and openness about the eyes, that told of generosity and good temper. The attire of this great personage was as plain as that of any one of the twenty grandees, who, in their long mantles and immense breeches of brown silk, sat near him, upon their heels, with their faces bent to the earth : indeed, if there was any difference, the emperor was the plainest attired, for while the grandees wore two swords each, Ogosho had but one, his sole mark of distinction being a bunch of different-coloured ribbons, which served to tie up his hair.

Now, although my acquaintance with courts was limited, I still knew sufficient to feel shocked at the demi-

godlike hauteur with which Ogosho gave audience to
those even of his subjects who possessed power of life and
death within their own states. Some ten or twelve were
then at court to make presents, to do which, each was
made to crawl upon hands and knees through one of the
small gates in the lattice-work to the royal foot-stool,
where, having remained for several minutes with his forehead upon the ground, without so much as a nod from
the imperial head, or a rub of his own caput from the
imperial foot, he crawled slowly back again, and thus
satisfactorily finished his audience.

Most interesting to us, however, was the audience given
to a company of miserable Portugals and Spaniards, at
whose head was our enemy, Don Pessoa. At the sight
of this man, Will Adams trembled with rage ; and verily
I believe, if I had not placed my hand upon his mouth,
he would have jeopardized our safety by some rude
speech.

"By my soul," he muttered, "it is mortal shame for
one who has faced a whole armada of such scum to keep
his tongue at anchor, for I doubt not the knave is here
to do us evil."

"Nay," I whispered, "remember the words of the father, and thy promise."

"Tut, tut," he replied ; "but listen, Melichor, for thou
knowest the speech of these savages better than I."

The Spaniard, having done homage after the same
slavish fashion as the princes, which caused me great
wonder in one of so haughty a nation, held above his
head a written paper, which the Father Rodriguez, who
stood near the emperor, took into his hand, and read
aloud in the Japanners' own tongue. It was a supplication from the Spanish Viceroy at Goa for three boons :
first, that Ogosho would so extend his protection to the
Christian priests, of all orders, that they might have the
free disposal of their houses and churches, and not be
molested ; secondly, that amity might continue between
his Japan majesty and the King of Spain.

"The which are but moderate demands, and should,
in Christian charity, be granted, scum though they be,"

whispered Will to himself, who was even then meditating preferring a similar request upon the parts of the
Dutch and English. Accordingly, when his majesty signified that these petitions should have the best consideration of the council of state, Will smiled good-humouredly,
for he regarded it as a good omen. But at the next request he growled, "The scurvy, greedy sea-rats," and
became so enraged that he would have forced a passage
through the lattice-work had I not placed my hand upon
his mouth, and held his arms. But at his indignation
the reader will not wonder, for thus it ran—

"That, as an evidence of his friendship for the King
of Spain, his majesty would not permit certain Dutchmen,
who had landed in Japan some time before, to reside in
his territories, but would drive them out."

At this the emperor held up his hand as a sign for the
father to discontinue ; when, with a look of good-tem-
pered astonishment, he said—

"Nay, this thing is not possible : *Japan is an asylum
for people of all nations. No man who hath been driven by
accident, or taken refuge in my dominions, and conducts himself peaceably, shall be compelled against his will to abandon
the empire ; but if his will be to quit, he is allowed to depart.*"

"A right noble answer to the base knave," I whispered.

"Words, mere words, Melichor ; or how is it that we
have been kept here like wild beasts in a cage," replied
Will.

"Knave's work, knave's work, as we shall see, Master
Adams," said I.

Ogosho's answer being translated, Pessoa seemed
mightily perplexed ; but, bethinking himself, replied—

"These Dutch are refractory and rebel subjects, who
have set at nought the power, and have fled from the
rule of his most catholic majesty ; and therefore it ill becomes the great Emperor of Japan, who himself so well
knows the wickedness and misery caused by rebellion, to
treat with favour, traitors and rebels to the authority of

a sovereign with whom his majesty professes to maintain relations of amity."

"By my soul, but I would like to tell this King of Japan, before the rascal's own face, how we have drubbed his murderous countrymen out of the Netherlands," I muttered.

"Aye, aye," muttered Will, "and I misdoubt me if he and his crew wouldn't get a few strokes from the rods they are pickling for us."

Ogosho, however, having listened to the father's translation of Pessoa's reply, said angrily—

"By the ghosts of my fathers, these foreigners are daring, to dictate to us the government of our empire, and to command whom we are to receive, and whom we are to exclude from our dominions :" adding, however, more mildly, "know that it matters not to us what quarrels and wars distant people have among themselves : our care is alone for the peace and welfare of the children of the sun-goddess ; and so long as strangers, be they whom they may, pay obedience to the laws, and, by their fair and honourable dealings, promote the convenience and enjoyment of my people, it matters not to what nation they belong, or to what power in the west they are nominally subject."

At this reply, Pessoa seemed so sorely perplexed and disappointed, that he would have sneaked from the presence, had not several of the Japan lords, who, for private reasons of their own, supported the Spaniards and Portugals in their general desire to prevent all other nations but their own from getting a footing in the land, thrown themselves at the royal feet, and advocated the granting of this presumptuous petition ; but at this Ogosho, losing all patience, arose from his seat, and cried out passionately to his nobles—

"Get thee from our presence. Have we not said, and are our commands so light ? *I tell thee that if devils from hell were to visit our dominions, they should be treated like angels from heaven, so long as they conducted themselves according to the laws laid down by ourselves and our royal predecessors.*"

The crest-fallen nobles immediately crawled backwards from the hall in dismay; but the intercession having given Pessoa time to think, he said—

"It is not alone, O great prince, because these Dutchmen are rebels to their own king that they should be sent away from this happy land, but because they are sea-thieves and murderers, who live by plundering the ships of all countries, and therefore, if suffered even to live, will seek to prey upon the people of Japan; whereas, if they be exterminated, not only will your majesty's justice be executed, but an example set to the rest of their countrymen, who will assuredly be prevented from following in their footsteps."

"O thou liar of first magnitude," cried Will, and that so loud that the whole court startled with surprise.

Ogosho, however, either not hearing, or not choosing to hear, replied to Pessoa—

"Truly it is good and friendly of the King of Spain to send so far, and we thank him; but as justice must be meted out to all nations alike, we shall command our council to examine into the affairs of these rogues of Hollanders, and see that they are punished as they deserve."

So saying, his majesty made a sign that the audience was at an end, and Pessoa and his steel-clad followers crawled backwards from the presence.

"It is, then, *this* villain," said Will, "who has worked us all the mischief, and the emperor—"

"Directed that you should be placed here, my son, so that, whilst you might hear the charges brought against you, without your accusers knowing of your presence, you should know that which you had to answer," said Father Rodriguez; adding "but follow me."

We obeyed; and in another minute, to the indignation of the lords present, *stood* before his majesty, who, notwithstanding the angry frowns of the courtiers, seemed mightily tickled, that while the envoy of a great king had humbled himself to the dust, two poor shipmen should but doff the hat and bend the body very low, which was no more homage than we paid to our generals.

As for Will, when the father begged of him to go down upon his knees, he lost all patience.

"Nay, nay, father," said he, "the knee of an Englishman is as stiff as a mainmast to all but God and his own queen ;" which, being translated, his majesty, with a good-humoured smile, as if refreshed with the novelty of a little honest bluntness, signified that we might remain as we were, and that was in an upright position, with our eyes fixed, and our hats in our hands.

Then his majesty, through Father Rodriguez—for although Will knew enough of the language to understand what he heard, he was not ready enough with his tongue to express all he wished—put the following questions, which, it will be seen, Will answered with as much skill as boldness—

"From what land do ye come ? is it not far away ? and what moved ye to come to this our empire of Japan ?"

To which, placing his finger upon England, in a map of the world which the Jesuit had spread upon the mat before him, Will replied—

"England, a country as rich as Japan, and ruled over by a great queen whose power makes her equal to any other sovereign in the world, be he great as he may ; and who, moreover, has long sought friendship with the potentates of the Indies, by reason that her country possesses much merchandize, and other products, that the Indians know not of, and which her people are desirous of changing for those commodities which are alone to be gotten out of the east ; and, moreover, that such dealing together of the peoples of the east and the west will benefit both."

Then, his majesty desiring to know if the English had wars, Will replied—

"Yes, with the Spaniards and Portugals, who desire to gather to themselves the trade of the whole Indies, and to do which they stop at nothing that is base or treacherous : but with all other nations the great queen is at peace."

Then, to his desire to know in what the English had

faith, and whether their bonzes held the same faith as
the Portugals and Spaniards, Will replied, that his countrymen believed in one God, that made heaven and earth,
the same as did the people he had named, but their
religion was different in its form, inasmuch as they worshipped God only, and not saints and images ; whereat
the Jesuit seemed angry, but said nothing.

Then taking up the map, and finding from the father
how many thousand miles Japan was, both from England
and the Netherlands, he desired to know by what way we
had come so far ; and when Will endeavoured to trace our
course upon the map, and that, too, through the Straits of
Magellan, of which he had never till then heard, his majesty lifted up his eyes with astonishment, and expressed
his belief that it must be a lie ; whereupon Will, forgetting the personage before whom he stood, waxed red in
the face with anger : seeing which, however, and fearing
some imprudent speech, the father said something to his
majesty, which we did not fully understand, but which
made him clap his hands to his sides and laugh aloud, as
if, forsooth, to call a man a liar had been a piece of wit.
Getting the better, however, of his mirth, he demanded
to know what merchandize our ship contained ; when
Will, who had an eye to the interests of his employers,
not only called over the list, but, believing that his
majesty was favourably disposed towards us, there and
then humbly begged permission that the Dutch, who were
his good masters, and the English, his countrymen, might
have leave to trade with his subjects, as did the Portugals and Spaniards ; whereat the emperor made no reply,
but, rising from his seat, ordered us to be taken from the
prison.

" By my soul, I believe I've gone a little too far with
that respectable old savage," said Will as we marched
from the hall of audience.

"Truly it was a venturesome plunge ; yet, to my
thinking, his majesty did not seem displeased at thy
petition : moreover, Master Adams, to my wonderment,
he said not one word about our piracy and thievishness."

" Aye, aye, Melichor, he did not put up his back, but

the nature of the cat is still there, and he will play with us till tired, and then, perhaps, kill, if not eat us."

" Nay, nay, Master Adams, the old gentleman means to befriend us ; for marked ye not the replies he gave the knave Spaniard ?"

" Tut, tut, Melichor, they are a treacherous race, given to blood-lapping, and this I have heard before.   I tell you we are on a quicksand, and may trust alone to God's providence," replied Will.

And shortly after we had passed through the city gates we came upon a scene not easily to be forgotten.

We were approaching the place of public execution, to which, just before us, marched a criminal upon his road to eternity.   First came a man with a pickaxe, and then another with a shovel, these being grave-diggers ; then a man bearing a large tablet, whereupon was written the offence for which the criminal was to suffer (viz. the stealing a sack of rice), and which was afterwards to be set up over his grave ; then came the criminal, his hands bound behind with a silken cord, and a paper upon his back, upon which again his offence was written ; then followed the executioner, with a drawn sword in one hand and a cord in the other, accompanied by soldiers with their pikes pointed towards him, indeed the very head of the weapon resting upon his shoulder ; the van being brought up by a great number of persons, among whom were many gentlemen, chiefly youths of noble birth, who, as soon as the poor man's head was struck off, tried the temper of their swords upon the body, which they not only hewed into pieces, but, placing the pieces one upon another, wagered with each other who could best cut them through at one blow.

Now this terrible scene I would not repeat here, but that I saw it with mine own eyes (indeed, I believe it was to terrify us that they made us wait for more than an hour to look upon it), and it was only one of many cruel scenes that go to shew the real nature of these Japanners, whom it is the object of many foolish people to over-cry as amiable and good, whereas, from all I saw, they are cruel, proud, voluptuous, and revengeful to the greatest degree.

8

CHAPTER XII.

To whom did those burning black eyes in the norimon belong? Where could I have seen the features of the haughty King of Tango? were the thoughts uppermost in my mind, as we were led onwards, after witnessing the barbarous scene just related, and so I said—

"Didst observe the lady in the state-chair, Master Adams, and believe thou hadst seen her before?"

"Not I, Melichor, for my eyes were fixed upon that savage-looking king, for in him I called to mind the son of old King Foyne," replied Will.

"Aye, aye, it may be so, but he was not called King of Tango," I replied : and, being only half convinced, I asked the chief of our guards, who replied, that his majesty was the person whom Will took him to be, but that, for his services to Ogosho, that prince had recently promoted him from his joint royalty to the larger undivided sovereignty of Tango.

"And the lady in the gilded norimon?" I asked interrogatively.

"The betrothed of the king's brother," was the curt reply.

"By the bones of my grandfather, if this king be our keeper I'll wager we shall find more of thorns than roses in our beds," put in Will.

"Nay, Master Adams, I doubt me if we have much to fear now we are under the protection of Ogosho himself."

"Tut, tut, shipmate ; to my thinking the change will prove as advantageous as a jump mid ocean from a burning caravel."

"This is churlish, this is churlish, on thy part, Master Adams, for of a verity it must be better to have dealings with the lord than with the slave."

"We shall see, we shall see," replied Will thought-fully; and shortly afterwards we arrived at a Sintoo temple, into which we were taken, and from that moment our condition became improved; for although we were as carefully guarded as before, we were better fed and lodged, nay, even permitted to walk (accompanied by one of our guards) through the beautiful groves and woods in which this mia was embosomed.

These mias (*Anglice*, dwelling-places of immortal souls), as likewise the monks who occupy them, are supported by the benevolence of pious Sintoos, who, living, make handsome presents, or, dying, bequeath large endowments to their favourite temple and its priests.

Well, having passed several days among these yellow-robed, beardless, long-haired, but jovial priests, whose queer, stiff, oblong, lacquered caps, as they stood out from their foreheads, somewhat resembled a fleet of small ships, we should have had a merry time, but for our anxiety as to our probable fate, of which we could get nothing from our guards; indeed, such is the cat-like nature of these Japanners, that they delight in torturing their captives : so when, upon the twentieth day of our lodgment in the temple, Will, who had long sought in vain to establish a confidence between himself and the guard, addressing that worthy, said—

" Harkee, my master, I have nought to complain of as regards your feeling, except that it is my belief that it is the custom in these latitudes to fatten prisoners before they are slaughtered."

The chief replied, " It is sinful to eat animals who may be made to work, for such would be an unpardonable waste of food."

" Ugh," whistled Will, taken aback at the reply, " the shark talks as if we were oxen."

" Tut, tut, Master Adams, the man is but the mouth-piece ; the words are those of his superiors," said I, fear-ing some imprudent outburst.

" Aye, aye, Melichor, true is it that ' out of the mouths of babes and sucklings cometh wisdom,' and truly am I an ass, for discipline is good even in an enemy," said he laughing; but adding, as, to our astonishment, Father Rodriguez entered the room—

" Whew, what news have we now ?"

" Naught that is bad, much that is good, my son."

" God forgive me that I ever doubted thee, father : say, is it not to thee we owe being shifted from a dungeon to this berth, which is fit for the great Drake him: self ?" said Will, warmly shaking the Jesuit by the hand.

" Nay, not so, my son, but to the King of Tango."

" My father, thou art not given to wit-chopping, and so are we the veriest of asses, for truly had we set this kinglet down as our enemy," said Will.

" A proof that we should no more judge of the kernel by the shell, than man by his countenance," said I.

" Nay, be not in haste to throw aside that wise principle," said the father.

" Aye, but by mine honour I will though ; for once having worked myself out an ass by that course of calculating, I will henceforth judge men by their acts, not their faces," replied Will.

" Then assuredly thou wilt be betrayed; for, not to advantage thee, whom he does not love, but to circumvent one whom he hates, did this king intercede in thy favour with the great Ogosho."

" Then I pray thee, father, read me this riddle," said Will.

" Know ye, then, that the King of Tango is at present at feud with the Don Pessoa: their former amity originated out of merchandising together, whereby both benefited. Well, in the last year of the Emperor Tiego, and at the time when the Christian brethren were suffering both fire and sword at the hands of their direst enemies, among whom may be counted this King of Tango (then junior King of Bungo), a great noble, who had embraced the Christian faith, was murdered—I can call his execution by no other name—with many members of his family. One, however, a daughter, escaped the slaughter, and, under my charge, took refuge on board Pessoa's ship, which happened to be then at Bungo ; but the king coming to a knowledge of her hiding-place, commanded Pessoa either to give the lady into his hands, or for ever leave his dominions."

" And as a soldier he answered the tyrant, no doubt, knave though he be," said Will.

" He was in a dilemma: for to refuse to resign the girl was to endanger the commerce of his country, as likewise his own private interests, while to comply was to betray a newly-converted member of the flock of Christ into the hands of a butcher."

" Tut, tut, father ; did the sordid wretch weigh pelf in the balance with the girl's life ?"

" Thou art somewhat impatient, my son," replied the father ; adding, " he did send her back to the king, but not till he had received a solemn assurance that her life should be held sacred. Such a condition, however, was unnecessary, for the Lady Mary possessed a warm friend in the queen, to whom she is akin."

" The Lady Mary—she who is betrothed to the king's brother ?" I said, interrogatively.

" The same, my son ; although it is not to the brother, but the infant son of the king, the Lady Mary is betrothed, for she is the inheritress of great wealth and lands ; hence another reason why she was safe in the hands of her father's assassin."

" But matters being thus amicably settled, how arose the feud between the king and the knave Spaniard ?" interposed Master Adams.

" Thus, my son ;" and the father continued, " Don Pessoa, during the short time the fair convert was aboard his ship, became smitten with her ; and he kept the secret within his own breast until recently, when, an opportunity occurring, he prayed of Ogosho himself, that, following the example of many of his countrymen, he might take unto himself a native wife ; and the boon being granted without even the name of a lady being mentioned, he at once boldly preferred his suit to the Lady Mary, who was in attendance upon the Queen of Tango ; and this daring coming to the ears of the king, so great was his rage, that, had not Pessoa been in some sort under the favour and protection of Ogosho, he would have slain Pessoa and the whole of his crew, who were then at his chief port."

" And but the devil protects his own, there would have been one great knave the less," said Will.

" But as, fearing the emperor, the king could not destroy Pessoa, to circumvent his plans his majesty carried the lady with him to the presence of the emperor, when, having told him of the Don's boldness, the emperor became so irate at a Spaniard's aspiring to the daughter of one of his greatest families, that had not Pessoa been then at court in the quality of an envoy from the King of Spain, he would have driven him from the empire. As it was, however, he received him coolly, and thus was it that he the more readily listened to the counter-statement of the King of Tango in your favour."

" It is a sign of a fair wind, father, when knaves get to loggerheads," said Will.

For my part, although I spoke not, I felt my hatred increasing for the Spaniard, and chiefly for his aspiring to the hand of the Lady Mary, though why it should concern me I then tried in vain to discover. I could not believe that I loved Maud Saris less, or less desired to hear the pealing of our wedding bells ; yet could I not but believe that the fascinating Japan girl still haunted my mind, if, indeed, it had not sunk deeper. " Heaven protect me from disloyalty and fickleness," thought I ; and verily the thoughts of Master Adams must have been akin to mine, for, observing my silence, he said, in his good-natured, bantering, boisterous manner—

" What, ho, there, Melichor ! hast got thy brains athwart this poor wench's raven eyes ?"

" Nay, nay," said the priest, with a smile ; but there was meaning in that smile ; " it will never repay my poor services by meditating the robbery of the godliest sheep from my poor flock ; one, too, who is vowed to the service of the church ; but," he added, " I had almost forgotten my mission, which is, to bring thee, Master Adams, and thee alone, to a private audience with the emperor."

The news was too good for Will to delay an instant,

so they were soon gone, and I left alone, pondering upon the words of the Jesuit. Why had he volunteered the information that Lady Mary was vowed to the church? who asked him? Not I. Could he, forsooth, dream for one instant that I, a vagabond, a miserable stranger, a prisoner in the land, could aspire so high? Tut! the thought was foolish. Yet that brought the remembrance that these Portugal and Spanish adventurers regarded the highest personages in Asia as beneath the meanest in their own ranks. Their merchants and sailors had married with Japan women. Yes, the wily priest did deem it possible; for it was his business to calculate the remotest chances of any interference wherein the interests of his order were concerned. Moreover, this girl was closely associated with those interests; for had he not called her the godliest sheep in his flock? by which, doubtlessly, he meant the 'call'-sheep, the lurer of others into his fold: and this opened my eyes (for I became suddenly very clear-visioned) to his real interest in her—to the reason that, in addition to Pessoa being a Spaniard, this Portugal Jesuit acted covertly. It was summed up in a few words: it was against the interest of his order that she should marry; but then, again, how could *he* prevent it, when one of his antagonists was a despotic king, the friend and favourite of one of the most absolute sovereigns in the world? Aye, truly, that *was* a knot to unravel; and in that endeavour I fruitlessly busied my mind until aroused by the return of Master Adams.

CHAPTER XIII.

WE START FOR JEDDO, AND MEET WITH A GREAT LADY, WHOM WE SERVE.

"THE old cat, the tiger-cat, we are as mice beneath his paws!" exclaimed Will, throwing himself upon a mat.

"What now, Master Adams? has this Ogosho hoisted the knave Pessoa's colours above ours?" said I.

"Nay, nay, not that; but the old savage is playing with us: there's no bringing him to the fore. He will neither that the Spaniards shall intrigue against, nor that we shall be otherwise than well fed, and kept at anchor in a calm during his pleasure," replied Will.

"But at least we are in no danger of being hauled up to thieves' crosses," said I.

"Aye, aye, Melichor, and that is all the sea we have made, and that, too, after having run me the gauntlet of a whole fool's catechism. Aye, faith, he put me as many questions about the English and the Hollanders, as if belike he was about to turn scribe, and do into his own barbarous tongue a complete history of the two countries, their wars and their troubles, their habits and customs, and, to boot, the family history of one Will Adams, about whose mother, father, wife, family, profession, means, past and future, he was as curious as if he had taken the place of one of Queen Bess's sergeants learned in the law, and was examining him upon his trial for high crimes against her majesty, her state, and dignity."

"But the end on't, the end on't: how finished he?"

"By asking me, in tones like the purring of a cat, whether I would like to pay a visit to my shipmates and countrymen."

"Thanks be to God, then."

"For why, Melichor? and I ask it not profanely; for holding to my lips a bottomless cup, into which he had poured hope in and out at the same moment?" said Will angrily.

"Nay, Master Adams, but for this, that our shipmates are still above ground," said I.

"Aye, aye, and for that I am heartily grateful; but it raises my ire that the end of all the questionings was nothing more than a performance of one of those ape-like grins with which these Japanners seem to be born and die."

"Be not impatient, Master Adams; for believe me the wind is shifting, and we shall weather the gale yet," said I.

"Thou art young and sanguine: for myself, God help me! I sometimes believe I shall never quit this cursed land," he replied, in a tone of despondency that surprised *me*, who had seen him the only one of high heart, and exhaustless spirit and hopes, when a whole fleet had been downcast; but now he was like a bird in a cage, dependent upon the will of a despot, even to his slightest movement: there was no room for his restless, energetic mind, which had begun to feed upon itself: but this he better expressed himself—"Throw me mid ocean in a cockboat, in a hurricane, with but God and myself for my reliance, and my spirits shall emulate the waves themselves; but in this accursed cage my mind and body will rust to death."

At length, at the end of another forty days, the wind did shift, nay, turn right round in our favour; for Master Adams was summoned to another audience with the emperor, who, after again questioning him for about two hours, told him that we were at liberty to visit our old ship, which, greatly to our astonishment, he further said was then in the port of that city, where it had been brought to be destroyed.

Need I say how gladly we accepted the boon, or how joyful we were at finding our old shipmates, not only alive, but in health. Would that the pen of a Master Shakspear or Jonson were mine, to describe the volcanic joy upon their side. They wept like children or women (as for that, so did we), for they had heard that we had long since been crucified as pirates and thieves. And here I cannot help remarking how easy it is for some people to shed tears, or, at least, how transient is the feeling that produces them; for, not long after, when the question arose about the disposal of a certain sum of money among them, these same weepers, one and all, arose in open mutiny against Master Adams, who had been so greatly their friend; but of that more anon. At our meeting we were very merry, and, moreover, returned thanks to God that we had come together again; but as Master Adams ever had the interests of our merchants at heart, he speedily began to inquire as to what had chanced since we had been parted; and finding that directly after our leaving the ship every article of any value had been stolen, so that our shipmates were then nigh unto starving, he resolved at once to crave audience of the emperor, and lay his complaints at his majesty's feet; and this he did the next day, when Ogosho, getting into a great rage, commanded that the rogues should return all the stolen articles; but as this could not be, by reason that the robbery had happened so long before, and the goods had been distributed in so many different directions, his majesty further ordered that the royal treasury should pay unto us five thousand reals, and, moreover, in his own presence was the coin brought, and delivered into the hands of Master Adams, to distribute among our poor men. So, taking this money back to the ship, Master Adams was received as if he had been an angel from heaven, for the miserable fellows were sorely pressed with hunger. Thus, by the benevolence of the emperor, were we relieved. At the same time, however, he ordered that we should remain with our ship at Sarai till he sent us further orders, which happened at the end of thirty days, when Father Rodriguez brought us a command to proceed with our ship along the eastern coast of the province towards Jeddo, to which city Ogosho, with the whole of his court, was about journeying. And great was the delight of all, for although we would have preferred permission to direct our course homewards, we were glad of any change from inactivity.

"Great is the gratitude of our poor fellows for thy many kind services, and from my soul I thank thee, and promise to return them, if ever I have the opportunity," said Will, shaking the Jesuit by the hand, who replied—

"My son, I have done but my duty, and require not thanks ; but, an' you *will*, you *may* even now do me no small service."

"Then be what it may, father: save only it interfere not with my fealty to Queen Bess, thou mayst count it accomplished," said Will.

"A person in whose welfare I am interested would voyage with thee to Jeddo, that he may escape an enemy who is all-powerful in this city."

"Enough, father : whoever he be, he may claim our best cabin," replied Will.

"Aye, even the *best* cabin it must be, my son ; and if I have any claim upon thy gratitude or honour, let him have his will, whatever it may be—so that it endanger not the ship—without espionage of any kind."

"My hand upon it," returned Will.

Then, as the father went over the side, he said—

"Keep a good look out, and soon after the great bell of the city has sounded, the boat will be alongside. Now farewell, my son, and may the Virgin give thee a fair voyage."

"It isn't all taut this. I misdoubt me but there's a spar or two loose in the rigging ; night work is dark work, in more shapes than one, Melichor," said Will, as the priest left us.

"Of a verity it is a mystery, Master Adams," I replied musing.

"And all mysteries are, to say the least, suspicious ; but we must e'en await the result, Melichor." And so saying, he went to busy himself with the necessary preparations for our voyage.

But here, as the reader may think it strange that Will did take so much upon himself while the captain was on board, and in sound health, I must remark, that as Master Quackernack believed we all owed our preservation to him, and, moreover, seeing that he had been appointed by the emperor as a kind of governor over us all, from the moment of our being brought together again, the captain insisted upon resigning all command into Will's hands, a piece of nobleness which met with the liking of our entire party.

Before sundown that same day there came on board a Japan pilot, learned in the seas about there, with some ten sturdy sailors, and this by command of the emperor, nominally for our convenience, but, I have little doubt, as much to prevent our endeavouring to leave the country and directing our course homewards ; but be that as it may, these fellows were very civil, and obedient to the orders of Master Adams, which was fortunate for his promise that the stranger should be received with as much privacy as possible ; so, as it was determined that we should not sail till next morning at daybreak, what by his jovial, goodnatured bearing, and heartiness of manner, combined with several bowls of hot saki, and a few pipes of the forbidden tobacco, in which the men took great delight, Will easily managed to make them turn into their berths at least an hour before kokonats (midnight), as, indeed, the whole of our own crew, with the exception of Master Quackernack, myself, and Will, who agreed to keep the night watch between us.

For more than an hour we kept watch, listening with anxious attentiveness to any sound that came to us through the murmuring of the rolling waves as they dashed against the ship's sides. At length the city bell sounded, and, shortly after, we heard the sound of oars plashing in the water : a few minutes more, and a boat reached the side of the ship. Casting the light of a small lantern into the boat, we saw that it held two persons, one of whom was a boy, the other, to our surprise, was in the robe of a Canusis (Sintoo priest) ; then, throwing a rope-ladder into the boat, the ends were held by the rowers, and two persons immediately afterwards stood upon deck, but, either from the cold sea air, fear, or joy, I know not which, neither could do more than just chatter a few thanks.

"The poor fellows are weather-bound in the tongue, Melichor: haste thee for a cup of saki," said Will.

At the word saki, however, he in the priestly garb shook his head, and whispered timorously—

"The noble Sama is good, but his servant would be alone."

"My master would not be seen or heard till the ship is on her way," said the other.

"Aye, aye, then alone it is," said Will, leading them to the cabin which had been provided for them. But when they reached the door, he who had last spoken suddenly, but with as much gentleness as the action permitted, took the lantern from Will's hand, at the same time both bowed down and turned their backs upon him, as is the politeness of the country, then entered the cabin, and closed the door in Will's face.

But Master Adams, not at that time being sufficiently acquainted with the customs of the land to distinguish between politeness and rudeness, turned upon his heel, and, in angry tones, exclaimed—

"Whew! but for my promise I would teach you somewhat of courtesy, my masters."

"Tut, tut, Master Adams; as well might a lion be cross with a kitten, as a pilot-major of Queen Bess's fleet chastise a priest and a boy, pagans though they be," said I.

"By mine honour thou art in the right, Melichor; but," he added, "I was not best humoured at the sight of this Canusis, for I fear me the Jesuit is but making a cat's-paw of me in this matter, which may mean treason to the emperor."

"Nay, nay, Master Adams," said I, "it is churlish to doubt at every turn the honesty of one who hath done us such good service."

"Tut, tut, lad, thou art in thy green age, while I am old enough to know, that though, like the breechless Scots, these Portugals and Spaniards have ever a dagger at each other's throats, they nevertheless join in hatred to the heretic, be he Englishman or Hollander."

"By mine honour, Master Adams, you do the Father

Rodriguez less than justice, for truly must he have charity who could thus save this Canusis, who is of the deadliest enemies of the order of Jesus," said I.

"Now, indeed, hast thou sent the bolt into the bull's-eye. No, no, lad, there is some mystery hidden here; for never till that blessed time comes when the wolf will lie down with the lamb, will a Portugal priest, of his own free-will, put forth a hand to save a Protestant or a Pagan. Nay, nay, thou goose; again I tell thee, there is more than meets the eye, and Will Adams is the cat's-paw," replied Will; adding, however, savagely, "But hark ye, Melichor, that paw wears a gauntlet of such metal, that belike the chesnuts will stick to the fingers while the priest whistles for them." And in such like converse did we pass the night.

So we began our voyage, tantalised by a mystery; and for five days we continued our course in sight of land, during the whole of which time our mystery kept to his cabin, his wants being supplied by his own boy, from whom the Japan sailors managed to discover that his master was a Canusis of rank, and fortunate for us was the discovery; for, being very noisy, and, after the nature of their race, given to drunkenness, the knowledge that so holy a personage was on board kept them in awe, if not order: indeed, upon more than one occasion these men requested the boy to beseech of the holy man to come forth from his cabin, and officiate at a sacrifice to the sea-god, who might thereby be induced to grant them a good voyage; but, no less to their astonishment than indignation, these requests were invariably evaded; whereupon the belief became current, that the angered deity would punish us all with shipwreck.

Now the foregoing was very curious; for upon the twentieth day of our voyage the clouds grew black, the wind shifted, and the waves exhibited such sure symptoms of a coming storm, that the native sailors in a body begged of the boy to pray to our mysterious passenger to come forth, and help to arrest the anger of the sea-god, and again came a refusal; which, although it raised

the ire of the Japanners, they still continued steady at
their posts, as the vessel tacked about, threading her
course between granite rocks, coral reefs, and jutting
points, upon which she momentarily threatened to split ;
but for a time all went well.

At length, however, the boldest shipman felt a tremor
at his heart, for surely never in any other sea had been
seen such a hurricane. The very world seemed shaken
by a war of elements that seemed to promise universal
destruction. The fearful roaring of the wind—louder,
far louder, than during our ordinary typhoon—discharges
of thunder that might have deafened a world of giants,
and broad sheets of forked lightning, that gave a demo-
niacal expression to the countenances of the men. Still
again, as yet, every man kept to his post. Master Adams
at the helm, by the side, but above the Japan pilot, with
his bared head, long hair flowing in the wind, and his
large flashing blue eyes, stood amidst thunder, wind,
lightning, and a deluge of rain, like another Ajax ; and
such was the energy and determination expressed upon
his features, that the men would not for shame have left
their posts. But we were within sight of a great city ;
the winds beat inland with such terrible violence that
(afterwards we heard) above a hundred houses were
thrown to the ground, nearly the whole were unroofed
and trembled to their foundations. Then the sea, aroused
by the commotion, kept rising, till it burst its boundaries, undermined the great wharf, beat down the stone-
walls as if they had been paper, and sunk and shattered
hundreds of barques that were moored in the harbour,
while the superstitious inhabitants, frantic and maddened, ran to and fro, endeavouring to appease the god
of the storm by flourishing about their heads lighted
fire-brands.

The sight proved too much for our Japan sailors ; they
ran from their posts, clamouring vehemently for the
Canusis to come forth and appease the storm god ; and in
another instant we should have foundered, but for Master
Adams, who shouted, in a voice that could be heard even
above the noise of the elements—

" To your posts, as you value your lives ; and the
priest, if need be, shall be dragged forth.   Go ye, Melichor, and bring the fellow on deck ; for an' he can do
nought else, he can take a turn at the pumps."

To hear was to obey ; and on the instant, and without ceremony, I burst open the door of the priest's cabin
—and the mystery was unravelled.   Before me, in the
garb of a Canusis, except that the helmet-cap had fallen
to the ground, in fervent prayer, upon bended knees, with
eyes uplifted, and holding an ivory crucifix in her hand,
knelt—" the Lady Mary !"

" God's providence ! is it possible ?" I exclaimed.   But
doubtlessly, imagining from my entrance, that the ship
was sinking, she cried—

" Jesus, Mary, protect our souls !   We are lost."

" Nay, lady," said I, taking her hand : " it may be
given to you to save us ;" and I told her of the Japanners'
determination, and Master Adams's order, that she should

come upon deck, and sacrifice to the sea-god ; but with
a look partly of supplication, partly of resignation, she
replied—

"Sama, I may willingly resign my life into the hands
of Him who gave it ; but, forsake him—never."

"Lady, for thy life, for all our lives, hasten : these
men need not be deceived, nor thou compromised. Let
them make the sacrifice, while thou prayest to the only
true God ; but come—" and giving her the helmet, nay,
placing it upon her head, I led her forth, whispering that
her *incognito* might even still be preserved. The last
words reassured her ; then, with a presence of mind
which I afterwards found to be the most marked feature
of her character, she adjusted the crape vizor, so as to
hide her features, and with a bold, firm step, walked upon
the deck. The fears of the superstitious men became
instantly calmed, and they fell upon their knees. Then
bidding them to arise—while two proceeded with the
sacrificial rites, that is, threw overboard a barrel of saki
and a number of copper coins—she knelt, and with uplifted hands, prayed, not to their god Kompira, but to our
Saviour and the Virgin ; and, not to speak profanely, the
prayer of that enthusiastic yet gentle girl must have
reached heaven ; for within an hour the storm fiend became powerless, the elements at rest. Hollanders and
Japanners (shipmen of all nations are superstitious) gazed
lovingly and gratefully upon the devotee, for they felt
that she had saved them from destruction. Of course the
feeling was but momentary with the Europeans ; but the
Japanners bowed their foreheads to the ground, as if
their Canusis, as they believed her to be, was too holy to
be gazed upon by mortal eyes : nor did they arise till she
had sought her cabin. Moreover, for the rest of the
voyage, although it was troubled by much foul weather,
and lasted many days, they continued cheerful, obedient,
and, wonderful to relate, temperate.

But that night, when the tempest had subsided, when,
in charge of the watch, I stood with my back against the
bulkhead, can I describe my thoughts? Scarcely. I

longed to reveal my discovery—my secret—to Will; but
no, I dared not : it was not my own.

Then I catechized myself. Why did *I*, Melichor von
Santvoort, feel so great an interest, such a burning
anxiety in this young Japan maiden? Could it be that
I loved Maud the less? Nay, nay, Melichor, *that* thou
must not believe. And after suchlike fashion did I pass
the night.

The next day we were riding in a dead calm : Will
and I sat in our joint cabin. I had been overhauling
the events of the previous day. I had spoken of the
storm, the wrecks on shore, the devastation, the behaviour of the crew,—of all matters but one, the one
nearest my thoughts ; and that Will opened up, by
saying—

"But, Melichor, hast thou no speculation anent this
precious Canusis?"

"Me, me?" I replied, hesitatingly, for I felt half-
ashamed of keeping a secret from him : "not I, Master
Adams ; what now is there for speculation about this
priest? surely thou art not even at this time thinking
him in league against thee with Father Rodriguez?"

"Tut, tut, thou goose ! Canst not see that this priest
is no priest?"

"No priest !" I repeated.

"No more than I am a mermaid ; but an' I am a
judge of the article, it is a woman," replied he, laughing.

"A woman ! truly it is a strange conceit ; but why
thinkest thou this?" I said.

"Firstly, for the most *un*reasonable of reasons, that
she hath no tongue ; secondly, that she hides her face
with yon crape, after a fashion that did none of the
priests we saw in our temple quarters ; and lastly, because she was entrusted to us by a priest, who, having
mischief in hand, knows that the best instrument with
which he can carry it out is a woman," said Will, again
laughing.

"An' this be so, Master Adams, our honour is concerned ; for the good father hath thy word that the
cabin of this stranger be free from *espial*," I replied.

"Tut, tut! didst ever know Will Adams break his word? Still, hark ye, Melichor, it is my belief that this sham Canusis is some fair dame, whom the father has beguiled from her home, and is sending on to Jeddo, that hereafter he may have a companion to aid him in his labours." At this my cheeks burned with indignation, and I replied warmly—

"Not so, by my soul, Master Adams."

"Thou art warm in the lady's cause: but look you, here is her boy;" and at the same moment that he laid his hand upon my arm, the Japan boy entered the cabin, and having looked first at Will, then at me, with a bow till his forehead nearly touched the ground, begged the Sama who had entered the cabin during the tempest would honour his master with a visit.

Taken aback by this unexpected request, I hesitated to reply; but Will, turning to the boy, said—

"Return thee to the holy *man*, and tell him the Sama is following at thy heels;" adding to me, in English— "Fie on thee, man, for keeping a secret from thy comrade and shipmate; for verily I believe thine ears have received more than thy tongue hath chosen to repeat. But hie thee to the cabin of this she pagan, for my curiosity is as ardent as a maiden's desire to know who is to be her future husband;" and no less to avoid Master Adams's banter, than anxious to avail myself of the invitation, I instantly obeyed.

The maiden was sitting upon a travelling mat, reclining her back against a bamboo pillow, still in the dress of the Canusis, but free from the helmet cap, which permitted her raven hair to rest upon the floor. Upon my entrance she gracefully bent her body forward, and, with her hand, motioned me to be seated upon another mat near to her, and her face becoming suffused with crimson, which, to my thinking, tinted her complexion even like the bloom upon a peach, she said, with downcast eyes and faltering voice—

"Peace be unto the noble Sama, and may his heart find no place for hard thoughts at the boldness of a

9—2

maiden! But, alas! it is the hounds that teach the deer to fly."

"Truly, lady, even hounds might be pardoned for chasing one so fair and beautiful," I replied.

"The Sama has a silken tongue, but it was not to hear such soft words that his handmaiden presumed to request his presence, but to thank him for his ready wit, by which she was saved from disgrace, nay, perhaps worse, if it be possible that anything worse could happen to a maiden of Japan."

"Lady, the poor service of thy servant meriteth not these words of thanks: rather hath he to crave thy pardon for his rudeness, unintentional and unpreventable though it was," said I, quite satisfied that I had made a very pretty speech, after the fashion of the easterners; and I believe she thought so too, for with a smile, albeit rather melancholy, which penetrated to the heart of the coxcomb before her, she replied—

"Enough, Sama, thou hast earned my everlasting gratitude; but," she added nervously, "is it even suspected by others in this ship that the Canusis is other than he seems?"

"Lady, I may not deceive thee: *it is.*"

"Then thou, Sama, hast disclosed my secret," she said quickly, catching my arm.

"By my soul, no, lady, but Master Adams—"

"The auge (pilot), Adams?" she said interrogatively.

"He, and he alone, lady. Yet even he suspects not that the lady he carries is of so high a rank as the chief friend of the Queen of Tango."

"That is good, very good; and thanks be to God it is so, for from the Auge Sama I have nothing to fear. No, no," she muttered, almost to herself, "the Auge Sama is a bold man, a brave man, a good man."

"Aye, lady, and albeit his curiosity may be great, of too much honour not to remember his promise to the Jesuit father that thy secret, even as thy person, was to be free from molestation."

"Yes, yes, for he is a good man; but," she added, "he may see me at another time, in another place; and what then will this good man believe, nay, what thyself, O Sama, of the Christian maiden, the daughter of a noble Japanner, who he will remember once so far forgot her sex, religion, and rank?" and as she spoke she glanced significantly at her attire.

" That dire necessity alone could have compelled her—"

But, placing her fair hand upon my arm, she interrupted me, saying—

" Stop, Sama ; I have resolved. Lend me thy patience for a time, and thou at least wilt no longer wonder at my having adopted a course that even the priest should have shrunk from but as a last resource. Listen."

I bowed obediently, and she commenced the following truthful but terrible history.

CHAPTER XIV.

A TERRIBLE HISTORY.

" KNOW, O Sama, that among the earliest converts to the teaching of the sainted Xavier, were the king and nobility of Bungo, and chief among the latter in rank and power stood my father's father. Thus was I born in the faith ; for although my grandfather was dead at the time of my birth, my father, mother, and grandmother were still among the most earnest of the followers of Christ, and the protectors of his church ; and that they suffered not in the early persecution of the Christians, they were indebted to the great honour in which my father was held, not alone by his own king, but that king of kings, the mighty Tiego.

" But, alas ! the King of Bungo, growing old, associated with him in the government his son, the present King of Tango, who, never having been more than nominally a Christian, and that only to please his father, no sooner found himself the dominant ruler, than he took no pains to hide his hatred of the new religion and its followers ; and when, at the latter part of his life, the

great Tiego directed a persecution against the Christians,
the young king of Bungo was found first and foremost in
his efforts to uproot the new religion from the land.

" For some time, however, the tyrant was compelled
to postpone his fell purpose; for although the greater
part of his nobles were Christians, they were both loyal
and powerful; and in the full consciousness of their in-
tegrity, they held themselves in no danger, but especially
my father, who believed himself additionally secure, from
the fact that the queen was his near kinswoman.

" The slightest excuse, however, is sufficient to bring
into play the passions of a tyrant; and so, upon the occasion of a trifling street quarrel between some Sintoo
priests and Christians, the flames which had so long been
smouldering burst forth. Churches were pulled down,
the public cross, which the holy Xavier had erected, was
burned, the fathers themselves ordered to quit the kingdom, and the people to return to their national idolatry,
or die.

" The tyrant, however, but little knew the hearts of
his people, for at the very commencement of the tempest
they, one and all, mean and noble, enrolled themselves
in a brotherhood called the Confraternity of Martyrs,
each pledging himself not only to continue the usual
practices of prayer, fasting, and penance, but to suffer
loss of property, banishment, or death, joyfully, for the
name of Jesus : and nobly did they keep their vows, even
to the little children, those blessed innocents (who were
destined to play a prominent part in the coming persecution), to whom the fathers tendered a pledge especially
adapted to their tender years.

" This confraternity so enraged the king, that whereas
hitherto he had only harassed the lower class of people,
he now boldly attacked two nobles, brothers, who had
been baptized by the names of John and Simon, by sending to them an officer and a bonze, who were ordered to
insist upon their recantation of the faith, or suffer the
penalty of death. Without an instant's hesitation the
brothers spurned the bonze from them ; nay, even when
the officer, who wished to befriend them, prayed, they

would but *feign* compliance with the king's decree, have the ceremony of recantation privately performed at their own houses, or bribe the bonze to allow it to be *supposed* he had received their apostacy, they still refused : nay, when John, who was the first to suffer, was dragged to the bonze's house, and the superstitious book was set upon his head by main force, as the token of his apostacy, he protested so loudly, so vehemently, that the officer had no alternative but to slay him.

" Leaving the chamber reeking with the blood of one friend, the officer proceeded to the house of Simon, whom he found in converse with his mother. The sight of their happiness, and the consciousness of the terrible errand upon which he had come, so unmanned him, that he wept aloud, and, falling upon his knees, prayed of the lady to exercise her maternal influence, so that Simon should comply with the king's commands, and thus save herself the anguish of losing a second son, and himself that of imbruing his hands in the blood of another friend.

" It was a terrible moment, O Sama ! The appeal thrilled through that mother's heart. For a time she was dumb ; but at length the Lord gave her strength, and she answered ' That, being herself a Christian, she would rather lose her son, than he should lose his soul.' And although, at this noble reply, the officer became annoyed, and charged her with obstinacy, he at once left the house, being unable to carry out the king's commands. Soon afterwards, however, another friend of Simon's entered, charged with the same errand. Knowing its purport, Simon received him with an affectionate smile, thanking him for that token of his friendship, whereby he should be prevented dying by a meaner hand, and then prostrated himself in prayer before an image of our Saviour crowned with thorns, while his mother, as a signal that the occasion was one of joy, called for warm water that he might wash. This ceremony being finished, the mother fetched Agnes, the young and beautiful wife of her son, who, although exulting in the coming martyrdom, could not prevent her tears, but, falling at her husband's

feet, she blessed him, and besought him to cut off her
hair, in token that she would never again marry. Simon
complied, saying—'My beloved wife, and thou, too, my
mother, it is but a short time I go before thee.'.

" Then Simon was led forth to the hall, where the execution was to take place, and having distributed his
rosaries and some other little presents among his friends
and disconsolate servant, as he bent his body before the
picture of the Saviour, his head fell to the ground, when
the mother, with the courage of a Maccabee, taking up
the head of her beloved son, exclaimed—

" ' O dear head, resplendent now with celestial glory !
O happy Simon, who hast had the honour of dying for
Him who died for thee ! My God ! Thou didst give me
Thy Son ; take this son of mine, sacrificed for the love
of Thee.' "

" This is terrible, O lady," I said, sickened at the tale.
But in the relation she had become excited ; her enthusiasm for the glories of martyrdom had absorbed her horror, so, holding up her hand, she replied—

"Stay ! listen, Sama ! I am narrating a terrible history : as yet you have heard but the opening. Listen !"
and she continued—

" Then came the grieving wife, Agnes, to weep, as
became her weaker nature, bitter tears over the relics of
her husband ; but, lo ! shortly afterwards entered an
officer, bringing with him Magdalen, the wife of John,
and Lewis, a little child whom the latter had adopted as
his own, who solemnly proclaimed to them that they
were all to die together.

" Then at that awful time began to be shewn the glorious spirit that filled the breasts of the Christian
brethren ; for with joy the condemned embraced each
other, praising, blessing, and thanking God, not only that
they were to suffer for his Son's sake, but that, like Him,
they were to die upon the cross : and then, robed in
their best attire, they set off for the place of execution in
palanquins, which the guards had provided for the purpose, and having reached the fatal spot, Jane, the mother
of Simon, prayed of her executioner to bind her limbs as

tightly as possible, that she might thus share the anguish which the nails inflicted upon those of Jesus. Then, filled with the divine spirit, she preached from the cross with so much eloquence, that the officer, fearing the effect of her words upon the people, stabbed her at once ; and thus perished one who might have been worthy of following our Lord.

" Magdalen and the child Lewis were the next to suffer ; but the child being bound so violently that he could not refrain from shrieking, the officer asked him if he were afraid to die, when the child replied by desiring that they should set his cross up opposite that of his parent, when they would see. With this request the officers complied, and for some minutes the two regarded each other in silence, when the mother, summoning all her strength, said—

" ' Son, we are going to heaven : take courage, and cry Jesus, Mary, with your latest breath.'

" ' Mother, you shall be obeyed,' replied the child, and the next instant they were transfixed with spears. But the last has to be told, Sama: the young, the fair, the beautiful Agnes, the companion, the playmate of my childhood ; oh, how can I describe the end of that blessed being ! During the foregoing scenes she had remained kneeling in prayer ; no one would molest her : her very executioners wept that they were bid to mar so much beauty : their hands were powerless to do their office. So thus finding that no one sought to bind her, she laid herself gently and modestly down upon the cross, where for an hour she rested, waiting calm and serene, as if pillowed upon an angel's bosom, even smiling with joy at the ruffian who at last was bribed by the executioner to do the deed, as he lifted the spear that struck her soul from earth to heaven.

" Thus, O Sama, have the women of Japan died, and thus calmly, joyfully, will they again die for the love of God." And the beautiful enthusiast clasped her hands, and, looking upwards, prayed silently for the souls of those whose history she had been relating to me.

But, reader, let me take thee by the button-hole for a

minute. Should any of you be so squeamish that you would rather that such terrible relations had been left out of this narrative, let me tell you that the present writer is not a maker, but a relater of a sad and sober history ; and, moreover, that as it is from the past of a people that their future may be guessed, I have thought it proper to give these same relations, and that, too, as they at this present stand in the Japanners' own history, and the writings of the Jesuit fathers, who have printed them in all the chief tongues of Europe. But to resume my narrative. When the lady had somewhat recovered from the excitement which these memoirs had caused her, she said—

"But the blood of that family only whetted the appetite of the tyrant, for, not long after, the mother, the wife, and children, all died, either by the sword or upon the cross. Yet, though the blood now flowed freely from those heaving fountains, Christians' hearts, it did not stay the zeal of the higher nobles, whereat the king became so enraged that he sent for a celebrated bonze to re-convert them ; but his services were useless, for they were unattended, or, when attended, the Christians, in defiance, still wore their beads. In vain the king commanded, and the queen received the bonze with every possible reverence and submission at the palace ; the ladies of the court, however, refused obedience : they would neither listen to the bonze, nor remove the rosaries from their necks, and although, with some, imprisonment, and even starvation, was tried, it failed to shake their faith. Then the king grew sullen with his courtiers, all of whom were prepared to suffer a fate similar to that of the brothers ; and thus at length it came.

"The king had paid one of those visits to his great chief Tiego, which the emperor so frequently and jealously required from his nobles, and had returned, leaving at the royal city of Osacca, the queen and her ladies, especially those nearest her heart, of which I was first and foremost.

"It was upon his return that he determined to strike a blow at the Christians. He began with the bravest and most powerful of his nobles, one who had earned undying glory both by sea and land. Yea, Sama, for this powerful lord Thomas, who had been baptized by the sainted Xavier, he sent an invitation, couched in the most honied words, and when he came into his presence he showered upon him honours and words of praise, and gradually led the conversation up to the hated subject of Christianity ; but knowing with whom he had to deal, and that to convert by argument would be like the conquest of a kingdom, as many nobles would follow the lead of the renowned Thomas, the king called in the aid of the learned bonze, whose arguments and sermons had failed to convince even the ladies of the court. The pagan priest argued and prayed of the lord Thomas to recant ; the king implored, offering him fresh dignities and wealth as the price of his compliance. To all this the brave soldier listened till his patience became exhausted ; then he, who would have died beneath the banner of his king with joy, conscious that he died in the performance of his duty, replied—

" ' I have listened, O king, till my indignation consumes me : now hear my answer. As a soldier, as a subject of an earthly monarch, I should have deserved crucifixion— the most disgraceful of our punishments—for deserting the banner beneath which I had fought : then should I not be worse than the most despicable of human beings, if, for fear or favour of that monarch, I could desert that King of kings, to whom, on the day of baptism, I swore allegiance ? Then know, O prince ! now and for ever, that my hatred to traitors is as great as my hatred to treason, and I will cheerfully resign my possessions, family, and life, rather than be false to that banner which is so filled with immortal life, that if even now hurled to the earth, must, at some future time, rise triumphant over the land.'

" Too indignant to reply, the king left the apartment, and the Christian lord, knowing what must follow from such a speech to such a man, retired to his house, sent for a Christian father who was hidden in the city, and prepared himself for death. It was in vain that his well-

wishers urged of him, for the sake of his family, who
would otherwise be involved in the same ruin with him,
to seek safety by flight, for to all their prayers he had but
one answer, viz.—

"'Know you, my friends, that so far from flying from
martyrdom, I would go to the end of the earth to seek
it. Moreover, too much love have I for my dear children,
to wish to deprive them of a blessing which I myself
covet above the empire of the world.'

"The following day this pious lord received a present
of fish, and an invitation to dinner, from the governor of
the city, who was a great favourite of the king's, and
knowing full well the ominous meaning of such an invitation, he took an affectionate farewell of his wife and
family."

Here the lady sobbed aloud as she said—"The rest is
soon told, Sama.

"While sitting at table the host held forth a sword,
and desired to know his guest's opinion of its capabilities
for the striking off of a human head. Thomas, having
examined the blade, replied calmly, that it was ex-
cellently well fitted for such a purpose, and the next
moment the governor laid him dead at his feet."

"But the family, the family of this lord, surely they
escaped the fate of this noble man, lady?" I said, wrought
to a strange excitement by this terrible narrative.

"Thou shalt hear : listen !" she replied, when she had
recovered from the hysterical state in which this relation
had thrown her, adding—"But a few hours afterwards
the brother fell by the same sword ; the mother and the
two sons of Thomas were also condemned ; while his wife,
Martha, her daughter, and eldest son, were, from some
caprice, exempt from the sentence. But, Sama, the remembrance of that tragedy unnerves me. I can tell no
more, at least at present :" and she fell backwards exhausted, when the boy, or rather girl, for, like her mistress, she wore the male garb, beckoned to me to leave
the cabin, and flew to her assistance.

That tragedy, which the Lady Mary had failed to

repeat, has since been told in those letters to which I
have before alluded, and thus it runs—

"Martha, while she wept over her cruel fate, called
her grandchildren, and, embracing them tenderly, told
them, that as their father had died for Jesus Christ, so
she and they were now to do the same, and then to go
and live with him in heaven. The children quietly
answered that there was nothing which they wished for
better ; asking, at the same time when it was to be?

'Now,' she said ; adding, 'so go and take leave of your
mother, and prepare yourselves for death.' With smiling
countenances the children hastened to obey ; and having
distributed their toys among their playfellows, and made
some parting presents to their nurses, they clothed themselves in the white robes which Martha had taken care
to provide for the occasion, and knelt before their mother,
saying—

" ' Adieu, dear mother, we are going to be martyred.'

" The mother was weeping at the instant as if her very

heart would break ; but fearing to discourage her children, or cast the shadow of her own maternal grief over their coming hour of trial, she embraced them, saying—

"'Go, dear children, and, remembering Him who died for you, tread courageously in the footsteps of your father and uncle. Behold them stretching out their arms to help you : behold the saints and angels, with crowns prepared to set upon your heads : behold Jesus Christ Himself inviting you to his most sweet embrace : and when you reach the place of execution, shew yourselves to be indeed his followers, by your contempt of death. Fall on your knees, loosen your collars, join your hands, bow down your heads, and cry out, Jesus ! Mary ! with your latest breath. Oh, how wretched am I that I cannot be with you in that hour !"

"Then," continues this letter, "hiding her face in the arms of her little ones, the poor mother burst into an uncontrollable fit of weeping, moving the very soldiers to such compassion, that, fearful of yielding to their sufferings, they tore the children from her embraces, and almost threw them into the palanquin which was to convey them and their grandmother to the place of execution. During the short transit thither, that venerable Christian took care to occupy the little victims in prayer and pious ejaculations ; nor did she cease her guardian care when they reached the fatal spot, for she stood and saw them one by one butchered before her eyes ; and then, advancing with a grave and stately pace, she, in her turn, submitted to the sword."

Truly so touching a story has not been written since the days of the first Christian persecutions ; and yet it is but one of many to be found in these letters, *the truth of which in the main, even allowing that they may be slightly coloured, is beyond doubt.*

To resume, however, my narrative. In less than an hour the lady again sent for me. She had recovered from the violence of her emotions, and having hastily told that tragedy which I have repeated in detail, she continued—

"Of the three who had been spared, the mother died

of grief, the son and daughter were detained in the
palace in honourable confinement, but day by day expecting their doom. That doom, however, was averted.
Yes, with grief, with shame be it said, by the brother,
who, to save his own life, and that of his sister, became
an apostate, and, as his reward, was appointed to an
office about the tyrant's person. In the fierceness of
his nature, however, he had resolved to slay the king,
and one day, while hunting, made the attempt. He
failed, was seized, and condemned to the mutilation òf
his right hand. He suffered the punishment, and then
appeared so repentant that he was again taken into
favour ; and thus, throwing the tyrant off his guard, by
the aid of the good Father Rodriguez, he rescued his
sister, and, together, the three escaped by night to a
Spanish ship in the harbour.

"Once on board the friendly vessel, the good father,
who had suffered many pangs that one of so goodly a
family of martyrs should have endangered his soul by
apostacy from the faith, implored of him to seek re-
baptism, and his sister, upon her knees, aided the father,
but the wild youth, sullenly turning to the father, said—

"'Say, O priest ! is it permitted to the followers of
Christ to seek revenge for deadly injuries to their
honour?' and the reply being in the negative, the youth
said—

"'Then, O my father, will I not return unto thy flock
until my honour has been satisfied ;' and after this his
re-conversion was never alluded to, even by the father."

"But that Spanish ship?" said I inquiringly, remembering Father Rodriguez's story.

"Was commanded by Pessoa. That youth was my
brother ; and so far thou hast heard the history of the
unfortunate Mary, to whom the great God, for some wise
purpose, has denied the crown of martyrdom, for which
she longed."

"May heaven forfend, lady, that such should be thy
fate. So much beauty, so much earnestness and enthusiasm, were intended by God to benefit the world by its
existence, not by its annihilation."

" Sama, thou hast not the warm blood of Japan in thy
veins, nor canst thou be of the goodly material from
which martyrs are made, so thou canst not believe that
I exist but to perform a mission."

" May Heaven forgive me, lady, for preaching such an
unchristian doctrine, but truly thy real mission should
be revenge upon those who have caused such suffering to
thee and thine."

" It is, it is : thou art right, Sama, it is revenge ; but
of such a goodly revenge, that even the proud children
of the sun-goddess have never dreamt of ;" and as she
spoke, her eyes sparkled, her brow seemed bold, and her
limbs quivered in every fibre. " But," she said, " MY
story has really to come. Listen, Sama ;" and she then
repeated what the father had before told us, viz.—

" The day after we had been taken on board the ship,
the tyrant sent an envoy demanding that we should be
given into his hands, which, after some negociations for
our future safety, was done ; and, greatly to our surprise,
we were received with courtesy, nay, installed in our old
ranks in the palace, my brother near the person of the
king, and myself near that of the queen, to whom, indeed,
we were partly indebted. The real cause, however, of
the change in the tyrant's temper was the death of
Tiego-Sama, which happened about that time ; for upon
his demise the great Regent Ogosho held the power of
the state, and it was known to all that he was not only
favourable to the Christians, but greatly loved the good
Father Rodriguez.

" Then a heaven-like happiness seemed to be dawning
over the land : the war in Corea was stopped ; the Christian princes and their followers called home ; and thus
the almost expiring church became revived, for the cross
was once more held aloft, churches were built, and the
doctrines of Christ preached aloud ; as for our tyrant, he
also seemed to be about to become a convert.

" It was shortly after this, O Sama, that thou and thy
companions were cast upon the shores of Bungo, and that
the two kings and their courts visited the ship, and then
so much of evil was there left in the nature of the young-

est, that, but for his father and the noble queen, thou wouldst have been crucified ; and, indeed, that thou wert ultimately saved was entirely owing to the jealousy of the growing influence of Pessoa with Ogosho, that had arisen in the king's heart.

" But to conclude my story. When Ogosho had defeated the first attempts of the nobles and princes who resisted his usurpation of the supreme power, he turned his attention to the trade with foreigners, which he wished to encourage for the good of the empire. Amongst the leading Portugals in the nation was this Pessoa, who being brought much into his presence, at length had the hardihood to demand permission to marry a Japanese lady, as had done several of his countrymen. Ogosho sanctioned the demand, giving him a written permission, but without naming any lady. Taking advantage of this, Pessoa filled up the blank with my name, and then returning to Bungo, impudently demanded of the king that I should be given to him in marriage. But, enraged at this great presumption, the king drove him from the palace, threatening to destroy him and his ship ; and about that time the young king was promoted to be King of Tango, and, moreover, to the government of Fuisimi. For security against the plans and schemes of Pessoa, he conveyed me with him to that castle ; and because he knew that in my heart I must detest him for his cruelties to my family, I was kept in a kind of splendid imprisonment with him, and apart from my noble mistress, who was at the court of Ogosho. With him I travelled in a norimon from the castle to Seruga, and then my heart leaped with joy, for I thought to be once more with the queen. Alas ! I was disappointed, for' my protectress, my friend, had left that city for Jeddo.

" Upon our arrival at Seruga, great was the king's vexation to find the Spaniard at the court of Ogosho, in the character of an envoy from his sovereign, the King of Spain ; and as to ruin him in the emperor's favour was the great object of his heart, he laid bare the plans that they had long before concocted together to get thee and thy companion crucified, and, thus, by the quarrel be-

tween these two bad men, wert thou saved; but then
happened, also, his great opportunity to increase his own
riches and power.   Although, by having one castle and
town within the dominions of the king, my father had
been his subject, and so within his power, the greater
part of his wealth and lands being within the province
of Quanto, over which Ogosho held hereditary rule, the
bulk of his wealth, at his murder, became at the mercy of
Ogosho, the liege lord : so to obtain these into his own
hands, he besought two things of the emperor ; first, that
for my brother's attempt upon his life, which he had himself so severely punished, he should be denied all right
to the succession ; and secondly, that I should become
the wife of his infant son."

  " Nay, it is not possible that the generous Ogosho
should have granted these monstrous demands," I said.

  " Sama, Ogosho could not do otherwise, for war has
again burst forth : the great admiral of the empire, Tsucamidono himself, one of the guardians of the Kubo-
Sama, Fide Yori, is in arms at the head of a vast army ;
so Ogosho complied, rather than strengthen the already
strong force of his enemies by another king : indeed, it
was only after the king's audience with Ogosho that I,
for the first time, became aware of his long-brooded
schemes.   It was then he told me that the emperor had
resigned his right of guardianship over me into his hands ;
that he was about setting out with the army to meet the
rebels to the authority of Ogosho ; and lastly, that upon
the very next day the marriage ceremony should be performed.   Stunned with the intelligence, I spoke not ; and
deeming me sufficiently humble and submissive to his will,
he departed from the palace, leaving me without restraint.
Recovering my self-possession, I sent for the good Father
Rodriguez, told him my fears for the safety of my brother,
who was at Jeddo, and whose death-warrant I could not
doubt had gone forth, for the tyrant will no longer permit one to live who may at any time become reinstated
in the great prince's favour ; but that which, to me, was
the most terrible, was, that my vows to heaven of a life
fo charity and devotion to God and the church, might be

foully broken, and I involuntarily become guilty of per-
jury that would ruin my soul."

At the last words, I know not why, a chill, a dull heavy
sensation, fell upon my heart ; but I said nought, and the
lady continued—

" The good man counselled my escape to Jeddo."

" To Jeddo, lady ! it is even to that city Ogosho and
his court are now hastening."

" To Jeddo, Sama, and for three reasons ; first, that I
may put my brother upon his guard; secondly, that I may
ask counsel of my beloved friend, the queen ; and lastly,
that after secreting myself for a sufficient time, I may, if
necessary, demand justice at the feet of Ogosho, who,
when state-policy no longer darkens his memory, may
remember that my father, the Christian Lord Thomas,
was once the friend of his heart. Ah, me ! I determined
upon adopting the father's advice, and would have traversed the whole distance in the disguise of a bikuni
(begging-nun), begging my way step by step over mountain and hill."

" Nay, lady, such would indeed have been martyrdom,
for it would have killed thee," I said, gazing on her fragile frame, which still quivered with excitement. But
looking me steadfastly in the face, with something that
in another visage I would have called scorn, she replied :—

" Sama, I am told that the people of the western sky
are brave ; what then are their women ? have they the
souls of mice ? But it must be so, or thou wouldst not
have uttered such words. I tell thee, the women of
Japan are fit to be the mothers of heroes ; for when their
goal is before them, like the hunted deer, they fly toward
it, never stopping till they reach it, or are overtaken by
death."

" Nay, lady, thy heroic spirit would have succumbed ;
thy fragile strength——"

" Not so, Sama, the Spirit of the great God is in my
heart ; and even as he lent aid to the sainted Xavier, to
traverse the pathless wilds, scale mountains, and wend
his way through cities filled with scoffers, without guide

or money, foot-sore, ill-clad, and starving, so would he
have strengthened the limbs of a weak but fervent girl,
the energies of whose soul are devoted to His service ;
but," she continued, "it was not the will of the great
God that I should thus be put upon my trial.   The good
father procured me the habit of an idolatrous Canusis,
(which may Heaven forgive me for wearing) ! and so
placed me at thy mercy and honour."

"Where thou art as sacred, lady, as if in the arms of
thy parents, for thy will shall be our law : command, and
thou shalt be obeyed."

"Enough !" she replied, with a queenly air ; "and as
the Sama would merit my gratitude, wherever he may
meet her let him forget that he had ever seen her before,
and the poor hunted girl may yet find the opportunity of
repaying him, or his countrymen, for this service."   And
thus ended this strange conference.

CHAPTER XV.

I MEET WITH AN UNPLEASANT SURPRISE, BUT SAVE A KING'S LIFE.

"BESHREW me, Master Melichor, but I am no less envious of thy long confessional, than consuming with curiosity to know the history of thy fair penitent," said Will
laughing, as I rejoined him in the cabin.

"But hast no curiosity to know the name of our fair
passenger, Master Adams ?"

"No, Melichor, by mine honour, no ; for, I take it, the
women are much alike throughout this queer land."

"Nay, thou art wrong, Master Adams : the Lady Mary
is like no other woman in the world," said I.

"The Lady Mary ! what meanest thou ?"

"That it is she who wears the guise of a Canusis," and
as I repeated to Will the leading points in the history I

had just heard, he listened attentively, exclaiming, as I concluded—

" God's mercy ! 't is a sad tale. Poor lass ! poor lass ! But it was sorry management of the Jesuit not to have entrusted us with the secret. Did he think, a murrain on him, that we should have done her harm, or have refused our aid ? Tut, tut, these Jesuits, like moles, seem born to grope their way alone in the dark."

" Again thou art prone to do the good father an injustice, for while to keep her secret might have been to the lady's advantage, it could not injure us," said I.

But as Master Adams was at that moment called away about the navigation of the ship, the conversation was suddenly dropped, nor was it resumed, for, by reason of the rocks, channels, and foul weather, he had enough to occupy his mind the remainder of the voyage.

In five more days, after a dangerous and very tedious passage, we reached within a few miles of the city of Jeddo, and, by night, the lady and her servant went ashore in a small boat, and that in such regular order that none on board, with the exception of Master Adams and myself, could have had the slightest suspicion that she was other than what she seemed. The next day we arrived at Jeddo, a city in which we were destined to live for ten years, and that, too, with so few events of importance happening, that I will hasten over that time as briefly as I may.

Upon our arrival we found that Ogosho and his court had reached the city some days earlier. So great was the exultation of Master Adams—for he never doubted that we should now receive permission to leave the country— that at the earliest opportunity he craved and obtained an audience of Ogosho ; but although that prince received him with favour, and, moreover, made another gift of money to our company, he still refused us his permission to quit the land. Many months passed away, keeping us all in a state of suspense ; by reason of which idle life, several of our men growing mutinous, demanded that, as officers and men were prisoners alike, and therefore of the same rank, each should be his own commander, and

that the money given by the emperor should be at once
equally divided among us all : so, as there was no law to
prevent, and the native authorities would not interfere,
the money was divided, and each became at liberty to go
his own way within the land, which, for some reason,
must have been pleasing to the emperor, for thereupon
he ordered that each alike should receive a yearly pension
in money and rice.   This kindness, however, I afterwards
discovered had been obtained by the intercession of
Master Adams, who day by day grew in the favour of
the emperor, and this by reason that his majesty took
great delight in the mathematics, geometry, and the art
of navigation, all of which Master Adams was fully competent to teach : indeed, by the end of the two years, notwithstanding that he could not get permission to leave
the country, so powerful had he become at court, that
even our old enemies the Portugals and Spaniards, were
necessitated to apply to the English pilot for any favour
they wished to crave of Ogosho, and by granting these
demands, which he did in most instances, Master Adams
set them an example, by returning much good for the
great evil they had done, and the greater they had attempted to do him and his companions.

Now Ogosho, being loth to be far apart from his
English teacher, bestowed upon him a small residence
within the walls of the palace, and which adjoined the
great house occupied by the King of Tango while the
latter prince was in attendance at court, and in this house,
during the two tedious years I have chronicled, did I pass
my time, living for the greater part—that is, with the
exception of the small pension allowed to me by the
emperor—upon the charity of my friend Master Adams,
himself by no means well to do, for at that time the
emperor had conferred little but the honour of his countenance upon him, and this caused me to become very
restless and unhappy ; for inasmuch as none but enemies'
ships came to the land, I had resigned all hope of returning to Holland or England.   I longed for some active
employment, not only for the good of my body and

the Lady Mary, who, with shame I confess, had certainly
weakened the impress that had been made upon my heart
in England, and this much-desired occupation came to me
at length, after the following manner :—

I have said that the great house of the King of Tango
adjoined that allotted to Master Adams : it did, but it
was upon the side of the large and magnificent garden,
from which it was separated by a deep, wide, vast ditch.
Now, by the side of this ditch I was wont' to wander
alone, meditating upon the past, and the probability of
my ever again reaching Europe.   Well, one evening, as it
was nearly dusk, while peering into the beautiful gardens
upon the opposite side, I saw some person stealthily
approaching the edge, indeed, so stealthily, that my curiosity became excited, for those were the king's private
gardens, and I watched his movements narrowly.   He
came nearer.   Surely, I thought, that figure is known to
me, although indistinct by reason of a row of cypress
trees.   Still cautiously he walked onward : I kept pace.
At length we both reached a spot where upon each side
was a huge tree, whose boughs and foliage met and
became entangled with each other.   In an instant, as if
it had been the rigging of our caravel, I clambered up
the trunk, and then, through a break in the foliage,
recognised, after a period of nearly two years, the features
of—the Lady Mary !   Why was she there, and in the
same garb, too, that she had worn when on board our
ship ?   If again in the power of the King of Tango, why
that disguise ?   But after a moment I remembered her
vow of revenge ; and knowing the thirst, the panting,
undying longing for revenge that forms so great an ingredient in the nature of the Japanners, my heart sick-

knew not; and then, partly, perhaps, from the prickly
thorns which had drawn my blood, and partly from some
little fear at being found where I became suddenly conscious I had really no right to be, I became somewhat
alarmed.   My fears for myself, however, quickly vanished
in my admiration of the beautiful scene around me,
which, notwithstanding the mantle of night was gradually
enveloping the landscape, I could see.

The gardens, which were about one English mile
square, were dug out of the earth, or might have been a
cistern, and were reached from the castle by a balustraded
flight of stone steps; the walks were paved with sea-
pebbles, of variegated colours, while the trees, flowers,
and flowering shrubs were of the rarest kind, many being
twisted by art into very fantastic shapes, some being
gigantified to several times their natural size, and with
their branches growing into the back-windows of the
castle, while others were dwarfed into mere miniatures.
Then a pellucid stream ran murmuring through the whole,
the banks of which were decorated with artificial rocks
and fountains, from which leaped gold and silver fish, the
work being studded with gilded imitations of butterflies
and other insects.   Then there was a beautiful mia, or
temple, dedicated to the king's patron saint; and this
temple, which was surrounded with tall, bushy, flowering
shrubs, stood within a few yards of the bathing-house,
which, from the issuing steam, I could see was being
used, and probably by the king himself.   The latter
thought awakened me to the necessity of caution; so I
crouched down among the shrubs, there to remain till
the occupant of the bathing-house had taken his departure, and greatly vexed that I had allowed the person
whom I believed to be the Lady Mary to draw me into
these forbidden grounds.   Scarcely, however, had I, as I
thought, hidden, when the door of the bath-house stood
open, and the keen, black eye of a slave seemed fixed
upon my hiding-place.   As, however, he almost immediately returned within the house, I hoped that he had not
seen me; but the door again opened, and the king came
forward, attended by the same slave, to whom, as he

came from the house, his majesty gave some command, when, with the bound of a wild-cat, the slave instantly sprang upon the shrub, and clutching me by the throat, dragged me forward to the feet of the king, who, however, to my great surprise, no sooner recognised in me one of the foreigners he had befriended, than he laughed outright, perhaps at my distress, perhaps with joy to find no greater enemy : but be that as it may, he at once commanded the slave to unhand me ; and well for him that he did so, for the next moment the words—"Die, thou slayer of women and children," hissed through the air, and a glittering cattan would have stricken his head from his shoulders, had not my hand arrested the assassin's arm, and so turned the weapon, that the flat side felled him to the earth stunned.

Foiled in the attempt, and taking advantage of the care which the slave and I were taking of the king, the assassin fled, where no one ever knew ; but that assassin, —it was the Canusis, the Lady Mary whom I had

watched, and who had been hiding within the temple till
the king should quit the bath-house : and thus, as my
fears had been right, so had my hopes to save her from
the crime being strangely realized; and that neither king
nor slave had recognised her seemed certain, for her face
was hidden by the darkness, and the thin dark veil that
hung from her cap.

Now by reason of the blow from the cattan having
been very heavy, the king was nearly an hour before he
came to his senses : then, however, having given many
orders, and offered a large reward for the discovery of the
assassin, he turned to me, saying—

" As for thee, O stranger of the western skies, the gods
must have sent thee into the garden for our protection :
therefore attend us in the morning, and great shall be thy
reward."

Then, rejoicing at the king's ill-wind which had blown
me good fortune—for notwithstanding his majesty's laugh
at my discovery in the bush, I verily believe it was his
intention to punish me, I made my bow—and left the
apartment into which we had conveyed the king from the
garden.   As, however, I was passing through one of the
great ante-rooms, I had to stand aside for the queen, who,
having heard of her husband's danger, was about visiting
him, attended by her ladies, in one of whom imagine my
astonishment to see the Lady Mary, not now in the dress
in which she had attempted the assassination, but in the
ceremonial attire of a court lady ; but, alas ! no longer
with bold, firm step, bright eyes, and face mantling with
the rich blood of health.   No ; the eyebrows were knitted
together, the lips pale, the step faltering : indeed, she
seemed an altered being : then her voice also was changed,
at least so it seemed, for, passing near, very near to me,
she appeared to hiss rather than speak—

" Be silent, O Sama !" but the look—it haunts me now
—was one that implored silence. She passed onward. I
left the castle in a dream—aye, a horrible dream—a
waking nightmare. Was it possible that I could have
been bewitched by a being, a woman, whose life was devoted to so foul a mission as murder ? a crime that, in my

eyes, the tyranny of the king and the sufferings of the lady could not justify. Again, was I not an accomplice? knowing, but not divulging whose hand it was that for ever held the sword of Damocles over the sovereign's head : and that Master Adams discovered not my secret was a wonder, for when, upon returning to his home, he accosted me—

" Fie, fie, Melichor, to look thus like a man about to be keel-hauled, when it is said thou hast made thy fortune by preventing an act which, villainous as it was, would have done the world some good."

" Made my fortune ?" I repeated, for want of other words.

" Thy fortune, aye, for truly thy longing for some active service, will now be gratified by this King of Tango, as a requital for thy good service, and yet thou art as glum as if thou wert the accomplice instead of the frustrater of this assassin."

" An accomplice ?" I repeated with a start, for the words were ringing in my mind.

" Tut, tut, Melichor ; canst thou do nought but echo ? truly thy wits are a little out of order ; so at present we will no more of this, but make a stoup of saki, and drink to the health of our friends at home, for I, too, have news."

" Hast got permission for us to quit this accursed land ?" asked I.

" Nay, I said not that ; yet is it both good and bad : good, as thou shalt hear hereafter ; but bad, inasmuch as it bringeth the death of the gallant Master Davis, who, when we left the Texel, was about sailing under the Stadtholder's commission, with Houteman's fleet, and, moreover, who was as brave a seaman as ever set foot on sea-plank."

" Aye, aye, Master Adams : he who made the two voyages in '55 and '56 in search of a North-West passage ? But this is sad news. But how couldst thou have got it ?" said I.

" Listen, Melichor, and hear how that these smiling, loving knaves are nought but a race of bloodhounds thieves," said Will. Then continuing. "From what I can make out from a certain knave pilot, who has but recently reached Jeddo, it appears he was engaged some two years ago by a party of ninety Japanners, chiefly nobles, to sail with them in the quality of pilot, he being a seaman ; that is, as seamen are here. Now the purpose of these knaves seems to have been pirating ; and so they directed their course along the coasts of China and Cambodia, but without meeting with any success; till at length they foundered upon the coast, but no lives were lost, and being in so goodly a number, they seized upon a smaller junk, in which, much discouraged, they endeavoured to make for home, and so, between Bantam and Batavia, they fell in with a ship, which I make out to be the 'Tiger,' commanded by Master Davis. Well, upon this meeting many civilities took place. Then some of my countrymen went on board the junk, and some twenty-six of the Japanners aboard the 'Tiger,' and together they feasted and drank. The piratical Japanners, however, in the junk, having concerted measures beforehand, set upon their visitors, the Englishmen, and slew all who could not jump overboard. At the same time the others boarded the 'Tiger,' and fought with such fierceness and courage, that they seemed to throw themselves upon the English pikes, and even when the men of the 'Tiger' had driven them from the half-deck down into the main cabin, they there fought with such obstinacy that the combat lasted five hours, when finding that they should be beaten, they set the cabin on fire, and continued to fight with the flames roaring about their ears. Then Master Davis, fearing they would fire the whole ship, brought down a couple of great guns loaded with cross-bars, bullets, and case shot, and did such execution among them, that one only out of twenty-two escaped, the rest being torn and shattered to pieces. The victory, however, was dearly purchased, for in the fire the greater part of the 'Tiger's' men were slain, and with them the gallant Master Davis, my old comrade and shipmate. The only one who escaped was the pilot, who threw himself into the sea, and, after

floating about for a day and a_, night, was picked up by a
Chinese junk, by which means he has arrived in Jeddo:
but now, Melichor," he added, with a great tear upon his
weather-beaten cheek, "a cup of saki to the memory of
an old shipmate, as gallant a gentleman and as good a
navigator as ever lived."

"But the good news," said I, when we had drunk to
the memory of Captain Davis; "the good news: hast
then persuaded the emperor to let us depart?"

"Nay, nay,—not all, but one, one alone: with me he
will not part, nor with any but Master Quackernack, who,
when he pleases, may sail in the next Chinese junk which
leaves Firando."

"Then out upon such news an' thou callest it good,"
said I.

"Nay, nay; thou art impatient, Melichor: the wind
may blow from that quarter yet; so, as we can't get what
we would, let us take what we may, and herein lies the
good. The Captain, Master Quackernack, will carry with
him this writing;" and so saying, Will pulled forth from
his pocket, a letter written in fair large characters, and
ingeniously addressed—

"To my unknown friends and countrymen, desiring
this letter, by your means, or the news, or copy of this
letter, may come into the hands of one or many of my
acquaintances in Limehouse, or elsewhere, or in Kent,
in Gillingham by Rochester."

The contents of this letter, which has since become
famous as the cause by which the English first reached
Japan, were a complete history of our voyage and troubles since leaving Holland, with further particulars of all
the advantages the merchants might obtain by sending
their ships to that empire. This letter, moreover, contained another directed to his wife; and as Will read the
contents of that to me, his bold face became flushed, and
tears rolled down his cheeks, for which he attempted an
excuse after the following fashion—

"Look you, Melichor, when God gives tears to a man,
I believe it's to make him feel a little better than a man.
Like a woman, it may be—God bless 'em; so that we

should know what a woman feels : and, hark ye ! I believe there is some invisible string between husbands and
wives, who are parted lovingly, so that, being pulled at
the same time, they shed tears together, and now it's my
belief my wife is crying at the same indefinite hope that
we shall meet again,—God bless her.   I never knew how
much I loved her, and the children, till, after having resigned all hope of ever seeing them again, it glimmers
once more, like a little star upon a dark night."

Now I have to chronicle little else of that night, than
that we both shed tears till we grew ashamed of each
other ; that we drank more saki than was good for us,
but greatly pleasing to our Japan servant, who had
hitherto been disgusted at our temperance ; that we went
to our beds dreaming of home ; and that in my dreams I
concocted a letter for Maud Saris, which the next day,
from memory, I copied out in a fair bold hand.

CHAPTER XVI.

I AM APPOINTED TO A POST IN THE KING OF TANGO'S
HOUSEHOLD, AND MAKE A JOURNEY WITH THE QUEEN.
—WILL REMAINS AT THE COURT OF THE EMPEROR.

" THERE is at least, then, one good thing indigenous to
the land of Japan, and that is the goodly plant gratitude,"
said I to Master Adams, the next morning after my interview with the kinglet of Tango.

" Hast then found the road to fortune as I promised
thou shouldst ?"

" Aye, even so, if it be the same which leads to Osacca,
to which city I am to go with the queen, in whose suit
this kinglet hath given me an office, which hath in it
something of a captain of guards, a little of the footman,
and much of the spy."

" A spy ! lad, it is not a goodly office."

" Aye, Master Adams, for although rather hinted than
insisted upon, it is expected that I shall keep watch upon

the movements of that sweet lady, the queen, of whom
this king seems mighty jealous."

" Jealous ! then by my honour his majesty shews but
little wisdom by entrusting her to the charge of a goodly-
looking lad like thee," said Will laughing ; adding, " then
the king goes not himself to Osacca ?"

" Nay, he cannot ; for to-morrow he leaves this place
for a distant province, which is now invaded by the rebel
regents, whom he is to keep amused till the great Ogosho,
having paid his first state visit to the Mikado, can rejoin
him. But sadly it grieves me, Master Adams, that after
so many toils and much suffering together, our courses
are now to turn to opposite points of the compass."

" True, lad, true ; it grieves me : still, we may not
complain, but endeavour to shape our course to the wind
that blows, and wait patiently till we may quit this barbarous land."

" True, Master Adams ; yet since thou art in such
favour with the emperor, he might, for the asking, give
thee leave to shape your course to Osacca, for the golden
cobangs of this King of Tango will suffice both our
wants."

" Nay, Master Melichor ; it is better that I should remain here, where, in due time, I may yet serve thee, our
countrymen, and myself to boot, for but this morning the
wise Ogosho sent for me to the palace, and set me a task,
the doing of which, although it will require all my wits,
when done, may advantage all."

" Would he have thee teach him the English tongue ?"
I asked.

" Nay, nay ; thou canst not guess. It was this. First
he told me that he had ordered my pension to be increased to a sum sufficient to support me here after the
fashion of a general ; then he desired that I would build
him a ship after the English fashion ; and so determined
is he to have his will, that when I told him I was no
carpenter, and ignorant of the craft, he laughed, and
asked me what I had done with my eyes, when so many
had been built just beneath my nose, as I had often told
him when answering his questions about my birth-place

and bringing up : to which, as I could but reply that I had not learned the craft, he laughed again, and bid me set about the work at once, saying—

" ' Let the auge (pilot) command the emperor's servants to find him all he wants in material, and men, and money, and set about the work. Let him do his endeavours as if he was serving a friend ; and if, after all, it be not good, no matter.' "

" A right good answer ; and did I prevent thee doing him so great a service, I should be as much thine enemy as I am now thy friend, for the ending must be good."

" Aye, Melichor, for it may earn us our liberation from this land, and be the means of establishing a commerce for our countries, a thing that is at my heart, no less to spite these selfish Portugals and Spaniards, than for the benefit of those who have English and Dutch blood in their veins. So we will even pass this night together as jovially as if we had just made a safe harbour and a profitable port for our merchandise." So, after the fashion of the previous evening, we whiled away the hours more in merriment than in wisdom.

The next morning I received from the King of Tango, by way of present, a wardrobe befitting one who had now the right of wearing two swords, and held an office in a great man's household ; and, indeed, my habiliments fully required this reinforcement, for, but for the kindly offices of a series of strings which held them together, they would long before have parted company ; and such was my pleasure at the gift, that by dint of constant practice I soon learned to wear loose gowns and straw shoes, whose only attachment to the feet was by means of buttons between the toes ; but to get accustomed to the fan, which is as much a part of the Japanner as his own head, and has imprinted upon it a list of roads, and the fares of public carriages, norimon men, and public porters, I had no small difficulty, for it was ever in my head that a fan was as seemly in the hands of a sailor, as the farthingale and kirtle of a tirewoman. However, determined to make the best of the matter, I kept the thing stuck in the girdle of my petticoat robes, packed the remainder in a kind of trunk, which the Japanners call an adofski, and which the servants fastened upon my horse, took a hearty leave of Master Adams, who wished me " God's speed," and repaired to the palace of the King of Tango, where I found the procession, for that it was, rather than a travelling suite, ready to set out.

Thus was I fairly established in the service of the *King* of Tango. I have hitherto, and shall throughout this writing, give that prince and others of his rank the royal title ; but that my readers may not understand that to mean a person of so great importance as the sovereigns of Europe, they must know that the Japanners call them Tonos, and that the title of king was bestowed upon them by the Portugals, because, although few possessed greater wealth than an English earl—for instance, my Lord of Leicester, Southampton, or Suffolk—they each possessed sovereign power, such as making war, and that of life and death over the lords, barons, and meaner sort within their realms ; although, at the same time, they were subject in the like manner to the richest and most powerful prince of their own order, who, although sometimes called the Kubo-Sama, as was the young Fide Yori, then in honourable imprisonment at Osacca, sometimes the Tycoon, and at others the Ziogoon, still, by whichever name, was and is a despotic prince, *nominally* acting as the lieutenant-general of the *nominal* emperor or Mikado, but positively *over* the prince who holds the latter ancient and sacred title, and is sole despot of the realm.

Now the moving of the court and retinue of one of these kinglets is not to be imagined by those who have not witnessed the like, except indeed they have seen the march of an army of some twenty thousand persons, and to that it may be compared, if we omit the commissariat and cooking utensils, for the meals are provided on the road at the different towns and cities through which it is to pass ; and as this may be done in proper order and with decency, moreover, so that at no one place two of these great retinues may meet, messengers are sent onwards a week, a fortnight, and frequently a

11

month before, in order to stick up in the public places, placards announcing that at such and such a time the king or great lord will pass through, or stop at a particular place ; further, to give timely notice to the keepers of the public inns, that they may be prepared to supply the necessary food, for all of which, I must add, these tradesmen are paid a fair and liberal price, according to the bills of fare set down by the laws of the empire.

Now by reason that the King of Tango wanted all the force he could muster for the wars, the retinue of his queen was but small, consisting indeed of but four thousand persons ; still this number, as they did but march at the rate of four miles a day, took a considerable time to pass through the gates of Jeddo : indeed, the last body, for they were divided into companies of from one to four hundred, did not leave the city till the following day. With that body, however, which formed the immediate guard and attendants of the queen and her court ladies, and consisted of at least a thousand persons, I travelled, about five hundred yards in advance of the queen's norimon, or state chair, on a led horse, by the side of an officer, who commanded the party, and was also upon a led horse. This person was an elderly man, of goodly looks and bearing, that is, for a Japanner, a chadamodo, or noble of the first rank, and called Yorimon Dono, the first word being his surname, and the latter his title of courtesy, which, like the word Sama, when appended, had the signification of lord, or sir. Moreover, from his golden spurs of European make, and the golden medal, and heavy chain of the same metal, which hung upon the linked armour which covered his breast, I conjectured that he must have been one of the nobles who accompanied the two young princes as ambassadors to the Pope, in '82, and with whom he had received, from the hands of Sixtus the Fifth, the knighthood of the gilded spurs ; and my conjecture was correct, for I soon found that he was called by the name given to him at the baptismal font by the Jesuit father, *i.e.* Martin, and thus was he always called by Europeans *Sir* Martin, a title of which he was ever proud, justly, perhaps, deeming a Christian knighthood of greater honour than his Japan lordship.

Well, as I have said, by the side of Sir Martin of the Golden Spurs I rode, and that, too, a long and wearisome time, along great roads, across mountains, including the sides of that wonder of the world, the Fudsi Jamma, which these Japanners so honour, that they have it painted upon their fans, the walls of their houses, and at the bottom of their culinary utensils, as if, forsooth, they were never weary of gazing at it. This mountain is of wondrous height, and is an extinct volcano, and was to me chiefly amusing, from the fact that the jammaboos, or mountain priests, spend a great part of their lives in ascending and descending its heights ; a toil which is considered by them to be a work of religious merit, and therefore commendable to the gods. Then the towns, villages, rivers, and roads, which I have before mentioned as being most to be admired and wondered at for their cleanliness and order, astonished me more on this journey by the vast multitudes of people to be found thereon, and the strange scenes to be witnessed, and which served greatly to cheer me, under the disappointment of not being able, in the slightest degree, to get a glimpse of the queen, or the ladies of the court, among whom I hoped to have seen the Lady Mary ; for notwithstanding the shock given to my feelings by her wicked and unwomanly attack upon the king, and, moreover, the hypocritical concern she had exhibited at his danger, when attending the queen so soon afterwards, those eloquent eyes, that pale brow, and queenly gait, still haunted me : and all this feeling I was convinced was disloyalty to the fair Maud in England ; but it was the truth, and so I confess it ; human nature is weak, and I was not better than my kind. At length, shaking off this desire to catch a sight of the lady, because I found all attempts fail, I found some amusement in the human nature which we met with at every turn, and which may serve my readers as a kind of panorama of the inhabitants of Japan.

First, then, not only were their superstitious

11—?

bespoken by the numerous images of gods and goddesses at every turn, and upon every hill, but upon the door of almost every hovel was painted a god. Upon others were affixed half sheets of paper, with the figure of the ox-headed, black-horned givon, the meaning of which is, the ox-headed prince of heaven, and which is placed there to charm away that terrible disease the small-pox. For the same purpose, as well as to frighten away other diseases, some doors were decorated with a monstrous figure of a countryman, all covered with hair, and with a huge sword in his hand, with which it was ready to battle with and keep off misfortunes of all kinds. Upon others were pictures of dragons, or devils, with open mouths, large teeth, and fiery eyes, whose frightful appearance they believe will keep off the envious from disturbing the peace of their families. Then, among the lesser charms, were branches of particular trees, to bring good luck, or keep off evil spirits; indulgence-boxes, called offari, made of thin boards, and filled with small sticks wrapped in pieces of white paper, which they purchase, upon their pilgrimage to the sacred town of Isye, of the Sintoo priests, and which, by being placed over the door, are believed to bring happiness and prosperity. Upon other doors were long slips of paper, with short prayers written thereon, and, indeed, many others too numerous to mention.

As for the living beings, who swarm upon these roads like bees, to say nothing of the processions of the princes, nobles, and government officers of all kinds you meet by turns, going to and fro, there are, firstly, three kinds of pilgrims, the chief of whom are those upon their way to Isye, to obtain remission of their sins, and purchase the indulgence-boxes, or offari, I have mentioned, and, for the greater part, being of the poorest kind, travel upon foot, crying to travellers, with bowed heads and low submissive voices, " Great lord, be pleased to give the poor pilgrim a senni towards the expense of his journey to Isye." And so great is the belief in the merit of these pilgrimages, that children, if fearful of punishment for their misbehaviour, will run away from their parents, go to Isye, fetch an offari, which, upon their return, is deemed a sufficient expiation of any fault they may have committed. Again, so numerous is this order of pilgrims, that hundreds are obliged to pass whole nights lying in the open fields, exposed to wind and weather, some for want of room in inns, others out of poverty, and numbers are found dead upon the road, when, if they have not their names and places of abode somewhere about their persons, as is the custom of all natives when they travel, for fear of sudden death, their offari, if it be on their return from Isye, is carefully taken up and hidden in the nearest bush or tree.

Then some of these Isye pilgrims are vagabonds and strollers, who thereby get their living, and have quaint conceits by which they seek to amuse : sometimes four will join together, all clad in white, in imitation of the kuge, that is, the courtiers of the sacred mikado, when two of the party will walk forward with a barrow, adorned with fir branches, and cut white paper, in which is placed a figure emblematic of some historic legend, whilst a third, carrying a commander's staff, and his person adorned with bunches of white paper, dances before the barrow, singing a song, and the fourth goes begging in the front of bonzes, or by the side of passing travellers.

Another kind of pilgrims is the siunse, a set of vagabonds who visit the thirty-three Quanwon temples which are spread over the empire. These people travel in parties of two or three, singing from house to house, and are clad in white, with beads hanging around their necks, upon which the names of their temples are written : and so easily do they get their living, that great numbers devote their lives to perpetual pilgrimages.

Then, again, there are to be met with many people upon private pilgrimages to particular temples, who run about, even in the hardest frosts, with no apparel whatsoever, saving a little straw about their waists : these miserable beings, however, are to be pitied as the victims of their superstitious paganism, for they make these painful journeys in pursuance of religious vows, which they

promise to fulfil in case they should obtain from the god
relief from some fatal disorder, for themselves, their
parents, or relations, or obtain deliverance from some
other great misfortune they were threatened with.   It is
necessary that these people should have good wind, for
they are almost perpetually running.

Those who are charitably disposed may well satisfy
their hearts, for the race of beggars is legion.   One tribe
of these have their heads shaven, and to it belong some
of the most comely damsels in Japan, who are of the
order bikuni, that is, nuns.   All of these girls are attached
to some one of the many nunneries at Meaco, or elsewhere, to which houses they pay a portion of their earn-
ings, by begging and otherwise, as an acknowledgment.
The greater part of them are the daughters of poor
parents, so that when I say, further, that none but those
who are handsome are admitted into the order, it will
serve as another proof of the ungodliness and immorality
of these people, whose *innocence* has been so much over-
praised by the Jesuit fathers, and *others of later date*, who
have written letters, but therein have unfairly said nothing of these things, nor that some of them are bred up
as courtesans, but, having served the time for which they
were apprenticed, buy the privilege of entering into this
religious order, there to spend the remainder of their
lives and beauty ; and the following is the fashion after
which they pursue their calling :—

They live two or three together, and make an excursion
every day a few miles from their houses, when they watch
for people of rank who travel in norimons, cangos, or on
horseback, and, facing one of these, they accost him,
singing rural songs ; and thus they procure so much
money, that although their heads are shaven after the
fashion of their order, they are enabled to dress themselves in caps or hoods of black silk, with a large hat and
rich quilted gowns, that the loss of hair is not noticed.

Another of the religious begging orders to be met with
in travelling in Japan, is that of the jammaboos, or mountain soldiers, so called because they are at all times
rmed with swords.   These do not shave their heads,

but follow the rule of the first founder of their order, who
mortified his body by climbing up high mountains.   They
have a general who resides at Meaco, to whom they are
bound to take yearly a sum of money, and who is their
fountain of honour, and distributes dignities among them.
On the road they are most commonly seen posted near a
temple, from whence they accost travellers in the name
of its patron *kami*, or saint, and as they give forth short
discourses, they, at the same time, rattle a long staff,
which is loaded at the upper end with iron rings, and at
intervals blow a trumpet made from a sea-shell.   Sometimes, indeed most frequently, they watch for a person
making the difficult ascent of a steep hill, when, knowing
they cannot easily escape, a troop of these jammaboos,
their children, and the before-mentioned bikuni, suddenly
pounce upon him, and with their rattling, singing, trum-
peting, chattering, crying, make such frightful noises,
that the poor pedestrian has but little choice between
bestowing alms or going out of his senses.   Another
means these begging priests have of making money, is by
telling fortunes, conjuring, and professing to discover
where lost goods may be hidden.

Other religious beggars are to be met with, shaven and
clad after the fashion of Buddhist priests, sitting or
standing, generally in pairs, pretending to read aloud
passages from their Fokekio, or Bible.   Others are found
sitting near running streams, making the *siegaki;* that is,
they take a green branch in their hands, and murmuring
some words with a low voice, wash and scour it with
shavings, upon which are written the names of certain
deceased persons, which they believe gives relief to the
souls confined in purgatory, and this they perform for
any person at the small charge of one senni.

Even now I have not done with the religious beggars,
for there are three other tribes.   One whose members sit
upon the road all day long, singing a hymn and beating
a bell with a hammer.   Another, the brotherhood of
which stand in the fields before a small altar, upon which
is placed an image of the god Quanwon, or the picture of
Amida, the supreme deity of departed souls, or Semaus,

the head keeper of the prison where the souls are confined, or of Dsisoo, the supreme commander in the purgatory of children ; and some others, wherewith, and by some representations of the flames and torments prepared for the wicked in a future world, they endeavour to move the passenger to charity.   Lastly, others stand by the roadside, pictures of misery and woe, having made a vow not to speak during a certain time.   Now whether it was that the countenances of these silent beggars were not sufficiently woe-begone and dejected, I know not, but certain I am, that their business prospered the least of all, which further convinced me of the truth of an old opinion of my own—that if virtue be its own reward, it must, in many instances, be very easily satisfied.

Then the religious orders, in Japan even, have not all the begging to themselves, for very numerous were those of the laity, and many were their claims to charity.   Some were sick and lame, a great number with sore eyes, a complaint so common in this country, that there is one, and have been two, very powerful orders of the blind, who are for the greater part the musicians of the country ; some decrepid, some very doleful, some very comical, others praying, some singing and playing upon what they believe to be musical instruments, and others flying wonderful kites, or performing juggling tricks.   But of a truth, to end this account of begging, there was a good sprinkling of every kind of beggar to be found in the whole world, and *herein* are these savage Japanners wonderfully civilized ; and I would establish the maxim, that the greater the number and ingenuity of beggars in a country, the greater must be its civilization.

But these beggars, religious and lay, are not the only pests upon the roads in Japan, for there are also swarms of minor tradespeople of both sexes, adults and children, who offer for sale almost every conceivable article of a small kind ; amongst others, pocket-gods, chiefly for the poorer class ; all kinds of eatables, cake, boiled roots, road-books, fans, straw shoes both for horse and man, ropes, and strings of the same material, tooth-picks, and many other things.

Then there are the letter-carriers, who run in couples, so that, should an accident happen to one, the other can proceed with his packages, and who at certain distances find relays to meet them ; and these men, or rather their business, is considered of such importance, that the train of the greatest prince must give way for them to pass. Then the numerous pack-horses and waggons drawn by oxen, for no oxen are killed or cow-milk is drunk in the country, it being considered,—apart from the Sintoo and Buddhist religions, which forbid the killing of such animals for food,—a sin to do the first, because they are useful as beasts of burden to man, and equally so to use milk, as God sent it alone for the nourishment of calves.

Then, among minor miseries—and minor only as regards the size of the animals—is the swarm of barking, snarling, cur dogs, who may not be removed, or even hurt, for they form a kind of corporation of themselves, being under a royal charter, and having an officer to guard their interests, and who alone may punish them when guilty of too much insubordination.

Having named the annoyances, I will mention one of the curious sights of the journey, namely, that of seeing the fields covered over with nets, to keep off the cranes, for, notwithstanding the mischief these birds do to the crops, to frighten one is a crime, but to kill one, except the slayer be the emperor, or the bird be for his majesty's own use, is punishable with death, and that because, like the tortoises, they are reckoned as happy animals in themselves, and are believed to portend good luck to others by reason of their long life ; and so great is the veneration that these people have for this bird, that the great and wealthy have pictures of them all about their houses, and the lower classes of men never speak of them except as " My great lord crane," which in their language is " O Tsurisama."

But to resume my narrative. It was after several days' travelling, and without meeting with any incidents worthy of note, excepting the quaint people themselves who crowd the roads, that we arrived at Meaco, one of the

most singular capital cities in the world, and which for
its greatness, luxury, and superstitious inhabitants, may
be likened unto Rome itself.

CHAPTER XVII.

MEETING OF THE ZIOGOON AND MIKADO.

As we entered the city, my head grew dizzy with the
noise and excitement, for the great streets were crowded
by the followers of nobles and princes, who were entering
from different quarters, with numberless artificers and
labourers, soldiers and servants.   Then the houses were
alive with bustle ; the public squares, the spacious porticos
of public buildings, were swarming with living creatures
engaged in the work of preparation for the coming sight
(the meeting of the two great potentates) : great scaffold-
ings were being erected upon every vacant space of
ground, and from the windows of the houses, shops, and
manufactories, at least all those which were in the direct
line through which the processions were to meet.   Houses
and streets were festooned with flowers, decorated papers,
and variegated lanterns ; idols of various shapes, repre-
sentatives of the different gods, were either being repaired, reburnished, or regilded ; stores of refreshments
were being laid in, wherewith to regale friends who were
expected from all parts of the empire.   New and magnificent umbrellas of state were being carried to the palaces
of the nobles, and fanciful fans to the houses of the well-
to-do, from the different workshops.   Gentlemen with
gilded arms upon their faded and well-worn garments,
two swords in their girdles, and pretensions which burst
through their means, and exposed their pride, were
strutting the streets in the vain endeavour to borrow for
themselves, or the one servant who walked behind, carrying an extra pair of straw shoes, some piece or pieces of
finery, and, alack ! in many instances, necessities.   Tradesmen, who, notwithstanding their great wealth, dared not

for their lives at other times to have been seen with that
mark of gentility—the sword—now, under the guise of
hiring themselves as servants to princes or nobles, were
gaily strutting home with one newly-purchased, and the
noble or princely badges which would enable them to
wear them in their girdles, and so pass through the meaner
and less-privileged crowds among the ranks of the soldiers : indeed, the din of preparation must have resembled that made by the people of the Netherlands for the
grand reception of Philip of Spain upon his first visit,
and when they thought, and tried to believe, they loved
the tyrant ; or those made by the good citizens of London
to receive Queen Elizabeth, when she went to the church
of Saint Paul to return thanks to God for the destruction
of that same tyrant's invincible armada.

Such was the din that assailed our ears, such the sight
that met our view, as we passed through the city to the
palace prepared for the Queen of Tango's reception, which
was, in fact, but an offshoot, or one of many palaces
which compose the great freestone fortress in the northern
quarter of the city, which, although once the dwelling of
the Mikado, had for a considerable time been set apart
for the residence of the Kubo-Samo Ziogoon, or Emperor,
as the Europeans name him, during his periodical state
visit to do homage to the holy Mikado, his nominal master,
but virtual slave.   Then, strangest of sights to be seen at
the head·quarter of heathendom, the very incarnation of the
Mikado and his sacred court of heaven-descended Kuge,
where, it is said, there are no less than five thousand
pagan temples, and countless images of Sintoo and Buddhist deities—was the great number of Franciscan and
Dominican priests, who, in defiance of the laws promulgated by the Emperor Tiego, had passed from Manilla
and New Spain into Japan, rebuilt churches and monasteries, and were then ardently seeking that martyrdom,
which, alas ! their insolence and audacity so soon after
procured them.

This Meaco, or Kio, as the Japanners call it, is situated
in a highly-cultivated plain, and is from north to south
about three miles long, and from east to west two miles

broad.   Its surroundings charm the eye, for they consist
of beautiful green hills and mountains (these being thickly
dotted with temples and images of gods), out of which
arise numerous rivulets and springs, all of which flow into
one great river, which runs its course, through the middle
of the city, where the united stream is crossed by a magnificent bridge.

Of the inhabitants, of whom there are nearly two millions, fifty thousand consist of dames of *more* than doubtful virtue, Sintoo priests, and the kuge, or members of
the Mikado's court.   This great city is the very seat and
head in Japan of all its virtues and vices, the very fountain from which the good and bad spring through the
land.   First, as the great magazine of manufactures ; for
there they refine copper, coin money (which bears the
arms of the Mikado), print books, weave the finest stuffs
with gold and silver flowers, make the rarest dyes, the
most ingenious carvings, musical instruments, pictures,
japanned cabinets, all things that are wrought of gold,
silver, copper, and steel, the richest and most costly dresses
—for in Meaco the fashion, if any fashion there be, is set
agoing—all descriptions of toys and puppets, whose heads
move of themselves : indeed, there is nothing that may
not be bought in Meaco, or if not to be bought there,
when introduced, however ingenious or clever it may be
in its construction, that an artisan cannot be found to
imitate and improve upon ; and as all articles produced
in this city are of great esteem throughout the empire,
nearly every other house is a shop, or a manufactory, and
the trade carried on is of fabulous amount.

This city is again the very fountain and mainspring of
the superstition of the empire ; for not only is it the
manufactory of ceremonials and forms, but of temples
and deities which meet the eye at every turn.   Its surroundings stupefy with the essence of heathenism ; its
newest suburb is remarkable for the number and magni-
ficence of its temples, one alone of which is said to contain a thousand idols, in the shape of hydras, men, birds,
devils, magicians, all with a larger or smaller number of
hands, arms, and legs : in another suburb is a mountain

inhabited alone by monks, whose laws are remarkable for
their severity, but whose town is a sanctuary for the most
flagrant rogues.

Meaco also boasts a Pantheon, which is accounted the
most magnificent building in Japan : this structure contains two thousand and six hundred statues of gilded
bronze, each in a splendidly decorated temple of its own,
many of these idols being representations of emperors
who have received deification. The greatest and most
magnificent of these is the Daybod, and which in size, as
well as cunning artifice, equals the great images of the
ancient Egyptians, for each thumb is so great that it could
not be embraced by the arms of the largest man, while
its feet, hands, mouth, eyes, forehead, and other features,
are in just proportion, and as perfect and expressive as
the portraits of the most renowned painters.

Another monument in this city is the magnificent temple
and tomb built by the Emperor Tiego.   The entrance-hall
is four hundred feet long, and three hundred feet wide,
and paved with jasper, while great pedestals of the same
material are placed at regular intervals upon either side :
at the end is the peristyle of the temple, which is ascended by a flight of steps.   Upon the right stands a
Sintoo monastery, the chief gate of which is encrusted
with jasper, overlain with ornaments elaborately wrought
out of silver and gold.   The nave of the temple is supported by lofty columns and pilasters : moreover, there
is a choir, like those in Romish cathedrals, with seats, and
a grating around, wherein male and female choristers
chant the prayers.   Within the temple the idol of the
great Tiego was worshipped as a god, while, in mockery
of the impiety, his son and heir, Fide Yori, was at the
same time held a prisoner in the great castle of the neighbouring town of Osacca.

Then Meaco is also the seat of the arts and sciences,
and in one quarter, in imperious pride, resides the highest
caste of the empire, viz., the kuge, nobles of the blood of
the Mikado.   These kuge, who are the only authors in
Japan, dress after a distinctive fashion, and are so proud
of their birth, that the great princes of the empire, upon

their journeys to and from Jeddo, invariably avoid Meaco, in order to avoid paying that homage, which any of these kuges, however beggarly, may by law demand, and the princes dare not refuse.

Much that is curious, and much that may be questioned, has been written about this Mikado, by people who, being themselves lovers of the marvellous, have liked to fill the wondering ears of others ; such, for instance, as that divine honours are paid to him : that he is not allowed to breathe the common air, nor his feet to touch the ground ; that he never wears the same robes twice, nor eats a second time from the same dishes, which, after each meal, are broken, for should any person attempt to use them he would be certain to die of inflammation of the throat ; neither are his beard, hair, or nails ever cut, poor gentleman ! except when he be asleep ; and, moreover, that so high and mighty is he in the world of spirits, as well as in that of mortals, that, annually, all the gods of Japan wait upon him, and spend a month at his court ; by reason of which the month in which their godships are presumed to be away from their several businesses, is called by the people by a name which signifies the month "without gods."

Now, that all this be true I will not vouch, indeed it is my fervent hope that it be not, for I should be right sorry that a gentleman existed in this world deserving of so much pity. As for the Japanners, they at least *pretend* to believe all this ; and certain it is, that to humour the people, the Ziogoon, or real emperor, has fairly divided the empire with the Mikado ; that is, he has made himself the substance to his holiness's shadow : for while the Mikado is at the head of the learned and priesthood, the Ziogoon commands the armies, and takes unto himself the revenues of the empire, at least all but those of Meaco, which, out of reverence for the Mikado, is held to be a separate and independent principality. Then, while divine honours are paid to the sacred prince, his time is considered to be of so much value to the gods, that the Ziogoon kindly manages for him the whole business of the kingdom. Again, all honours and titles spring from

the Mikado, but all pay and power is in the hands of the
Ziogoon, and no great war may be made, nor any important law be promulgated, without the Mikado being con-
sulted.   It is never known that he refuses his consent.
In fact, the Mikado is a great bladder of air, painted, decorated, and always floating a short distance from the
earth, revered by the people, who are superstitious ; regarded by the nobles and gentry as the fountain of honour ; titular alone, but of marvellous value in the eyes of
this vainglorious, proud race ; and kept afloat by the Ziogoon as a plaything, which, by amusing the minds of his
different subjects, may prevent them from looking too
narrowly into the source of his own rule, which was
originally derived from the Mikados when they were the
only emperors, and the Ziogoons their lieutenant-generals.
Moreover, it is possible that his holiness may be thankful
that so much business is taken from his hands : for, apart
from his multifarious duties of sitting still for many hours
a-day, without moving to the right or to the left, the
government of his numerous priests and literary relations
—who, it is reported, are the most difficult to keep in
order, even more so than his numerous concubines—the
time taken up in entertaining all the gods of Japan upon
their annual visits, he is blessed, or punished, as it may
be, with no less than twelve lawful wives.

I have said that the end of our journey was to be
Osacca.   It was ; but then females are alike curious and
fond of sights in all nations ; and so her majesty, the
Queen of Tango, had determined to witness, *en route*, the
great doings at the sacred city, or she had been especially
so commanded by Ogosho, who, usurper as he was, wished
to swell to its uttermost the greatness of his state at his
first visit to the imperial descendant of Ten-sio-dai-sin,
the chief of the demi-gods and founder of the dynasty.
But be that as it may, the queen and her suite took up
her lodgings at the palace then preparing for the Emperor
Ogosho, his empress, and heir, who made their entry into
the city five days after our arrival.   How I passed my
time during that period I have little to say, except the
many efforts I made to obtain even a sight of the queen

or her ladies proved fruitless. On the day, however, when the sovereigns met, I was more fortunate, for as the greater part of her men-at-arms were sent to swell the emperor's train, I was chosen, with Sir Martin of the Gilded Spurs, to command her body guard : thus my place was near that of her gilded norimon ; but, greater to my delight, near also to that which held the Lady Mary, whose beauty now so far outshone the magnificent robes and jewels which she wore, that my eyes were blinded to the material, or even colour. This I know, that she then looked neither the hunted gazelle panting for her life, as on board the ship ; the melancholy victim of her own sad story ; the revengeful woman seeking the death of a tyrant ; nor, worse, the hypocrite pretending obedience and duty where she had attempted murder, and must for ever hate. I had seen her in the ante-room with the Queen of Tango, and now I am writing of that peerless beauty I am loth to quit her for another subject. Yet must I tell the reader of that meeting of the two sovereigns. Insomuch, however, as I was too much en-raptured with the lady to notice all with my own eyes, I will, in order that I may give an accurate description of the pomp and outward show of these rival courts, re-peat, from the report of an eyewitness, one Conrad Cra-mer, who did publish the same some few years since.

The golden norimons, or state hand-coaches of the Queen of Tango, and her ladies, were drawn up upon the side of the great ditch which surrounded the castle : these were attended by some three hundred attendants and guards of the king, in the state liveries and uniforms, bearing the banners and arms of his royal house : with these, at some distance apart, were stationed myself and Sir Martin.

The whole of the streets between the Palace of the Mikado and that of Ogosho, which were strewn with white sand, were lined on either side with the mixed guards of both sovereigns, and were all clad in white, two-sworded, with helmets of black lacquered metal, and holding in their hands steel-headed pikes ; and the scaffolds, windows, and house-tops were crowded with the millions awaiting to see the return of Ogosho, who, having visited the Mikado the day before, was now about to bring back with him that honoured prince, upon whose face so few of that multitude had ever set their eyes, and at length they came as follows—

First, numerous porters, with black, lacquered, and gilded chests, containing the Mikado's luggage ; then the maids of honour of the Mikado's ladies, in green nori-mons, studded with brass nails ; then twenty-one nori-mons of black and gold, carrying the attendants of the kuge, or lords of the Mikado's court ; then twenty-seven norimons, bearing the lords themselves, with their foot-men carrying their umbrellas of state, attended by one hundred pages, clad in white, and twenty-four mounted gentlemen magnificently attired and armed to the teeth, with saddles of gilded lacquer, and covered with tiger-skins, with trappings of crimson silk : as for their horses, their manes were tied up with gold, their breasts covered with silken network, and their shoes done about with the same material, each horse being led by two footmen, who bore umbrellas fringed with scarlet cloth of gold, each horseman being accompanied by eight pages in white. This richly clad and attended guard was followed imme-diately by three chief wives of the Mikado, each of whom was carried in a gorgeous vehicle, decorated with figures of beaten gold, and drawn by two black bulls, which were covered with a network of crimson silk, and led by hal-berdiers : behind came a footguard and a host of pages, followed by black norimons, each having numerous guards, pages, and footmen, carrying umbrellas.   These contained the great ladies.

Afterwards came the presents, viz. two stools inlaid with plates of gold, a large sea-compass, two great golden candlesticks, two pillars of ebony, three cabinets of the same wood, garnished with gold, two golden basins, and a pair of richly gilded, varnished slippers.

Then came several men with large iron rods, to beat away all who might be in the road ; followed by the im-perial sambreys, or life-guards, the most richly attired and finest-looking men in the empire ; then, in magnificent vehicles, and with many thousands of gentlemen, pages, halberdiers, and others, the Ziogoon Ogosho and his long train of attendant lords, each of whom had, in his turn, attendants, pages, guards, and followers innumerable.

Next came the Mikado's concubines, each in a vehicle drawn by a single bull, also attended and followed by hundreds of gentlemen, pages, soldiers, and footmen; after these, a large body-guard of gentlemen, who formed the escort of the forty-six princes of the Mikado's blood and house, each of whom was carried in an ebony norimon, decorated with ivory and gold, and had borne before him a magnificent umbrella. Then, alas for those who had ever heard the sweet sounds of European music! came the grand band of the Mikado's palace, made up of tabours, timbrels, copper basins, and bells, the noise of which must have been mightily pleasing to the holy potentate, for, immediately behind, he followed in a little wooden structure, made like a sedan-chair, but much larger, with windows upon all sides hung with embroidered curtains. Its roof was arched, and had in the midst, upon a great buttress, a cock of massive gold, with his wings spread in a field azure, with several stars of beaten gold about the sun and moon. This throne was carried by fifty gentlemen of the Mikado's retinue, all clad in white, with bonnets of the same colour upon their heads. The Mikado's guard, who carried large umbrellas and gilded pikes, was led by an officer upon horseback, who rode near the throne, armed to the teeth, and bearing a target struck through with seven arrows. Last of all came a great number of soldiers, footmen, and other attendants. That the latter had come at last I was heartily glad, for while the two potentates and their respective suites passed, all bystanders were compelled to bow their foreheads as near to the earth as the crowded audience would admit, and the show from beginning to end lasted some nine hours. I was as heartily tired of the real thing as doubtless are my readers at the mere description. Now, when the Mikado had crossed over the drawbridge, all those great ladies who had taken no other part in the ceremonies of the day than that of

lookers on, and were of sufficient rank, or had their
lodgings within the fortress, followed; and among these,
the Queen of Tango's party were the first, to the no little
delight of at least *one* of her officers.

Now as I shall have but little to note about this
Mikado, I will only add my belief that his majesty must
have been the greatest benefited by this visit; for during
his stay at the castle, not only was he waited upon in
person by the warlike and wise Ogosho himself and his
heir, but Ogosho, at parting, presented him with two
hundred marks of gold, one hundred rich garments, two
great silver pots of honey, five catties of the rare wood
calambar, two hundred pieces of crimson serge, five pots
of silver full of musk, and five horses of the finest breed,
all richly trapped; and Ogosho's heir, the young prince,
made his majesty presents of no less value. I am not of
an envious temper, but, alas! I thought if I had all these
things and our good ship again, to what profit might they
be turned in London or Amsterdam; and I believe, upon
the night of the day of the Mikado's departure with these
good things, my dreams were made up of the Lady Mary,
the rich presents of Ogosho to the Mikado, and—shall I
write it? yes—Maud Saris, whose clear sweet face
haunted me, and for one hour with whom I would still
have given the whole riches of Japan. Yet, oh inconsistent Hollander! had the choice been offered, I could
not, for my life's sake, have made up my mind which of
those fair creatures I would have chosen. Now all this
I set down for the purpose of encouraging others, who
may be as wavering as I was, not to be ashamed of freely
confessing, at least to themselves, their faults, and that
too, without the slightest attempt at reservation, inasmuch as a guilty mind is ever haunted by ghosts of its
own creation; for at length, no matter when, like a
secret in a woman's heart, they will force themselves
forward, and that, too, notwithstanding every attempt to
keep them down by means of the nether world's pave
ment—good intentions.

CHAPTER XVIII.

I MIX MYSELF UP WITH THE JAPANNERS' POLITICS, AND
GET INTO DIFFICULTIES.

THREE days, and the show was at an end; the over-
excited spirits of the people had fallen to zero; the
streets were dirty, the houses disfigured with scaffoldings
and remnants of faded finery: indeed, the city, the
inhabitants, the houses, were, as Master Shakspeare hath
it, "stale, flat, and unprofitable;" but by reason of this
the theatres (which are common), tea-shops, and saki-
houses, became crowded with persons, seeking to fan
their spirits up again to the artificial height from which
they had fallen. Yes, all, every thing, everybody, was
dull, myself, perhaps, the dullest of all, for it was a point
of ceremony that the queen and her following should not
quit the city till after the emperor, and, for some reason
not known to me, Ogosho delayed his departure.

But why was *I* so dull? why did I look back with
regret even upon those many months spent in prison
with Will Adams? Well, because a hope had sprung up
in my heart that the thoughts and feelings of the Lady
Mary were reciprocal. But was it not presumption in a
mere foreign adventurer, the temptings of my own
vanity? Perhaps so: still I would at the time have
quarrelled with the man who had thus said. But presumption I did not believe it, for (even as the Roman
citizen deemed himself more than the equal of a barbarian
king), so at that time, Europeans, who would have licked
the feet of their own petty chiefs, believed that they
were wrought out of better materials, a superior clay, to
all and every one of these great races, by the side of
whom their furthest ancestors would have been as mush-
rooms. And albeit this may not be true, and may, nay,
must be, the cause hereafter of much bloodshed from mis-
understandings, as every cock thinks himself the chief
upon his own dunghill, I did believe the poor wandering

Hollander to be more than the equal of the daughter of one of the most princely houses in Japan: moreover, I thought the lady could not be otherwise than of a like opinion. Then, again, I had been raised to some Japan rank: she was also a Christian, and from that I extracted hope. But again, was she not the betrothed of a prince? Aye, but to that she herself was averse. " But, my friend," asks my reader, "had you no twitches of conscience touching English Maud?" In reply, I will tell the truth, and shame the devil. Know, then, that the education I had received among shipmen, one half traders, the other half pirates, in intention, if not in fact; long absence from Europe; deep sufferings; many heart-burnings; the common practice of intermarriage between European adventurers and the ladies of the land; the apparent certainty of detention for the rest of my life in Japan; all tended to soothe a not very rebellious conscience, embedded as it was in a very sanguine mind. Then, again, Maud in all probability believed me dead, for loss of life was a less uncommon event than it is even now: then why should I throw away the substance for the shadow? And, moreover, I endeavoured—remember, only endeavoured—to believe that I should have accorded to her the same latitude. And thus, while I admit it would have been more knightly to have resolved upon a lonely and unwedded life, I am yet of opinion that such resolutions are more frequently made than kept.

At length, however, the din of preparation, the running to and fro of officers, soldiers, servants, and the Canusis, or Sintoo priests, belonging to his household, all bespoke that the Ziogoon had fixed upon a day for his departure. It came, and the van-guard of his train marched out of the town, leaving within the fortress only his majesty, the body-guards, and his personal train, among whom were several Canusis, who were to follow the next morning.

Towards the middle of the day I received orders from the Queen of Tango, through Sir Martin of the Gilded Spurs, the only gentleman of her following who had the

privilege of speech with her majesty, to prepare the
party under my command to quit the castle immediately
after the Ziogoon. This duty occupied me till late in
the afternoon, when, tired of the din and bustle, and
somewhat oppressed by the heat of the weather, I sought
relief and quiet in the splendid garden ; and after wandering in solitude for about an hour, I threw myself
upon the banks of a silvery stream which ran through
the grounds, and within a hundred yards of a small
temple : from the latter, however, I was hidden by a
high ridge of ground, upon which were planted a double
row of cypress-trees ; and there, as I lay watching the
sports of the gold and silver fish, and listened to the
murmuring and rippling of the water, I was aroused by
the sound of footsteps, when, I know not why—for it
was no affair of mine, nought but sheer curiosity, I
believe—I arose to my feet, and, clambering up the
ridge, through the foliage of the cypress-trees, saw that
the new comer, whose back was turned towards me, and
who wore a yellow robe and shipshaped helmet, was
nothing more than a Canusis, when, vexed at the interruption of my reverie, I should have returned to my
former position, but suddenly there was a rustling among
the flowering shrubs, in which the temple was embedded :
another Canusis came forth, and the first hastened forward to meet him, and, to my astonishment, in another
instant they were locked in each other's arms.

Now, having no faith in the brotherly affection of
Sintoo priests, who, as a rule, regard each other after the
fashion of rival cats of the masculine gender, my curiosity
increased ; and so, under cover of the trees, I crept along
the ridge till I reached sufficiently near the temple to
hear their voices. The one seemed in tones of anger and
disappointment, the other in those of supplication, but
so soft, so musical, they brought to my memory the
Canusis our passenger—the Canusis who had attempted
the assassination ; and, assisted by sight of the short
slender figure, I soon had not one atom of doubt remaining that the Canusis whom I had first seen was—the
Lady Mary ! and in one instant curiosity changed to

jealousy, and I was about to rush forward, but, fortunately, the folly, the imprudence of such a proceeding
coming concurrently into my head, I simply stood still,
fearing either to advance or retreat, and thus did I un-
wittingly become an eavesdropper.

I heard but little, for both spoke in undertones, but
what I did hear alarmed me for the lady, for the dis-
jointed words, "Kubo-Sama," "the Castle of Osacca,"
"the tyrant of Tango," warned me that treason was con-
cocting. But then my jealousy arose to fever heat, for,
in words of the warmest affection, she besought her companion to hide within the temple till the following day,
when Ogosho and his train would have left the city.
Then, as the lady came forth cautiously from the shrub-
bery, she started suddenly, exclaiming—

"We are betrayed, I have been followed!" and not
doubting that it was to me she alluded, and hearing the
rattling of a sword against its scabbard, I stood up to
prepare. But no; coming along the other side of the
ridge, and making towards the temple, I saw the chief
Canusis of the palace, the favourite of the emperor; and
as in an instant it occurred to me I might be of service
to the lady, I fell upon my knee behind the trees, and
watched for my opportunity. Resuming her presence of
mind, almost as soon as she had uttered the exclamation,
she said to her companion—

"Hie thee within; remain silent; this may be but
accident; the priest may suspect nothing, may pass
without recognising me for other than I seem." Then,
shading her face with the black silk, she advanced, with
her head bent forward as if in meditation, and with the
ambling pace assumed by the Sintoo priests.

The chief Canusis came forward at a similar pace, his
head also was bent, but his lynx eyes were fixed upon
the lady's hand, which was pressed upon the bosom of
her robe, and *whatever* it was she guarded so carefully,
that the priest seemed to me to be determined to get into
his own possession.

A few paces more, and they met, and that, too, so
near to me, that, by stretching forth my hand, I could

have touched either.   The lady, in her assumed character
of a subaltern priest, salaamed, and would have passed
onwards, but the chief, standing in her path, and, with
a malicious smile, pointing to some of the emperor's
guards who I then for the first time saw in the distance,
evidently awaiting his call, said—   '

"That the bonzes of Christ permit their followers to
wear the holy robes of our mia priests is not to be wondered at, for they are artful ; but that the chief lady of
the Queen of Tango's court should so far forget her
maiden modesty and high rank, is indeed a marvel."

The lady trembled but for an instant, then replied, as
she now boldly gazed in his face—

"Priest, then thou knowest me : still, if thou art what
I _know_ thee to be, a lover of gold, thou wilt keep that
knowledge to thyself."

"Alas, lady ! thy secret, the object of my coming here,
is known to another, and to one who has sent me hither,
and me, a Canusis, that none other may share his knowledge."

"Another !   Of whom speakest thou ?   Who has power
to command the services of the chief priest of Ogosho ?"
she asked with alarm.

"Ogosho himself," said the priest in a soft tone.

"Then, indeed, am I lost," she replied in despair.

"Not so, O lady ; for it is even for thy benefit alone
that I am here."

"These are but words, priest."

"Lady, the great Ogosho has long sought an interview
with thee."

"What words are these ? read me the riddle.   How
could the master of the empire seek without finding from
her whose very life depends but on his breath ?   Nay,
priest, the great Ogosho had but to command to be
obeyed."

"Not so, lady : the builder of a mighty fabric does not
blunt the edge of the tools with which he is working : in
a word, he would not openly cross the path of the King
of Tango, albeit he would save thee from a fate thou
dreadest."

"Again, I say, thou speakest in riddles."

"Art thou not destined to be the bride of the Prince of Tango?"

"Alas! even so, if death does not happily intervene."

"The great Ogosho pities, and would save thee, by placing thee far above the reach of his king and his baby son. Lady, thou art the jewel of his hopes: he would have thee grace his household with the presence: the honours and lands of thy illustrious parents should be restored."

"Stay, priest: listen to *me*," she said with flashing eyes: "the honours, the lands *I* seek are not of this world."

"Nay, not for thyself, but for—" the priest halted in his speech, and the lady, with a quick glance at the temple, said—

"Whom?"

"He whom thou lovest as thine own life," replied the priest, adding, slowly and maliciously, as he pointed his finger, "he who, even now, is hiding like a deer from the hounds."

The certainty that her whole secret was known now lent her additional courage, albeit the courage of despair, and she replied—

"Ah! then we *have* been watched, the gardens are filled with hounds who scent the deer. Priest, draw off these same dogs for but half-an-hour, and thou shalt have gold enough to outweigh thee in the scales."

"A lesser reward will serve thy purpose, lady; but *one* word from thy lips and the all but stricken deer shall be the honoured prince."

Gazing wildly, as if frenzied, and scarce knowing the meaning of her question, she said—

"Priest, *that* word!"

"One of compliance with Ogosho's prayer; one that shall make him happier in his own heart than he is in the eyes of the world; one—"

"That would deliver my body to shame, and my soul to everlasting perdition," she replied; adding scornfully, "it is well for thee that thou hast thine hounds within

call, and that the life of one more precious than mine is
within thy power, or I would, woman as I am, smite thee
to the earth ;" and her hand played with the hilt of a
small dagger just concealed within the folds of her robe.

"Alas, lady ! that thou shouldest be angered with thy
servant, who is but the mouthpiece of one who places at
thy feet an offer that it has been the wont of the highest
and most peerless ladies of the land to accept as the joy
and ambition of their lives, and which it is madness to
reject ; but thou art—"

"A *maiden of Japan*, and a *Christian*, and in *that* unity
thou hast my answer," she replied.

"Then, if this be thy answer, lady, I pity thee ; for
though the madness of the Christians makes martyrdom
for their false faith honourable, even with them the death
of a traitor to their sovereign is damnable, and of everlasting infamy in all creeds."

"Traitor !" she repeated aghast.

"Lady, I would rather that my tongue should be torn

from my mouth than offend one upon whom the great
Ogosho would bestow such honour; but the words must
be spoken: thou hast but a choice between the palace of
Ogosho and the death of—" (as he spoke he again pointed
to the temple).

"Words, words, priest," she replied haughtily; adding,
"these threats avail thee not, for of this of which thou
speakest thou hast no proof, and without, not even Ogosho
dare sacrifice the lives of the people of Japan."

"Lady, thou hast the beauty, but art wanting in the
wisdom of the serpent. Behold the proof;" and as the
priest spoke he snatched from between the folds of her
robe a packet of papers, and at the action I could scarcely
keep down my indignation, or restrain myself from seizing the dastard's throat. The lady, I thought, would
have struggled with him to regain that packet, but, glanc-
ing at the soldiers, she resigned herself to despair, and,
throwing herself upon her knees, she, in piteous tones,
implored him to restore the packet.

"The sharpest weapon of a fair woman should be her
tongue: the letters of traitors are dangerous to her as naked
swords in the hands of infants, so it is well for thee as it
is; but thy fate is, nevertheless, now in thine own hands.
See, thy first request is granted." So saying, he made a
signal with his hand, and the guards withdrew: then he
added—

"Now, lady, the hounds are drawn off, the deer may
fly: but get him where he may, he cannot escape, when
I so will it, paying the penalty of his crimes. Yet his
life—his fate—is in thy hands."

All hope seemed lost. Frenzied by despair and fear
she again fell upon her knees, saying—

"Be it as thou wilt; but give me back that paper."

"*And*—" said the priest, sardonically.

"I will (may God forgive me!) sacrifice life, soul—
all."

"At length, then, hath reason returned: the papers shall
be restored to thee inviolate and unopened."

"God of mercy, thanks from my soul! Give it me,
give it me;" and she held out her hands.

" Yea, lady, *when* thou art within the walls of the palace at Jeddo," replied the rogue meaningly.

" Priest, dost dare doubt my plighted word ?" she cried angrily.

" I would not doubt thee, lady ; but words being as empty air, this paper leaves not my possession until thou hast performed thy part of the contract ; nay, not even at the command of the Christian's God himself," replied the priest exultingly, holding up the paper, and retreating a few paces towards the ridge.

" Blasphemous wretch !" exclaimed the lady ; but suddenly the paper left his hand : indeed, for some time my fingers had been itching to get at him ; and finding him so near, I sprang from behind, and, in an instant, had him upon the earth, with his own robes so tightly twisted around his head and mouth, that I believed he could neither see nor speak.   The lady gave a slight shriek ; but, with a woman's ready wit—at once seeing from whom the aid had come—spoke not, for fear that, by my replying, he might recognise my voice ; so, silently, I secured him to a tree, by twisting his robes round the trunk ; and this being done, she beckoned me to follow her.   We entered the temple together : she looked around, and then exclaimed—

" Thanks be to the great God, *he* has escaped."   Then to me she said—" The packet, the packet, noble stranger ! and may the God of heaven reward thee, for the gratitude of my heart would be small reward for so great a service as this.   But the packet, the packet : it is as the very life-blood of many princely lives : give it me ;" and she held out her hand.

" Thy pardon, lady ; but if this paper be of such importance, it is safest in my possession, at least until the departure of the Ziogoon and this cowardly priest, who hath neither seen my face, nor heard my voice," I said. But she hesitated to reply, and I added, " Surely the Lady Mary cannot doubt the honour of her servant ?"

" Thy pardon, noble Sama : I will entrust my life to thy honour : let it then be as thou wilt.   But now let us return by different paths, and at night I will send for

thee." So saying, she left the temple, and, resuming the
meditative walk of a Canusis, she returned to the palace,
and I to my apartment ; when, examining the packet, I
saw the superscription was to the Kubo-Sama, the young
Fide Yori, then imprisoned at Osacca. With something
like a feeling of jealousy, I asked myself who is this
nameless *he*, so loved by the lady? But why—why
should it trouble me? for even if not her lover, would
she bestow her affection upon me—me, forsooth—after
scorning the son of a king, and the advances of an
emperor? Tut, tut! surely my plain Dutch mind was
becoming besotted, to dwell for an instant upon such a
play-house kind of heroine being fit for the wife of a
Dutch trader. But although I could no more prevent
such thoughts than I can now refrain from confessing them, after a long contest between that Dutch head
and Dutch heart, the latter, which, it must be remembered, had been moulded in honest England, obtained
the victory, and set the head a pondering how it could
best serve such a heroine, for heroine she was ; for never
before had woman of Japan been known to refuse an
offer of a share of the heart and palace of the Ziogoon.
Alas ! that after-history has to reveal that that virtuous
refusal, by arousing the latent hatred of Christianity in
the breast of Ogosho, should have been one of the earlier
springs of that terrible and extraordinary persecution
which afterwards broke forth, and continued till the
Christian faith, its priests and disciples, were swept from
the empire.

Now this document, which was becoming so trouble-
some to me, was folded within an envelope about six
inches long by two and a-half wide, fastened down by
some adhesive material, impressed with a black stamp at
the point of juncture, and addressed upon both sides.
While I was turning it over, and making many attempts
to guess its contents, I was interrupted by a young
woman—the same who had attended the lady on board
our ship—who begged of me to go with her to her mistress ; and, requiring no second invitation, I followed the
girl to the lady's apartment, which was placed at the

extreme end of the building, and one of the chief of those
appropriated to the use of the Queen of Tango and her
household.

The room was neither large nor lofty, but the walls
were highly japanned and inlaid with golden representations of the mountain Fudsi-Jamma, and figures of the
Japanners' emblems of long life, tortoises and cranes.
The chief part of the apartment was, as in all Japan
drawing-rooms, a recess, called the toko : it was formed
in the wall just opposite the door, and fitted with shelves
of rare and costly wood, upon which, and in front of a
gilded picture of a god, stood a richly ornamented vase
of choice flowers ; at the foot of this toko were several
mats, one upon the other, of fine texture, the upper mat
being fringed with gold ; and upon this seat, esteemed
the most honourable in the room, the lady bade me be
seated.   She was sitting in the middle of the apartment,
but, when the girl quitted, she arose, and, first looking
about the room as if fearful of eavesdroppers, she took
both my hands in hers, and with tremulous voice said—

. "Noble Sama, the packet."

I placed it in her hands.   She examined it as if to see
it had not been tampered with ; then placed it within
the folds of the rich satin robe which had replaced the
priestly garb she had worn in the garden, saying—

"The Sama is noble, truthful, and brave : he should
have been a great warrior ; but, alas ! the poor orphan
whose eternal gratitude he has earned can never repay
him, for he has saved from death—worse, dishonour—
some of the noblest in Japan."

"Lady, the knowledge that I have succoured thee is
reward sufficient: but tell me, is *he* who gave thee this
packet of thy kindred ?"   It was a churlish question, but
there was a devil in my breast who prompted it.

"The Sama asks that which will neither benefit *him* to
know, nor *me* to answer," she replied angrily ; adding,
"but the people from the western sky love gold : he shall
be rewarded for his services."

The tone rather than the words themselves stung me
to the quick, and I replied—

"In what has thy servant offended thee, oh! dear lady, that we should be compared to the greedy swine of Portugal and Spain, or have earned thy frowns instead of those smiles which alone he deemed sufficient reward?"

"True, O Sama," she replied sorrowfully: "the smiles of the orphan should be valuable, for they are rare. But," she added, "the night is wearing, and it is neither seemly nor safe for either that we should be thus alone. I sent for thee, not solely to obtain this packet and to offer my gratitude, but to pray of thee another and a somewhat dangerous service."

"Lady, my heart's blood is at thy service if it be not against the interests of Ogosho."

"Nay, Sama; fear nought against thine honour: I ask only that thou wilt keep this packet in thy care till I crave it from thee at Osacca, to which city we go to-morrow, for the Canusis will seek to obtain it from me."

"It is a traitorous letter, lady," I replied; feeling, as I must admit, some qualms at again having possession of so dangerous a document as I believed that to be.

"Ah! then the western stranger *fears:* it is enough," she replied angrily, when, although not admitting her right to be offended at my objecting to risk my goodly body, I really felt ashamed of myself, and, holding forth my hand, said—

"Give me the letter, lady, and while I have life it shall not leave my keeping till thou demandest it."

Then, putting it in my hands, she said—

"But remember, Sama, I am placing at thy mercy the lives and honour of myself and others, who, if thou servest them faithfully, can fully reward—"

"Lady, I seek not reward," said I, interrupting her; but not noticing my words, she added with vehemence—

"And so great will be the service to myself, that aught, within my power to give, thou shalt not hereafter ask in vain, or I refuse."

Oh, what wild hopes rushed through my foolish, frenzied brain at the words!—words uttered, perhaps, without meaning, as wide apart from that to which my vanity pointed as the poles themselves; but to smother my thoughts, hopes, feelings, and still anxious for her safety, I replied—

"But, lady, from this priest, who hath been so foiled, hast thou nought to fear? Will he not proclaim to the emperor that he saw this packet, and to whom it is addressed?"

"For his life he dares not: it would be to admit *that* which Ogosho never pardons, that he had made a discovery, yet could not prove it; in a word, that he had failed," she replied; adding, "yet that he may not, by some villainous means (for he will leave no effort untried), obtain possession of the packet, is the reason alone that I entrust it to thy honour and care."

"But again, lady: the Ziogoon loves thee, and will assuredly entrap thee into his power."

"Nay, Sama; fear not: great as the regent whom you term Ziogoon, he is too wise to excite the enmity of the King of Tango."

"This King of Tango," I repeated, as a question that had long tormented me arose first in my mind—"this King of Tango, lady? It was from this king that, more than two years since, when thou soughtest our ship, thou wast flying?"

"And the Sama *wonders* to see the persecuted orphan again, and of her own free will, in his court," she replied: adding, "let him listen. Then, as this day, the Sama performed a great service, for he rescued me from the power of the king, enabling me to reach Jeddo. Once there, I sought the good father Rodriguez, who had reached the city before me. He, who is greatly in the favour of Ogosho, besought for me his protection. Ogosho granted me an audience, and, in tears, I related my story to him; and the wily prince, alas! for purposes of his own, commanded the King of Tango to postpone the marriage—the hateful marriage—till the boy-prince had advanced in years, and, in the mean time, that I should remain under the protection of the queen. But," she added, "this wonderment, Sama, has it but now arisen in thy mind?"

"Nay, lady, long since; when, when—" but the words would have suffocated me.

"When thou sawest me in the ante-chamber with the queen, upon the day of the attempted assassination of the tyrant," she replied, putting the words in my mouth with a coolness that not only astonished, but so disgusted me with her audacity, that my love fled in an instant, and I was provoked to say—

"But the assassin, the Canusis, was *he* permitted to escape?"

For an instant she seemed amazed, surprised: her eyes flashed; but, recovering herself, she innocently asked—

"Canusis! How knowest thou that it *was* a Canusis? the assassin was not seen."

"Lady," I said sternly (although I do not know what right I had to be stern), "I stayed the assassin's blow; for, in *my* country, let the provocation be what it may, there are but two powers to whom the punishing of the guilty is delegated—God, and the law."

Then, for a moment, she gazed at me as if I had been her deadliest enemy; at least I thought so; but, taking my arm, she replied—

"Sama, I *know* thou didst not see the assassin's face." When, as I was about replying, she interrupted me, saying—"Listen, Sama: the bell tolls the kokonats (midnight). Now remember thy promise, and may the great God take thee in his keeping:" when, dumbfounded at her coolness, and unable to reply—for her manner, her dignity it was that spoke with her tongue—I made a lowly obeisance, left the apartment, and, seeking my own bed, or rather mats, laid down to sleep—no! to wonder at the strange being I had just quitted, and to wonder still more that she had cast a spell over me that—that—well, not even the thoughts of Maud Saris could rescue me. And that night I had but troubled rest, for so fearful was I of the packet's being found in my possession, that, at fitful intervals, I would awake, and start upwards upon my mat, and look earnestly about me, as if the Canusis himself had been in the room.

CHAPTER XIX.

WE LEAVE MEACO AND REACH OSACCA, BUT I AM SUR-
PRISED BY THE JESUIT, LOSE MY CONSCIOUSNESS, AND
FIND MYSELF WITH THE LADY MARY.

THE following morning we left the sacred city, and
before sun-down arrived at Osacca, which, although but
a distance of about fifteen miles from Meaco, is approached
by a road so lined with houses and densely populated,
that it is difficult for foreigners to discover where the
one begins or the other ends. That the boundaries, however, are well marked by the Japanners themselves there
can be no doubt, as Osacca is one of the five imperial
cities of the great Tiego-Sama, and independent of the
jurisdiction of the Mikado, whose positive government
is confined alone to Meaco and a portion of its suburbs,
that being all remaining to him of that vast empire over
which his ancestors once held supreme power.

The imperial city of Osacca, which is of great size and
substantially built, stands upon the banks of the river
Jodagawa. It teems with humanity, and, in consequence
of the many small rivers, and one great canal which runs
through its streets, and so enables goods and merchandize
to be landed at the very doors of the houses, it had long
been a great mart for trade; but when Tiego erected
upon its eastern side a fortified palatial castle, it assumed
the rank and dignity, and afforded all the advantages and
vices, of a fashionable capital, even to rivalling its neighbour, Meaco ;— luxurious living, sensual pleasures,
theatres, plays, mountebanks, jugglers, and, indeed, all
that could draw money from the pockets of a population
so numerous as to be able to raise, within a few days, an
army of eighty thousand men. And as at that time the
titular Kubo-Sama lived in the castle built by his father,
Tiego—for as yet Ogosho had not been guilty of any
cruel act against his granddaughter's husband—more than

half that number of troops, all devoted, it was supposed, to the usurping regent, encompassed the castle, and manned the fortifications of the town, *nominally* to do honour to the young prince, but *virtually* to prevent his falling into the hands of the rival regents, who were in arms in different portions of the empire, and so well knew, as Master Shakspeare hath it, " that a king's name is a tower of strength," that they were for ever intriguing to get him in their own keeping ; and many were the broils that were continually happening in the streets and public ways, by reason of these intrigues, for the population were about equally divided between the factions of Ogosho, and that of the young Kubo.

Now to the great surprise of our whole party, no sooner did we arrive at the city than we were met by an officer of the King of Tango, who told us that the king himself was already there in the capacity of commander-in-chief for Ogosho, and that upon leaving Jeddo he had set forth the report that he was about journeying to another part of the empire, in order to cover his real design of marching by an unusual route to Osacca, which city it was his belief the rebel regents intended shortly to besiege, and endeavour to obtain possession of the young Kubo-Sama, with whom it was suspected they had some secret means of holding constant communication ; and thus did I get the unpleasant news that speedily I might find myself at the very head-quarters of the san-guinary civil war, of which I had heard so much ; which, with the knowledge that I had in my possession, to say the least, a dangerous document, did not, by any means, increase the soundness of my first night's slumber in that city.

The apartment in the great official castle of the King of Tango appropriated to my use was upon the north side of the building, and had one large window, with a balcony so low, that, at high tide, it touched the waters of Joda-gawa, which washed the northern walls. Having taken possession of the room, and arranged my sleeping-mat, I sat down before a large tray of sweetmeats, fruits, hot water, and saki, and as I partook of the good things

before me, meditated upon my fortunes, the strange
chances that had converted a matter-of-fact Hollander
into a luxurious Oriental, the probability of my ever
reaching my native land, and Will Adams, Maud Saris,
and the Lady Mary.

The latter it was, upon whom my thoughts were chiefly
fixed, for as I sat, with that precious document like a
nightmare upon my bosom, I momentarily expected to
see her; but as the time passed on, and neither messenger
nor lady came to relieve me of the incubus, I became
covered with a cold sweat, for was it not possible that I
might be robbed of it during my slumber? After waiting
till quite tired out, and the noise of the bamboo canes,
which the sentries and watchmen rattle to mark the hour
of the night, telling me how hopeless it was that either
the lady or her messenger would visit me before morning,
I prepared for sleep. So, having drawn over me the
extra gown which served for night gear, I placed a large
screen before the window, when suddenly I heard a
scratching at the paper panes. The noise startled me
for an instant, but believing it to be caused by some
houseless dog that had clambered into the balcony from
the river, I proceeded to lie down, but the scratching
continued.

"A murrain on the animal," I muttered, and, jumping
up, pulled aside the screen, and opened the window, when
—gods of romance and mystery!—in the coarse gown of
a small trader of the city there stood before me—the
Jesuit!

"Father Rodriguez, here, and in *such* guise!" I exclaimed.

"Hush!" he said, placing his finger upon his lips; then
adding, in a whisper, "when the wolves are prowling, and
the flock is in danger, it becomes the shepherd to be on
the alert."

"How, father? what meanest thou? What danger can
threaten the fold of Christ while the Christians are bask-
ing in the sunshine of Ogosho's favour, and the father
Rodriguez is the favoured friend and counsellor at court?"
I asked.

" Were I not the latter I had not been here : but listen. Hitherto, Ogosho has cared but little, either for the faith of Christian or pagan, but recently the hated councils of the King of Tango, the increasing strength of the friends of the Christian prince, Fide Yori, the bitter remembrance of the boasting Spaniard in the late reign, and lastly, and

more forcibly than all, the representations of a certain Canusis that a lady whom he loves resists his overtures, on the ground alone that the teaching of the Christian fathers forbid her compliance, has determined him to follow in the footsteps of Tiego, and to let the blood-hounds of persecution loose : in a sentence, the chief of those bloodhounds is the King of Tango, and hence the reason he is entrusted with the command of Osacca. But, my son, many of this king's own powerful princes are of the true religion, and therefore it behoves him to act warily ; the more so, that the Ziogoon has received in-formation of an intended attack upon Osacca by the Fide

Yori party, whom he means first to defeat by means of
Christian as well as pagan princes, and then, under guise
of punishing rebellion, to send forth fire and sword among
the Christians, who, he believes, favour the rebels."

"But yet, father, are the canons of thy conscience so
supple that they will permit thee to play the traitor to
thy great friend and adopted sovereign ?"

"I am but the instrument of heaven—the minister of
a cause, for which to die is martyrdom most blessed : still
would I serve both persecuted and persecutor ; the first,
by warning them against giving aid to the rebels ; and
Ogosho, by saving him the lives of his subjects : and," he
added, "thus is it I am here, to crave of thee, my son, a
night's shelter, for I would not have it known that I am
in the city."

"Enough, father, thou art welcome both to shelter, and
such refreshment as may render it agreeable," I replied,
but, I must confess, greatly against my inclination, for I
had small taste for the crown of martyrdom, which,
should he be a traitor, and discovered in my apartment,
would in all probability be bestowed upon me by Ogosho
or the king of Tango.   Making, however, the best of the
matter, I placed before him the remnant of my repast, of
which, when he had partaken as ravenously as if famished,
he proposed a loving cup of saki.   I agreed : he filled the
cup, I pledged him, and have but a dim recollection of
what afterwards took place.   I must have feared for my
packet.   Did the father speak of the Lady Mary?   Did
he tell me the document had been seen by the Canusis
through the partings of the robe with which I had covered
his head?   Did he insist upon my giving him the packet?
Did I refuse?   I know not ; but I remember that suddenly I fell backwards, powerless to move or to speak,
yet seemingly conscious that the father endeavoured to
take it from me : that a struggle began ; that rage gave
me again the use of my limbs ; and then I had him
clutched by the arm.   But it must have been a dream ;
for, opening my eyes, the bright golden sun was shining
in the room, and—and—the lady herself standing by my

side, smarting with pain, for her arm it was that I had clutched.

" Father of heaven, where am I ?" I exclaimed. But putting her finger upon my lips, and looking nervously around the room, she said—

" Hush ! The Sama has been in the land of dreams many hours, for the sun is high in the heavens ; but the paper ?"

The paper !—and a cold sweat bathed my brow : the dream—Had I lost it ? I looked wildly around the room. The Jesuit was gone ; but putting my hand in my breast, it alighted upon the packet : it was safe. I examined and found it intact ; and so, with no little delight, I placed the accursed document in her hands. But then, gazing on her glowing face, its bright beauty, her queenly form, I rejoiced that I had had the great privilege of serving her.

" May the great God reward thee, noble Sama, for this service !" she said, securing the paper within the folds of her robe.

" Lady, there is but one reward I crave ; and that—"

" Thou shalt command," she said, interrupting me. And oh, how my foolish heart bounded ; for like lightning the hope, the belief, ran through my heated brain, that she knew, nay approved—perhaps returned—my love : but how from fever-heat down to zero ran my blood, how tingled with chagrin my heart, when she replied—

" Beneath the far distant western skies the noble Sama has left those who love him, and to whom he would, and shall return ; for the queen will join with her friend and kinswoman in praying of the king to free him from this land of his exile."

" Alas ! lady, the land of my exile, though even of chains, is the only land wherein thy slave can be happy ; for it alone contains the bright beauty of the Lady Mary."

" Alas ! alas ! the Sama is still among the dream-clouds : he knows not what he says : his words are words only— not from the heart, but the lips," she replied playfully. But then, the memory of my foolishness rising to fever-heat, I exclaimed, as if I had been one of Master Shak-speare's players—

"Oh, lady, is it thus the daughters of Japan torture those who love them? Love! yes, lady; I love thee, and would make thee my wife." At last I had passed the rubicon.

"Hush! hush! the Sama is still among dream-clouds— the fogs of this land are in his head," she replied, putting her finger to her lips.

"Lady, I am, like thyself, of noble birth."

"Noble! yes, the Sama *is* noble; he is better; he is good—brave; but these words, what are they that they should fall in the ears of the betrothed bride of the Prince of Tango?" she replied with dignified hauteur.

"Lady, to thee that marriage is hateful," I said. Then, with flashing eyes, she replied—

"Sama, thou art right; it is, and will never happen."

"Then, lady, may I hope?" I said.

"By the great God it is given to all to hope; yet to build even hope without a proper foundation, is to erect a palace upon a bed of sand : and such is thine, if thou hopest to wed one who is vowed to the church."

"Lady, that vow is not taken."

"With lips, Sama, no; but the vows of the devoted have their springs in the heart. Yet," she added, "this thing thou askest is not possible; for though even the bride neither of prince nor church, my father's daughter lives but for one object, the performance of a vow."

"Lady," I exclaimed, my love being somewhat cooled as I thought with what savage earnestness she still sought the death of the king, "revenge belongs alone to the God thou wouldst outrage." But placing her hand on my shoulder, and gazing in my face earnestly, inquiringly, she said—

"Stay, Sama, thou art still among the dream-clouds."

"Nay," said I, interrupting her; but, placing her hand upon the letter, she gave a sudden shriek, crying—

"We are lost—the Canusis."

My back had been towards the door. I turned, and but for the lady, I believe, should have jumped into the river; for the old Canusis, the confidante of Ogosho, stood at the entrance with a meaning and malicious smile upon his face. The lady, however, with more presence of mind, snatched the letter from her bosom, for what purpose, except to tear it into shreds, I know not. But whatever that purpose may have been, it was frustrated by our unwelcome visitor, who, old as he was, with the bound of a deer sprang forward, and in an instant had possessed himself of the fatal document.

I caught him by the throat, and would have strangled the knave ere I would have removed my grasp; but the lady at once, with a look of resignation, said—

"Unhand him, Sama; it is the will of Heaven! I am lost."

At her request I loosened my hold of the priest, and he said with a malicious smile—

"The lady is wise, for the guards of the king are without the room, and in an instant may be here. Yet is there no danger for her if the western foreigner's words of love are truth."

"What meanest thou?" I said.

"That the Sama, if he hath not the heart of a woman, proclaim himself the bearer of this letter."

"Priest, I thank thee. Lady, be it so," I said, with that readiness for self-sacrifice for which my love seemed to be making me remarkable.

"Heaven reward thee, Sama, but this may not be; nay, it would be useless, for well the priest knows that it is not for myself I fear."

"Lady, those whom thou lovest and for whom thou fearest are saved from harm, for this hath the great Ogosho promised, even before he reads their names in this paper," replied the priest.

"Priest, the hateful meaning of thy words are plain, but already hast thou had thine answer," she replied firmly.

"Lady, once more, ere it is too late, comply with the prayer of Ogosho, and this letter shall be again in thy possession, and thy friends free from harm: refuse, and the hatred of the great Ogosho will be shown, not alone to these traitors, but to the whole of the Christian dogs in the empire, by whose extermination he will be revenged

for those doctrines, which alone have taught thee to refuse
the highest honour which it is in the power of the emperor to bestow, and which a woman of Japan has never
dared to refuse."

"Priest, as I *have* said, I *now* say—the daughters of
my father's house hold their lives at the will of their king
and emperor ; but their honour is held alone from God,
to whom I pray for deliverance ;" and, as she spoke, she
held the little crucifix before her, kissed it, and mur-
mured a prayer.   At which the priest, losing patience,
stamped his foot, saying—

"Be it so, lady ; yet even now shalt thou be saved
against thy will, but the blood of thy friends be upon
thine own head."   And scarcely had he uttered these
words, when the room was filled with soldiers.   The
lady advanced some steps forward, as if to resign herself
into their rude hands, but, to my surprise, the priest said—

"Lady, this is no place for thee : depart :" then to the
soldiers—"Bind the hands and feet of this Christian
rogue, and away with him to the gokuya."

"Stay ; it is I—I alone, who am guilty," said the lady ;
but the reply I heard not, for in another minute I was
packed as close as a bale of cloth, and carried from the
apartment.

CHAPTER XX.

I AM CHARGED WITH TREASON ; THE KING IS ENRAGED ;
THE CANUSIS IS DISCOMFITED, AND THE LADY MARY
ACTS VERY STRANGELY.

THE gokuya (*Anglice*, Hell) fully merited its name, being
a miserable apartment, some twenty feet long by about
ten feet wide, and lighted and ventilated above by a small
grating in the roof : moreover, crammed into the place
were some twenty other offenders of the lowest class.   But
to give you a full notion of this prison, which is one of

the institutions of the empire, I must tell you that the door is never opened, except for the ingress or egress of prisoners, who, while there, are forbidden any kind of amusement or occupation, whereby they might alleviate their misery : they are not allowed to take with them their sleeping-mats, pillows, or gowns ; their girdles, whether they be of silk or cotton, are replaced by straw-bands, the wearing of which is alone a mark of deep disgrace. The filth of the place is removed through the same hole in the wall by which the food is introduced. The meals are of the coarsest kind ; and although the miserable inhabitants are permitted to purchase or obtain them from their friends, no person can receive such food without it be in sufficient quantity to supply the wants of the whole of the inmates. But, last and most terrible of all is, that, while confined in this room, all are outlaws, that is, not punished for any offences committed against each other ; so that the strongest giving laws to the others, it resembles a cage of savage beasts, each of whom have just sufficient of the lowest attributes of humanity to make brutality more brutal.

In such a place, amid the hideous mockeries, laughter, and jeerings of a number of blaspheming wretches, was I confined. Determined, however, to bear it with a good grace, I preserved my temper till they had fallen asleep, and then, left to my own thoughts, I began to think over the events of the past few days, and full employment it gave me. First came my own danger, then that of the lady and her friends ; and with one of those friends—he who had given her the letter in the garden temple—I had but little sympathy, as, but for him, I should not have been placed in that predicament—a murrain on him ! Then there was I—a plain matter-of-fact Dutchman—moving about among all the mysteries of a romance. Truly, I believe the wildest romances must have had their origin in fact, if, indeed, life, truthfully seen, is not even itself a romance. But the mystery ! Who was that stranger in whom the lady had taken such an interest as to endanger her life and my own ? How did the old Canusis derive the secret of their meeting ? More

important to me—How did he discover that I had been
the person who had nearly smothered him in the garden?
Had there been a hole in the garment? Then the Father
Rodriguez, what had become of him? Why had he so
mysteriously vanished? Why had I fallen asleep while
conversing with him? Had he drugged my saki? but,
if so, why—for what purpose? And, trying to solve
that last problem, I at length fell off to sleep.

My dreams were of the danger of the lady. At one
time I saw her incarcerated in a dungeon awaiting some
barbarous punishment for treason; then I saw her, as
the morning before, anxiously awaiting to obtain possession of the letter. But, awakening, I found a soldier
by my side, who, having first cut the cords which bound
my legs, commanded me to follow him. I obeyed. Outside the door I found a small detachment of his fellows;
and these, having placed me between their ranks, so that
I was surrounded, marched me to the bath-house in the
garden, and, standing around the water, they bade me
perform my ablutions; after which they marched me to
the presence of the King of Tango, who was sitting upon
a mat in his hall of audience, with his lords and great
officers upon either side upon their heels: behind sat the
queen and some of her ladies: chief among the latter was
the Lady Mary. At this I was rejoiced, for I saw her
free and unharmed; although, at the same time, I must
confess to a sensation of chagrin, that I was evidently
about being made the scapegoat. Before the king stood
the Canusis, who no sooner saw me than he said—

"This, oh King of Tango, is the vagabond stranger
who, regardless of thy great favour in bestowing upon
him an office, has dared to set his mean eyes lovingly
upon a lady of thy queen's court; nay, even upon her
destined to be the bride of thy son:" whereupon the
Lady Mary advanced a few steps, as if to address the
king; but his majesty, who, for reasons best known to
himself, wished to alter the charge against me, said—

"Nay, father priest, we will not believe this thing, for
it would dishonour us in the person of our son's be-

trothed ; nor is it necessary, as thou hast a more heinous crime with which to charge him."

" The powerful king is loyal to his supreme lord, the great Ogosho, against whom and his government this mean rogue has been plotting treason."

" Thou liest, priest : not for my life would I do aught against the great Ogosho, to whom I owe a debt of gratitude," said I. But the Canusis, regardless of my speech, declared that he had seen a follower of one of the rebel regents place a letter in my hands ; that he had by force taken it from me, when he found it to be directed to the Kubo-Sama Fide Yori, with whom to hold communication without the permission or command of Ogosho was a crime worthy of death. Further, he stated that I had again taken the letter from him, nearly at the cost of his life ; but that the gods had ultimately enabled him to again recover it from me, and that, in my own chamber in that castle, " and just, too, oh king," he concluded, " when the rogue was seeking to drag within the meshes of his treason the lady of whom I spoke, and who can doubtlessly account why she should have sought the chamber of this man"—a fabrication of lies that bewildered me.

" If, oh holy man, thou canst prove this crime, the punishment shall be speedy ; but doubtless thou canst show us this letter."

" Nay, oh king ; that letter is alone for the eyes of Ogosho ; and in his name I demand that this rogue shall be delivered over to the imperial troops, who may take him to the presence of his majesty, that, either by words or torture, he may be made to confess the associates in his treason," said the priest.

" How ! wouldst thou command us in our own government ?" said the enraged king ; adding to one of his officers, " drag the letter from his girdle." But the priest, unwilling to undergo such indignity, and seeing that all attempts to save the lady herself had failed, pulled forth the letter, and, upon his knees, gave it into the hands of the king, who frowned terribly as he saw the superscription.

Then the Lady Mary hastened forth, and, throwing herself at the feet of the king, said—

"It is thy handmaiden alone, oh king, who is guilty, if guilt there be : this noble Sama is innocent." And then, to the chagrin of the priest, she repeated all that had passed in the garden with the Canusis ; not, however, mentioning one word about the stranger who had given

her the letter. But the king, who had hitherto endea-voured to shield the maiden, now said sternly—

"Lady, either thou, this stranger, or the priest, have played us false ; and if it be as I suspect, that either has been the bearer of treasonous intelligence to the castle of Osacca, no power on earth, save that of Ogosho, can save thee ; and he was about to tear open the envelope, but the priest, coming forward, said—

"Stay, oh king : on thy loyalty to the great Ogosho, open not that letter : its contents are alone for his eyes." But, disregarding this, the rude soldier prince ran his fingers about the paper. It was so closely sealed that it

occupied him nearly a minute.   To me—to all—that minute was hours.   The Lady Mary watched resignedly as
regarded her own fate, but with bloodless lips and glistening eyes in fear for that of others.   The Canusis gazed
in moody, sulky silence, as if its opening would defeat
some wily plan ; I, as if I had made my peace with heaven, for not one glimpse of hope remained in my breast.
But at length the document was opened ; the king stared
at it for a moment, turned it round and round, then,
with an expression of gratified surprise upon his face,
said—

"Rogue priest, what means this jugglery? How darest
thou to gratify thy mean hate of this stranger, pass thy
tricks upon us?" and, as he held it before him, the lady
bent forward, her eyes strained, and clasping her throat
as if to suppress her rising emotions.   The priest gazed
stupidly, tottering and gnashing his teeth with impotent
rage, for he had been foiled.   I, with foolish astonishment, for all this pother had been about nothing, at least
so it appeared to me, for, lo ! the envelope so treasonably
addressed was

EMPTY !

The Canusis was the first to speak.   His bravado was
gone.   At the best, it appeared that he had played with
a powerful prince, to gratify some hatred against me ; or
why had he prayed of the king not to open the document?
At the thought of the punishment which the latter in
his rage might award him, he fell upon his knees crying
bitterly.

"As I hope hereafter to enter the realms of the kami,
oh king, thy slave has had no hand in this : that envelope
held a treasonous letter ; for in my duty to my sovereign
I opened it ;" adding, as he lifted up his hand in awe—
"May the gods protect us from devils : magic has been
at work."

"Fool, or rogue, or both, get thee hence from this city
of Osacca, for if thou art found within these walls by the
hour of kokonats, I will have thee in the gokuya," said
the king ; and for this leniency I could not account at the

time, otherwise than that he rejoiced at the lady having been thus saved from falling into the hands of Ogosho, for such would have happened, had the expected treasonous letter been found. The priest, astounded and humiliated, crawled from the presence without another word ; when the king, addressing me, said—

" Hollander, thank thy gods for this escape. Thou art free." But to my consternation, before I had time to thank his highness, the Lady Mary, who had remained gazing upon the empty envelope in speechless horror, cried wildly—

" Let not this rogue escape, oh king : he is a traitor." But suddenly, as if, in her hatred to me, she had said too much, she gazed around her wildly, and then, overcome by a tempest of conflicting emotions, she swooned at the foot of the throne. The king, the queen, the court became alarmed, the physicians were sent for, but in consequence of her last mysterious words, I, oh unfortunate scapegoat ! was, by the king's command, again led away to confinement.

CHAPTER XXI.

IN WHICH I VERIFY THE ADAGE THAT LISTENERS HEAR NO GOOD OF THEMSELVES, YET SAVE MY LIFE BY EAVESDROPPING.

Now, verily no human being could have been treated more like a shuttlecock, for scarcely had my guards conducted me back to the horrible gokuya, than one of the king's officers came and bade me follow him. I submitted to this fresh blow from my battledore, fate, by obeying in silence, for I but little cared whither he led. When, however, I found that he had conducted me to a small apartment, the windows of which opened like doors upon the great gardens of the palace, and in very polite tones told me the reason of my release, I was no less surprised than gratified. His story was to the following effect.

The Lady Mary, recovering almost immediately from her swoon, and not seeing me in the presence, desired to know if I had been set free ; and being answered in the negative, and also informed that she herself had made some grave charge against me, she fell at the feet of the king, and prayed of his majesty to release me at once, for that her words had been uttered during the madness of the moment, when her senses were wandering ; whereupon the king, who, I believe, had secret reasons of his own for complying with her wildest caprice, complied there and then, ordering me to be taken from the gokuya to that room, where I was to remain during his pleasure.

When the officer had delivered to me these commands, adding that I might walk in the gardens to exercise my limbs, if I so chose, with many bows he quitted the room, leaving me to my only resource under such circumstances —meditation ; and at once I sat down to reflect, cast up my reflections, and extract therefrom, if I could, some clue to all this mystery. But as, to a plain matter-of-fact mind, riddles and mysteries of all kinds are obnoxious, so to the same minds are they most difficult of unravelling. Before my last interview with the king I had puzzled my brain to discover why the Jesuit had come and gone from my apartment so mysteriously : that, however, was now solved, for there could be no doubt that, having first stupefied me with some drug, he had purloined the packet ; and very cleverly he had performed his task, for although he had abstracted the kernel he had replaced the shell without one visible crack.

Now, as his theft had in all probability been the saving of my life, as also that of the Lady Mary, I had every reason to be thankful I had been outwitted. So far so good ; but what could have been his motive ? That, however, defeated all my pondering and reasoning to discover. But what did it matter to me who had every reason to be satisfied with the result ?

Then I recalled to mind the mental agony, the fears of the lady ; first, her evidently terrible dread that the letter should meet the king's eyes ; then, most strange, the gaze compounded of rage and horror, with which she met

14

empty envelope, for the loss of the very document, which, if it had *not* been abstracted, would have condemned her and her friends to certain death, seemed to have caused her more agony than her previous peril. Truly, I could only account for it by her having believed that I, whom she had trusted, had taken the precious paper for the purpose of turning it to a treacherous use : hence the cause of her exclamation and swoon. And I liked this explanation, for it led my vanity to believe that her sufferings had arisen from the fear of having been deceived in one she—well—loved.

But to continue my narrative, and chronicle events as they happened. About two hours after the officer had quitted my apartment, and I was standing at the window, meditatively gazing upon the magnificent gardens before me, suddenly I heard the sound of footsteps, and, turning my head in the direction of a path shaded by camellias of uncommon height, I saw the form—I could not be mistaken, although his back was turned towards me—of the Jesuit Father Rodriguez. "More mystery ; but I will discover something this time," I muttered, as I remembered his desire not to be seen in Osacca. And suiting the action to the word, I ran down the steps, and, entering an avenue of cypress trees, walked noiselessly forward, when, although I could hear nought they said, I *saw* he was in earnest conversation with—the Lady Mary. I could not be mistaken, for now their faces were turned towards me, and fearing they might see me, I stooped down, but, instead of advancing, they retreated, and that, too, so quickly, that I lost sight of them.

Vexed at having been thus foiled in satisfying my curiosity, I sought relief by walking about the gardens, and for nearly two hours amused myself with the gambols of the gold fish in the ponds, the spouting waters of the fountains, and at the hideous grimaces of a great god with a thousand arms and legs ; but so did my mind dwell upon myself and fortunes, that I but dimly saw aught but visions of the past, my home in England, my ambitious hopes, the voyage from the Texel, the bright genial face of Will Adams, whom I longed again to join, and—and—well, it must be confessed, the lovely, pensive face of the Lady Mary; for she was the phantom which haunted my mind, sometimes loving, though ever fearing, that, like the beautiful land itself, that placid countenance was but the treacherous surface beneath which lay hidden volcanic emotions and passions. Yet, as the foolish moth is drawn irresistibly to the flame which is to consume it, did my heart seek the mysterious beauty. With such thoughts was my mind occupied; aye, so deeply, that I scarcely noticed that a dense fog (Japan is, beyond all countries, the land of fogs) was filling the land; but again the sound of footsteps fell upon my ears. I listened: I could not see, for the fog-film was too thick; but so distinctly could I hear the footsteps that I became certain the pedestrians, whoever they were, were walking through an avenue of cypress trees and flowery shrubs near me, and which led to the mia, or chapel. The fog, the trees, obscured me from view, so I crept along the outer side of one of the rows, listening attentively. As I have said, there were two persons; moreover, they were walking towards the mia. My curiosity became excited; nay, I fear it was jealousy, for I but little doubted that the Lady Mary was one of the twain. I kept pace with them till they entered the little building, where, just beneath the portico, and within a few inches of my ears, they stopped to finish their conversation. I then distinctly recognised the voices: one was that of Sir Martin the Christian, the other monstrously like, though somewhat hoarser, thicker, quicker, than that of the Lady Mary; but the conversation—well, it was *that* which satiated my curiosity; nay, chilled my blood with horror, caused me to feel as might a man while undergoing the process of petrifaction, or being changed into stone limb by limb. The pith is this. The Lady Mary—she who has such hold of my heart and mind—was deliberately laying down a plan for my assassination. Yes, she was boldly declaring that the false knave of the West (meaning me) had himself extracted the fatal letter, and had made such use of it with some high personage (I did not hear whom), that the conspiracy had been discovered, and for that reason it was necessary for the safety of the conspirators, that he (I) should die, aye, and that very night, and that, too, by means of the hara-kiri, a process which, translated, has the pleasant sound of the happy despatch.   Further, I made out that the twain were to enter my apartment, and, by persuasion or force, cause me to rip up my own bowels.   I had heard enough : my first impulse was at once to seek an audience of the king, but, oh soft-hearted Melichor ! there was yet love enough for the intended murderess remaining to make me fear the fearful doom that the disclosure would bring upon her, indeed, to shift the wind of my intention ; and so I determined to hasten back to my apartment, and snatch up my sword, muffle my face within the folds of my gown, and, at all hazards, made an attempt to escape from the palace.   But suddenly the precious couple came forth from the temple, when, fearing discovery, I remained motionless until their footsteps had become out of ear-shot.   Then, with some difficulty having forced my way through the now thicker fog to the door-windows of my room, I entered, and in disgust, horror, and the most bitter feelings, I threw myself upon the mats, and sought relief by giving way to the most idiotic emotions.   I had heard no person follow me into the room, yet suddenly I felt a hand upon my arm, and looking up, oh mystery upon mysteries ! there before me, calmly beautiful as ever, but with a glittering cattan in her hand, stood the she-wolf, the Lady Mary.   At the sight I leaped to my feet, and, starting backwards many paces—indeed, knowing the purpose of that weapon, its sight caused me a sudden colic—cried—

"Ah ! truly thou art quick enough ; but beware, for neither thou nor thy friend shall leave this room alive."

Whereupon, with much astonishment depicted upon her countenance, she replied—

"Has the Sama again been in the dream-clouds, or is he possessed with the 'fox' (mad) ? for truly it is not possible he can fear a woman."

"Oh thou fiend !" I thought ; yet, ashamed at having betrayed fear of a woman, I said—

"Lady, I know thee, and for what purpose thou art now here."

"To save thee from the vengeance of those whose anger thou hast incurred. But hasten, place this cattan beneath thy gown, and follow;" and she gave me the sword. But still believing she was only veiling her purpose under a decoy, I said—

"Woman, again I say I _know_ thee, and am not to be decoyed to the slaughter."

"Alas! alas! thou art ill," she said; adding, "what thoughts possess thee? But speak not—no, not one word, for, by my hope of heaven, I am here to befriend thee." And so earnestly did she utter these words, that I followed her through the intricacies of the palace till we came to a door, which I recognised as being that of my former apartment; and when we had entered, she said, as she pointed to the window which abutted over the river—

"That is the only means of escape from the palace: there a boat awaits, which will conduct thee to a place of safety."

But still I hesitated; for was not the river a fitting place for assassination. Perceiving my doubts, she led me to the window, and pointing to the men in the boat, in one of whom, to my surprise, I recognised the Father Rodriguez, said—"Can the Sama still doubt the honesty of her who would die rather than one hair of his head should be injured?"

These words—the tones in which they were uttered— were sufficient, even had I *not* recognised the boatmen, for, as if by enchantment, my fears, doubts fled, and, having placed her hand to my lips, I descended into the boat, when the father, putting one of the sculls into my hand, said in a whisper—

"For thy life not a word till we are off the river."

Less than an hour at the oars brought us to the water-steps of one of the great warehouses, where it appeared the Jesuit had his lodgings.

No sooner, however, had we entered the father's apartment, than, unable longer to suppress the bitterness of my wrath towards one whom I believed had caused me so much misery, I said—

"Whatever may be the goodness of thy motives, the darkness of thy ways has caused me great suffering."

"Those ways, my son, have been but as necessary means towards an end; and this time have they been the saving of thee from destruction."

"By my soul, priest, I understand thee not: therefore, if thou canst speak in nought but riddles, in God's name hold thy peace," I replied angrily; and that anger bringing us together yard-arm and yard-arm, he proceeded to tell me how it was, that, against my will, I had been pulled to and fro like a play-house puppet.

"Know then, my son," he began, "that thy troubles were greatly of thine own bringing about: for although, in the garden at Seruga, thou so bravely rescued the Lady Mary from the Canusis, thou didst the work so clumsily, that he saw thee; and having done so, at once resolved upon recovering the packet, and effecting thy ruin."

"How, my father, couldst thou have had knowledge of that scene in the garden?" I asked.

"My office, which keeps me near the person of Ogosho, and his majesty's great regard for his servant, gives many opportunities for using eyes and ears that are never closed, never shut. *How*, no matter: sufficient that I *did* hear the Pagan priest relate the history of his discomfiture to Ogosho; and further, I heard the Ziogoon command him to follow the Queen of Tango to Osacca, and endeavour, by all means, to recover possession of the packet, but *so warily*, that the Lady Mary should not be compromised, at least so publicly, that he should be compelled to include her among the list of traitors he knew, or more than guessed, to be enrolled therein. The Canusis obeyed, and reached this city even before you; and from that hour watched his opportunity. He knew not, however, that I had heard this, nor that I was at hand to frustrate his designs by forestalling him in the possession of that packet."

"But, my father, how is this possible? How knewest thou that I had possession of the paper?"

"Because, my son, knowing the Lady Mary was to be entrusted with it, its great importance, and, let me add, being aware of thy honesty and attachment to the lady, and also that she would be too wary to keep such a document in her possession after the adventure in the garden, and knowing that thou wast the sole person to whom she could safely entrust it, it required but small shrewdness to guess that it would be found in thy possession; and of all this the Canusis had knowledge; but though very cunning, the pagan was *not* aware that *I* knew it."

"But the Lady Mary, father, was *she* cognizant of thy design?"

"Not so; for so zealously are the Christian fathers watched where the King of Tango holds his housekeeping, that I could get no speech with her, at least in time to warn her : hence, my son, the reason of my first appearance in the boat."

"Then thou drugged the saki ?"

"It was a means to an end ; but the ingredient, though effective, was innoxious : moreover, by drugging the saki, and abstracting the contents of the packet, I saved thy life, no less than that of many noble men and women."

"But the letter : what has become of that ?"

"Nay, it matters not ; it is safe."

"But it matters much to me, for by both parties am I regarded as a traitor ; and from two sets of knaves is my throat in danger by this chicanery of thine."

"Tut, my son ; had that letter been found upon thee, thy life would not have been worth an hour's purchase."

"By my honour, father, it would have been of greater value than now, when, in place of *one*, there are *two* daggers at my breast."

"Tut, tut, my son, *thou* needst not fear."

"I say thou art in the wrong, father, for scarce an hour since, my doing to the death was planned by that fascinating tigress."

"Tigress ! whom meanest thou ?"

"The Lady Mary. Aye, and with her the Christian noble, Martin."

"The Lady Mary ! impossible, my son," said he, with surprise ; "but, but," he added, "truly the danger, the fear for others who are most dear to her, and her indignation at thy apparent treachery, may have made her frantic."

"Verily, but a small consolation for me, father. Mad people should be chained up."

"My son," replied he, after a moment's thought, "this thing is not possible ; it is thou who art mad : for did not this lady save thee again from the gokuya ? has she not even now saved thee from that assassination with which thou chargest her ?"

"That she plotted my death, my own ears are the witnesses ; though by what inscrutable means she was so speedily inclined to change her intentions is to me still a mystery."

" My son, let it suffice thee for the present to know
that the lady again believes in thy honour; nay, that she
is aware of the abstraction of the letter."

" Thus, then, it was in consequence of thine own ad-
mission that *thou* stolest the paper, that she kindly re-
prieved *me.* Truly, father, I know not which I owe the
most—hate or gratitude—for bringing the dagger to my
throat, or, when there, rescuing me from the weapon,"
said I bitterly.

" I said not that *she* sought thy life; I said not that it
was *her* from whom I had saved thee : but, mark me, son,
I do say that thy only safety is in remaining hidden
beneath this roof, at least for a period."

" More riddles, father ; for who in this barbarous land
can seek *my* miserable life ?" said I.

" First, Ogosho, who will be played upon by the chief
Canusis, who hates thee for having foiled his plans; secondly, the Christian knight Martin, who thinks that
thou hast purloined the letter, and given it to the King
of Tango, whose ignorance he believes was only apparent,
and put on to hide some hidden scheme of vengeance
upon the whole Christian community. From the latter
danger, however, to-morrow's sun will rescue thee, for
the lady herself will prove to him that his belief is ground-
less ; but from the enmity of the pagan priest thou must
remain here *perdu.*"

CHAPTER XXII.

I SOLVE A MYSTERY, AND WELL SERVE THE QUEEN OF
TANGO, THE LADY MARY, AND THE JESUIT.

THUS had I been plunged into and extricated from great
perils, without myself being to blame or praise for the one
or the other. Now I was to be incarcerated in the Jesuit's house, that I might avoid other dangers which ho-
vered over me. But having sufficient regard left for my

life, miserable though it might be, and knowing discretion to be the better part of valour, I resolved to take the father's advice, and make myself as comfortable as circumstances permitted. Accordingly, for many days I ate, drank, slept, and patiently awaited better times.

The days, however, passed very monotonously, for few were the hours of companionship which the father bestowed upon me. What he did with himself for the greater part I was at a loss to discover : that he was engaged, however, in some secret affair I did not doubt, for although he knew it not, I was fully aware that he received constant visits from men whom, from their long brown robes, I took to be merchants and traders of the city, and, by reason of such visits, I thought the sly old gentleman had other and more profitable transactions than the cure of souls, at least till one day, overhearing two of these visitors in conversation, I recognised the Portugal tongue, and thus guessed them to be brethren of the same order as the father, who, being under the ban of the law, and so unable to perform their religious functions publicly, met in secret at the house of their superior, Father Rodriguez, under the guise of merchants ; but as, however ardent my curiosity, it was really no manner of business of mine, I never questioned the father ; indeed, if I had, I do not believe he would have satisfied me. Still, being given to observation, I could not help remarking that each day at sundown he regularly walked in the large garden at the side of the house (the reader will please remember that the back fronted the river), and that the walk invariably lasted about two hours, whether the day was one of sunshine, rain, or fogs : that he always seemed pleased, nay, even joyous and lighthearted, upon his return. Well, putting this observation to the fact that he had very earnestly begged of me (ostensibly for my own safety) never to walk in that garden, a suspicion haunted me that things were not quite taut ; in fact, that he was helping in the brewing of a conspiracy against Ogosho, for well I knew that his sympathy, like that of all the Christian natives, was with the deposed Prince Fide Yori. So, so—well, I will make a clear breast of it—my curiosity led me to *watch* him. Accordingly, one evening, I followed in his wake, taking care to keep myself out of sight, which, by reason of the trees, bushes, and tall underwood, was not difficult, till I saw him approach the large bath-house, in front of which he walked to and fro for about five minutes, I suppose. For an instant I must have turned my eyes in another direction, for suddenly he disappeared, and greatly to my chagrin : for if I followed the path between the place where I was hidden and the bath-house, the door of the latter being open, we might meet, an accident not by me desired; and so, as I could do no better, I waited for about half an hour ; but then, curiosity getting the better of prudence, I crept softly towards the bath-house and listened. All was silent save a certain dull murmuring sound, which appeared to be caused by the wind upon the waters of the river. I entered the bath-house, but *there* nothing was to be seen save tubs, hot-water pipes, and other apparatus for bathing ; and being at my wit's end, I stood still to think. The murmuring which I had believed to come from the river sounded louder. I held my head forward, as if to strain to the greatest extent my sense of hearing, and becoming convinced it arose from beneath, I laid my ear upon the ground. I could not now be mistaken : it was the sound of human voices, and I started to my feet with no agreeable sensations, for I no longer doubted that conspirators had met in some cellar beneath, or that Father Rodriguez was with, of, and among them ; and more than ever my curiosity became excited. I desired to know more, but I wished I had' known nothing ; for should I be found there by the conspirators, my life would be worth but a small purchase. Then it occurred to me to find the secret entrance to the cellar, for through that the father must have so suddenly vanished ; but after a few minutes of useless examination, I prudently resolved to return to the house. I left the bath-house, but, in the excitement of the moment, took a wrong path, and did not discover my error till, by the rustling of the wind upon the water, I found myself near the river, nay, heard the sound of oars. I stopped, for it might be the arrival of more conspirators. I stooped among some bushes and listened. A boat or barge rubbed against the free-stone water-wall ; and, the moment after, my fear changed to indignation, for I heard the voice of my enemy, the chief Canusis, who, as his companion got ashore, said—

"Now, get thee to this bath-house, and, having secured the secret entrance of which you speak, hasten back, so that we may at once to the water-gate, and so confront the rats in their very hole."

"Oh, oh," thought I : "then I am right : there are conspirators in that house." But then it occurred to me that while the Father Rodriguez was upon one side, the Canusis was upon the other ; and in an instant my choice of sides was determined upon : so, keeping at a short distance in the rear, I followed this rogue, who I more than suspected to be a confidential servant of Sir Martin of the Gilded Spurs, till he entered the bath-house ; when, stealthily following and looking through the half-opened door, I saw

the fellow stoop down near the largest tub, and examine
what had appeared to me to be an ornament, namely, a
large tortoise of copper, inlaid in the flooring. Lifting
up one of the scales, he took from his girdle a key, and,
placing it in the lock, turned it twice : in fact, he was
doubly locking from the outside. the entrance mentioned
by the Canusis, and thus, I had no doubt, was entrapping
the conspirators. Now, disliking such foul work, I sprang
forth, seized him by the throat, snatched the key from his
hand, and threatened, if he uttered a word, to strangle
him ; but the poor wretch was too much terrified to speak,
and as I had neither thought nor time to ask any questions I secured his arms and legs so that he could not
move, by means of his own robe, a portion of which,
stuffed in his mouth, served also as a gag : then, placing
the key in the lock, lifted the tortoise trap, when finding,
as I expected, a flight of narrow steps, I descended ; but
the next moment my legs were lifted from the ground
and my body thrown violently backwards : thus did I
make my appearance among the conspirators ; aye, conspirators truly, but who were conspiring for their own
salvation. In fact, I had profaned a *meeting of Christians ;*
for there were the Father Rodriguez, the Lady Mary, and
the Queen of Tango, who, though alarmed at my abrupt
entrance, were still upon their knees, with rosaries before
them, and in attitudes of fervent prayer ; also the Christian noble, Sir Martin. The latter it was who had given
me such a rough welcome, and who, holding me by the
throat, exclaimed as I fell—

"Miserable dog, thou hast betrayed us !"

The ladies were too greatly alarmed to speak, but the
Jesuit, recognising the intruder, and more in anger than
in fear, arose from his kneeling position, and taking Sir
Martin by the arm, said, as calmly as if he had been proceeding with the service—

"My life upon it, noble Sama, you have naught to fear
from this Hollander." The knight let go his hold. Then
to me added, " But thou, my son—"

" Stay, father ; I pray thee listen," said I, interrupting
him. " The Canusis of the emperor hath discovered the

time and place of these thy secret meetings, and is even
now, while I speak, at the water-gate, prepared to arrest
or confront you all. The entrance above was doubly
locked from the outside by a rogue whom I found in the
act, but who now lies speechless and immoveable." :

My words at the same time gave agony and relief.
Hearing the fellow was secured, they one and all followed
the queen in repeating the common prayer of thanks of
the Christians of Japan—

"Jesu Maria! Jesu Maria! in the hour of their danger
thou art ever at thy children's call."

"But the rogue above must be secured : will the Sama
aid me?" said Sir Martin, who was the first aroused to
the necessity of immediate action.

I complied. Ascending together, we blindfolded the
man, and, between us, carried him into a room at the
upper part of the father's house, where we left him, and
there he remained, upon a scant diet of rice, cake, and
water, until the Christians again became sufficiently in
the ascendant to be regardless of any harm his tongue
might attempt to do them. As we returned to the cellar
we met the father and the ladies, who were disguised in
the long brown garb of merchants. Advancing some steps
before the Lady Mary, the queen, taking both my hands
in her own, with a look and in tones which still cling to
my memory, said—

"The queen has not words to convey to the Western
Sama how great are her thanks for the service he has this
night performed."

"The great God alone, O Sama, can picture to thee the
gratitude which swells our hearts, and makes words useless
to express our thanks," said the Lady Mary, kissing my
hands.

My heart leaped to my mouth : I forgot the would-be
murderess, every thing but the last act ; and as, under the
guidance of the Japan knight, they left the house, all I
could say was—

"May God ever preserve thee from thine enemies,
lady : *me* He has more than rewarded by having granted
me the privilege of saving thee."

The Jesuit and myself ¡were now alone, and when he
he had offered up a prayer for their escape, he said—
"Well hast thou done, my son, and from my soul I
thank thee."

"But, father, if these pious meetings be traitorous in
the eyes of the king, then art thou not safe, for assuredly
they, as well as the place and hour, are known to the
Canusis, thine enemy."

"The pagan priest believes not these meetings are held
for the practices of our holy church, but suspects them
to consist of the enemies of the usurper Ogosho, *those* who
are even now seeking to drag him from the throne : he
knows, also, that the Lady Mary is, by her birth, of the
Christian, or Fide Yori party : but could he prove that
she had attended a meeting of the adherents of the young
Kubo, he would again have that claim upon her which the
loss of the document you wot of took from him.   Thus,
my son, have you again foiled him, for without the most
convincing proofs of her guilt, he fears to, nay, dares not,
demand the lady from the king, her protector."

"But the queen, father, for even she trembled as if she
had narrowly escaped some terrible peril."

"The royal lady's fears, my son, were rather for the
safety of her kinswoman than for herself ; for, notwithstanding his fits of jealousy, so devoted is her husband
to her, that she tempers even his great hatred of the
Christians, whom he would exterminate an' he could,"
replied he ; adding, "but still she would dread his coming
to the knowledge that she attended the secret meetings
of the brethren."

"But it is said the king knows his wife has been converted : if so, she would have but little to fear from his
knowledge that she attended these meetings."

"The tyrant, my son, permits her practice of the holy
faith, but in her palace alone : did he know of this meeting with Sir Martin it would doubtless excite his jealousy.
This the Canusis knows ; so, could he have confronted
her majesty in the company of Sir Martin, he would have
held the discovery so *in terrorem* over the Lady Mary,

that she would have sacrificed herself, perhaps, to Ogosho, in order to save the life of her mistress."

" The life of the queen ! is it then possible, father, that this king is so insensate a wretch ?"

" Aye, my son ; into many dangers has his jealousy thrown the beautiful Grace (for by that name has she been received into the Christian church). God help her ! but I fear that in one of his jealous fits he may yet slay her ; —her, the beautiful, the good, the pure ; so strong in the faith, so earnest in her devotion to the welfare of her Christian brethren, that she is now the chief buttress of the church in this city," replied the father ; adding, " but of this enough."

And the remainder of the evening was spent by the father in prayer and meditation ; by myself in thinking upon the events of the day ; of that kiss upon my hand, and the donor, the beautiful assassin, for whom I had strange feelings, and with whom I should have been madly in love : but, comical as it may seem, the truth is, I could not—and I tried very hard—get out of my head a notion that the symbol upon a lover's seal, of an arrow piercing the heart, was much more to be admired than the real performance of the hara-kiri at the compulsory instance of a lady love.

CHAPTER XXIII.

HISTORIC TRAGEDY.—THE DEATH OF A CHRISTIAN QUEEN.

THE events of the next two years were but few worth recording ; those few, however, were of so serious, so solemn a kind, and so illustrative of the old adage, that truth is stranger than fiction, that I would impress upon the mind of the reader that, as here set down, they are in no degree the coinage of the present writer ; but after this, should he or she remain in doubt, I may refer them

to the Japanners' own history, which has been done in
the languages of the Portugals, the Spaniards, the
French, the Hollanders, and the English, wherein is
related the sad story of the beautiful Grace, the Christian
Queen of Tango :—but to resume my narrative.

From what fortunate cause I know not, but certain it
was, that from the night of the escape from the cellar,
the persecution of the Christians in Osacca slackened.
Some would have it that it was owing to the visit to
Ogosho's court of one Don Rodriguez, sometime Governor-General of the Philippines, and who had successfully
interceded for his fellow-religionists.   Others asserted
that the King of Tango, coming to the knowledge of the
narrow escape of his queen and her chief lady from falling into the hands of his liege lord Ogosho, had been so
rejoiced, and his heart thereby so softened, that her
majesty had been enabled to mould it somewhat in
favour of her Christian brethren.   And the latter was
my belief, for within three days after the escape, it was
signified to me, through an officer of the royal household,
that by reason of the queen's great regard for me, his
majesty had reinstated me in his service, and commanded
my return to my old lodgings in the palace.

Where the happiness of the whole people depends
upon the breath of one, the changes from deepest grief
to liveliest joy are sudden, nay, even instantaneous.   So
was it in Osacca ; for, lo ! the Jesuit fathers were now
seen again in the streets, the native Christians openly
attended their church, and the beautiful Queen Grace
became so enthusiastic in the cause of the faith, that she
publicly performed the duties enjoined by the fathers ;
she gathered around her at the palace the children of the
poor, and, in token of her following of Christ in the
proper spirit of humility, washed them with her own
hands, instructed them in the holy mysteries, exhorted
them to virtue, and so made numbers fervent Christians ;
and, moreover, that she might the better prosecute her
religious studies, she herself learned to read and write
the Latin and Portugal languages, and, indeed, altogether
followed out so precious a course of life, that she became

15

regarded as a saint, and was dearly beloved both by Christians and infidels.

Thus, then, did the native converts buoy themselves up with a hope that their Millennium had arrived ; but, alas ! they were building upon a foundation of sand. The volcano which was so soon to deluge them with its wrath was even then fermenting. The confederate kings of the party of the young Kubo-Sama, Fide Yori, gained several victories over the armies of the usurper, Ogosho, whereupon the latter commanded the King of Tango to march to his aid, with all the troops that could be spared from the defence of Osacca, and then came the first shock ; for although nearly as many Christians adhered to the cause of Ogosho as to that of the young Kubo-Sama, so doubtful was the King of Tango of their sincerity, that, prior to his leaving for the imperial camp, he displaced Sir Martin of the Gilded Spurs from his post of overseer of the palace, and established in his stead one Jocativo, who, being a bigoted Sintoo, and, moreover, devoted to the king, was not likely to show too much favour to the Christians, or even to his mistress, the queen, over whom the jealous tyrant had left him complete control ; at least whenever she quitted the palace-gates, through which she could never pass except under the escort of Jocativo.

For some weeks after the departure of the king from Osacca, matters went on within the palace without much alteration, except, indeed, that I now had more opportunities of seeing the queen and the Lady Mary ; for, be it remembered that the women of Japan, unlike their sisters in other Asiatic nations, are permitted social intercourse with the other sex. At length, however, a cloud settled over the horizon : alarm sat on the faces of the many, joy on the faces of the hopeful few : soldiers were drawn from within the palace, and every other possible source, to man and defend the walls of the town ; and these troops, barely three parts of whom were of the Sintoo or Buddhist faith, were fearful and suspicious of the remaining portion, who were Christians ; consequently many were the broils between them, the more frequent, as the officers, fearing to lose their services, did not punish either.

The cause of all this was, that spies had brought intelligence that Augustine Tsucamidono, King of Fingo, and great Admiral of the empire, and Xibunizo, King of Omi, were marching upon the town with a vast army. But to my sad story.—The enemy were in sight, the siege had commenced, and Jocativo, who, to do him justice, was no less brave than skilful in his capacity of chief commander of the troops, made a noble defence for many days, during which time he had planned, and caused to be successfully executed, several sorties ; but his bravery and skill were unavailing, for, at last, the enemy effected a breach, and entered the city, driving the defenders before them. Foreseeing this defeat, Jocativo had, early in the day, sent orders to his second in command at the palace to have every place of possible entrance trebly guarded, and not to permit a living soul to go without its walls ; and thus were the inmates, myself among the rest, kept for hours in a state of terrible anxiety, awaiting the result.

I have said that the king had conferred upon me a command of a party of his guards. Well, prior to his departure, my office had been rather nominal than real ; but afterwards, when the great body of the troops had been withdrawn for the purpose of defending the walls of the city, the general, Jocativo, stationed me with a party of fifty men in the outer court of the queen's apartments, where I did duty ; or rather, nothing but walk about, posting and relieving sentries at the various outlets. Upon the fatal day, however, our suspense was at last broken, by the appearance before the walls of Jocativo in full retreat at the head of a scant remnant of the guards ; and scarcely had this party been admitted, when an officer of the admiral's army, Sir Martin of the Gilded Spurs, who, at the commencement of the siege had gone over to the enemy, appeared before the walls. Faint and haggard, begrimed with blood and dust, Jocativo answered his summons ; and to Sir Martin's demand that the Queen of Tango should be given up

to the victorious admiral, returned a bitter and bold
defiance.

This was sheer madness, for the place could not hold
out a single day; and though, with the instinctive
resignation to the will of their superiors so common to
Japanners, the whole garrison remained silent, they
prepared to die; but, after what fashion? In hand to
hand fight with the enemy? No; but as I will now
relate.

When the general, Jocativo, had replied to Sir Martin,
he went to the bath-house, where he remained for about
half an hour—not more: then, attended by several of
his superior officers, all with naked swords in their hands,
he passed me, but with an expression of fear, determination, horror upon his countenance that startled me.
Where could he be going? What was about to happen?
I knew not, nor even then dreamed. Now the apartments, or, rather, separate house of the queen and the
ladies, was raised from the ground by pillars of about
two feet in height. In this space, beneath the house, I
saw men arranging a number of small barrels in lines,
but so near to each other that they touched, and that,
too, all of them; and, with the exception that the
countenances of these men wore a blank and chapfallen
expression, they were proceeding in as business-like an
order as if they had been filling the hold of a merchan-
dize-ship. Curious to know the meaning of this labour,
I asked; but the only reply I could obtain, was—

"Obeying the command of the king."

The answer was indefinite enough, but still I felt no
alarm, till a portion of the contents of one of the barrels
fell upon the ground: then the horrible truth arose all
at once to my mind. I exclaimed—

"Great God! they are about blowing up the building,
the residence of the queen and the Lady Mary:" and at
once bidding defiance to all forms, I passed the sentries,
ran through the passages, and reached the queen's hall
of audience.

The apartment was filled with soldiers, but, forcing
my way between them, the following scene presented

itself. Jocativo and two officers of the next rank were kneeling, but weeping bitterly, holding their hands before their faces : a group of the queen's ladies were also upon their knees, with their faces in their hands, and loudly sobbing: a sacrifice was preparing : the soldiers with their naked swords were the attendants ; the generals the sacrificial butchers ; but the victim—at whose feet, clutching the hem of her garment, and with a sorrow and grief that had passed the power of speech, knelt the Lady Mary—was the beautiful Grace, Queen of Tango, who stood erect, but rather with the martyr's resignation in the present and undying hope in the future, than the defiance of a heroine, with her hands placed upon the head of her favourite friend, whom, in tones whose melody now rings in my ears, and an angelic sweetness of expression, a very heaven of hope beaming from her eyes, she was blessing. But for a moment I will retrace my steps.

Jocativo, finding defeat certain, and having received the admiral's message, hastened to his mistress with a sealed packet, which the king, upon the eve of his departure, had given to him. Its contents were commands, that, in the event of the enemy besieging the town, and the probability of the queen's being taken, to strike off his mistress's head, and fire the palace. Revolting as it seems, the command was holy in the eyes of a Japan general ; holy too, in the eyes of a queen, a devoted wife, who knew no will but that of her husband.

When the fatal document was read aloud before her whole court, the queen was the only person unmoved : nay, when her friends and attendants fell to weeping, tearing their hair, and giving way to the wildest despair, she gently chid them, saying—

"Be not thus afflicted, oh my children ! Death to a Christian soul is but the passing from a temporal life to one that is eternal." Then, when she had again blessed the Lady Mary, and her other friends, she commanded the generals to obey their master's order, without fear or sorrow.

Jocativo, kissing the hem of her robe, said—

"Would, oh beloved queen, that the lives of ten thousand of thy slaves could answer for thy precious life; but our master's orders are imperative. Yet, madam, thou diest not alone, for thy servants are resolved not to survive a crime which the laws of the empire, and the obedience we owe to the king, compel us to commit. No, they dare not live when they can no longer serve a princess whose great virtues they revere and Japan adores."

To which, in sorrow and pity, rather than in anger, she replied—

"Know you not, my friends, I am a Christian ; and that, therefore, there is nothing in death to alarm me, for the true religion enjoins me to obey the orders of him whom our laws have made the master of my life ; but at your determination to destroy yourselves I shudder, for, alas ! what will then become of you for all eternity ? Therefore I implore of you with my last breath that you be content to execute the orders of your king as concerns me, and not sacrifice your own lives; for although such is the law of Japan, in that it is unjust, and will not excuse you before the tribunal of Him who alone has the power of life and death."

The officers remained silent : they dared not comply :—they were too full of sorrow to refuse.

Then, turning to her ladies, she again affectionately bade them an eternal farewell, and exhorted them, as they had loved her, to quit the palace immediately. Some of those who were Christians only, prepared to depart, for the sad tragedy was coming to a close. One alone still knelt at her feet in silence—it was the Lady Mary ; the grief of the others had been violent, hers had been silent ; but to the last exhortation she replied—

"Grace, beloved friend, my Saviour forbids me to die, my heart forbids me to live ;" then lifting her hands she said—

"Come what may, I will not leave thee ;" but overcome by her conflicting emotions, she fell forward senseless. At this I advanced : the soldiers obstructed the way, but the queen waving her hand to them, they stood aside. I caught her in my arms, and Grace, sweetly smiling her approval, said—

"Thou at least, oh Sama, art free to depart: take her hence to the camp of the admiral: her life is too precious to be sacrificed; her soul must not be endangered by self-murder." One living kiss upon the warm lips of the senseless girl, and the queen led the way to her own execution. I heard nor saw no more; but by the aid of some of the Christian attendants, who, perhaps from obedience alone to the queen's command, perhaps from religious feeling, but, I believe, chiefly from love of their own lives, were about to fly the palace, I carried her to the court-yard, and, placing her in one of the royal norimons under female charge, led the party forward, and in about half-an-hour, partly by persuasion, partly by force, we had made our way, amidst the multitudes of civilians and soldiers who thronged the streets, to the chief gates of the city, where our further progress was stayed by an advanced body of horsemen, led by two men, the one Sir Martin of the Gilded Spurs, who now openly wore the emblems of the Christian soldier of Japan, viz. a white surcoat over his armour, embroidered with a red cross and three nails, and a small tablet in front of his helmet, upon which was engraven the word "Jesus;" the other, a young man, nay, a youth, of slight figure and diminutive stature, who wore no Christian emblem, but, armed to the teeth, and with a long naked sword in his hand, sat his horse with the ease and firmness of a warrior, and the dignity of a king.

Upon first perceiving our party the two leaders galloped in advance of their troops to meet us. They were known to the bearers of the norimon, for they put down their load, and, at once recognising me, Sir Martin, turning to the youth, said—

"It is the western Sama, who hath done us so much service; and, by the God of my father, but badly have we rewarded him:" whereupon the youth dismounted from his horse as if to perform the ceremony of welcome; but as the men moved aside, and he caught sight of the tenant of the norimon, he gave an exclamation of delight, which was reciprocated by the Lady Mary; but the first sensation of delight at the unexpected meeting being passed, he said, as he frowned savagely at me—

"*Thou*, my sister, and travelling under charge of this stranger! Is it, then, as I have heard?"

"But for this noble Sama, my brother would now have no sister, for the queen"—

"The queen! the queen! What of the beauteous Grace? How fares she? But we forget our duty: it is to the queen's rescue we are hastening," said this impetuous boy, almost in a single breath; and not waiting for a reply, he would have remounted his horse, but at that instant a great explosion shook the town, and made the earth beneath us tremble.

"Alas! alas that I was born! The queen, our Grace, has passed to heaven," exclaimed the lady, covering her face with her hands. That explosion told its own story, at least to the bystanders: help or aid was fruitless. For a minute they stood mute with horror: then the Christians fell upon their knees, and, with uplifted hands and hearts, prayed to heaven. The youth alone exhibited no outward signs of either prayer or grief; but terrible was his brow, blood spirted from his nether lip, and that hand—that mutilated hand—he held before his eyes for an instant; the next, he coolly ordered his party to advance towards the great castle of Osacca to meet the main body of the army of the admiral, which was just without the town. To me he said haughtily—

"Whether I have most to thank or hate thee, I may not now judge; but for the present I will relieve thee of the charge of this lady."

"This is unjust, oh, my brother."

But stopping his sister, this wild young savage said—

"When was it, oh, my sister, that the maidens of Japan were taught rebellion against the chiefs of their families? Yet," he added, addressing me, "I would not have thee believe that we are ungrateful, oh, stranger; so for the present I crave thy company." And without another word from him, and before I could reply, I found myself in the midst of a party of soldiers, being led I knew not whither, or whether as friend or captive.

But of that explosion, of Grace the queen : well, her last moments are thus chronicled :—

"She was led forward to her oratory, and after fervently praying for some minutes, with a countenance smiling, as if she had heard the most agreeable news,

told the general, Jocativo, that he might execute the king's orders at his will.   The general then, having intreated her forgiveness, she knelt down, and, as she pronounced the sacred names of Jesus and Mary, her end was accomplished.   Thus died the handsomest and most accomplished woman, and the most fervent Christian in Japan."

The pendant of this terrible illustration of the savage nature of these Japanners was as follows :—

"After death they covered the queen's body with a cloth of gold, filled all the apartments with combustible materials, and, while the chief officers shut themselves in a room, and ripped themselves up, another set fire to the gunpowder beneath; and thus, by the fearful explosion which speedily reduced the whole pile to ashes, gave an ominous welcome to the incoming troops of the victorious admiral."

CHAPTER XXIV.

THE SPEEDY VICTORY OF THE CHRISTIAN ADMIRAL IS MARRED BY A MORE SPEEDY DEFEAT, AND I AM AGAIN THE FOOTBALL OF FORTUNE.

Now, in our progress to the palace, it struck me as very remarkable, that while the whole population—Christian, Sintoo, and Buddhist—put themselves forward vigorously at the appearance of the conquering soldiers, not one European father was to be seen; and that, too, though the party to which in their hearts they were most affected was now dominant. For my own part, I had but small reason to be thankful for the change of rulers; for no sooner did we reach the great castle of Fide Yori, who was so speedily to be proclaimed the sole ruler of the empire, than Sir Martin of the Gilded Spurs, upon the part of the conqueror, repaid me for my services to the Lady Mary, by saying—

"The Sama is free to depart. Let him not enter the castle, for his life is endangered."

"How!" said I; "what words are these? Let the noble Martin explain. Who would strike at the life of his servant?"

"Words are but words; they are not armour which will protect his life from the dagger. Sufficient for him to know that he has angered one who can bear no control, yet whose anger may, in a few days, become gratitude." And before I could answer, the Christian knight rode forward into the castle. Astounded, I stood aside, and was nearly ridden over by the savage young lord, who,

as he rode by the side of his sister's norimon, bent his
eyes upon me with a glance that pierced to my very soul.
It was enough, however, to recall me to prudence; and
so, letting the troops pass, I made my way to the house
of the Father Rodriguez, whom I had not seen for a long
time. He was alone, therefore I at once recounted to
him, in indignant tones, my day's adventures, my services
to the Lady Mary, and her brother's grateful return.

"Still, harbour not anger in thine heart, my son, for
this youth is maddened by many wrongs," was his reply.

" How, my father, is it I who have wronged him, that
he should seek my life ? for I make no doubt that it is of
this young viper the Christian knight cautioned me to
beware."

" Even so, my son ; at least, so he believes ; and that,
too, in the most tender part—his honour ; for he is of
proud and illustrious rank, and believes that in the poor
wandering sailor of the west he sees one who has more
hold upon his sister's heart than he approves."

" Would that this thing were ; but, my father, if even
so, how can he, who has been so long parted from his
sister, have come by this knowledge."

" My son, I know not. There may be another, whose
jealousy, having been aroused by you, may have whispered
in his ear."

" Is it possible, father, that he of whom you speak is
the Christian knight ? for none other could have imagined
this thing."

" My son, of me it is useless to inquire, for I know
not ; so enough for the present, for my soul is trembling
with sorrow—with fear." And so earnestly did he utter
these words, that, being alarmed, I said—

" What meanest thou, father, by fear ? Is not the
Christian party triumphant ?"

" Alas ! my son, we shall be involved in one common
ruin, for this attack upon the town is premature and ill-
advised.   Even now I have sure information that Ogosho
and the King of Tango are within a day's march with an
overwhelming power, and thus I tremble for the fold of
Christ, for upon the Christians will the vengeance fall,"

replied he mournfully : and the reason that no European priest had been forward to welcome their friends the victors, at once forcing itself upon my mind, I said—

"Hence, then, the cause the shepherds were not found this day at the head of their rejoicing flock."

"It would have been madness, my son: it would have been to have thrown aside the last hope ; whereas now the Emperor Ogosho will, by their forbearance, and the impossibility of his proving that the Christian ministers have had aught to do with welcoming his enemies, at least not be able to regard and punish it as a rising only of the Christians, as indeed it is not, the greater portion of the admiral's crew, as well as the population of this city, being of the idolatrous faith."

"Oh, would that I were free of this accursed land of broil, tyranny, and bloodshed," I muttered.

"Remain here, my son, and thou hast little to fear, for thou wearest the livery of the King of Tango."

"Father," I replied angrily, "it is not that I fear for myself, but that I cannot get from my mind's eyes the vision of that dying queen, her cruel death by the order of her husband, the danger of the Lady Mary, who, if these fears of thine be realized, may also die by the hand of her savage brother."

"My son," said the father, as he arose to leave the room, "'sufficient for the day is the evil thereof:' we are in the hands of God; but my heart is sad, sorely grieved at the death of that queen, whose blessed face and acts will never be torn from the hearts of her subjects, many of whom even now await me, to offer up prayers for the repose of her soul :" and the father quitted the room.

It is not my intention to write in detail the history of that period, but merely to give those events which affected either myself or Master Adams : sufficient, therefore, to chronicle, that the prognostication of the father became realized, and that as follows :—

The great admiral and his brother king, having received false intelligence that the armies of Ogosho had been defeated, determined at once upon an advance upon

Osacca, hoping, by getting possession of the young Kubo-Sama's person, thereby to put an end to the war. His success we have seen. Before, however, he had time to rebuild the battered fortifications, or strengthen his force, the King of Tango appeared before the place, at the head of the very flower of Ogosho's troops—troops, also, who were flushed with victory, for the intelligence brought to the admiral proved false : his colleagues had all been defeated.

Now, when the admiral heard of the investiture of the city by so great an army, and, at the same time, of the defeat of his brother generals, he at once determined to evacuate his position, and, if possible, to fight his way through the enemy ; and this, by reason of the inordinate spirit which his own great reputation and personal bravery had instilled into the breasts of his soldiers and officers, he might have accomplished : but his very virtues proved his ruin, and thus it happened.

It had ever been a sacred custom of the Japanners never to set out on a military expedition without first having sacrificed and prayed to Mantiffen, the god of war, for success. Upon the morning of the day the great sortie was to take place, the troops, as usual, were regularly drawn up before the image of the god, and every man lowered his arms and bowed low in token of homage and adoration ; but in the midst of this, the very commencement of the ceremony, the admiral, attended by several of his chief officers, and wearing the Christian emblems, entered the temple, and, commanding some Christian soldiers to break in pieces all the idols of lesser note, he himself seized upon Mantiffen, and hacked and hewed at the image until its head fell from its shoulders ; and thus, having exhibited his indignation at idolatry, he commanded the troops to offer up prayers to the real living God, and then led them, not to victory, but, by reason of the anger of the Sintoo portion of them at the indignities offered to their god, to defeat, and himself and brother king to chains and captivity : and all this did not take more than three days from the time of their triumphant entry into the city.

As for me, as usual my luck was directed by the devil, for no lesser influence could have caused me to become so mad that I must rush to the palace with the wild hope of saving the Lady Mary, and that, too, in the nick of time that the enemy entered from another side ; when, as madly, I attempted to do mortal combat with some dozen soldiers, who at length, having disarmed me, saved my life because I proclaimed myself an officer of the Queen of Tango, who had escaped by a miracle ; to which the polite reply was—

" If, as this rat says, he was with our beloved queen at the time of her being called to heaven, the king may wish to question him ; and as the life of the miserable wretch is of little consequence for a few days, he may keep it in his wretched body till the king has time to order otherwise."   So was I then thrown into a small cellar-like room in companionship with six sacred dogs, whose temporary kennel it had been made, and whose keeper was for the nonce appointed my gaoler.

In this place I was kept for several days upon an
allowance of food, which, although scanty enough, was
considerably diminished, as with a portion I was compelled to purchase the goodwill of my four-footed companions, who, regarding me as an interloper, would let me
have neither peace nor rest upon any other terms. As
for the gaoler, like all officials in Japan from the highest
to the lowest, he kept his own counsel with a pertinacity
so stern and uncompromising, that, notwithstanding my
questions, I could learn nothing of the daily progress of
affairs, or get from him a hint as to the probable fate of
the person, in whom I took so much interest, viz. myself.
When I put a question, he bowed and laughed ; if I grew
angry with him, he bowed and laughed; if I surmised
that it was the intention of somebody to have me assas-
sinated, he bowed and laughed the more; but when I
inquired the fate of the great admiral, whether he had
been killed or taken prisoner, he *neither* bowed nor
laughed, but kept a stern, and, to my thinking, a sad
silence.   Had the Jesuit Fathers been expelled the city ?
No answer. Did he know whether the Father Rodriguez
was still in the city, and would he inform him of my imprisonment? At this he stared and kept silence; but when
I took from my girdle a golden cobang, he held out his
hand, took the coin, and he bowed and laughed more
than ever ; but what was more to the purpose, promised
compliance. He kept his word ; for the next morning
the good father himself stood before me.

"Thanks to the Virgin, my son, thou art yet alive," said he.

" Rather say, *not dead,* father ; though better if I were,
for life is scarce worth having upon the tenure mine
seems to be held in this accursed land."

"Peace! thou knowest not what is best for thee, my son."

" Say, my father, is it good to live in a dog-kennel
upon starving rations, half of which I have to part with
to save my legs from the teeth of these fiendish dogs?"

" Be not ungrateful, my son ; this incarceration has
been good for thee.   Since you entered this place, that
which I feared hath come to pass ; the city has been
reddened with the blood of high and low."

"Sayest thou so? then the *Christians have* been made the scapegoats of this rising."

"No—yet, yes, my son; for, as a body, the brethren have been unmolested, and even now are free to exercise the practice of their religion; but the cloven foot, the hidden hatred, has been exhibited in the greater punishments and cruelties practised to prisoners of the faith than to those who are still idolaters; for while vast numbers of the pagans have escaped unscathed, all who were Christians have been immolated."

"But the lady, the Lady Mary?"

"Is safe."

"Thank God! But her brother, the young savage?"

"Either dead or fled, for he is not among the slaughtered."

"And he who caused the tragedy, the great admiral, what of him, father?"

"Alas! my son, he is no more, but his martyrdom marks for ever a glorious epoch in the blood-stained annals of the Christian church in Japan," replied he; adding—"at the first onset the great admiral's usual good fortune forsook him, for both he and the King of Omi, his friend, were surrounded by the troops of the King of Tango. The first prisoner taken was the king of Omi. As for the admiral, with such desperation and bravery did he do battle with the enemy around, that he kept them at bay till they were well nigh exhausted. But of those then in arms against the immortal prince there were but few who had not fought and bled beneath his victorious banner in the Corean war: moreover, although by imperious duty arrayed against him, they still so loved their old commander, they but parried his blows; nay, several times drew back, that, by ripping himself up, according to their barbarous custom, he might avoid the disgrace of falling beneath the swords of meaner persons than himself, or, worse, being captured, and so be dishonoured by a public execution. At this there was commotion in his soul: the temptation was great, but remembering God's ordinance against self-murder, he threw down his sword, saying—

" " 'Even do with me as thou wilt ; but, in the sight of God, humiliation is worthier than honour.'

"The victors being thus compelled to seize and bind him, with weeping eyes and saddened hearts led the fallen chief into the presence of the King of Tango ; and even he, remembering the former greatness of the prince before him, and who had once been his friend, trembled with grief as he demanded of him whether he was penitent for the great crimes he had committed in disturbing the tranquillity of the empire.

" 'Penitent to my God for numberless sins, but rejoiced that I am about to die for having observed my oath of allegiance to the Emperor Tiego and his heirs. What that oath was, well *thou* knowest, O king.' And at these words the chief of Tango turned aside with shame, for he was also one of those forsworn princes who had solemnly vowed to the dying Tiego never to forsake his son Fide Yori; but not noticing his shame, the admiral continued—

" 'Now, O king, I have but one request to make at thy hands.'

" The king arose impatiently, for he feared the prisoner was about to ask for his life, but the admiral said—

" 'Nay, Sir, it is not my worthless life that I ask, for had not the law of God forbidden, I had never been brought alive into thy hands to-day. All I pray of thee is a Jesuit father, who may prepare me to die as becomes a Christian.' "

" This was granted ?" said I.

" Not so, my son : the king made no reply, but ordered the admiral to be heavily laden with chains, and thrown into prison till the hour of his execution ; but his request was referred to Ogosho, and barbarously refused. Augustine, thus left destitute of all human succour, threw himself upon the mercies of God with such a generous confidence, that, far from quailing before the prospect of an ignominious death, he rather exulted in the thought of being thus brought into closer imitation of his Lord and Saviour."

" Is it possible, father, that the generous Ogosho will take the life of this noble prince and good Christian ?" said I.

"Alas! my son, or rather should I say, glory be to God, it is over," replied the father; adding, "The King of Omi and Augustine, have been condemned to be beheaded, yesterday the sentence was carried out with every sign of hate and fear. As they proceeded through the streets, bound like the vilest criminals, and followed and surrounded by a mob of hired ruffians, a herald rode before them carrying a placard, upon which was written the sentence, and loudly proclaiming at intervals that they were punished in that manner for troubling the repose of the state; but oh, my son, amidst the jeers and revilings of the mob, how great was the contrast between the conduct of the *heathen* King of Omi and the *Christian* prince Augustine; nay, the difference was gloriously visible: the faith in which they severally trusted was written upon their features; for while, filled with the human pride inculcated and cherished by his idolatry, the King of Omi was so overwhelmed with shame—a shame which for him had no hidden value to compensate for its exterior bitterness—he covered his face with his hands and wept, as if in the depth of despair; Augustine, on the contrary, counted his beads with a serene countenance that brought tears into the eyes of many of his enemies: and, as a disciple of a religion which places humiliation above honour, and gives to virtue in disgrace a precious consciousness of its resemblance to the Redeemer of mankind, he not only met every insult with the calmness of one who felt that *sin* alone could really lower him in the eyes of God, or the estimation of good men, but with an air and manner which shewed alike his vivid hope of future bliss, and the greatness of his consolation." —But here the good father stopped, and covered his face for a moment: the relation was too much for him. As for me, with tears in my eyes I said tremulously—

"But, were none of the Christian fathers permitted to pray with the prince in his last moments?"

"None, my son; but at the eleventh hour the officers permitted the assistance of a native Christian, whom I

despatched to him, and from him I have the account of
his last moments," replied the father; adding, "to this
his fellow-Christian, the prince, declared that he died, not
only content, but full of joy; for having confessed and
communicated before going to battle, he had since done
all that had been suggested to him as a fitting preparation for this solemn occasion. At the last moment, some
of the bonzes wished to perform in his favour the superstitious rites customary upon such occasions, but rejecting
their offer with scorn, he took a picture of our Lady
into his hands, and set it three times upon his head, a
mark, you may know, of the greatest honour and esteem
that can be paid to any thing or person in this land. In
fear, trembling, and tears, died the King of Omi; but
when Augustine's turn came, without change of countenance or colour, he fell upon his knees, earnestly re-
commended his soul to God, and, while the Christian's
death-cry, 'Jesus, Mary,' trembled upon his lips, his
head was severed from his body. But," continued Father
Rodriguez, "the narrative unmans me : we will have no
more of it now. For thyself, fear not : thy liberation
is at hand. Now, my son, farewell till to-morrow." And
so saying, the good priest left me meditating upon the
life and death of the great admiral, of whom another
Jesuit has written—

"Such was the tragical end of Augustine Tsucamidino,
King of Fingo, high admiral of Japan, generalissimo of
the imperial armies, after having twice conquered the
Corea, made China tremble, and caused the most powerful of eastern monarchs to sue for peace from the Ziogoon
of Japan. From the first hour of his conversion to the
day of his death, he had been the unwearied promoter
of the Christian religion, and its most zealous and fearless defender against the machinations of its enemies.
His military talents, his high renown, his wealth and
power—all had been devoted to this one great object;
and he died at last, scrupulous of the oath which he
had taken to oppose every attempt at usurpation on the
part of the self-created Ziogoon Ogosho."

The pendant to this personal history affords a good

illustration of the state of society among the Japanners of that period.

After the death of Augustine, a letter was found in the lining of his robe addressed to his wife and children, in which he expatiated on the submission due to the decrees of heaven : and exhorted them with zeal and tenderness to remain faithful to the one God.

Augustine's family, notwithstanding his death, retained hopes of recovering their rank.   The eldest son, a boy twelve years of age, had taken refuge with an old friend of Augustine's, the King of Nangato ; but that cowardly prince, thinking to make his peace with the Ziogoon, struck off the head of his guest, and sent it at once, by his ambassador, to Ogosho ; but, to their surprise, so great was the indignation of the latter at this act of villainy, that, but for a ready lie, which Ogosho may or may not have believed, it would have cost them and their master dear.   The exculpatory story was, that the young Prince of Fingo, having been stopped while endeavouring to escape, had, in despair, ripped himself up.

That, in ordering the execution of Augustine, Ogosho was actuated by dread of the great general and statesman, and not the *man*, is certain ; for notwithstanding it is the custom for the whole families of state victims to be included in the same death-sentence, he pardoned and restored to their blood, wealth and position, his wife and children.

CHAPTER XXV.

I AGAIN FALL IN WITH WILL, WHO RELATES THE STORY OF HIS GOOD FORTUNE ; BUT TELLS OF SAD NEWS FROM ENGLAND.

THE whole of the next day I anxiously expected a visit from the father : he did not, however, come, and so I remained awake nearly the whole night, pondering as to the cause.   The succeeding morning, however, he made his appearance, and that, too, with a bright countenance, and brighter intelligence, for he brought me liberty.

My heart was full of joy and gratitude : I thanked him, but he said—

"My son, I merit not these words; for, alas! the power of the Portugals and Spaniards, clerical and lay, has passed into other hands—into those of one through whom all must now petition the Ziogoon, and to whom alone thy thanks are due."

"More riddles, my father," said I, with astonishment.

"This time, my son, the riddle will at least not raise thy anger ; but follow me hence from this den."

Need I tell how willingly I followed his lead to his own house, at the very door-step of which, to my surprise and delight, I saw Master Adams ; but whom, having shed his European dress for the costume of a Japanner of rank, I did not recognise, until, coming forward and taking both my hands, he said—

"By my soul, Melichor, lad, this is the happiest moment I have come across since our parting."

"God bless thee, Master Will : but this unexpected meeting hath robbed me of my wits."

"Aye, aye; yet God's providence be thanked that thou hast a head left to keep them in : but an' thou hast had sorry feasting lately, so let's e'en make up for lost time, ere we lay our tongues yard-arm and yard-arm about our doings in each other's absence." So we passed into the father's state-room, when, leaving us to chat over the past together, the good priest quitted the house.

Well, of course we had so much to say that we were for some time in great confusion as to whereabouts to begin ; so, after we had for some minutes been questioning and cross-questioning each other, without being able to get answers that we could at all put into a straight understandable line, Will said—

"We are getting our brains among the shoals, mate, so let us change our tack : suppose I bring my tongue to an anchor, and keep my ears open, while thou unwindest thy yarn."

Whereupon, readily agreeing, I related, to the best of my memory, the whole of the adventures that had happened since our parting, saving and excepting the tender feelings I had endured for the Lady Mary, and which, somehow, in fear of his blunt nature and bold opinions, I could not get out of my lips, and which I was afterwards sorry for, because, after having heard all I had to say, he chose to pass his opinion of the Lady Mary after such a fashion, and in such language, that, an' he had been another man, we should have got to high words.

"But," I said, in conclusion, "prythee, Master Adams, tell me how it comes that I am indebted to thee for my release from yonder dog-hole ; for that it is to *thee* I nothing doubt."

"Aye, aye, lad, all in good time ; but, as I have lately experienced, to build a ship you must begin with the keel, so will I commence at the beginning, for no good can come of a ship or a yarn that makes its course stern for'ards : so now to begin.

"Well, first I'd have thee to know, that, for the first twelve months after we parted company, my time was occupied in building the ship for the Ziogoon ; and this, by dint of great memory of what I had seen in the

queen's ship-yards in England, and the help of many
Japanners, who built the queer-looking craft of this land,
and as many labourers and as much material—of the
latter there is no lack—as my necessity required, I did
manage to do, after a fashion, which, though it might
have brought tears of merriment to the eyes of English
or Hollander, so pleased Ogosho, that, forgetting his
great dignity, he capered for joy, and nothing would he
have but that I should make the voyage myself to Siam
in her."

"Verily, Master Adams, it was like making a chirurgeon to take his own nostrums," said I.

"Aye, lad, and so it was to my thinking; but as I
had honestly endeavoured to make the craft seaworthy,
and, moreover, had given to me a goodly number of experienced Japan mariners, I was fain to comply, and it was
God's providence that put the chance in my way ; for, as I
shall shew, that which came out of it helped on my
fortunes, which are now great as I could wish. Now,
although I was given command of the ship for the voyage,
it was only after a fashion, for those were put with me
who had orders from Ogosho to prevent my steering
altogether and entirely from these seas, and directing my
course to England. Well, it so happened, that, about
the time of our arrival in Siam, the chief, who was called
the white king, died, and was succeeded by his second
son ; but the new king was attempted to be put aside
by a certain great lord: the latter, however, failing
in his design, was put to death ; whereupon two hundred
and eighty of the lord's slaves, all of them Japanners, no
sooner heard of his execution, than they ran to the
palace, and, securing the king, compelled him to give up
to them four of his chief nobles, whom they believed to
have been concerned in their master's fall. This being
done, they murdered the poor nobles, and then made the
king sign, with his own blood, a paper of conditions and
privileges in their favour. But as the Siamese rose
against the Japanners, the latter, seizing upon all the
treasure they could discover, fled to the sea, some to one
ship, some to another, but the greater number to my

vessel, when I was perforce obliged to bring them back to
their own land; the doing which, and the successful
voyage, so delighted the heart of the Ziogoon, that he at
once conferred upon me a house, lands, and slaves, like
unto a lordship in England."

"Well hast thou done, then, as indeed thou saidst
thou shouldst, by keeping at the fountain-head, Master
Adams."

"Nay, nay, lad, be not hasty in thy conclusions; for, as
thou wilt hear, fortune has had her frowns as also her
smiles for me since we parted," he replied. "But," he
continued, "so pleased was his majesty with the ship I
had built, that nothing would content him but that I
must build him another, the which, after many months,
I did, and which, as the devil would have it, came in for
the use of his friends the Spaniards; for scarcely had the
second ship been finished, than it chanced that one Don
Velasco, the Governor-General of the Philippines, was
cast away upon the coast of Nipon, and his friend the
devil aiding him, caused the Japanners, high and low, to
treat him well, and make much of him, even to taking
him to the very court and presence of Ogosho; whereupon
the knave, finding he was so well received, put the same
demand as did once before the knave Pessoa, earnestly
beseeching of his majesty that, if he was friendly with
his master, the King of Spain, he would not permit the
Hollanders to reside in his territories, but would drive
them out, forby, in addition to being enemies to Spain,
their mal-practices on the sea, piracy, ought to be sufficient
to cause him to drive them forth."

"The Hollanders?" I repeated interrogatively; "of
whom spoke he? our shipmates? for surely none others
of my countrymen have found their way to this land?"

"Stay—stay, lad, I had forgotten I had not told thee
of the arrival of the 'Red Lion,' and the 'Griffin,' but of
that anon: my yarn is not quite ship-shape, but no
matter," and he continued—"Well, well, the Ziogoon
gave the rogue a reply that but little pleased him, for
neither telling him he would, or he would not, he
answered that it would be difficult to drive them forth,

for they had his royal promise to remain in Japan one year ; but at the same time he thanked him for letting him know what characters the Hollanders were, as it would keep his subjects on their guard : then, whereas his majesty wanted a favour, he offered him my new ship, furnished with all necessaries, to take him back to Spain, begging of the Don to request King Philip, his master, to send to Japan fifty miners, for he understood they were skilful in extracting silver in New Spain, because his own miners could not get from the Japan mines half the silver they were capable of producing."

" But the Hollanders, Master Adams," I said, burning with anxiety to hear of my countrymen, or, indeed, of any men, not being Portugals or Spaniards, who had recently come out of Europe.

" Beshrew me, lad, but thou wouldst lead a man to believe the Hollanders as clannish as the breechless Scots," he said, laughing ; then continuing, " Well, then, these countrymen of thine arrived in two ships, the ' Red Lion,' and the ' Griffin,' and thus it happened that they came to Japan. They were part of a fleet of thirteen ships, bearing nineteen hundred men, and three hundred and seventy pieces of artillery, which under Master Verhoeven were sent by the Stadtholder Maurice to give an account of a certain fleet belonging to the Portugals, which was about leaving Lisbon to take out to Goa a new governor. Foiled, however, by the Portugals' friend the devil, Master Verhoeven did but little, nay, nothing but made an attack upon Mozambique, and take from the harbour one carac laden with goods, after which he directed his course by Cochin to Johir, and so on to Bantam ; where, hearing from some Japanners who were in the harbour that certain Hollanders were here, he sent forth the ' Red Lion ' and the ' Griffin,' hoping thereby to afford us some aid, get a treaty of commerce with Ogosho, and also to fall in with the carac of Pessoa. Again, however, by the aid of his friend the devil, the knave, our old enemy, has escaped by one or two days, and is even now not far off this part of the coast, on his road to Macao, with

a very Indies of gold and silver, which would have
been to the profit of our merchants."

"But the news, the news: heardst thou not aught
from Amsterdam—from London?" I asked impatiently;
but at this he made no reply. I was shocked: he
must have heard some sad intelligence. He placed
his two elbows upon a table at which we were sitting
(rare luxury in Japan), and hid his face in his hands.
Nearly five minutes he remained thus, and then, as if
by a determined effort, he held his head erect; but he
ran his sleeve across his face—tears were in his eyes.

"God's mercy, Master Adams, what mischance hath
happened to move thee thus?"

"Tut, tut, it is passed," he replied; adding, "aye,
Melichor, there is news. First, of our old captain,
Master Quackernack."

"What hath happened to him?"

"Nothing; nothing more than a shipman and a
soldier's fate, Melichor. The Japanner junk in which
he sailed for China made its course to Malacca, when
falling in with the Verhoeven fleet, Master Quackernack
took service on board, and fell in the first action with
the Portugals, but he died gloriously, hand to hand
fighting with the enemy."

"Peace be to his soul, and honour to his memory,
for he was a good and gallant man, albeit the creature
of ill-luck." said I.

"I cry thee Amen; but would that his fate had
been mine."

"Nay, nay, Master Adams, we have now life and
hope before us; but why this melancholy mood?"

"I am unworthy of being a Christian, Melichor; I
have lost hope for the future:" and musingly, but
sadly, he said, "for it's better to be regretted than to
regret."

"What meanest thou? Thou saidst thou hadst news
from home: in God's name, what may it be?" I cried.

"Blank news, blank news, lad. It is of my wife—
the brave Mabel—the little fair-haired heroine, of
whom I told thee, Melichor," he replied; but, oh, so

wildly, so bitterly. The brave, cool sailor had evidently
kept his worst news to the last. His frame now trembled with excitement, as if the giving birth to a single
word was shaking his whole manhood.

My heart telling me what the reply *must* be, for want
of other words, I said—

"What of her? What of thy wife?"

"Melichor," he said slowly, sadly, sternly, "it must
be told to you alone, and then forgotten. She is—
God of heaven!" he added wildly; "I can scarcely
bring the word to my tongue—dead!"

Can I describe the scene that followed? No. The
effect of heart-searing sorrow upon a bold brave man, is
not describable: it must be felt alone. The word
uttered, he hid his face within his hands and sobbed
like a child. What I did may be imagined: I could
not speak. Alas that sorrow should find its antidote
in the wine-cup! no, not antidote, but a soothing and
temporary forgetfulness, a momentary Lethe. But,
whatever philosophers may advise, or moralists descant,
this, with some natures, is the only relief. I, who
abhor intemperance, who have never sought the wine-
cup as a solace in trouble, knew not what to do, or
how to soothe my friend; yet then, almost incontinently, placed a cup of hot saki before him; and I
was properly rebuked, for scarcely wetting his lips,
he threw it from him, saying—

"Nay, nay, lad; it is over now: the bitterness of
my cup of misery must not be soothed with what,
after all, is but the coward's refuge. In joy it is sinful, but in sorrow it is criminal, for it makes mountebank the grief which the Lord sends to chasten our
hearts."

Then, endeavouring to turn his thoughts into another
channel, I said—

"But, Master Adams, how fared my countryman, the
Hollander, at the court of Ogosho?"

"Well, well, Melichor; for taking my representations
now that I had become his friend, and to shew me, that
so long as I did not desire myself to leave his empire, by

my prayers and intercession he has granted the subjects
of Holland greater privileges and benefits than have
ever yet been held, even by the Portugals and Spaniards.
He has given them permission to have a factory at Firando, and, loading them with presents, sent them back
to Holland, with a long letter to the Stadtholder, in which
he promises, that at whatever port or haven of the
empire any Holland ships may put, his governors and
subjects are commanded by him to shew them all favour
and friendship, to their persons, their ships, and enterprise ; that, indeed, they shall be placed upon the same
footing as his own subjects."

"And thus, in the midst of thine own great trouble,
hast thou generously, by means of thy great services to
this Japan sovereign, opened up to my countrymen mines
of untold and unimaginable wealth.   It was well done,
it was well done, Master Adams."

" Yes, yes, Melichor ; as I am, and have long been,
the servant of the worshipful merchants, it was, after a
fashion, my duty, and being my duty, you see I didn't
desire any manner of thanks ; so we will have no more
on that head, an' it please you," he replied, adding,
" and, by God's help, my own countrymen shall have the
same advantages."

"And· after what fashion do the Portugals and
Spaniards take these concessions," said I.

" But scurvily, but scurvily, lad : like dogs, they now
lick the hand that has beaten them ; for such small belief
hath the Ziogoon either in their goodwill or honesty,
and that chiefly because he can't forget the boast of the
pilot about the king's conquests, or the insolence of the
Franciscan and Dominican friars, that he hath made it
so that all negociations about trade and other matters
must pass through my hands, and therefore these beaten
dogs do frequently come to me, almost upon their hands
and knees, to pray that I will get them the same
privileges as the Hollanders ; but, by my honour, that
will I never do. Still, for pity's sake, and being a fellow-
Christian (although, I pray to God, of a better sort), I
hold not in remembrance, at least to their disadvantage,

that they *have* been and are *still* our bitter enemies, for their friend the devil has made lashes of their own passions and avaricious practices, with which, sooner or later, they will whip themselves out from the land. But," he added, "anent my own countrymen, I have heard through the Hollanders that some worshipful merchants of London, headed by Sir Thomas Smith, have settled an Indish Company, and that many of my countrymen have a faction in the Indies; so praise be to God for ever and ever. I hope soon to hear of their coming here, for I have despatched a letter, telling them what power I have with the Ziogoon, and what advantages they may get by the coming for."

"Verily, thou hast been doing great things, not alone for the present, but for future ages," said I.

"Nay, nay, lad; get thee off that shoal. What I have done, I have done, but only as the instrument of chance: the praise is God's, and all the merit thereof, so no more upon that head," he replied; adding, "but now, Melichor, touching my rescue of thee. Well, having built another ship, the Ziogoon commanded me to make a voyage to Siam, and round about those outlandish coasts, with a great cargo of merchandize. So, before leaving Jeddo, knowing that thou wert in Osacca, I determined to put in here on my way, and persuade thee to share the voyage: but before weighing anchor, the news came of the great doings here, and knowing that thou wert likely to be in some danger, I applied to Ogosho to give me an order, under his own seal, to get possession of thy body wherever I might find it; and, by the Lord, it was lucky I had such foresight or thoughts ahead; for no sooner did I put in to this port, than our old friend, the Father Rodriguez, found me out, and said how that thou wert in jeopardy. But I need say no more, for, after getting such news, thou knowest what I would do."

"God bless thee, God bless thee, Master Adams," I said, shaking his hands.

"And now, lad, art willing for a trip to the land of the Siammers?" said he.

"By my soul, yea, and at this moment."

"Nay, nay ; we leave not for a few days; for there are to be great doings here upon the arrival of the Ziogoon."

"Well, well, Master Adams, be it an' thou wilt, it will be hard talking that shall persuade me to leave thee again while in this land," said I. And thus having settled upon the voyage to Siam, we spent the rest of the day in much small talk anent matters of the past, and speculations upon the future.

But to chronicle the state of society in which my narrative is set as in a frame—what a change in the aspect of the city during my imprisonment !

A calm had succeeded the storm. Now the streets, which had so few days before been devastated by fire and deluged with blood (among no people in the world is so much blood spilt in civil frays as among the Japanners, for, of the nature of tigers and hyenas, once lapped, their appetite is insatiable), were beginning to wear their holiday garments; rubbish was being cleared away; houses, not utterly destroyed, being patched up ; gay lanterns hung out ; silks thrown across streets ; scaffold-ings for sight-seers being erected ;—and all to give a loyal reception to the victorious Ogosho, who had com-manded a grand tournament to be given in honour of his victories over the rebel regents.

The King of Tango, having destroyed the two kings his enemies, and killed, dispersed, or recruited among his own army the rebel soldiers, had now time to think over his domestic affairs ; and bitter must have been the tyrant's thoughts, terrible the lashings of his conscience, for he had destroyed *her*, the only being he had ever loved ; which, now regretting, though perhaps only after the same fashion that a petulant child would the destruction of a toy, he sought to appease the saintly shade by bestowing favour upon the religion that she had so dearly loved. The Christian church was again opened, and the practices of religion encouraged more warmly than ever. Then, oh the monstrous hypocrite ! his grief for the death of his queen was as extravagantly shewn as if he himself had not been her murderer ; and hearing that the good father had collected some half-calcined bones, supposed to be those of the sainted Grace, with the intention of having them decently interred, he ordered the father to perform a funeral mass for her. The church was hung with black, and a *chapelle ardente* being placed before the altar, the mass was sung, and with so much majesty and devotion, that the tyrant, who with all his chief nobles was present, aped the crocodile, his better in nature, and wept; declaring also that the ceremonies of his native priests were far inferior to those in use among the Christians; and, wonderful to relate, even those who knew him so well believed that they had made one great sinner truly repentant, for at the same time he gave free permission to all his own subjects to embrace the Christian faith. But though this wretch affected to be so well pleased with the fathers that he presented them with a large sum of money, honour be to their memory, they accepted it not for their own uses, but to distribute among the poor.

But for myself—had not my troubles come to an end? Not so; for although I rejoiced in my heart that I was so soon to leave the city with Master Adams, and promised to myself much pleasure, my thoughts still so hankered after the Lady Mary, that they became the means of causing me years of misery, and that, too, after the following fashion.

On the morning of the tournament I made inquiries of the Father Rodriguez, but he, after his usual mysterious manner, checked my curiosity, telling me that of her I should hear before the day was out—aye, and do her a great service, had I the mind.

" But, my son," said he, " for dear life's sake, utter no word of this, even to thy friend Master Adams."

" God's life, my father, I will have no more of this; for what I may not tell him I will not do," I said hastily, for truly I had had enough of mystery.

" It is well, my son: I had forgotten that knightly feeling runs not in the blood of the Hollander; that the Lady Mary, in her great tribulation, need not seek the aid of the trader, albeit he is sworn to her service," replied the father angrily; and then the mountebank part of my nature arose to the ascendant, and I said—

" Danger ! what meanest thou, father, and how can I save the lady ?"

" My son, the king has chosen a successor to the martyred Grace. The Lady Mary is his choice."

" God of heaven ! is this possible ? But the lady—the lady—what says she ?"

" My son, she will die rather than be forced to this; but with thy aid she may escape both fates."

" How, my father, how ? tell me, and to the death I am at her service," the whole, instead of a part of my nature now being mountebank; for though I was of a firm, obstinate mind with everybody else, the name of the lady, as doubtless the reader by this time knows, ever made fool of Melichor von Santvoort.

" First, have I thy promise to give this aid ?" asked the father firmly.

" Aye, aye, man; but after what fashion is it required ?" I replied, and that surlily, for I felt conscious that my resolutions were of no more durability than ropes of sand.

" The lady has given out that she is sick, so that she may not attend the tournament with the king; so, after the show, at nightfall, when the streets will be all turmoil and tumult with the revelry, get thee to that cellar in the garden, where thou didst such service to the ill-fated Grace, by rescuing her friends from the heathen priest, and follow its course until thou comest to the river ; there, awaiting, thou wilt find a pleasure-barge, ready manned with rowers, who will be prepared to obey thy orders : command them to row the boat to the palace, beneath the window of the apartment where I surprised thee on the night of thy arrival in Osacca, and watch until thou seest the fluttering of a white fan, when, if possible, so dispose of thy men that they may not see too much of the lady, who will then, by thy aid—but remember, thy *sole* aid—descend, and at once enter the cabin, at the door of which thou must place thyself, so that by no accident any one of the rowers enter, as doubtless, out of curiosity, they may make some excuse to do, for they will be told that the lady is eloping from her parents with thee her lover."

"So that is the character I am to *assume*," said I bitterly.

"Aye, my son; and if thou art wise, ONLY ASSUME," he replied; adding, " then, when she is safe in the cabin, with all speed make for the great rice-fields near the mouth of the river."

" But how, oh, my father, can I see the rice-fields if the night be dark ?" said I.

" The rowers also have their instructions : they know the spot where you may both land : it is indicated by a large blue dragon lantern, near to which you will put the lady ashore."

" And then ?" I asked.

" And then, fear not, for there will be those at hand who will provide for her further safety. As for thyself, dismiss the boatmen, and find thy way on foot : it is but a short, although a circuitous distance," said the father ; adding, " now, my son, wilt thou do this thing ?"

As I have written before, the mountebank was upper-most, for the Lady Mary was in the case, and I answered "Yes."   But would that I had had the power of saying " No," for it would have saved me much misery.

CHAPTER XXVI.

I AM MIXED UP WITH A STRANGE ADVENTURE, BUT MAKE A DISCOVERY THAT COMFORTS ME, ALTHOUGH I AM ALMOST IMMEDIATELY KIDNAPPED BY AN OLD ENEMY.

O, Melichor, Melichor, why did fate give thee such a wooden head, or so soft a heart ? Why canst thou not escape these snares, which the evil one is ever setting to entrap thee into some misery ? Even such were my thoughts as I was hastening to witness the grand sights ; not, be it remembered, for the love of sight-seeing, but

17

that I might get out of the way of Master Adams, from whom I felt it impossible to keep the secret entrusted to me, and also that the bustle and noise should drown my thoughts. But this tournament. Well; the full details of the day are given by one of the Jesuit fathers, who, being present, afterwards chronicled them in his printed letters. Well; first premising that had the Ziogoon been tutored by Henry the Seventh of England, he could have found no better way of crushing the power of his kingly lords, I will give the reader the substance, if not the words, of the worthy father :—

"In order to make the tournament as magnificent as possible, a royal proclamation forbade the attendance of any lord who was unable to go to the most extravagant expenses in his equipment; and the nobles, on their parts, hoping to win the favour of the monarch, who was now considered invincible, the princes vied with each other in the splendour of their arrangements and the prodigality of their presents to the royal donor of the *fête*. The general of the forces made gifts to the amount of fifty thousand ducats; another expended twenty thousand upon his own equipment; a third made his appearance with fifty footmen, dressed in the most sumptuous silks of China; while another changed the colours worn by his train, and the fashion of their garments, no less than seven times in the course of the day. The procession was opened by seven hundred cavaliers, with their attendants in rich liveries; then came the monarch's sons, shining in gold and jewels (be it remembered that the Japanners rarely affect jewels); after them the emperor himself, surrounded by innumerable officers and others, mounted on a superb war-horse, and looking as if a shower of precious stones had fallen on his garments : indeed, it was not difficult to distinguish him in that crowd, for he showed himself by the majesty of his presence and the lustre of his habiliments—China silk, wrought in precious stones, with a scarf of inestimable value cast across the shoulders ; the housings, bridle, and frontlet of his horse, were all of silver and gold ; the reins were set in pearls, and

the stirrups of pure gold (verily, this king, as he sat upon
horseback, would have been a pretty piece of merchandize to have taken back to Amsterdam); a thousand
cavaliers of the royal household followed; and as soon
as the emperor entered the lists, the air was rent with
the acclamations of the multitude, who, mayhap, having
paid for all, were applauding their own generosity.
Then the lords of the tourney ranged themselves in their
respective positions, running two and two, and three and
three, against each other. The royal princes greatly distinguished themselves for their prowess, but to the
emperor himself, who ran the last, the victory was
awarded." But anent the latter, I would not for a pretty
sum have been the lord who had gained such victory
over those royal personages, notwithstanding the good
father who had chronicled this *fête*, says—"and well did
his majesty deserve the award by reason of his great and
superior dexterity."

Now, anent that golden and precious attire of the
emperor, as I stood in the crowd, I saw one man's eye
fixed upon the jewels, even as those of a wolf might have
been fixed upon a lamb in the farmer's safe keeping: and
looking earnestly at that man, by reason that, from his
dress, I knew him to be a Spaniard, I started with unpleasant surprise to see that it was our old enemy, Pessoa
—the knave Pessoa—whom Will Adams had told me
was on his way to Macao with his carac. What did
he do there? Was any mischief afoot? Tut, tut, he
had as much right there as I had. Still, I took it as a
bad omen; and as I walked away towards the house of
the Jesuit, I pondered over the matter, thinking at least
to inform Master Adams of *that;* for suddenly it occurred
to me, the knave, having escaped the Dutch ships, might
be hovering upon the coast in wait for Will's vessel,
which I made no doubt was a small craft, and, moreover,
that Pessoa had some knowledge of his voyage to Siam.
However, unfortunately, Master Adams was not in the
house; and although I waited till nigh the time I had
promised to keep my appointment, he did not return;
and so I went without seeing him. But now for that

which more immediately concerns myself and the arbi-
tress of my fate—the Lady Mary.

I had no difficulty in entering the bath-house in the
garden, nor in lifting up the artificial tortoise, nor indeed
in reaching the edge of the river, where, as the father
had foretold, I found a large state or pleasure barge,
manned by six rowers, who no sooner saw me than they
helped me on board, and, without a word, plunged their
oars, which were muffled, into the water, and rowed off
in the direction of the palace. The night was dark,
there was no moon, and what little noise was caused by
the plash of the muffled oars was lost in the ripple of
the water and the moaning of a good stiff breeze which
had sprung up. The palace was soon reached : I opened
the cabin door, that the lady might instantly disappear
upon coming aboard : then, to employ the men, I made
them thrust their oars into the water like poles, so as to
force the boat near the supporters of the balcony, while
I placed the others after the following order—two at the
bows, and one at the stern, to clutch the supporters
themselves. The night was pitch dark ; the tide was
low, so that the deck of the boat was about three or four
feet beneath the flooring of the balcony. No sooner
were we thus brought all taut alongside than I heard a
fluttering of silk : looking up, by the glimmer from a
small lantern which some person from behind held in his
hand, I saw the lady herself, and waving, too, the white
fan ; but, to my surprise, without waiting for my answer
to her signal, the next instant her hand rested upon my
arm, and, lightly as a fawn, she stepped into the boat,
and, without a word, glided into the cabin, as she entered
pulling the door behind her.

"Thank heaven," I muttered, "she is safe on board."

Taking up my position by the cabin door, I gave the
word, the men stood to their oars, and in another minute
we were in the middle of the stream ; and so far I had
no doubt of making a safe and speedy landing, for, with
the exception of a barge here and there, carrying homewards the more temperate revellers who were leaving the
feasts and drinking parties given in honour of the *fête*,

at an earlier hour than the rest, the river was clear. As
for the people on shore, even those whose proper duty it
was to watch the river, they were too much engaged to
attend to what might be passing upon the water.

Silently but swiftly we ran our course : it occupied
about an hour. We had reached the mouth of the river
—the great gullet, as it were, which opened into the sea
—when the glimmering of a lantern caught my eye.
Doubtless, I thought, some ship, whose voyage her
captain had delayed that he might witness the sights on
shore. This thought brought to my mind Master Adams's
ship : it might be her; and I felt delighted, as if near a
friend. But then I remembered Pessoa being in the
crowd. Was it his vessel? If so, it would be best to
avoid her. I did, and ran towards the shore, between
which and the aforesaid ship we were about midway. It
was darker than when we had started : the wind blew
boisterously, as if brewing a storm. However, for that
I cared but little, for we should reach the land in a few
minutes; but suddenly the plash of oars came upon my
ears. I could not see, but I heard a boat near at hand :
some person on board hailed us in the Japan tongue, but,
before I could frame a fitting reply, our boats grazed the
sides of each other : the next minute we were boarded
by some dozen men, several of whom turned on the light
of lanterns, which they held in their hands, but had kept
darkened. My rowers were paralyzed with fear. I
called on them to drive the pirates into the water with
their oars, not, however, leaving the cabin door, where I
stood, brandishing a pike which I had snatched up. One
half the sea-thieves attacked my crew, the other advanced
to the cabin : their object was evidently plunder. For
some minutes the contest was severe, and I kept them at
bay. I had stricken down two, when one cowardly
ruffian slipped behind me, and, pulling my feet from
under me, threw me upon my face : his knife was at my
throat, but the cabin door flew open, the knife was
dashed from his hand, and he fell with a groan. This
change of affairs gave courage to the rowers, and they
fought with so much vigour and determination, that at

length the cowards fled over the sides, some into their
boat, others into the water. I snatched up a lantern,
when by its light I saw—great heavens !—with her back
turned towards me, the Lady Mary in hand to hand
fight with a stout fellow, in whose voice and features I
recognized the traitor Owater. Astonished at the extraordinary prowess and strength of the lady, but alarmed
for her safety, I sprang forward, and, by one thrust of
my pike, sent the rascal into the water. But now came
another surprise; for seeing we had cleared the deck,
the lady, snatching up one of the oars, and ordering the
rowers to do the same, pulled heartily—aye, manfully—
till the boat was run right in shore, when my surprise
became turned to anger, rage, for the light from the
signal dragon lantern showed me I had been duped,
nay, made a cat's-paw of by the father. The lady was
no lady, but her own brother—he of the mutilated
hand ! Still I spoke not, for fear of doing him an
injury ; but when he had thrown a bag of money to the
rowers, and they had departed, seizing me by the arm,
he said—

" The Sama's wits are in a fog : he believed he was
serving the sister : yet it is so, for no greater service
could he do her than save her brother from the fate
of the great admiral, for which he was reserved," he said
savagely.

" Tut, tut. It was dishonourable, cowardly, to deceive
me."

" Dishonour ! coward !" he exclaimed, clutching the
hilt of his sword. The next instant, however, he added,
" But the Sama has served me well, and his anger is
nought—"

" Stay," I exclaimed, as a bright thought rushed through
my mind. " Tell me, man, didst thou not attempt to
slay the king in his own garden ? Didst thou not also
conspire to murder me ?"

" Both of these things did I do, Sama. Of the first I
will say nought, for it concerns thee not : the latter I
repent, yet would repeat, did I think now, as then, that
thou wert a rogue and a traitor," he replied fiercely ;

adding, "but that I regret, and will repay the injury with gold."

"Youth, I want not thy gold, but I thank thee; for this declaration, this proof that the lady thy sister is no assassin, repays me for the service I have done thee, though, to my thinking, the service was scurvily obtained."

"My sister!" he exclaimed; adding musingly, "then my acting was complete : but," he added fiercely, "have others this thought to her injury?"

"Nay, nay," I said, "not so."

"Good; but remember, Sama, that henceforth thou hast no such thoughts for my sister, whose blood can no more mix with that of the trader, than oil with water," he said savagely.

"Thou mad boy, the trader is as noble as thyself in his own land," I replied egotistically.

"Nay, the land of traders groweth not nobility," he said scornfully. "But," he added, "no more of this, Sama; those of my blood are not wont to accept of unpaid services, and, by my honour, since thou refusest gold, I will believe thou art noble, and so repay thee with brotherly love;" and he held out his hands, but, refusing to take them, I said—

"The hand of an assassin would be a dangerous gift and dishonourable to accept." Again his eyes flashed, and he clutched his sword-hilt.

"But," he added, "the Sama is angry, disappointed, and he uses words which, were it not for his services, would cost him his life. But farewell, stranger of the western skies : should we meet again, thou wilt know me for what I am, and, *knowing*, accept my proffered friendship." And as he spoke, two horsemen, leading a horse, came from behind a clump of tall trees, and, having spoken some words to him, he again and again clasped my hand against my will, and saying, "May the noble Sama's own God preserve him," leaped into the saddle and disappeared.

Thus, although I had no great liking for this young savage, I rejoiced at the chance that had taken so great a weight from my mind, and she, whom I had found it impossible to tear from my heart, notwithstanding I had believed her guilty, at least in intention, of such crimes, now became the object of my adoration. I felt that it was disloyal to Maud Saris, but then I am rather of a weak nature, at least in such things; and as I did not myself plant the feeling in my own heart, I therefore could not help it. Then, as I walked onward, intending to make my way through the suburbs into the town, I pondered upon the wily Jesuit, who had made me the means of rescuing this youth, who had doubtlessly been awaiting his doom; and I rejoiced at his success, for it was more than possible that the story about the intended marriage of the lady was mere romance; and my heart growing lighter, I said to myself—"Now for Master Adams;" but, I suppose, loud enough to be heard, for scarcely were the words uttered, when I felt my arms pinioned from behind, and a man replied—

"Nay, friend, if thou seekest ship service, by our Lady, thou shalt have enough."

I knew the voice, and my heart sickened: it was Pessoa's, into whose hands I had at length fallen; and, as the omen, the dismal thoughts of the morning, came across my mind, I submitted, as if to the stroke of fate: indeed I could not help myself, and so permitted them to throw me into the boat; and, as I lay sulkily silent, I heard that the ship in the roads was Pessoa's, who had been indeed, as I knew, to see the tournament; and that the boat party, when they attacked us, were waiting to take him to the ship; and afterwards I learned that the knave Owater, being left in command during his commander's absence, had attacked us, thinking it to be the pleasure-vessel of some lord, taking home its richly and costly-dressed owners, and that he would, in the absence of the captain, do a small stroke of business upon his own account. To do Pessoa justice, however, if, indeed, a man who acted from policy alone could be deserving of any praise, he no sooner returned to his own ship, and came to a hearing of the piratical attack which had led to the loss of three of his men, than he ordered the leader, Owater, to be put in irons. As for

my poor unfortunate self, I own that I had become so
despairing of all rescue, that I cared but little what
became of me ; nor did I grumble, or even speak, when
the knaves, upon taking me on board, loaded me with
irons, and threw me into the dirty hold of the ship,
leaving me the night to meditate upon my past and
future.

At daybreak I was awakened—for, even in my miserable plight, I slept—by the weighing of the anchor and
the bustle upon the decks ; and shortly afterwards two
savage-looking knaves of Portugals came, and, ironed as
I was, led me up the hatchway to the half-deck, where,
in a cabin strewn with valuable merchandize, and furnished fit for a prince, sat my worst enemy, Pessoa : and
when, at his command, the two men left the cabin, the
knave, addressing me with a smile of grim satisfaction,
said—

" Welcome on board my carac, comrade, for truly it
was a lucky chance that should find me an officer within
the same hour that I lost three of my best men." And
finding I made no reply, he added savagely, " 'Fore
heaven, man, it is child's play to sulk, for, by my soul,
thou hast but small choice between a good service
with fair pay and no great duties, and a trip in irons
across to New Spain, there to remain for the rest of thy
days."

" By my faith, there is little difference in the choice ;
so e'en as thou likest, thou knave, for I am within thy
power," said I.

" Nay, nay, man ; this humour will avail thee nought :
but I have thee at disadvantage, which should not be,"
said he ; and striking a gong, which brought the two
men again, he ordered them to unlock my irons, when
the relief was so great that I said—

" God's mercy, man, but I do thank thee for this."

" Aye, aye, and, if thou hast wit, will thank me for
greater favours yet : but get thee hence, and think well
over my offer. I want such an able fellow as thee, and thou
wantest fortune, which thou wilt find by serving me
faithfully." Then the men, as if divining their chief's

will, conducted me to a room on the lower deck, where were assembled the officers of the ship at their morning meal, and, from the hospitality shown me, I soon found that Pessoa's object was to gain me over to his service; nor will the reader deem me vacillating or inconsistent, when he finds that the knave succeeded. Indeed, he was master of the position; for by refusal I had the prospect of a life-long slavery; by acceding with 'simulated good-will, there was, at least so I thought, a prospect of desertion from the ship. How long, however, it was before that prospect became realized, it will be the business of my next chapter to relate.

CHAPTER XXVII.

HOW I SERVE UNDER MINE ENEMY, WITNESS A MASSA-
CRE OF THE JAPANNERS AT MACAO, AS ALSO THE
VENGEANCE TAKEN BY THE LATTER IN NANGASAKI
BAY, UPON THE SHORES OF WHICH I AM THROWN
WITHOUT CEREMONY.

I ACCEPTED service with Pessoa; indeed, I could not do otherwise: but it was with the resolve to make my escape at the first opportunity. Alas! that opportunity was five long years coming; five years of poignant cha-grin that I had been foolish enough to interfere in Japan politics; five years of hope deferred, of dreary imprison-ment by land and sea; for although well-fed, lodged, and paid, I was never permitted to go ashore, except when in Macao or the Philippines, to which places we voyaged. Wretched, however, as, to me, was this im-prisonment among a people whom I had hated from my childhood, the incidents which happened, at least those of importance to the reader, were few, and shall be quickly related.

The voyage to Macao was made without the occurring of any memorable event, except the death of the traitor

Owater, who thus escaped the disgraceful and well-merited
death which would have overtaken him had he fallen
into the hands of his countrymen, who never forgot that
he was the means of doing to the death poor Tom
Adams.   Upon arriving at Macao, the head-quarters in
the east of the Portugal traders and missionaries, Pessoa,
finding that, during his absence, he had been appointed
to its governorship, and having certain fears of meeting
with an armed ship of the Hollanders, resolved to forego
the next year's voyage to Japan ; and, by reason of my
understanding of merchandizing affairs, appointed me a
kind of clerk or secretary, with fair pay and provisions,
but no liberty to leave the precincts of the fort : indeed,
the soldiers were ordered to arrest, or, if need be, kill
me, if they found me beyond the said precincts without
the governor's written permission, which, I need scarcely
add, I never obtained.   The second year, Pessoa himself,
unable longer to deny himself the profits to be gained,
took a heavily laden and well armed ship to Nangasaki,
and returned to Macao with so large an amount of gold
and other valuable merchandize, that his appetite for the
annual traffic became greatly whetted.   Now I had accompanied him, but, while at Nangasaki, was kept below in
irons ; so that I had no means of holding communication
with the Japanners.   No sooner, however, had the ship
quitted the port, and got fairly out to sea, than Pessoa,
with savage politeness, set me free, and made many
excuses for the necessity of putting me in irons.

During our stay at Nangasaki, I discovered the real
object this man had in detaining me prisoner, which was
no less than that, at some time or other, I might act as a
kind of decoy-duck to get my friend Master Adams on
board his ship, and into his power, when, it is my belief,
he would have had that brave man murdered, so vastly did
he hate him for the footing he had obtained in the
empire with the emperor, and at the cost of the Portugals, who had to transact all their affairs through and by
permission of the Englishman.

I have now, however, to relate the causes which led to
my release from the thraldom of the Portugals, and in

that relation will be found a lesson for all times, what
English people or others may expect, if they attempt by
boastful language and dishonest means to coerce or use
after a piratical fashion these Japanners, who are, and
ever will be, of the nature of lynxes, foxes, and tigers,
and will exhibit it, too, in their dealings with Europeans,
who for the greater part, while they boastfully hold
themselves the superior race, foolishly deny the Asiatics
the universal egotism of thinking the same as themselves.

In the latter part of the third year of my captivity, a
Japan junk of war belonging to the Ziogoon put into the
port of Macao from stress of weather ; and Pessoa, finding she had on board a noble Japanner, who had been
sent by the Ziogoon as ambassador to Champa, in order
to establish further commerce with that country, as well
as to bring back a cargo of the precious gum called
calambac, gave his permission to the crew to remain in
the town until the winds changed.   But the ambassador,
officers, and men, finding the place greatly to their liking,
asked and obtained permission to pass the whole winter
there, and this was very well so far : but in the course of a
few weeks, so many other vessels filled with Japanners
put into the port, and from thence took up their lodgings
in the city, that Pessoa began to grow alarmed that they
intended to seize upon the town for themselves ; and
this fear being also held by the traders and Jesuits, the
latter endeavoured, at first by persuasion, to get them to
leave the port ; but the Japanners, finding they were so
well berthed, and, moreover, in such great numbers,
laughed to scorn the Portugals, who, being of a nature
as haughty and bloody as themselves, resented this treatment by harsh and contemptuous words.

For a time Pessoa, who did not wish to embroil himself with the Japan Emperor, for fear of losing his profits
by the annual traffic, took no notice of these doings ;
but at length from words they came to blows ; riots,
brawls, fights, became common, and at every scuffle the
Portugals seemed to be getting the worst, and consequently the Japanners more insolent, the governor began
to set in order and ready for fighting the whole of the

ship-men, soldiers, and others under his command : but at this the Japanners became but the more bold and insolent ; and one of their number even went so far as to head a small party, and led them into the house of a Portugal trader, which having plundered, they marched off triumphantly. Now this being a piece of daring that, if left unpunished, would have been followed by similar outrages, Pessoa sent an officer to the Japanners to demand that the chief thief should be given up to public justice, but success having increased their insolence, they refused ; whereupon the governor at once marched upon them, and a long and bloody hand-to-hand fight took place. The Japanners, however, finding they were being beaten by numbers, separated into two divisions, and, by a masterly though leisurely retreat, took possession of two great houses, where they barricaded themselves, resolved to fight to the last extremity.

Thus defied, and for a time foiled, Pessoa, who, to do him justice, knave Portugal though he was, re-organized his troops, and with them encircled the houses, so that not one of them could escape ; then sounding a parley, he summoned the whole party to surrender. They again refused, and he, being prepared with the proper materials, at once hastened to draw a great circle of fire around the buildings, to roast the enemy alive ; whereupon many of them came out and, throwing down their arms, were made prisoners. Unfortunately, among the captives was one who was recognised as having been one of the plunderers of the trader. Now Pessoa determined to make an example of this man, and so, marching him to prison, he then and there caused him to be strangled after the fashion of the Portugals, and in the presence of his captured countrymen, the latter of whom he set at liberty after the execution, thinking thereby that the news they had to take to their fellows then holding out, would be sufficient to terrify them into submission. These men, however, were so enraged at what they called the murder of their comrade, and they so influenced the passions of the besieged, that now one and all resolved to fight to the death.

This determination of the besieged so irritated Pessoa, that he at once put his threat into execution, by firing one of the houses ; then, as the smoke arose, the flames ascended, the timbers of the house began to crackle, the miserable wretches, with sword, pike, or musket in hands, leaped from the windows, burst open the door, and came forth half-choked, half-burned, and, maddened with rage, pain, despair, fought as if they had been devils from hell, or a whole jungle of wild beasts, and they fought only as men do fight under similar circumstances, but they were shot down to a man.   Alarmed at the fate of their fellows, the party in the other house surrendered at dis-cretion : they were marched off to the fort, and thus tranquillity was restored to Macao; but in the great heart of the Japan people, a spark of hatred was lighted against the Portugals that has never since been extin-guished, and, perhaps, never will ; for, among the Japan-ners, hatred and revenge is held a principle of honour, and never dies, but, collectively and individually, it passes down to many generations, the latest descendants feeling themselves more bound in honour to keep alive the flame than those with whom the original feud arose.

The conflict having been forced upon Pessoa, the victory weighed upon his heart heavier than a defeat, for the latter, if life had been left, might have been reme-died, and the affair would have had its ending, as it had had its beginning, in Macao ; the national honour, the revengeful feelings of the people, would not have been excited ; nay, such laws, after a fashion, rule the noble Japanners, that defeat might have been profitable to Pessoa, for the rioters would have been punished by their own laws.   Now the Portugal chief knew the people well, and, knowing them, had much to fear.   At times, he resolved never to set foot in the empire of islands again ; but, oh the cursed greed of gold ! the profit realized by the last voyage clung to his memory ; the time that had elapsed since then would also add to that to be gathered from another, by reason that the mer-chandizing Japanners would be the more anxious to give their rich gold for his goods.   Thus he could not resist

the temptation of another trip, nay, nought was there to
prevent but this unfortunate and fatal brawl.   Even
that, however, he believed might be softened down ; and
so he set at liberty his prisoners, and, after treating them
with munificence and hospitality, sent them home with a
paper, in which he had drawn up a lengthy account of
the whole affair, of course laying the chief blame to the
Japanners who had fallen in the fray, and persuading
their fellows and countrymen to affix their names and
seals to the document in corroboration of its verity.
That the Japanners, however, once in their own land,
had another version of the story to relate to their chiefs,
we shall soon see.

Well, permitting several months to pass, in order that
this terrible affair might be forgotten, Pessoa, nothing
daunted, equipped a galleon, and, with me as his secretary, a large body of armed men, and a more than
usually large cargo of saleable merchandize, set sail for
Nangasaki.   Upon our arrival in the magnificent bay,
Pessoa shewed many signs of his fears that the massacre
of Macao would be remembered to his disadvantage : the
watch was increased and doubly armed ; the culverins
and heavy brass guns were loaded nigh to the muzzle ;
pikes and swords were everywhere at hand ; so that, in
place of a peaceful trader, the good ship presented the
aspect of war to the knife.   Yet was this shewn on board
alone, for Pessoa sent to the governor a deputation of
two of his officers, and that, too, in the garb of peace, to
demand permission to exchange his merchandize with
the traders of Japan for their gold ; and further, another
lengthy statement of the riot at Macao, and its causes.
The officers had orders, also, to inform the governor that
a copy of the statement would be forwarded to the
Ziogoon himself.   The return of the deputation was
awaited for by Pessoa with great anxiety : he feared,
nay, prepared for an untoward result.

The officers returned with good news, with the permission desired, and many compliments from the governor, nay, an invitation that Pessoa would visit him.
The commander accepted the invitation, was hospitably

received, nought more was said of the Macao affair, than
of the inutility of sending to the Ziogoon the copy which
Pessoa had said he intended to forward to his majesty.
Pessoa was satisfied, and permitted himself to be persuaded, nay, even destroyed the document: the trading
commenced, and all went merry as marriage bells. But
the fear passed, the Portugals grew more insolent than
ever: they resumed their old trick of cheating, and many
bickerings arose between then and the Japan traders;
and thus affairs went on, without even preventing Pessoa
from lading the galleon with an amount of gold, and
other rich commodities, that had never been equalled in
any former voyage; nay, riches sufficient to satiate the
wildest avarice. So he resolved it should really be his
last voyage. It was: and thus it happened:—

I have said that the riches collected on board the
galleon were enough to have satiated the wildest avarice.
I was wrong. No amount that the ship could carry
was enough to satisfy these Portugals; for although
so heavily laden, they still lingered upon the coast,
loth to quit so prolific a mine, and day by day adding
to their stores: for although, at length, the commander
seemed satisfied, the men were not, but day by day
brought fresh excuses to prolong their stay; but that
Pessoa, so determined, so active, so good a commander,
permitted such delay, to the endangering of his own
safety, was a cause of wonderment to me. But then
he wished, when he had the opportunity, to humour
those fierce hearts, and moreover, he really believed in
the governor of Nangasaki's protestations of amity.

At length even the men's greed became satisfied,
and the vessel was got ready for sea; but, alas! the
golden hours had been wasted, the wind had died away,
there was barely sufficient left to float a feather, and
the galleon lay upon the waters like a log. But to
our disaster. Well, it was a dark January night, Pessoa
had thrown himself upon his couch, I lay upon another
in the same cabin—for although, while in port, the
Portugal had ordered me to remain on board and caused
me to be closely watched to prevent my escaping to

the shore, he treated me almost upon an equality with himself, hoping, thereby, ultimately to get me to decoy Master Adams into his power—when we were aroused by the rattling sounds of musketry. In an instant Pessoa was upon his feet, the next upon deck, and the next the drum beat to arms. Following the commander, I speedily found myself amid a hurricane of small shot; a number of Japan row-boats, with lanterns at their prows, were drawn up at a short distance in line of battle, manned with Japanners, who were firing volley after volley, rather at the ship than its crew. But bitterly must they have repented their folly, for Pessoa's gunners, taking advantage of the enemy's lanterns, made such good use of the culverins and great guns, that their petty weapons became speedily silenced.

Now any commander, not besotted with vanity and insolence, after receiving such proofs of the Japanners' real intentions towards him, would have put to sea at the earliest moment: but no; though the wind shifted more than once, out of sheer obstinacy and a spirit of defiance, he remained upon the coast, as if inviting another attack.—It came: and how was the mighty fallen!

It was a dark night, about a week after the first on-slaught: we were in a dead calm, and the huge galleon lay at anchor in a narrow channel near the mouth of the bay, when we were again aroused by the splashing of oars. The sounds seemed to delight Pessoa, for hastily donning his half-armour, he ran upon deck, saying to his men softly, as he passed them—

"More sport, my men; the heathens are at us again with their popguns."

I have said he wore half-armour; his contempt, however, for the enemy was so great, that in place of his helmet he wore but a velvet skull-cap. The men were speedily at the guns; every light was extinguished; not a word was spoken, and by this means, simulating an unconsci-ousness of the nearness of the Japanners, he hoped to lure the fleet of boats so within reach of the guns as to sweep them out of the water, and in deathless silence we awaited the approach of the enemy : but hours passed, and they came not, nay, they were as silent as ourselves. Many were the whispers as to the cause; great the anxiety and many the speculations as to what were their tactics ; but not till the first grey of the breaking day did we make the discovery : then, however, the heart of every man amongst us beat quickly. The galleon was in a trap, for, spread out nearly half-a-mile, in crescent form, but far from the reach of our guns, were some two-hundred row-boats, filled with half naked men, armed with swords, pikes, and muskets ; then, in the hollow of the crescent, but greatly in advance, were two enormous barges, lashed together, and their tops boarded, upon which was erected a great tower of wood, covered with the skins of newly-killed animals, and riddled with holes just large enough for the barrels of muskets : moreover, there were battlements at the top, from which they could keep up a perpetual and destructive fire upon the ship's deck, without in turn receiving a shot that could injure them.

As this monster tower slowly approached, Pessoa laughed to scorn the pagan invention ; but having first equipped himself in full armour, he commanded two demi-culverins and two great brass pieces to be loaded nearly to the muzzle with cross-bars, bullets, and case shot, and with a loud shout the gunners fired at the tower.

"Holy Virgin, the heathens are in league with the devil !" exclaimed Pessoa, as he saw the well-aimed missiles fall from the sides of the tower.

"Jesu Maria ! but a capful of wind, or we are lost," exclaimed the terror-stricken sailors.

"To your guns—to your posts ! for by the blessed Virgin, I will strike down the first who quakes before the pagan dogs," said Pessoa, jumping upon the half-deck, where, sword in hand, he stood fanning the energies of his steel-clad warriors, but who, nevertheless, were being mowed down by the Japanners' continuous and well-directed volleys from behind the wall of their tower. For two hours, the firing was terrible, the loss, however, being entirely on the side of the Portugals. Then slowly, but surely, like the approach of doom, and

vomiting forth bullets from every part, came this floating engine of destruction, till it grated ;the sides of
the ship—Then—

"To your pikes, to your muskets; the dogs give us a
chance; they mean to board us," cried Pessoa ;—and
bravely, nobly, the men obeyed the order. The Japanners had made one false step by not keeping up the
work of destruction from the tower; for now, as those
from the boats, with loud yells of defiance, like maddened
wolves, came over the sides, they fell backwards, pierced
to the heart, or with heads cloven in twain. How long
this lasted I know not: suddenly there was a cry that
the stern of the ship was on fire. The alarm was false
so far, but about fifty Japanners had succeeded in clambering upon that part of the deck. However, for such
an onslaught, according to the custom of that time, Pessoa
was prepared : he quitted the upper deck for a minute,
re-appeared, and the next the stern-deck, boarders and
all, were blown into eternity, for he had fired his hand-
piece into a barrel of powder. Then there was a temporary lull on both sides, and Pessoa, in a state of great
exhaustion, leaning against the bulk-head, seized me by
the hand, saying—

"By our Lady, man, but I thank thee for thy services
this day, and repent me of my sins ; and if"—but before
he could finish the sentence, another volley came from
the tower, more boats were around the ship, nay, she was
entirely surrounded, the half-naked savages, with their
gleaming swords and pikes, were fighting like devils :
still the courage of the gallant Portugals kept up. It
was now, however, apparent that all must surrender, or
be ignominiously butchered. Pessoa being convinced of
the hopelessness of continuing the conflict, drew a cordon
of men around the hatchway, and, while they defended
the position, he disappeared for a minute ; then coming
up he waved a crucifix which he held in his hand. It
was a dangerous experiment, but it succeeded ; for no
doubt believing him to be about to command his men to
surrender, they ceased firing, when, addressing his men,
he said—

18—2

" Nobly, my friends, have you this day upheld the honour of Christian soldiers, and by destiny, or the devil
alone, could we have been defeated. Let us not then
tarnish our glory by surrendering to these pagan hounds.
Let them not enjoy that wealth for which we have so
hardly toiled. I *will* not, nay, I *have* not," he exclaimed
vehemently, " asked you this : your deaths are *already*
appointed by a nobler means than the pagan sword."
He stopped an instant : all listened with intense anxiety :
it was an awful momemt ; and he said, " A prayer to
your God ; for in another moment you will be in eternity ;
the magazine is fired." Then, kissing the crucifix, he
cried, " Follow !" and leaped into the sea. Can I describe
the scene that ensued ? No. Prayers were hastily uttered by some, blasphemous oaths by others, wild yells
from the Japanners, who had seen their chief enemy
escape ; but on the instant, I, and I believe all, leaped
after the commander ; and the almost simultaneous explosion of the magazine proclaimed to the Japanners who
were fortunate enough to be in the more distant boats,
that hundreds of their countrymen had been shattered
into thousands of pieces : worse, that the rich argosy, the
immense treasures, had gone with the ship to the bottom ;
and more enraged at the loss of the treasure than the
sudden destruction of their fellows, they kept up such a
fire upon the wretched Portugals, who were now swimming for their lives, that of those who had been on board
that fated ship, not one, save the present writer, escaped
to tell the tale. The loss of the Japanners numbered
more than a thousand. And now, I pray, that when
hereafter others seek that beautiful bay, they may call to
mind how that, notwithstanding the fair surface of its
waters, and the sleek manners of the semi-barbarians of
the land, it was once terribly ensanguined by the blood
of Europeans ; and, moreover, for their own benefit, take
warning that what *has* been, *may* be again : the tiger of
a thousand years ago, is the tiger now : and so is, and
ever will be, till the crack of doom change the natures
of the easterns of all nations, but especially the Japanners.

My escape was little less than a miracle, for while my late shipmates were all stricken to death in the water by the bullets of the Japanners, I remained unscathed ; but that was, under Providence, by means of my being an excellent diver, which enabled me, with but little exception, to keep under water till I reached the rocky shore of a neighbouring island ; but once reaching land, I lay me down senseless with exhaustion. How long I thus remained I know not : when, however, I became

sensible, I found myself alone : the island seemed deserted. I was horrified at the sight of the number of bodies of Portugals and Japanners strewn along the shore, where they had been thrown by the waves ; but with sword, pike, or bullet wounds, which hideously proclaimed the manner of their deaths. Looking out upon the sea, I could not perceive one vestige of the noble galleon ; no, for with all her wealth she had gone to the bottom. At a long distance, however, from the land, the water was strewn with the boats of the Japanners, perhaps fishing for some of the bodies of their slain countrymen, with faint hopes that in some the sparks of life might not yet be quite extinguished.

The sight of these small craft told me that spot was no safe place for me, for should one of them chance to put in shore, my life would not be worth a minute's purchase : and so, having changed my Portugal attire for the garments of one of the slain Japanners, I endeavoured to walk inland ; but so weary, so bruised by the buffeting of the waves, that I had not proceeded a hundred yards, when I fell to the earth, exhausted by weakness and want of food, and fell asleep or senseless, I know not which. When consciousness returned, I found myself surrounded by a party of fishermen, pearl-fishers, who had evidently been using every effort to restore me to my senses. I asked where I was, but, unfortunately, in the Portugal tongue, to which I had been so long accustomed. This betrayed me, for the enraged fishermen, recognising the language of their enemies, would have slain me at once, had I not miraculously called out that I was the friend of the *Auge Sama* Adams. That revered name staying their hands, I related the story of my capture five years before, and begged of them to take me to any town where the pilot might then be living. The name of Will Adams, and my story, saved my life : it did, however, little more ; for, binding me hand and foot, after their fashion, they conveyed me on board their junk, telling me they were returning to Jeddo, where the *Auge Sama* then lived, and where they should be able to discover the truth or falsehood of my account of myself.

Well, when, after a dreary voyage of many, many days, we arrived in the harbour near Jeddo, these doubting fishermen humanely informed me that either my liberation or crucifixion—they knew not which—was at hand ; but the information did not in the least alarm me, for I knew that I should stand or fall by the truth or falsehood of my story. That the fishermen, however, scarcely credited my tale was certain, for instead of going at once to

Master Adams, they reported themselves to the governor, who at once sent two sub-officers to examine me ; and these officials, having listened attentively to my narrative, and put me through a torturing series of questions, took their departure, leaving me as they had found me, bound hard and fast : and thus for three tedious days and nights I remained in that miserable junk ; but on the fourth I heard the plashing of many oars ; then there was a great commotion upon the deck above, and speedily I heard— oh joyful sound !—the voice of Master Adams command- ing the fishermen to unbind my limbs, and bring me to him.   Too impatient, however, to await the execution of his orders, Will was in the cabin, knife in hand, the cords were sundered, and I was once more free : although so long and tightly had my limbs been bound, that I could scarcely make use of them.

"By my soul, Melichor, it makes me right glad to see thee, albeit it be in this plight : many are the months gone since I gave thee up for lost," said he, shaking my hand most heartily.

"Truly, Master Will, my escapes have been but little less than miraculous ; and but for thy name and present good service, I should have come but by an untimely end."

"Tut, tut, man, don't let us spoil our present joyful meeting by useless words, but get thee the use of thy legs, and let us quit this hole, for thou lookest as if thou wert at thy last gasp, and that too by starvation.   So come, come, and let us fatten up thy scarecrow visage as soon as may be," he replied.

Then, when I had for about ten minutes exercised my legs and arms, so that I could put them to their natural use—for the tight binding had sadly numbed them—by means of Will's assistance I got into a barge, which, from its equipments, decorations, and numerous liveried rowers, . I took to be the pleasure-craft of a prince.   We speedily reached the shore, where, awaiting us, with about fifty attendants, in the same livery as the rowers, were two handsomely caparisoned led horses.   Upon one of these Will assisted me to mount, then himself mounting the other, and ordering the men to so surround us that the crowd which (notwithstanding two runners with long bamboo canes went before us to clear the way) pressed closely to see the *Auge Sama* and his scarecrow friend, could not annoy me, we proceeded at a steady pace through the great city of Jeddo.

During our progress Will kept solemnly silent, but when we had reached the furthermost suburb, and he observed the surprise with which I gazed about me, especially when passers by stopped to pay the same homage to Master Adams as if he had been a prince in the land, he said—

" Aye, aye, man, thou art surprised, I see, to find that thine old shipmate hath brought his pigs to so good a market, but the explanation shall come anon, for truly it is but little better to listen, than to talk, upon an empty stomach."

" Truly, Master Adams, our fortunes have been vastly different, but God awards where award is due ; and from my soul I rejoice at thy prosperity. But," I added, " one question, my dear friend : knowest aught of the Lady Mary ?"

" Aye, aye, that do I, Melichor : poor lass ! poor lass ! hers has been a sad history. But I tell ye, man, not a question will I ask, not a question will I answer, till thou hast rationed thy carcass ;" and then, turning to the men, he gave the word to halt : indeed, we could not well proceed further, for we fronted the moat or ditch of a large house.

CHAPTER XXVIII.

Now, prepared as I had been to find Master Adams living after the fashion of a prosperous gentleman, I must confess to great astonishment at seeing and hearing that the poor pilot had been installed in the rank of a noble of the highest grade ; yet such was the fact. The estate to which he had brought me was called *Phebe*, and was a lordship conferred upon him and his heirs for ever, by the Ziogoon. The house itself was of vast size, moated after the fashion of a castle, magnificently decorated, and strongly built, surrounded by beautiful gardens, wrought after the Japan fashion into hill and dale, mountain and valley, with rocks, fountains, rivulets, flowering-shrubs, rare trees, and rivulets sparkling with gold and silver fish. Moreover, so great was the estate appertaining thereto, that it held upon it one hundred farms, and a goodly population, all of whom were Master Adams's slaves, and over whom he possessed the power of life and death, as if he had been a king. But if surprised at the *outer* appearance of the house and grounds, I was almost breathless at the grandeur of the interior, which, with the exception of having chairs and tables after the European style, was furnished like the house of a prince. But now, as I have to tell rather of the man than his goods, I will proceed with my narrative.

Well, according to his promise, Master Adams said but little until I had heartily partaken of the plentiful refreshments which he set before me in one of the largest rooms in the house, a room which, by the way, was, after the custom of the country, separated into two divisions by a painted, japanned, gilded screen, which reached the whole height and breadth of the apartment. When,

however, he believed I had fully satisfied the cravings of
nature, he said—

"To begin at the beginning, I must go back to the
time of thy sudden disappearance, now well nigh five
years. Well, as thou knowest, I was busily preparing
for my voyage to Siam—a voyage which grief for thy
supposed loss nearly knocked on the head. But at once
to my story. Thou mayest imagine my surprise on the
evening of the tournament to find thou didst not return :
still, I believed that no other injury had befallen thee
than what so often takes place in this land upon all occasions of public joy, viz., that thou hadst been found
amongst some party of noisy revellers, and, by consequence, been locked up for the night by the ottona
(street-keeper) ; but the next day, and the next, coming
without bringing thee, I became alarmed, and, by leave
of the governor of the city, sought for thee in the public
prisons ; but, as thou knowest, found thee not."

"But," said I, "the Father Rodriguez knew the affair
I was on : he must have heard from the rowers of the
fray upon the river."

"Aye, aye, man ; but the father—may his soul rest in
peace—"

"The father, Master Adams, what of him ?" I said interrupting.

"Died two years since, my friend."

"The world could have better spared a greater man,"
I interposed sorrowfully.

"True, true ; but we may not choose our companions
upon earth. But to continue my story. The father,
when he left thee on the day of the tournament, proceeded at once to Seruga, where he remained for several
weeks ; so from him I could gather no information respecting thee ; and great was my grief. Well, after
searching the city through—the prisons, the tea and saki
houses—I came to the conclusion that thou hadst been
drowned by some mischance in the river. When, however, the father returned, and he found that thou wert
missing, with tears in his eyes and grief upon his countenance, he told me the story of thy mission, and also

the story of the fray as he had heard it from the rowers, and of which we could make nothing, for the boatmen declared that they had landed thee safe. For a time, however, we suspected that this declaration was false, and only made to cover their having slain thee; and so I kept my eyes upon the fellows, till the father, hearing of the safety of the young lord, knew that the men's account was true. After this I could come to no other conclusion than that, after reaching the shore, thou hadst been slain in a fray with some party of drunken revellers, who, to hide their guilt, had disposed of thy body; and thus, compelled to give thee up as lost, I proceeded with my ship to Siam: and, although deeming thee dead, from that time—and each year has brought me greater wealth, the firmer friendship of the Ziogoon, and additional honour—my old comrade has never for a day been forgotten; nay, not even in the midst of many startling events and multitudinous affairs. Over these latter I must pass, to come to the present." Then, when he had taken breath, he continued—

" Now, my friend, with regard to that great knave, but enemy, though he was a gallant commander, Pessoa, when the fugitives arrived from Macao, bringing the news of the great slaughter of their comrades, great was the rage of the Ziogoon and his lords, nay, of the whole people; and, but for my advice, I believe a large armament would have been sent to destroy all the Portugals in Macao. As it was, when I told Ogosho that such an act might bring upon his land the armies of the Portugal and Spanish kings, who would be glad of such an excuse to play the same scheme of conquest, rapine, and murder, as they had in New Spain, he only determined, that when next Pessoa brought his carac to Japan, his people should have no manner of traffic with him.

" The time, however, that elapsed between the massacre at Macao and the Portugals again coming to Nangasaki, had softened the anger of the Japanners, without rubbing from their minds the great profits they made by the traffic; and so, had the Portugals not been more than usually insolent, which they were by reason that they took the good temper of the Japanners to be cowardice and fear, the trade might have gone on for years to come without interruption. Now, while loading the carac with the wealth with which it afterwards sunk, there happened to come to Nangasaki the commander of the men killed at Macao, and being determined upon revenging their defeat, he persuaded his kinsman, the King of Arima, to aid him. So the latter prince, with thirty small junks, made a night attack upon Pessoa's ship, and met, as thou knowest, with a repulse. *Then* Pessoa should have sailed, for the Japanners never forget or forgive failure. This defeat made the affair of national importance, for, coming to the ears of Ogosho, his majesty became so enraged, that he issued a decree for every Portugal in the land, merchants, bishops, and priests alike, to be massacred. That order was not obeyed, for again acting upon Ogosho's fear and natural prudence, I persuaded him to rescind it ; but at the same time, instructions were issued to the King of Arima to seize or destroy Pessoa, his ship and crew ; when the King of Arima, knowing that if, after so direct and imperative a command, he failed, he would have to rip open his own bowels, called a council of his best officers, and among them concocted a scheme for the Portugals' destruction. What that scheme was, or how it succeeded I need not repeat."

" By my soul, Master Adams, if thou thinkest that it was the scheme of the miserable Japanners that defeated that gallant crew, thou art in the wrong."

" Nay, nay, thou art as warm as if the Portugal had been thy friend instead of enemy," said Will, interrupting me.

" May the devil be praised when praise he deserves, Master Adams ; and so I tell thee that nought but the great obstinacy and the dead calm was the cause of the defeat of this Pessoa, who, albeit he lived a knave, died a noble gentleman," I replied.

" Well, well, Melichor, I will not gainsay thee, for I also know that thou art right," said Will : "but," he added, " enough of this knave ; now open thy lips upon thine own affairs." Whereupon I repeated my history

since our parting, taking care (I know not why) to say
nought of my feelings for the lady who had been the
cause of all my sufferings.

"And now, Master Adams," I said, "thou hast heard
the story of my captivity, canst thou tell me aught of its
cause—the young lord, he of the mutilated hand ?"

"Aye, thou shalt have it ; but first a cup of saki : then
the sooner my story is over the better, for it is a sad one,
and one I love not to repeat," replied Will ; so having
replenished our cups, he began—

"After the battle in which the great admiral and his
colleague, the King of Omi, were taken captive, the
Christian knight, Sir Martin of the Gilded Spurs, fled in
safety to the savage island of Jesso, which, it is said, is
inhabited only by men who are covered with hair : well,
it was to him, and by his means, that the Lady Mary's
brother fled after thou hadst helped him to escape from
the castle, wherein had he remained but the next day he
would have suffered death ; and great was the secret joy
of the King of Tango, thereat, for he desired not to take
the life of the brother while he contemplated making the
sister his wife. And shortly afterwards, the Ziogoon
Ogosho, the King of Tango, and many other of the great
princes, returned to the royal city of Seruga, where, now
that the rebellion was at an end, they intended to remain.
And after the lapse of two years the great Ogosho, to
show both his wisdom, and that he desired not the death
of those who had been his enemies, proclaimed an am-
nesty ; whereupon the young lord and Sir Martin both
returned to the city of Seruga, and there took up their
residence. The Lady Mary went to live with her brother, where, poor lass, she was safe from the persecuting
attentions of the King of Tango, to whom she was compelled to listen, if only to avoid the still more odious attentions of the Ziogoon, for, as the intended bride of his
chiefest prince and great friend, Ogosho dared not pursue
her, and so for two years matters proceeded, till about
twelve months since.

"Then it began to be bruited about the court that a conspiracy was being hatched for the destruction of Ogosho,

and the restoration of the young Kubo-Sama, Fide Yori, who was still confined in the state prison at Osacca. Moreover, the King of Tango learned, by means of his spies, that it was headed by his old enemy, Marabosi, the Lady Mary's brother ; whereupon, that he might discover the names of the other traitors, he went in person, at the head of a body of soldiers, to the young lord, but, to prevent suspicion, he left his troops at some short distance, and, accompanied only by his usual number of body-at· tendants, proceeded to the house as if, as was his wont occasionally, to pay the young lord and his sister a com- plimentary visit. Marabosi received him in the hall with the usual ceremonies, and then conducted him to the great apartment, where fruit, fish, and sweetmeats, were served up, of which, while he was partaking, Marabosi knelt to do homage to the rank of his visitor. As his majesty was concluding his repast, there arose a commotion in the streets, such as might have been caused by the trampling of the feet of armed men : still, whatever Marabosi thought, he paid no attention to the noise, till one of the king's attendants, at a sign from his master, approached the window, and the others, some twelve, began to form themselves in a circle around the young lord, evidently fearing that if his suspicion of their intention to arrest him was aroused, he would at once rip himself up, and so die, with the great secret (the names of the other conspi- rators) locked within his breast. But seeing this, nay, being prepared, he suddenly sprang through the narrow- ing circle, and with one blow of his cattan struck the king to the earth. The attendants were paralyzed : they stood motionless, staring at the dying prince. As for Mara- bosi, without attempting flight, but with savage delight gleaming from his eyes, he lifted up his maimed hand, saying—

" ' Twice have I attempted, the third time have I suc- ceeded : my father, my mother, my family are avenged. Since my ninth year has my life been devoted to this one object, and I die content. Tyrant, woman and child slayer, I now go joyfully to death, to the torture, for my courage can thy people no more shake than a wall of iron.'"

"By my honour, the death was deserved at the young man's hands, though it should have been given in fair fight. But what became of the lady his sister?" said I.

"Patience, Melichor, and thou wilt hear all," said Will; adding, "the king spoke not, for his death was almost instantaneous. Marabosi was secured, and the house ransacked from one end to the other. As for the Lady Mary, she was taken to the same prison with her brother; but her presence of mind will for ever be remembered, for, upon seeing the troops approaching the house, and at once conjecturing (for she knew it not before) that her brother must be implicated in some conspiracy, she broke open Marabosi's private cabinet, and, seizing all the papers she could find, escaped with them to the bathhouse, where, indeed, she was discovered by the soldiers; but—triumphantly pointing to a heap of ashes—she had effectually destroyed all the documents by fire."

"By heaven, I know not how sufficiently to admire this noble woman," I exclaimed.

"That great act hath obtained for her the admiration of all Japanners, even her enemies," said he. "Well, the scheme of the Ziogoon and his council (for the King of Tango was but their chief instrument) being thus foiled, and knowing no other means to obtain the names of the conspirators, they seized upon two of Marabosi's most intimate friends, named Tchouya and Ikeymon, and, with Marabosi, subjected them to the torture; but oh, Melichor, such torture that red Mary of England never dreamt of; but sanguinary, cruel as it was, it was insufficient to make one of these brave fellows betray their friends. Listen, man! these barbarians plastered all three over with wet clay, then laid them in hot ashes until the drying and contracting of the clay rent and burst the flesh into innumerable wounds: still, neither changed countenance, nay, Ikeymon became horribly jocose.

"'I thank thee,' said he, 'for I have had a long journey, and this warning is good for my health : it will supple my joints, and render my limbs more active.'

"This torture failing to extort a confession, they next made incisions of eight inches long in their backs, into which they poured molten copper ; which, when it became cool, they pulled out again, dragging the flesh with it ; but still no confession.

"' I thank thee,' said Tchouya, ' for thus showing me a new mode of medical treatment.' As for Marabosi, as determined as the others, he said—

"' My courage thou canst not shake : I defy thy inge- nuity. Invent new tortures ; my fortitude is proof against them all. I should be ungrateful otherwise. The object of my life is attained ; my friends are avenged ; the disgrace of my mutilated hand is wiped out ; and I die content.'"

Master Adams stayed to take breath ; and I will seize the opportunity of impressing upon my readers, that out of no morbid feeling, but simply by way of illustrating the character of the Japanners, it is that I repeat this sad but *most truthful* story of those horrible doings.

"But the Lady Mary : did they torture that noble woman, for surely she would have confessed what she knew ?" said I.

"Not so, Melichor, it would have been useless to have tortured her, or even for her to have confessed ; for in this land the *evidence of a woman* is worthless and unlaw- ful," he replied ; adding, "but speedily the day of exe- cution came, and all the relations of the three prisoners were doomed to the same death, some thirty—the Lady Mary among the number."

"God's mercy ! sayest thou, then, she was butchered ?" I exclaimed.

"Tut, tut, man, have patience ; I said not so ; for hear- ing of her doom, I fled to the Ziogoon, and at his feet begged her life ; and, in a sentence I tell thee, I succeeded, and she is even now well and prosperous."

"Thanks to God for that news," I exclaimed, wiping from my brow the sweat caused by my anxiety as to the fate of that noble creature.

"I cry thee amen to that," said he; "but the Lady Mary, although released, would attend the execution; and, rushing upon the very scaffold—for even the guards were too much affected by the scene to offer any resistance—she embraced her brother, declaring she would die with him.

"'Nay, sister, beloved and only remaining child of our noble parents, wouldst thon be guilty of *self-murder?*'

"The lady started with surprise, with joy exclaiming—

"'What words are these, oh, my brother? surely they are *those* which should come from the lips of a Christian.'

"'And from a Christian—an erring one, but still a Christian—they do come, my daughter,' said Father Rodriguez, coming from among a crowd of soldiers; adding, 'thy prayers, daughter, have at length reached his heart; he dies—'

"'In the faith in which he was born, and which, while revenge remained unsatisfied, he dared not practise, but from which he has never swerved.'

"'Then may God take me from this world at his holy will, for *my mission* is fulfilled, my brother dies in the faith,' she said; but to the close of this sad scene she joined in the prayers, and continued till the fatal blow was given : nature could do no more, and she was carried away senseless from those shambles.

"But one other incident happened at that great butchery, Melichor, which should be proclaimed throughout the world, if only to prove how deeply in the natures of these Japanners is planted the feeling of friendship," said Will; adding, "as the sad train of prisoners approached the scaffold, a man, richly attired, and armed with a couple of gold-hilted swords, rushed through the crowd to the officer who commanded the guards, and said—

"'Behold, I am he⁻ they call Martin of the Gilded Spurs, and the friend of Marabosi. Living at a long distance from this city, I have but recently heard of this dismal conspiracy. Hitherto I have remained in concealment, hoping the Ziogoon would pardon Marabosi; but

19

since he is condemned to die, I am come to embrace and, if need be—to suffer with him.'

" ' Thou art a worthy and a noble man : would that all the world were like thee : thou hast thy wish ; go, join thy friend,' replied the officer.

" Marabosiand Martin conversed for some minutes, the latter producing a jug of saki which he had brought beneath his gown. In this they drank to each other an eternal farewell : both wept. The stern Marabosi thanked his friend, who then, as he left, said, ' Our body in this world resembles the flower asagawa, which, blooming at peep of dawn, fades and dies as soon as the sun has risen ; but after death we shall be in a better world, where we may uninterruptedly enjoy each other's society.'

" After the massacre, Martin, presenting his two swords to the officer, said, ' To you I am indebted for my conversation with my lost friend ; and I now request you to denounce me to the Ziogoon, that I may suffer like him.'

" ' The gods forbid, thou noble man : thou deservest a better fate,' said the officer, refusing to take the swords."

" A stalwart fellow by my honour ;" but still harping on the old subject, I said, " But, the Lady Mary, the Lady Mary, what became of her, Master Adams ?"

"That which becomes of most ladies," replied Will, laughing ; " she *married*."

"Married ?" I repeated, and I thought the word would have choked me.

"Married ! aye, man ; it was her only choice : the sole condition upon which Ogosho would save her. He had an unmarried friend, whom he wished to keep near his person ; and believing that a wife would be the very chain that would fasten him for life to his throne, when I threw myself at his feet and craved him to pardon her, he sternly refused, except upon the condition that the lady would marry—"

"In God's name, *whom* ?" I exclaimed. *

.   " By my faith, thou shalt soon see :" and as he replied, he arose to go towards the door.

" No, no, stay," I said ; and as the thought rushed

through my brain, I exclaimed, "I see it all, Master Adams, she is—"

"My wife—only my wife. But what scares thee thus, man? dost think she has made a bad bargain?" he said, laughing. "But pardon me, dear friend," he added, becoming serious, "I was a dolt not to have known this. I see it all: and from my soul I am sorry this thing hath happened; but it was God's will, and no work of me, his servant."

Strange were the sensations that passed through my mind—hate, jealousy: no, no, not hate: the latter, perhaps; but they were evanescent. If either were to blame, it was myself, who had kept secret from my friend the love I entertained for the lady. Indeed, had it been otherwise, had he been cognizant of my affection, to have saved her life he *must* have taken her to wife; nay, of his own free will would he never have married again: the remembrance of his lost Mabel would have forbidden such a thought. And as all this stood vividly before my mind's eye, I caught him by the hand, saying—

"Pardon, pardon this emotion, my friend: thou art right: the will of heaven must not be questioned. May she solace thee for her thou hast loved and lost."

"Tut, tut, no more of that, man;" and as he spoke a tear stood in his eye; so quickly changing the subject, I added, "As for myself, I will seek what consolation I may by joining my countrymen, the Hollanders, an' thou wilt aid me."

"So be it, Melichor; but now we will seek the lady, who, forgetting not thy many services, will be thy hostess for many a long week," said Will.

"Nay, not so, Master Adams: believe me not churlish, but ask not of me that which would be unnatural. To-morrow I quit this house;" and for a moment he stood amazed, but then replied—

"An' thou wilt: an' thou wilt; and perhaps thou art right: but 'tis a hard matter that we should thus part after so long a comradeship."

And now my narrative is nearly at an end. I have only to record, that, true to my resolution, I departed

from Phebe the next day, without seeing the lady : and,
in company with Master Adams, soon arrived at Nangasaki, where my countrymen, the Hollanders, had set
up their factory, and, by the kindness of Will, obtained
from Master Henrick Brower, who was its first captain,
the appointment of secretary ; and at that town, busily
engaged in merchandizing affairs, I soon forgot the Lady
Mary ; and, shall I confess it, began once more to let my
mind dwell upon Maud Saris, who, however, I afterwards
discovered, had at that very time been married to an
English merchant more than two years. And great as
was the chagrin I felt upon the latter news, it at the same
time much lightened my remorse at my own disloyalty to
the fair Maud.

It was in the year of our Lord 1613 that I settled at
Nangasaki, and in the year '20, I returned to my native
Holland ; but as the events which happened in the land
during that interim were so vast, so tragic, and, moreover,
of such importance to the whole world, that they would
require many volumes like unto this, I can only give such
an outline of them as may tend to bring this narrative to
a proper conclusion.

Well, in the year '13 happened that which Master
Adams had so long desired, the arrival of *his* countrymen
in Japan, for it was about the month of May when Captain John Saris reached Firando, in the ' Clove,' which
was laden with such merchandize as the Japanners desired.
Upon his arrival the king of that part of the land gave
him, his officers and men, many great feasts, entertain-
ments, and amusements, whereby they passed away the
time until their countryman, the *Auge Sama*, had been
summoned from his estate of Phebe. Master Adams
then conducted the captain to Jeddo, introduced him to
the great princes, and to the Ziogoon Ogosho, who, at
Will's intercession, gave Captain Saris a long and friendly
letter to his King, James the First, wherein he gave permission to the English to trade with the Japanners to
their hearts' content ! and so, when the captain quitted
for England, he left behind him an established factory,
which consisted of six Englishmen, under the joint charge

of one Master Cocks and Will Adams, the latter being
endowed by the Indish company of merchants in England
with a yearly salary of one hundred pounds ; and thus
were sown the seeds of what might have proved a mighty
tree of wealth, with its branches touching all the countries
of the Indies, but God, or the inaptitude for traffic, or
the great distance from England, prevented. But that
the English factory did *not* flourish, as had the Portugal
and the Spanish, and then was beginning to flourish the
Dutch, was no fault of the indefatigable Will Adams ; for
not only did he protect his own countrymen against the
still ever-intriguing Portugals and the Dutch, whose
jealousy led them, in 1617, so far as even to attack the
English factory ; but in the interests of the latter, and for
the increasing of the wealth of the before-named Indish
merchant company, he made many dangerous but profitable voyages to Siam ; and this, too, although at the time
he was in such mighty favour with the Ziogoon that he
could have commanded whatever he had asked, within
the bounds of man's reason. However, for the English
then to become established in Japan was not to be ;
greatly, I think, by reason of their great avarice and
quarrelsome nature when away from their own land, and,
moreover, that the people sent out were not fitting
patterns of the great nation from which they had come,
by reason of their loose tastes and habits. But perhaps
if ever the English nation obtain another footing in the
Japanners' land, they will send out better exemplers of
themselves, men who will not go, as then they did, as
adventurers to make a fortune by one voyage, and care-
less whether they made wealth honestly or not, so that
they *did make* it, but merchants who will have at heart
the establishment of fair trading, and a mutual understanding and respect between the two countries ; and if
ever this be the case, then even, at whatever distance
of time it may be, will the name of Will Adams deserve
to be embossed upon their first treaty-paper in letters of
gold ; for he it was who first made not only the *name* and
greatness of his countrymen known to the Japanners, but,
by his own conduct and talents—and he was of such

character for manly honesty that should serve for a pattern to his countrymen for all time—respected and venerated.

Then, what is wonderful, as shewing the great influence of Master Adams, is, that the period—viz. between 1613 and 1620—when he did so much for Englishmen, was a period which, in the annals of Japan, is written in blood ; for in 1614 the civil war again broke out between Ogosho and Fide Yori, and raged so long, and with such fearful fury and hate, by reason of the Portugals and the converted Christians aiding Fide, that, till the terrible and memorable massacre at Nangasaki, in 1622, and the expulsion of the Portugals, and the entire rooting out and extermination of Christianity, the empire might be literally said to have run with the blood and been filled with the shrieks of the many many thousands who from time to time suffered tortures so infernal, so indescribable, that naught but a council of devils could have sent them into the imagination of man. Yet Will Adams was a Christian, and still, during great part of the period described, lived and prospered, aye, and fought hard for the prosperity of his countrymen.

Now, to bring my narrative to end ;—although from 1613 to 1620 I saw Master Adams not more than a dozen times, and that only when his business brought him to Nangasaki, we often corresponded, and remained upon our old terms of friendship, so that, although, when in the summer of the year 1620 I was surprised to receive a letter from him, in which he earnestly besought me to visit his house at Phebe, I readily complied, the more willingly that I believed that now my feelings towards his wife were changed.

It was a long and tedious voyage that journey from Nangasaki to Phebe, but at length it came to an end, and I reached the first farm upon the estate early upon a summer morning. I was riding briskly, at least as briskly as a Japan horse could take me ; the farmer, his wife, and children were standing near the door of their house ; but, wonderful ! a stranger, and they had no curiosity ; nay, they but lifted their heads, and then changed their position : it was to hide their grief : tears were in their eyes

They have lost some beloved member of the family. I thought I would inquire. I did. In as fitting words as I could string together, I sought to console them, but the man, turning to me, said—

"Thy words, oh Sama, are good ; but, alas ! when the gods call away the head of the house, who can replace him ?"

" We were hungry, and he fed us ; we were his children, but he chid us not for our faults, which were many. Alas ! alas ! to make two such men in the same age is a task too great even for the gods," wailed the woman.

They had evidently lost the head of the family—the grandfather of their children : to attempt consolation would be mockery, so I rode onwards : but at the next farm the same scene presented itself. I became alarmed. I hastened onwards, the very roads seemed filled with mourners. Could the good master of the estates, my friend, the noble Will, be departed ? No, I could not believe it : but in my excitement, being vexed with the slow pace of the animal, I leaped from his back, ran forward, reached the moat, passed the bridge, entered the house, and oh ! what a scene presented itself. The rooms, the passages, were crowded with servants, not boisterously lamenting, as is the fashion in Japan upon ordinary deaths, but with red eyes, fitful starts, half-suppressed sobs, and speechless.

" Thy master ?" I cried aloud : my fears would let me say no more.

One servant took me by the hand, and treading softly, stealthily, as if in fear of his own footsteps, led me forward through the house into the garden, and there, beneath the overhanging foliage of two cypress trees, upon a couch, but with its pillows so raised thnt the sufferer could take a last look of the blue sea which he so loved, and upon which he had spent so much of his time, laid senseless, speechless, the gallant, the noble Will. By his side, gazing earnestly into his eyes, as if to watch their opening, knelt his wife—but oh, how altered by sorrow !—a Bible in one hand, a crucifix in the other, and near her two

296   WILL'S GREAT SICKNESS.

lusty boys, whose features, though dimmed with sorrow,
and damp with tears, bespoke their parentage.

At my approach the lady turned, stared wildly in my
face, held out her hand, but spoke not. This silence
lasted some minutes: then she gave a half-suppressed
shriek of joy: he had opened his eyes; consciousness had
returned. Seeing me, a smile lit up his countenance. He
put out his hand.

"May God be thanked that thou art in time, Melichor."

"Nay, nay, Master—

"Old friend, I *am* sick to the death. I would have
lived longer, for the sake of her and these boys; but I
complain not: *He* knows what is for the best." Then,
waving his hand to prevent my speaking, and having
taken a moment to recover his breath, he said, and in
English—

"Melichor, thou knowest I fear not death: I have met

it face to face too often ; but I have a sin to answer for
that causes me fear."

" *Thou* a sin that should so trouble thee ?" I said.

" Nay, dear friend, listen, and give me thy advice, for
thou art of my own faith and of more scholarship.   I—
I," and his voice faltered, " I have grievously injured one
who may curse my *memory*—Mabel—my childhood's companion—the wife of my youth !"

Alas ! I thought his senses were wandering.

" Nay, Master Adams, bring it to thy memory that she
of whom thou speakest is a saint in heaven."

" Nay, nay, old friend, my senses are clear, for I am at
that lucid point where disease wanes into death.   The
report of Mabel's death was false : she lives : her cousin,
Master Saris, brought me the news, and even a letter
from her.   Oh, my friend, she has been grievously
wronged ;" and waving his hand, as he saw I was about
to speak, he continued, " I leave a will in my cabinet—"
but his voice becoming thick, he stopped.

" Nay, dear friend, if this be to have sinned, the angels
in heaven may do the like."

" Stay," he said ; " I have seen thee : it has brought
comfort to my soul ; for if ever it is thy fortune to return
to Europe, seek her out, make all known, but pray of her
not to curse my memory."   And then, moving as if to
get up from the sofa, he fell in his wife's arms, and the
brave seaman, the English discoverer of Japan, had passed
away.

Now my story is done ; for since I have brought the
reader to the last scene in the life of him who hath been
the cause of my writing, it would be but presumptuous
for me to say more than that, while I remained in that
house of sorrow, I found that the enthusiastic girl had
become the staid, noble, Christian woman almost of a
pious English household, that I obtained the will, wherein
I found that my friend had divided his property—at least
that which could be turned into money, for the estate in
Japan was inherited by the eldest of the two boys I have
mentioned—between his family in Japan and his family
in England, the latter, by reason of the greater value of

money in England, being double ; and then, taking a
touching farewell of the Lady Mary and her children, I
proceeded to the English factory, where, meeting with
one Master Pring, who was just then returning to his
own country, I gave him the will, and with it instructions
to inform Mabel Adams the true reason of her husband
having married again.

As for myself, I have only to add, that, after the passing of about three years, finding myself fairly to do as
regards worldly wealth, I returned to Amsterdam, and
have lived there till this present writing.   That I did not
go to England, was because, upon my arrival, I chanced
to meet with the master of an English ship, who gave me
to understand that Mistress Adams died of grief for the
death of her husband, and with as much love as if he had
never left her.   I hear that she lies buried in the church-
yard of Gillingham, in Kent, but that she is registered in
the church books, by some mistake probably, as Mistress
Elizabeth Adams.

THE END.

LONDON: CASSELL, PETTER, AND GALPIN, BELLE SAUVAGE PRINTING WORKS, E.C

CASSELL'S

CHILDREN'S LIBRARY.

NEW WORKS JUST PUBLISHED.

Æsop's Fables, in Words of One Syllable.
With Illustrations printed in colours. Handsomely bound in
cloth gilt, with gilt edges, price 3s. 6d.

Sandford and Merton, in Words of One
Syllable. With Illustrations printed in colours. Handsomely
bound in cloth gilt, with gilt edges, price 3s. 6d.

Peggy, and other Tales; including the
History of a Threepenny Bit, and the Story of a Sovereign. With
Eight Illustrations. Handsomely bound in cloth gilt, with
gilt edges, price 3s. 6d.

Old Burchell's Pocket: A Book for the
Young Folks. By ELIHU BURRITT. Illustrated with Twelve
Engravings. Bound in cloth gilt, price 3s. 6d.

New Stories and Old Legends. By
Mrs. T. K. HERVEY. With Illustrations printed in colours.
Cloth gilt, price 2s.

Owen Carstone: A Story of School Life.
With Illustrations printed in colours. Cloth gilt, price 2s.

The Story of the Hamiltons. With
Illustrations printed in colours. Cloth gilt, price 2s.

The Holidays at Llandudno. With Illustrations printed in colours. Cloth gilt, price 1s. 6d.

The Hop Garden: A Story of Town and
Country Life. With Illustrations printed in colours. Cloth
gilt, price 1s. 6d.

Algy's Lesson. With Illustrations
printed in colours. Cloth gilt, price 1s. 6d.

Ashfield Farm: A Holiday Story. With
Illustrations printed in colours. Cloth gilt, price 1s. 6d.

CASSELL, PETTER, & GALPIN,

BOOKS FOR CHILDREN.

Handsomely Bound, Suitable for Presents.

Little Songs for Me to Sing. Illustrated
by J. E. Millais, R.A.; with Music composed expressly for the
Work by Henry Leslie. Square crown (*Dedicated, by express
permission, to Her Royal Highness the* PRINCESS OF WALES). 6s.

The Child's Garland of Little Poems;
Rhymes for Little People. With Exquisite Illustrative
Borders by Giacomelli. Square 8vo, cloth gilt, 7s. 6d.

Bright Thoughts for the Little Ones.
Twenty-seven Original Drawings by Procter. With Prose and
Verse by GRANDMAMMA. Square 8vo, cloth gilt, 7s. 6d.

The Children's Album. Containing
nearly Two Hundred Beautiful Engravings, with Short Stories
by UNCLE JOHN. Square crown 8vo, 368 pages, cloth lettered,
3s. 6d.
"A charming book for youngsters; full of bright pictures on all manner of
subjects, and attractive reading in prose and verse."—*Bookseller.*

Cassell's Picture Book for the Nursery.
Royal 4to size, full of Illustrations, with appropriate Text for
Young Children. Bound in embellished boards, 5s.; bound
in cloth, with coloured centre-piece, 6s.

Dame Dingle's Fairy Tales for Good
Children. Handsomely bound in cloth, with gilt edges, 5s.;
fully coloured throughout, 7s. 6d.

DEDICATED TO THE PRINCESS BEATRICE.

The Children's Garden, and What they
Made of It. By AGNES and MARIA E. CATLOW. With several
Illustrations. Square cloth, 3s. 6d.

CASSELL, PETTER, & GALPIN,
UDGATE HILL, LONDON, E.C.; AND 596, BROADWAY, NEW YORK.

CHOICE READING AND GIFT BOOKS FOR YOUNG PEOPLE.

The Royal Gallery of Kings and Queens.
Embellished with Portraits of our English Sovereigns. Handsomely bound in cloth, 5s.

The Family Picture History of England.
Bound in embellished boards, 3s. 6d.; cloth, extra gilt, 5s.

Famous Events in General History.
Illustrated by a number of beautiful Engravings, and written with the special view to interest and instruct Young People. Crown 4to, in an embellished wrapper, 3s. 6d.; bound in cloth, extra gilt, 5s.

Remarkable Persons and Scenes of History.
Illustrated throughout with full-page Engravings. Fancy boards, 3s. 6d.; bound in cloth, extra gilt, 5s.

The Bible Picture Story Book. The
OLD TESTAMENT. Crown 4to, in embellished boards, 3s. 6d.; bound in cloth, extra gilt, 5s.

The Bible Picture Story Book. The
NEW TESTAMENT, uniform with the above, 3s. 6d.; bound in cloth, extra gilt, 5s.

The Bible Picture Story Book. The
OLD and NEW TESTAMENTS together, in One handsome Volume, bound in cloth gilt, 7s. 6d.; fully coloured throughout, 15s.

Famous Regiments of the British Army.
By W. H. DAVENPORT ADAMS. 3s. 6d.

Beatrice Langton; or, The Spirit of
Obedience. 2s.

The Story of Arthur Hunter and his
First Shilling. 2s.

Philip and his Garden. By CHARLOTTE
ELIZABETH. 2s.

Drawing-room Plays. 3s. 6d.

CASSELL, PETTER, & GALPIN,
LUDGATE HILL, LONDON, E.C.; AND 596, BROADWAY, NEW YORK.

CASSELL'S
FAIRY STORY BOOKS.

Coloured, Sixpence each ; Mounted on Linen, One Shilling.

The New Little Red Riding Hood.	Cock Robin.
Aladdin ; or, The Wonderful Lamp.	The Three Bears.
The History of Tommy Thumb.	Whittington and his Cat.
Cinderella; or, The Little Glass	Jack the Giant Killer.
Slipper.	Children in the Wood.
Jack and the Beanstalk.	&c. &c. &c.
Old Mother Hubbard.	

CASSELL'S
CHILDREN'S PICTURE BOOKS.

Sixpence, Plain; Coloured, One Shilling.

BIBLE STORIES.

1. The Creation, the Fall, and the Flood.	7. The Story of the Life of Jesus.
2. Abraham, Isaac, and Jacob.	8. The Book of Miracles.
3. The Story of Joseph.	9. The Story of the Death of Jesus.
4. Moses and the Israelites.	10. The Book of Parables.
5. Joshua and the Judges.	11. The Story of Simon Peter.
6. The Three Kings—Saul, David, and Solomon.	12. The Story of the Apostle Paul.

HISTORICAL STORIES.

1. The Early Britons and their Saxon Kings.	6. Sovereigns of England from James I. to Victoria.
2. King Canute, William the Conqueror, &c.	7. King Pepin's Fight with Wild Beasts, &c.
3. Richard the Lion-hearted and his Successors.	8. Famous People of the Middle Ages.
4. Henry V. and his Battles against the French.	9. Famous Discoverers.
5. King Henry VIII. and his Daughters Mary & Elizabeth.	10. Good Queen Bess and her Times.
	11. Napoleon Buonaparte.
	12. Celebrated Warriors.

CASSELL, PETTER, & GALPIN,
LUDGATE HILL, LONDON, E.C.; AND 596, BROADWAY, NEW YORK.

EDUCATIONAL WORKS.

The English Language in its Elements and Forms.
With a History of its Origin and Development. Designed for
the use of Pupils and of Teachers, and as a Book of General
Reference. By WILLIAM C. FOWLER. 8vo., cloth, 3s. 6d.

Lessons in English : containing a Practical Gram-
mar, adapted for the use of the Self-Educating Student. By
J. R. BEARD, D.D. 12mo., in cloth boards, 3s. 6d.

Pocket Pronouncing Dictionary of the English Lan-
guage. By NOAH WEBSTER, LL.D. To which are added Ac-
centuated Lists of Scripture and Modern Geographical Proper
Names. 18mo., cloth, 2s. 6d.

Arithmetic for School and College Use. With a
copious collection of Examples, and a Chapter on the Metric
System and Decimal Coinage. By T. PERCY HUDSON, M.A.,
Fellow and Tutor of Trinity College, Cambridge. 12mo., cloth,
2s. 6d.

The Elements of Arithmetic. By Professor WAL-
LACE. Crown 8vo., 1s. 6d.

Key to the Elements of Arithmetic. With Answers
to all Questions in the previous Work. 32mo., paper covers, 4d.

Arithmetic for the Young, inculcating the Science
of Numbers by means of Familiar Objects, in a Series of Easy
Lessons ; with copious Directions for Teachers. 12mo., cloth,
1s. 6d.

Cassell's Euclid : being the first Six Books with the
Eleventh and Twelfth of EUCLID. Edited by Professor WAL-
LACE, A.M., of the Glasgow University, and Collegiate Tutor
of the University of London. Crown 8vo., stiff covers, 1s.,
Cloth, 1s. 6d.

Key to Cassell's Euclid; containing the Enuncia-
tions of all the Propositions and Corollaries. 32mo , paper
covers, 4d.

The Elements of Natural Philosophy, for the Use
of Schools. By the Rev. SAMUEL HAUGHTON, M.D., F.R.S.,
Fellow of Trinity College, Dublin. Fully Illustrated. Bound
in cloth, 4s. 6d.

Hand-book of Natural Philosophy. With Cuts.
Foolscap 8vo. 1s.

Cassell's Lessons in French: containing a Complete
View of the Idioms of the French Language, in a Series of
Easy and Progressive Lessons. By Professor FASQUELLE.
New Edition, Revised and Improved. By Professor DE LOLME.
12mo. Parts I. and II., in cloth, each 2s. 6d., or complete in
one volume, cloth, 4s. 6d.

Key to the Exercises in Cassell's Lessons in French.
12mo., cloth, 1s. 6d.

Cassell's French Manual. Forming a Complete,
Simple, and Practical Guide to a *thorough* Knowledge of Speaking the French Language. By Professor DE LOLME. Crown
8vo., cloth, 3s.

Cassell's French and English Correspondence for
Boys. 18mo., cloth, 3s. 6d. ,

Cassell's French and English Correspondence for
Young Ladies. 18mo., cloth, 3s. 6d.

Cassell's Commercial French and English Corres-
pondence. With a Glossary in English and French of Ordinary Commercial Terms, and Formulæ. Cloth, 3s. 6d.

The French Reader; containing Extracts from the
Best Authors. Designed for the Improvement of Students in
Reading the French Language. New Edition. By Professor
DE LOLME. 12mo., cloth, 2s. 6d.

French-English and English-French Dictionary.
In One Volume, 12mo., half-bound, 3s. 6d.

Cassell's Lessons in German; in a Series of Easy
and Progressive Lessons. By W. H. WOODBURY. Parts I.
and II., 12mo., cloth, each 2s. 6d. Or complete in One Vol.
cloth, 4s. 6d.

Key to the Lessons in German. Revised Edition.
12mo., cloth, 1s. 6d.

The German-English and English-German Pro-
nouncing Dictionary. 8vo., cloth, 7s. 6d.

CASSELL, PETTER, & GALPIN,
LUDGATE HILL, LONDON, E C.; AND 596, BROADWAY, NEW YORK.

www.ingramcontent.com/pod-product-compliance
Lightning Source LLC
Chambersburg PA
CBHW060542030726
47498CB00004B/1285